'Maureen Lee is one of those hugely talented authors who writes great women for women readers. Her books don't just have one heroine, they have several . . . exceptional . . . [a] thumping multi-generational saga'   *Daily Record*

Maureen Lee was born in Bootle and now lives in Colchester, Essex. She is the author of many bestselling novels including *Nothing Lasts Forever*, *Martha's Journey*, *After the War is Over* and the three novels in the Pearl Street series, *Lights Out Liverpool*, *Put Out the Fires* and *Through the Storm*. Her novel *Dancing in the Dark* won the 2000 Parker Romantic Novel of the Year Award. Visit her website at www.maureenlee.co.uk

By Maureen Lee

Flora and Grace

Maureen Lee

An Orion paperback

First published in Great Britain in 2013
by Orion
This paperback edition published in 2013
by Orion Books,
an imprint of The Orion Publishing Group Ltd,
Orion House, 5 Upper St Martin's Lane,
London WC2H 9EA

An Hachette UK company

1 3 5 7 9 10 8 6 4 2

A CIP catalogue record for this book
is available from the British Library.

ISBN 978-1-4091-3732-0

Typeset at The Spartan Press Ltd,
Lymington, Hants

Printed and bound in Great Britain by Clays Ltd,
St Ives plc

The Orion Publishing Group's policy is to use papers
that are natural, renewable and recyclable products and
made from wood grown in sustainable forests. The logging
and manufacturing processes are expected to conform to
the environmental regulations of the country of origin.

www.orionbooks.co.uk

For Susan Lamb, Juliet Ewers, Kate Mills and Jemima Forrester
with enormous thanks

Part 1

Chapter 1

The Limmat Valley, Switzerland, 1944

It was spring, late morning. Flora breathed in the sweet, sharp air, closing her eyes and smiling blissfully. This must be what the best champagne tasted like. It made her feel quite dizzy. The sun was as yellow as a lemon in the powdery blue sky, and the train that had just left the station on its way to Zurich puffed white smoke as it became smaller and smaller, adding to the fairy-tale quality of the scene.

She collapsed on to a wooden bench, her long legs stretched out as far as they would go, arms resting on the bench's back, sorry to have just said goodbye to nice Mrs Rhona Charlesworth, the American-born lady from Zurich who came regularly to see Andrew and Else at the school.

St Thérèse's school had been established ten years before in memory of Mrs Charlesworth's daughter, Antonia, who had died of consumption. It was named after Saint Thérèse of Lisieux, a Carmelite nun, who had died of the same disease at the age of twenty-four.

Flora Knox had been at St Thérèse's since 1938, when she was eleven. Her parents were dead, and her Aunt Winifred had read an article in *The Lady* about the school for delicate children in Switzerland. Anxious to get rid of her niece, Flora had been despatched there on the pretence of having a persistent cough. The cough had disappeared shortly after her arrival and never returned. She and her aunt corresponded rarely.

After war broke out, Aunt Winifred hadn't bothered to

arrange for Flora to return to England during the months when it was possible to travel through unoccupied France. Once Germany had invaded that country, escape was impossible. Switzerland remained neutral, but there were occupied countries on every border.

Flora preferred to be left where she was. She hadn't enjoyed living with Aunt Winifred, who continued to transfer the school fees twice a year to a bank in Zurich; Flora's parents had left the money for their daughter's education, so her aunt wasn't out of pocket.

Another train was approaching, travelling very slowly along the lines that shimmered in the sunlight. Flora watched with interest as it came nearer, wondering if it intended to stop. The railway employee who had examined Mrs Charlesworth's ticket when they'd entered the station came on to the platform to watch. He was very young; about the same age as Flora. His uniform was much too big.

Flora would have to leave soon. A small bus would arrive shortly at the station to take her up and up the winding road as far as the Hotel St Aloysius, where Else would be waiting in the big Mercedes-Benz. The old car's engine was tied together with string, or so Else claimed. From there, the road turned into a bumpy earth path that led to the school – an old wooden convent, long ago abandoned, set within a small forest of tall evergreen trees. Else would have driven Mrs Charlesworth all the way to the station in Zurich if Andrew hadn't woken during the night with one of his horrendous headaches, which meant he would be confined to bed for the next few days. During that time Else wasn't prepared to leave the school for more than half an hour or so, not even with Flora in charge. It would have been irresponsible, she claimed.

The advancing train was gliding into the station, only the wheels making any sound; a dull *clickety-click, clickety-clack*, repetitive and hypnotic. It was a cattle train, a long line of slatted trucks. Flora lost interest and began to study her long, thin feet. She badly needed new shoes. She looked up when she became aware that the sounds coming from the train weren't made by cattle, but were human.

Oh, my God! She wasn't sure if she spoke the words aloud or not. She jumped to her feet. There were *people* in the trucks. She could see them here and there between the odd missing or broken slat; someone's shoulder, the top of a head, a pair of hands, the occasional white face regarding her with deep-sunken eyes. It was like something out of the worst of nightmares.

Agitated and horribly frightened, Flora began to walk alongside the train, waving her arms, wanting to help, wanting to make it stop, but the engine at the front was too far ahead. These people needed water and food. They were jammed together like – well, like cattle. The smell was atrocious; of lavatories, vomit and death.

'Where are you going?' she cried. 'Who are you?'

Nobody answered. The faces, the eyes, continued to stare. The sight would haunt her for the rest of her days.

'Signorina.'

Where had the voice come from? And was it her imagination, but was the train beginning to go faster?

'*Signorina.*' Louder now.

In the passing truck, hands were tearing away the wooden slats. More hands appeared. The wood snapped and splintered. A space was being cleared. A woman shouted desperately, 'Hurry!' The train had definitely picked up speed. Flora began to run.

A baby was thrust through the space. Flora ran faster and met the haunted eyes of another woman; black-haired, dark-eyed, desperate. 'Take him,' she gasped hoarsely. 'His name is Simon.'

'I've got him!' Flora grabbed the child from the woman's arms, stumbling backwards as the train hurried out of the station and out of her life.

She was on the bench again, shaken to the core, the baby on her knee. He was a big baby, quite a few months old. He wasn't crying, but she could tell from his little screwed-up face that he was in distress. Oh, and he did smell! His beautifully knitted lacy shawl was grubby, and he felt excessively hot. She moved the shawl to reveal dark red wavy hair. His eyes were a lovely clear green.

Flora lifted him on to her shoulder and gently patted his back. It just seemed the natural thing to do. 'There, there, Simon, darling,' she whispered. 'There, there.'

Everywhere looked exactly as it had done only minutes before: the station, the sun, the sky, the young railway worker, who hadn't moved a jot, everything. Yet nothing would ever be the same again.

Andrew Gaunt, a landscape artist of much promise, as he had been described after his first exhibition in London, had gone on to fight in the Spanish Civil War. He had been badly injured, and shortly afterwards nearly died of smoke inhalation when the church in which he had been sheltering was set on fire.

In hospital, he had fallen in love with his Swedish nurse, Else Landstrom, and she with him. The Civil War over and another world war about to begin, Else had taken her lover to Switzerland, where the pure air would be gentle on his scorched lungs and permanently weakened chest. A giant, broad-shouldered man with a thick thatch of hair that had turned white overnight, he was now thirty-five years old and little more than an invalid, mainly from the headaches that haunted him.

The problem of how they would make their living quickly arose when Andrew discovered he had no more interest in painting, and had lost the talent for it. Instead, he and Else started a school for frail youngsters, a place where they could spend just a few weeks convalescing, or however long was needed for the sake of their health. They resolved never to have more than twenty children at a time. It was then that they met Mrs Charlesworth, a resident of Zurich, who offered to fund their project in memory of her daughter.

For Andrew, the scheme became a fascinating experiment. Having been raised in the industrial Midlands, the only child of a mother with a penchant for reading the Bible aloud and a father who believed that sparing the rod spoiled the child, he was keen to see what a completely liberal upbringing would have on young minds.

The children at St Thérèse's were encouraged to express themselves without regard to what other people thought, to say whatever came into their minds, to spend the day in bed rather than attend lessons, should that be what they wished. He discovered that young people genuinely wanted to learn when left to their own devices; that they were quite capable of original thought when they hadn't been told what to think.

The former convent was a spacious, bright, single-storey building with numerous small rooms in which the nuns, who had gone to live in Africa, had slept, a large room where they had eaten, a chapel where they had prayed and a somewhat crude kitchen. There wasn't a bathroom, just a row of stalls, each containing a sink and a row of three lavatories that had been outside, but which Andrew had connected to the main building with a rough-and-ready covered passage.

It was nine o'clock in the evening; some of the children had gone to bed, some were playing table tennis in the dining room. The ones in bed might well be reading. Andrew or Else would tour the building later and douse the oil lamps. If anyone wanted to continue reading, they would have to do so by candlelight. At the present time, not counting Flora, there were only three girls and six boys, their ages ranging from eleven to fourteen.

The chapel had been deconsecrated and now served as a living room. Flora, just seventeen and almost an adult, usually stayed up late. She no longer attended lessons. Instead, she taught English language and literature with considerable verve and much throwing about of arms and rolling of eyes. Tonight, she would find it hard to sleep after the events of the day. She had just finished describing for the third or fourth time what had happened when she'd taken Mrs Charlesworth to the station that morning.

'I shall go back to the station tomorrow,' she was now saying, 'and should another train like the one today attempt to pass through, then I shall stand on the line and flag it down, giving the poor souls on board the chance to get off and be saved.'

'You will do no such thing, idiot,' Else said mildly. 'You will be mowed down. You will end up as bits in a box ready to be buried. And there's not likely to be another train like that. That one today must have lost its way, or something. It was a mistake.'

Else was small and pale, with wispy fair hair and wonderful blue eyes. She was as strong as an ox, capable of lifting absurdly heavy weights such as Andrew himself, on more than one occasion. He loved her more than life itself.

Flora was quite different. Tall and slender – perhaps a little too slender – she had silver-grey eyes that were flashing with anger at that moment, and very long blond hair that could also look silver in a certain light.

In their isolated ex-convent, little was known about the war except by Andrew and Else, who listened to the wireless in their bedroom. Until Andrew had told her earlier, Flora had been entirely unaware of the existence of concentration camps in other European countries where members of the Jewish race were being sent. She was horrified when told that the unfortunate passengers in the train were almost certainly Jews on their way to a camp in Germany or Poland.

'Mussolini,' said Andrew, 'despite being a Fascist, was not willing to imprison Italian Jews just to please his friend Hitler. But since Mussolini's downfall, Germany is now in control of part of Italy and is rapidly getting rid of the Jewish population. That is where the train you saw must have come from; Italy.'

'The woman who spoke to me, the first one, she called me, "Signorina",' Flora explained. 'But the one who gave me the baby spoke English – perhaps she did that because I had shouted in English.' Tears came to her eyes. 'Imagine how she must have felt, handing over her beautiful baby to a stranger.'

The baby, Simon, was half sitting, half lying in a wooden cradle an appropriate distance from the roaring fire. A handsome child with his auburn hair and unusual eyes, Else had guessed him to be about eight or nine months old and well looked after. His good-quality clothes had been removed and washed and were drying in the kitchen. Now he wore an assortment of much too big children's clothes. An old towel had been cut in four pieces to make nappies.

'He hasn't been circumcised,' Else had whispered earlier, 'so he might not be Jewish.'

'Poor little bugger.' Andrew shuddered. Instead of getting worse, as usually happened, his headache had got better as the day progressed. He wondered if it was the arrival of the baby, a change in routine, something out of the ordinary that had done it. Perhaps what he needed was a change in his life, in their lives, his and Else's, so that the headaches wouldn't come with such deadly regularity as they did at least once a month.

The baby was wide awake, unable to take his eyes off the dancing flames. After a bath, the fresh clothes, a meal of thin soup, apple purée and milk, all fed to him with a spoon, he seemed to have recovered from his ordeal on the train.

Tomorrow, Else would go to Zurich to buy baby food, a bottle and more clothes. He no doubt missed his mother, but he was being made an enormous fuss of, and that was enough to make him smile from time to time. Every now and again,

Flora would kiss him, hold his tiny hands or stroke his hair. She talked to him non-stop, telling him all sorts of things about herself, about Andrew and Else and about the school. The baby listened intently, his eyes locked on hers.

She was going to keep him for ever, she declared. 'He was given to me, and it is my duty to look after him.'

'But Flora,' Else argued, 'Simon will have had a father as well as a mother. Even if neither survives the war, there will be aunts and uncles, grandparents who will want him. As soon as this horrible war is over, your duty should be to find these people.'

Flora had looked momentarily nonplussed, but swiftly recovered her composure. 'How do I find them?' She shrugged, lifting her thin shoulders. 'The train came from Italy. So, who do we contact in Italy? His mother spoke English. What part of the United Kingdom does she come from? And she might be American or Canadian. How on earth would we find out?' She spoke quietly and reasonably. Flora rarely made a fuss, no matter how angrily or strongly she felt about something. She stooped over the baby and lifted him out of his cradle, pressing him against her breast. 'And Lord knows what sort of fate those poor people on the train are destined for. Who will know that he was given to me on the journey?'

'There are agencies,' Andrew murmured. He looked at Else and made a face. As Flora's teacher, it could only be his fault that she spoke like a forty-year-old. 'Organisations will have records, or can get them from other organisations. The Red Cross is one. They won't have you on their records, Flora dear, but in time they could well have Simon and his mother noted as having disappeared. There are probably ways they can be traced.'

Flora just smiled. The baby's arms had crept around her neck. She was convinced they were meant for each other. 'I don't trust agencies and organisations. It was an agency that took me to my Aunt Winifred after my mother and father died and insisted that she have me, when she didn't want me at all. I would have been far better off adopted or put in a home.'

Now Andrew smiled. 'But then we wouldn't have had the pleasure of your company all these years, Flora.'

'Nor me yours,' Flora conceded. 'I don't know how you have put up with me for so long. I know how stubborn and awkward and impatient I can be.'

'That is the way I have encouraged you to be,' Andrew said. 'Why should children automatically think that adults are always in the right when they could well be in the wrong?' But she was probably correct in what she said about the baby. The chances of locating his wider family were remote. As for the poor mother, she could only have given him to Flora in order to save his life.

The war was at a crucial stage. Having invaded Italy by way of Sicily, the British forces and their allies were gradually making their way northwards. Early in June, thousands of troops of different nationalities had crossed the English Channel and landed in Normandy. They began to fight their way across France. With the Russians attacking through Poland and the Allies advancing north through Italy, the German war machine was being assailed on all sides. There was every likelihood that the war would be over within the year.

In the little school of St Thérèse, cut off from everyday life, things continued as normal. There'd been no shortage of food or other necessities. Baby Simon thrived. Flora, who'd shown no aptitude for such work before his arrival, was constantly knitting him clothes. The finished garments were clumsily made, full of knots and dropped stitches, but the baby wore them without complaint.

It was September, and Andrew and Else were on the veranda watching the children climb trees and kick balls to each other. The girls had pitched a tent and intended sleeping in it that night. In front, a brilliant sun was setting in the dusky

sky. The Hotel St Aloysius, the only sign that other human beings existed on the planet, was like a doll's house in the distance far below them.

Andrew felt that his health had improved enough for him to travel, to find somewhere warmer for them to live, once this terrible war was over; perhaps even to paint again.

'I would like to stroll along a golden beach with the blue sea frothing at my feet,' he said somewhat poetically.

'What about our school?' Else enquired.

'It's not *our* school, Else, although we started it, but Mrs Charlesworth's. I'm sure she will find someone else to run it. Dozens of men would jump at the chance of living in such a remote, peaceful place after the violence of a war.'

'And women,' Else reminded him. 'The war was violent for everyone.'

'And women,' Andrew hastily agreed. He didn't want to be thought a misogynist. 'If you are agreeable, I shall suggest that Mrs Charlesworth engage a married couple. If she wants us to stay until she finds a replacement, then we will. We can't let her down.'

'Of course we can't.' Else slipped her small hand into his large one. 'I am agreeable, though I shall miss the children terribly. I do wish we could have some of our own, Andrew.'

Andrew sighed. 'Me too. But you know, there's time. We are both still in our thirties. We'll just have to try harder. And there was something I was going to suggest, any way.'

'And what's that?'

'That we take Flora and Simon with us. I doubt if Flora's aunt wants her back. In all these years, she has shown little interest in her niece. I have looked upon Flora as ours for a long time. She has no one close, and neither has Simon – at least, not that we are aware of.'

Else's lips twisted wryly. 'You're wrong, darling. Flora and Simon have each other.'

'But the two of them can't possibly manage on their own.'

He paused and sighed. 'And, in my humble opinion, it would be a very bad idea for them to try.'

Flora had designated the first of August as Simon's birthday. On the day itself, she had made a cake bearing a single candle and they'd eaten it after tea and sung 'Happy Birthday'. The other children loved him. He was everyone's baby brother, a happy child, full of life, tottering all over the place on his little fat legs, chattering away at ten to the dozen.

He was becoming spoiled, Else thought, but when she mentioned this to Flora, she pooh-poohed the idea. She didn't deny he was being spoiled, but couldn't see that it would do him any harm.

'I wish someone had spoiled me when I was a baby. As it was, my mother and father weren't there most of the time, and I was looked after by landladies, bit-part actors and stage-hands.' Flora's parents had belonged to a group of travelling actors based in Scotland who had toured that country and the North of England. They had died when their van crashed in the Scottish hills. Flora, aged six, was in the back wrapped in blankets, and had survived the accident. She made the remark without resentment, as she did whenever she spoke about her Aunt Winifred's unwillingness to take care of her. She had grown used to her lonely situation, and it no longer bothered her.

Simon was being cuddled on her knee. She gave him a tight squeeze and he giggled. 'When he grows up, maybe he will spoil *me*,' she remarked.

'Are you still determined to keep him?' Else asked.

Flora put her head on one side and said thoughtfully, 'If it's humanly possible, then yes.' She stood the little boy on her knee and they rubbed noses. 'I love you, love you, love you, Simon Knox,' she sang.

Simon giggled again. 'Love you, Flo,' he sang back.

Else sighed. Simon Knox! Any minute now Flora will claim

to have given birth to him. She somehow doubted if the mother would ever come back.

It was Christmas, and Allied troops were approaching Germany from different directions with the aim of coming together in Berlin.

'I think the end is in sight,' Mrs Charlesworth remarked when she arrived on New Year's Day to stay for a few days. She was a stout, comfortable woman who wore a maroon velvet turban throughout her visit. She was never seen without a hat. Flora had wondered if she was bald, but tufts of grey hair were visible on the back of her neck.

She had agreed to advertise for another couple to run the school as soon as the war was over. 'Travel will quickly be back to normal, the trains running and the planes flying. I am longing to visit my sisters and my brother in New York. In fact,' she said soberly, 'I might even decide to stay on there. I have been a widow a long time now, and lost my only child many years ago.' Mr Charlesworth had been the head of an American bank. 'It's only friends keeping me in Zurich.'

'Friends are far better than relatives,' Flora assured her with all the wisdom of a seventeen-year-old. 'Friends grow to like each other. With relatives, it's the other way around.'

Chapter 2

For the sake of all concerned, Flora desperately wanted the war to end, but could see no reason to alter the course of her life when it did.

She was therefore taken aback when she discovered that as soon as it was over, Andrew and Else genuinely did intend to give up the school and travel.

'Hopefully after a while we will find somewhere less isolated, and with a more comfortable climate, to settle down,' Andrew said, adding that he and Else dearly wished that she and Simon would join them on their travels. 'We would become a family,' he said warmly.

'But I want to stay here,' Flora wailed. 'I thought I would stay for the rest of my life.'

'Flora, my love,' Andrew said calmly, 'you are only eighteen. There is a big world out there for you to experience. You don't know a single person your own age, either male or female. The only adults you meet regularly are me and Else. You have never seen a film or a play, or gone to a dance or a party – I mean proper dances and parties, not the sort we have here.'

'I don't want any of those things,' Flora said sulkily. Andrew could tell she was upset, scared to leave the school and the protection it offered. For all her confident and assured manner, the tragedy of her early life must have affected her; the death of her parents, living with her miserable aunt in

London, then being despatched to Switzerland – actually on her own, at the age of eleven, with a list of the trains she had to catch pinned to her sleeve. Else had gone to Zurich station to collect her, and found her hiding her tears behind a fit of temper at the lateness of the train. She was enormously brave.

'Why can't *I* take over the school and run it?' she asked now. 'I've been helping you and Else for years.'

'Because you are much too young for the responsibility,' Andrew said patiently. 'It requires a couple, so that the responsibility is shared. And Else is a nurse. Some of the pupils arrive quite run-down. They have to be looked after. You couldn't possibly manage alone. Why won't you come with us, Flora dear?'

Flora shrugged and didn't answer.

She didn't like to tell them that she wanted Simon to herself; they wouldn't approve. Else and Andrew loved the little boy, adored him; and he loved and adored them back, though it was Flora he loved the most. If they lived together, the four of them, in an ordinary place, an ordinary town or city, then Flora would be encouraged to go to the parties and dances that Andrew spoke about, and to see the films and plays. The time would come when she would feel obliged to go to work. And who would look after Simon then? Else, of course, while Andrew was in his studio, painting, Simon would come to regard Else as his mother, while Flora was merely a woman who played a much smaller part in his existence.

In all her life, Flora had never loved anyone as much as she loved Simon. And she loved him not just for herself, but on behalf of the mother who had entrusted him to her care.

Once they became independent, she and Simon, money would become a matter of concern. She had not long turned eighteen, and her education was finished; so how much was left of her parents' legacy? Indeed, had there been a legacy? Perhaps there'd only been enough money for her education.

The minute the post was back to normal, she would write to her aunt and enquire.

Andrew had placed the wireless in the living room, where everyone could listen to the British Broadcasting Corporation relay the news of how the war was progressing. They all understood English perfectly and would cheer when it was announced that Paris had been reclaimed, then Brussels, Belgrade, Athens . . .

Germany had been bombed mercilessly, entire cities almost disappearing beneath the weight of numerous raids. Late in March, American forces captured two important enemy airfields. Winston Churchill himself was reported to have crossed the Rhine with the 21st Army Group. Soviet troops entered Austria. Concentration camps were liberated and vast horrors exposed. Flora half expected Simon's mother, having survived her own horror, to turn up wanting her son back. She would surely be able recall the place where she had handed him over to a stranger.

At the end of April, it was revealed that Adolf Hitler had killed himself and the children shouted for joy. To all intents and purposes, the war was over. For Andrew, it only proved that there was no such person as God. A real God would never have allowed such an evil man as Hitler to exist. He had turned his formerly civilized country into a monstrous killing machine, allowing it to perpetrate an evil unknown to humankind until then.

The entire school was invited to a party at the Hotel St Aloysius. A party seemed only fitting, as letters had begun to arrive at the postbox in Zurich to say that parents were withdrawing their children from the school. It would be a celebration and a farewell party combined. Perhaps because a certain terrible period in the history of the world had ended and a new one was about to begin, parents wanted their children safely home while they thought about the future.

Else let down the hem of Flora's only decent dress, removing lace from an old one to sew around the neck. Flora's thick, silvery-blond hair was washed, arranged in a swirl on top of her head and secured with a mother-of-pearl slide.

'You look very pretty,' Else said when she had finished. 'But you need some up-to-date clothes. Everything you have has been altered in one way or another as you have grown bigger.'

Flora had no wish to look pretty, nor did she want more clothes. All she wanted was to stay where she was for the rest of her life and look after Simon. She said as much to Else.

'And do you think,' Else replied, 'that when Simon grows up he will also want to stay here for the rest of his life?'

Flora had no idea. She found it impossible to look so far ahead.

Two French women, sisters called Juliette and Anne Clemence, arrived one day at the end of May with Mrs Charlesworth to look around the building. They were only young, in their twenties, and had an even younger sister who had been born with a brain defect. They wanted to turn the convent into a school for girls who had a similar defect.

Mrs Charlesworth didn't mind the school being used for a slightly different purpose than the one it was originally intended for. 'As long as it helps children,' she said privately to Andrew and Else – and to Flora, who was also listening. 'Consumption is no longer as prolific as it once was. Also there is talk of treating the disease with these newfangled antibiotics. Nowadays, patients are better off in hospitals, where they can be cured.' Until the recent discovery of antibiotics, there had been no known cure for consumption.

The Clemence sisters would take over the building in August, giving the present occupants just over two months to make other arrangements.

*

Their first port of call would be the South of France, Else told Flora. 'We will travel in the car, which is big enough for us all.' She seemed to take it for granted that Flora and Simon would come with them.

Flora had written to Aunt Winifred to tell her the school was closing. Her aunt had shown no interest in her as a child. Now she was eighteen, an adult, she might not care if she ever saw her niece again. If that was the case, she and Simon would go with Else and Andrew. She had said nothing about the little boy to her aunt.

The next time Else went into Zurich, she brought back a letter. Flora was in the kitchen, sorting things out for when the Clemence sisters came.

'It's from your aunt by the look of it,' Else said. 'It's post-marked London.'

To Flora's surprise, the letter was quite friendly. Her aunt wrote that she was looking forward to her niece coming home, and had apparently transferred twenty-five pounds into a Zurich bank to pay for her fare and any other expenses she might incur. *I still live in the same house in Crouch End*, she wrote. *It wasn't touched during the air raids. You can have your old room back. By the way, I no longer have a lodger. I look forward to seeing you again, Flora, dear.*

'I didn't know she took in lodgers,' Else said when Flora showed her the letter.

'She had two when I was there,' Flora explained. 'The first was a lovely lady called Isobel, who was a model and lived in the basement flat. After she left, a man called Johnnie took her place.' She frowned, remembering. 'Johnnie hated me. I think he was the reason she sent me away; to please him. He wanted my aunt all to himself.'

'But he was only the lodger!'

'I wouldn't be surprised if he was more than that,' Flora said with the benefit of hindsight. She had a rather muddled

19

memory of the man, with his swarthy skin and jet-black hair. 'Lucas – his name was Johnnie Lucas.'

As they spoke, Else was looking more and more disappointed. 'Does this mean you and Simon will be going back to London?'

'Well, yes,' Flora said cheerfully. She had loved her room on the second floor of the house in Crouch End. It was at the top of a hill, and looked out over hundreds, if not thousands more houses, their roofs an amazing assortment of colours. Forever the optimist, she promptly began to look forward to returning to the only other place she could call home.

Else put her parcels on the kitchen table. Flora had been clearing out cupboards and wiping shelves. Outside, Simon was attempting to climb a tree, but the trunk was too big for his arms to go around. He was alone, all the other children having returned to their homes. In a few weeks' time, Simon would be two years old, albeit on his unofficial birthday. He could be heard talking to himself – he had a considerable vocabulary for a child so young.

'Should I throw away everything that's cracked, even if it's only a hairline?' Flora asked Else, holding up a nice white jug.

Else gave the jug a brief glance. 'It's a lovely shape, but I only want to leave behind things that are perfect.' There was a crash as the jug was thrown in the bin. Secretly, Flora was enjoying smashing dishes.

'What will your Aunt Winifred think about Simon?' Else asked, nodding at the little boy through the window. 'She doesn't mention him in her letter.'

'She'll love him,' Flora said with utter certainty. 'How could anybody not love him?' In fact, she didn't feel the tiniest bit certain. She merely assumed that her aunt wouldn't be cruel enough to turn her niece away just because she'd turned up with a child – a handsome and completely adorable child.

Else said, 'I think we should visit Zurich a few times over the next few weeks, Flora, and do some shopping. We'll have lunch and ride on the trams. You need to get used to mixing with people in a city. Otherwise you'll feel like a fish out of water in a big place like London when you're there for good.'

It was August, the war had been over for nearly three months and the woman on the train had not returned for her baby.

'It means he is mine,' Flora said to herself. 'For ever mine.'

It hurt, really hurt, to say goodbye to Else and Andrew after so many years together. In fact, it hurt so much that Flora was on the point of changing her mind and going with them until she remembered the reason why she hadn't wanted to go in the first place.

Else took her in the Mercedes-Benz to Zurich station to catch the train to Paris, Andrew in the back with Simon on his knee. Flora knew her decision was the right one when she noticed how tightly Andrew was holding on to the child, as if he never wanted to let him go. Mind you, he didn't want to let Flora go, either.

She was assured that, should things go wrong in London, all she had to do was send a telegram and Andrew would come at the drop of a hat and rescue her. Flora had one of those rare moments when she wanted to cry, but was determined not to.

On the train, Simon appeared very conscious of the vast change in their once quiet and uneventful lives. 'We are going on a long journey,' Flora had told him earlier, and he'd looked suitably impressed. He sat very still on her knee after pulling her arm around him like a cloak to hide behind, gazing at the other passengers in the compartment with the same sort of wonderment as a visitor would from another planet on seeing human beings for the first time. He had seen so few people in his short life, and those were mainly children, mainly speaking English. He sucked his thumb and peeped through

Flora's fingers while clutching his favourite toy, a teddy bear whose name was Rufus.

The woman seated opposite was charmed. 'Are you his nurse, or his mother?' she asked Flora, after poking the little boy in his stomach several times. It was supposedly an affectionate gesture, but Simon clearly didn't know what to make of it. The woman spoke German, the language used in that part of Switzerland. Flora knew enough to have a reasonable conversation.

'He's my cousin,' she replied. 'His parents died in the war.' She would have loved to have claimed to be Simon's mother, but then she would have had to invent a husband, and he would have to be dead because Simon couldn't possibly be illegitimate and looked upon as a bastard. It would have become terribly complicated. This way, if people asked she would say Simon's mother and father had died recently in an accident, as her own parents had. She would tell Aunt Winifred the truth, of course. The passport Andrew had acquired for Simon by illicit means was tucked in Flora's new handbag.

She felt uncomfortable at the way the two young men in the window seats kept looking at her surreptitiously over their newspapers. She got the same look in Paris while queuing for a taxi, and the man in front insisted she take his place, helping her, Simon and the suitcase inside and doffing his hat courteously. There was no denying the admiration in his eyes, and it dawned on her that it was because she looked pretty.

Else had told her when she was ready for the journey, wearing her new blue wool dress, white shoes and gloves, and a white hat that was little more than an organdie bow. 'You're a sight for sore eyes, Flora. Isn't that what they say in your country? I have always thought it a most peculiar compliment.'

In Paris, the taxi had taken them from the Gare de l'Est to a hotel in République where they would spend the night. Flora would have loved to have gone for a walk around the city, but Simon was exhausted. They had a light meal in their room and afterwards she read him stories; sweet, gentle fairy stories because he was too young to know about wicked witches and child-eating wolves.

The view from the window was of the side of another hotel, and Flora spent the evening watching the little boy sleep clutching Rufus, and listening to the sounds of the city: the traffic, an accordion being played somewhere out of sight, sometimes accompanied by the haunting voice of a woman singing, and passers-by arguing loudly, late into the night. She vowed that one day she would return to Paris and explore it properly, perhaps with Simon when he was older.

Early tomorrow morning, they would travel by taxi to the Gare du Nord and catch the train to Boulogne and the ferry to Folkestone. From there, another train would take them to London. They would arrive in Crouch End at about tea time. Flora couldn't wait.

Chapter 3

Aunt Winifred was expecting her, but not so much that she could be bothered to come and meet her one and only relative at Charing Cross station. She opened the door of the house in Crouch End, not looking the slightest bit different to how she'd looked when Flora had left seven years before. Of course, Flora had grown from a child to a woman in those years, whereas Aunt Winifred had merely gone from being thirty-nine to forty-six, which didn't seem nearly as long.

She could easily have been taken for fifty-six, and had always looked older than her age. It wasn't that she had grey hair, or that her long, oval face was heavily wrinkled; it was more that she bore the expression of a woman born out of date. Even in photographs as a child she had had an oddly serious look, as if she couldn't wait to age.

Flora could actually recall her wearing the clothes she had on now, or very similar: a droopy grey skirt totally out of fashion, going by the skirt of her own fashionable frock, and the ones she'd seen women wearing on the journey; a lighter grey blouse with the inevitable black cardigan over it, despite it being a beautifully warm, summer day. She wore the same jet earrings and a long necklace to match. Her eyes were muddy brown. The entire house, Flora recalled, was as dismal as her aunt's appearance, full of dark furniture with dark walls. She had always imagined it was how a funeral parlour would look.

'Flora!' Aunt Winifred clumsily embraced her niece, who was overwhelmed by the scent of the eau de cologne she had always used – Wild Bluebell. 'Did you have a frightful journey, dear?'

'It was tiring,' Flora conceded. She was longing for a cup of coffee, but from now on would have to make do with tea. She had never known Aunt Winifred to use coffee.

'Are you hungry? I have a small meal made, only sandwiches for now.'

'That would be nice.' Flora couldn't be sure if her aunt was deliberately ignoring the presence of Simon, or had genuinely not noticed he was there, standing by the suitcase, waiting to be kissed and made a fuss of. It had happened numerous times on the boat and the trains they had travelled on, and he automatically expected it to happen again with this new lady.

'And who's this?' Aunt Winifred took a step backwards, unable to avoid any longer the presence of a strange child on her doorstep.

'My name is Simon,' the little boy announced gravely. He lifted his arms to be picked up, but Aunt Winifred took another backward step and it was Flora who picked him up instead.

'I will explain about him later,' she said.

'Of course, do come in.' The woman looked flustered. 'I'll put the kettle on.'

'So, you see,' Flora was saying two hours later. Simon was tucked up in bed in the room on the second floor. 'I feel as if he was a gift from God, who chose me to look after him.' This rather dramatic statement wasn't exactly true. Andrew had never taught his pupils anything about religion, and had made no secret of the fact that he didn't believe in God. The children left the school uncertain as to whether or not God existed. Flora still wasn't sure herself.

Her aunt's house was part of a long, seemingly endless

terrace. It had three large bedrooms, an attic room where Flora would sleep, a bathroom, three downstairs rooms and a basement. It was where her father and Aunt Winifred, his sister, had been born.

Flora had forgotten how lovely the garden was in summer. The French windows of the living room at the back were open, and the scent of roses drifting in was overpowering, delicious. Gardening was Aunt Winifred's hobby, as well as knitting garments on very fine needles from complicated patterns that took ages to complete.

She was knitting now, and sniffed delicately. 'So, you are saying that Simon is Jewish?'

'Almost certainly, though he hasn't been circumcised, thank goodness. Andrew claims it is a diabolical practice.'

Aunt Winifred had turned pink with embarrassment. 'I wouldn't know, dear,' she said distantly.

'Tomorrow, will it be all right if I move another bed into my room, so Simon and I can have one each? Tonight, just for once, we can sleep together.'

'As you wish, Flora. I must say, I wasn't expecting you to bring a child home with you. I'm not used to small children. You didn't arrive until you were six, and you were a very quiet little girl.'

'You will soon get used to him,' Flora assured her, ignoring the reference to herself. 'He is the best little boy in the entire world. Before you know it, you will love him madly.'

Aunt Winifred didn't exactly fall in love with Simon, but she became fond of him. She would chuck him under the chin when they first met in the morning, and do the same when he went to bed at night. She never picked him up or cuddled him. He called her Auntie Win, and tried to pull her hair or do things to her face that she always managed to avoid. A few weeks after their arrival, she bought him a spinning top from Hamley's Toy Emporium in Regent Street.

Simon appeared to be quite happy with London. Flora often woke to find him at the window in their bedroom, gazing intently at the spread of roofs outside.

'See the smoke, Flo,' he would say gravely. Smoke fascinated him, the way it leaned to the right or to the left in the wind or, on a still day, streamed upwards in a straight line. Sometimes it was white, or it might be grey or black. Occasionally it was mixed with little red sparks, or came out in puffs if a fire was being started. Like smoke signals, Flora thought. 'I love smoke, Flo,' Simon would say. 'One day, will Auntie Win let me light the fire downstairs?'

'Not until you're much older, darling.'

One of the first things Flora did was to establish if there was still money left for her by her parents. 'I don't want to start work until Simon is ready for school, which won't be for another three years. Is there enough to keep us both until then?' she enquired anxiously of her aunt.

'Not quite,' Aunt Winifred replied. 'But, Flora, you are my niece. I am more than willing to let you stay as long as you . . . as you and Simon . . . want. And,' she added generously, 'I will give you a personal allowance of, say, twenty-five shillings a week.'

Flora treated her to an effusive hug. 'Thank you, Auntie dear.'

Although she would always miss Andrew and Else, she was glad that she had returned to London, having decided she wasn't suited to leading a wandering existence with a small child in tow. She discovered that she enjoyed crowds, noise and the hustle and bustle of city life. Two postcards had already arrived, one from the South of France with a picture of Nice, in which the sea was a highly unnatural blue that Flora didn't fancy one bit. The other was from a place called Menton, which she thought looked terribly dull, whereas London was truly fascinating now that she was seeing it as an adult.

We are about to move on, Andrew had written, *and look for somewhere more interesting to live, a place with more character. Else sends her love to you both.*

There was a row of kisses that could only have been put there by Else; Andrew wasn't the sort of person to send kisses.

The lovely summer was turning into a hazy golden autumn. Flora took Simon for long walks in the second-hand pushchair bought with her allowance. Sometimes it was just around Crouch End, to Priory Park and up and down Nelson Road, which was long; they lived at the very top. It was incredibly steep, and she would run down like a madwoman, the pram's wheels clattering on the pavement, Simon screaming with delight. Going up again was a bit of a struggle, and she was usually exhausted by the time she reached the top.

Other days, they would go on the bus to places like Buckingham Palace or Hyde Park, have tea, or milk in the case of Simon, in Lyons Corner House in Oxford Street. Simon loved travelling on the bus or the underground trains, his green eyes shining with excitement at the various sights he could see from the open windows. He must have thought that Flora would miss seeing the brightly coloured shops, the pretty flowers, the dogs he longed to stroke if he didn't point them out, banging sharply on the glass with his forefinger and squealing, 'Look, look, look, Flo. *There!*'

'I see, darling.' Flora would hug him, overcome with love.

When on foot, she would try to avoid passing the buildings damaged, or even demolished altogether, in the wicked air raids on London. How could she explain them to Simon? And they made her feel uncomfortable and ashamed. She was British, yet had avoided every single part of the terrible war that had ended so recently. It didn't seem right to have missed the bombing, the rationing and the pain and anguish suffered by her fellow citizens. Mind you, rationing was still in force and it was amazing, the small amount of food each person existed on. She and Simon had acquired a ration book each, and Aunt Winifred had registered them with Worrall's Grocers in Crouch End Broadway. Apart from gardening, Flora quickly discovered that her aunt was rather lazy, and it was she who collected the rations every Tuesday.

Luke Carr, a remarkably handsome young man whom she'd met in Priory Park where he was walking the family dog, Bertha, and who lived at the bottom end of Nelson Road, told her that the population had never been as healthy as they had been during the war. They weren't able to overeat, and it had done everyone good, in particular having to go without sugar. He also described the Anderson shelter in the garden where his family had slept for nearly six years.

'It's still there,' he told her. 'It used to have bunks in. You can come and look at it, if you like. Nowadays my dad uses it as a workshop.'

Mrs Carr, Luke's mother, was as thin as a scarecrow and incredibly glamorous, with waist-length black hair. She had three younger children, another boy and two girls. The Carrs' house was exactly the same as Aunt Winifred's, but inside couldn't have looked more different with its pastel-painted walls, vividly coloured curtains and modern furniture. It was full of the children and their friends.

Gloria Carr would have loved to feed them all. 'But it takes me all my time to feed my own lot out of the rations. I'm sorry I can't ask you to stay to lunch or tea, Flora. But I do have a bar of chocolate for Simon. Come along, Simon darling. Sit on my knee. Oh, I do miss having small children. I would have had ten if Thomas had let me.'

Simon would go to her willingly. He was a friendly child; the opposite of shy. Flora would sometimes wonder if, deep in his young brain, any memory remained of the time he had spent with his mother, particularly on the train – the 'train of death', as she was inclined to think of it.

Thomas, Gloria's husband, worked in the City buying and selling stocks and shares on behalf of his rich clients. Evenings and weekends he spent in the Anderson shelter – a damp, smelly structure half underground with vegetables planted in the soil on top – making ornamental model boats that he gave away to anyone who'd have one. Flora was given a ketch with dark red sails for Aunt Winifred, who must have only pretended to be pleased when it was presented to her; the following day Flora discovered it had been placed on the tallboy in her and Simon's bedroom.

It seemed no time before Luke's mother was referring to Flora as his girlfriend. But there was nothing romantic about Flora and Luke's relationship. She liked him and he liked her, and that was all.

Luke had always planned on going to university to study chemistry, but the war had come along and, just prior to his eighteenth birthday, his call-up papers had arrived.

'I was quite happy to join the army, navy, or air force, but instead I was sent down a mine in Wales,' he told Flora disgustedly. 'When I wake up, I can still smell coal dust.'

Now he was twenty-one, and was starting a degree course at Manchester University, commencing on the first of October.

'Will you write to me?' he asked.

'Of course,' she promised.

'Can I have a photo of you to take with me? Would you mind if I told people you were my girlfriend?'

'I wouldn't mind a bit.' All she had was a passport photo taken in Zurich, in which she thought she looked as ugly as a witch. She had two new photos taken; one by herself for Luke, and one with Simon to send to Andrew and Else when she had an address for them.

She missed Luke quite a lot after he'd gone, and began to

look forward to Christmas when she would see him again. His letters arrived weekly, and were becoming more and more amorous. Flora would have liked to write amorous ones back, but felt too embarrassed.

She became friends with his sister, Millie, who was seventeen and mad on films. Millie bought the *Picturegoer* magazine every week, read it from cover to cover and knew all sorts of personal details about every well-known film star. She was shocked to learn that Flora had never seen a picture in her life, and was only too willing to introduce her to the silver screen, as she called it.

'I think you should see Humphrey Bogart first; he's gorgeous, in a really ugly way. Spencer Tracy's the same. You couldn't exactly call him handsome. Cary Grant's incredibly charming, and Tyrone Power must be the best-looking man alive.'

'Aren't there any women in films?' Flora enquired.

'Of course; there's Betty Grable − her legs are insured for thousands of dollars; Dorothy Lamour, Katharine Hepburn − she's reputed to be Spencer Tracy's mistress.' Millie shook her head dismissively. 'But the women aren't even as faintly interesting as the men. I'm determined to marry a film star one day. I'm actually saving up for a plane ticket to fly to Hollywood.'

'Honestly?' Flora was impressed.

'Anyway,' Millie went on. 'Humphrey Bogart's latest film is on in the West End. It's called *To Have and Have Not*. It got marvellous reviews. Shall we go and see it at the weekend?'

Flora said she couldn't wait.

The leaves began to fall in Aunt Winifred's garden, and the roses died. She tidied it regularly, cutting the heads off the flowers, collecting the leaves and brushing the little paved path.

'It won't look pretty again until it snows and the holly

berries appear,' she said one day late in October, 'and then it won't be for long.' She had entered the room from the garden through the French windows. She removed her boots, took them into the kitchen and came back wearing slippers. 'I do feel sad when everything dies.'

'But they don't die completely, do they?' Flora remarked with a smile. 'I mean, they're still alive underneath the soil, and start growing again when spring comes.'

'I suppose so, dear. But they're not visible, are they?'

Her aunt looked extremely miserable. Flora wasn't surprised. She led a remarkably dull life. Three afternoons a week she went to play bridge with friends. One afternoon, the friends would come and play bridge with her. Miss Herriott was a spinster, like Aunt Winifred, and the other two were widows. Apart from her aunt, all these ladies were in their sixties, possibly older. In the evenings, she stayed in knitting and listening to the wireless. Since Flora had arrived, she didn't even leave the house to do the shopping. Flora tried to persuade her to go to the pictures, but she refused. For herself, the cinema was a wonderful, magical invention; she would have gone to see a different picture every night of the week if it had been possible.

'Why did Isobel leave?' Flora asked one night.

'Isobel?' Her aunt frowned.

'The model who lived in the basement flat. You and she used to go and see musicals together. She would sing the songs afterwards. I remember she had a lovely voice.' Her aunt had seemed so much happier and more alive in those days.

'Ah, yes,' her aunt nodded. 'Her name was Isobel Devlin. Her young man was a dancer, and managed to get tickets half-price. The shows were lovely. Noël Coward, Ivor Novello.' Her eyes lit up. 'The songs were lovely, too "I'll See You again" and "I Can Give You the Starlight". They were my favourites. Ah, yes, those were the days . . .' She sighed dreamily. 'Isobel used to invite me to the fashion shows, where she wore the most beautiful clothes.'

'Why did she leave?' Flora asked again.

'Her mother became ill; she had to go back to Liverpool, a place called Bootle. But we've stayed in touch. We always exchange cards at Christmas.'

'Could I write to her?' Flora asked eagerly. 'Tell her I'm back home?

'Of course, dear. I'll give you her address.'

Since coming home, Flora had often wondered what had happened to Johnnie Lucas, who had taken over the basement flat after Isobel, but she had disliked him so much that she wasn't prepared so much as to mention his name.

The weather was becoming colder, and Flora didn't possess a winter coat. Aunt Winifred produced a black sealskin jacket smelling of mothballs out of a wardrobe in one of the spare bedrooms, making the surprising announcement that it had belonged to Flora's mother, who must have left it there by accident.

'It should fit you,' she said. 'Your mother was the same build, though not so tall.'

At this point, she left the room and Flora tried on the jacket in front of the wardrobe mirror. She blurred her eyes, but the figure in the mirror still looked exactly like her and nothing like the mother she was trying to resurrect.

She sat on the bed. She didn't think about her parents all that often. After the accident in which they had both been killed, she'd been so stunned that she'd found it impossible to believe they were dead. But when the time came, and she realised this wasn't a play that they were in, that the stage curtains had closed on this particular act and would never open again, the six-year-old Flora had wanted to die too. But she hadn't known how to make that happen.

Sitting on the bed now, twelve years later, Flora wondered

if, had she known of the ways a person could commit suicide, she would have done it. 'I reckon so,' she murmured. She hadn't wanted to live any more without her mum and dad.

But she had lived. And it wasn't until that morning on a railway station not far from Zurich, when a baby had been thrust into her arms, that she'd understood there'd been a reason for her to stay alive.

She felt in the pockets of the coat, hoping to find a crumpled handkerchief, an odd earring, some memento of her mother. But there was nothing.

Chapter 4

It was almost Christmas, and Luke Carr was home from university. He'd hardly been in the house a minute when he came to see Flora, who found herself surprisingly pleased to see him. They kissed in Aunt Winifred's hallway, if not passionately, then something close to it.

'It's lovely to see you again, Flora,' he said huskily. 'I've missed you badly.'

'And me you,' Flora replied, just as huskily.

'Where's that horrid little boy you always seem to have with you?' Luke cried. 'Much to my surprise, I've missed him too.'

Simon toddled out of the living room. 'Me not horrid,' he said, eyes twinkling. 'You horrid boy, Luke, not Simon.'

Flora grabbed her coat, and Simon's, and they all went for a walk. Her aunt wasn't very keen on visitors, and Luke had never been any further inside the house than the hallway.

This was the first peacetime Christmas for seven years, and shop owners had decorated their windows with pretty lights and bright colours. Crouch End had suddenly become a dazzling and enchanting place, and Simon loved it.

And so did Flora. She held Luke's and Simon's hands, and thought what a wonderful world it was.

The Carrs were having parties on Christmas Day and New Year's Eve. Aunt Winifred had helped Flora make a dress from

a remnant of red crêpe material she'd bought in Petticoat
Lane. It was plain and very elegant, or so Flora thought. She
was really looking forward to the holiday. Else and Andrew
had sent her a glorious scarf from Morocco. As fine as a
spider's web, it was all the colours of the rainbow and would
look good with her new dress. For Simon there was a wooden
jigsaw that Andrew had made. It turned out to be a lorry when
put together.

Mrs Charlesworth in New York sent a diamante brooch
shaped like the Statue of Liberty, and a jack-in-the-box for
Simon. Her colourful card said that she was very happy, and
glad that she had decided to leave Zurich. *Now I am with my
own kind*, she wrote. Flora asked Luke to take a photo of
Simon to send to Mrs Charlesworth, who had been extremely
fond of the boy.

Else had written to say that they were thinking of settling in
Morocco, in a city called Casablanca.

*It's beautifully warm here, very cheap and a really fascinating
place to live. There's actually a film called* Casablanca *– you
must try and see it. We have rented a lovely pink house with a
roof garden, and Andrew is trying to get an English-language
school started, but hopes to have time to paint as he feels greatly
inspired again. You and Simon are always welcome to come and
stay.*

She had added an address for Flora to write to.

Flora had also heard back from Isobel Devlin in Liverpool,
who'd expressed herself absolutely delighted to receive her
letter. She lived in a place called Pearl Street, such a pretty
address.

Of course I remember you, Flora, she had replied. *Fancy
having to ask! I remember us being very good friends. If I recall,
you also wanted to be a model when you grew up. Well, you're*

grown up now, but you didn't say what you are doing. I really would love to see you, darling. If you are ever able to spare a few days, you are very welcome to stay with us in Liverpool. We have a spare bedroom, so can easily put you up.

She must be very popular – two invitations to visit! Flora hadn't mentioned Simon in her letter to Isobel – it was just too complicated to explain. She was always very conscious that she was telling lies when she said he was her orphaned cousin, but not only did the real truth sound too far-fetched, she didn't want people to know how she had come by Simon. It was too personal, and she wouldn't tell Simon himself until he was much older.

A parcel arrived for Flora on Christmas Eve, containing a pretty rose-quartz and silver necklace. There was a note from Isobel inside that said it had been given to her twenty years before by a Polish count. *He wasn't a very rich count, or the jewels would have been more precious. I haven't worn it in ages, and I'm sure it would be better off decorating a much younger neck than mine.*

On Christmas Day, the party at the Carrs' started at three o'clock with a buffet lunch. Flora took a dozen mince pies that Aunt Winifred had made as a contribution towards the meal. Simon was presented with a giant pedal fire engine that had belonged to the Carr children when they were little. It had been renovated and repainted bright red by their father. The little boy was delighted, though Flora had no idea where he would play on it – Aunt Winifred would never allow it in her garden, and Simon couldn't very well pedal it up and down Nelson Road; going down, it would run away with him, and pedalling back would be beyond him. The lorry jigsaw that Andrew had sent was far more sensible, if just a bit too young for Simon's sharp brain. He'd been able to put it together in a matter of seconds.

Later in the afternoon, Georgina and Thomas Carr went to a cocktail party with friends in Muswell Hill, more of the children's friends arrived and dance records were played as well as games such as postman's knock and charades. This was the sort of party that Else and Andrew had talked about; nothing like the ones they'd had at St Thérèse's school. Flora felt a little nervous, but still managed to enjoy herself.

Luke kissed her whenever they came across each other in the crowd of young people, who were gradually becoming quite wild as they chased each other from room to room playing some mysterious game of their own, followed by Bertha, the dog, barking madly. By this time Simon, with Rufus in his arms, had fallen asleep in the fire engine that had been brought into the kitchen, and Flora refused to leave him in case he woke up and was frightened, or someone fell over him in the excitement, Luke was attempting to keep some sort of order.

In the midst of the chaos, Flora decided to go home. She transferred a sleepy Simon to his pushchair, and Luke promised to bring the fire engine with him next day, when they would go for a walk in Priory Park.

At home, Simon was put to bed straight away, and Flora spent the evening with her aunt listening to a wonderful play on the wireless, *An Inspector Calls* by J. B. Priestley. Aunt Winifred produced a bottle of sherry, and they had a small glass each. It made a tranquil end to an extremely hectic day.

Or so Flora thought. She was woken up in the middle of the night by the sound of the telephone ringing. She had known there was a telephone in the hall downstairs, but this was the first time it had rung since she'd come to live there. For some reason – due perhaps to the lateness of the hour – she found the ringing horribly sinister. Outside, it was completely quiet and the ringing seemed to be the only sound in the world.

Eventually it stopped, and Flora wondered if the phone

had been answered. She got up, checked that Simon hadn't been disturbed and opened the door of her room. Downstairs, she could hear her aunt's voice, but not what she was saying. Not wanting to eavesdrop, Flora closed the door and went back to bed. For the rest of the night she only half slept, and couldn't get the ringing of the telephone out of her head. Who had called her aunt at such a strange hour?

Next morning, she waited for Aunt Winifred to explain who the call was from, but she said nothing, and from this Flora gathered that she was expected to say nothing either.

Two days later, leaving Simon fast asleep in his bed on the second floor, Flora went to the cinema with Millie and Luke Carr to see Spencer Tracy and Katharine Hepburn in a picture called *The Keeper of the Flame*. It had a complex and mysterious plot. Back in Crouch End, they discussed it in the Carrs' kitchen over a cup of coffee.

'It reminded me a lot of *Citizen Kane*,' Millie remarked with a knowledgeable air.

'Me too,' Luke nodded just as knowledgeably. 'It's all about undeserved power used badly.'

Flora hadn't seen *Citizen Kane* and said as much, whereupon Millie promised to take her, no matter which cinema it happened to be on at.

Luke looked glum, and reminded them that he wasn't likely to be around. 'I'll be going back to Manchester soon.'

'Don't worry, brother dear, I'll look after your beloved girlfriend for you,' Millie told him with a sweet smile. 'Oh, and by the way Flora, bagsy me be your bridesmaid when you get married.'

Flora and Luke didn't speak much as they walked up Nelson Road to her aunt's house. *Married!* Flora was sure that the path towards marriage should be much more meaningful and ardent than it had been so far. She prayed Luke wouldn't do anything silly like propose; she truly wasn't ready for it, and hopefully neither was he.

At the gate, he merely kissed her sedately. Perhaps he'd been just as taken aback by Millie's words as she had.

Inside the house, she was about to go into the living room to announce she was home, but paused outside. Voices were coming from inside the room, and one was a man's.

She frowned, changed her mind and hurried upstairs. Simon woke when she entered the room, though only to mutter a few words. ' 'Night, Flo,' without even opening his eyes.

Flora kissed him tenderly. ' 'Night, darling.' She stroked his forehead and returned downstairs. Her aunt was listening to the wireless, and an announcer on the BBC was reading the news. Was this the man's voice she had heard?

'You're home early, Flora,' her aunt said.

'Not really.' She was actually quite late, but couldn't be bothered arguing. It must have been the newsreader that she'd heard when she came in. 'If you don't mind, I'll make myself some cocoa and go to bed. Would you like some?'

'No, thank you, dear. You know,' her aunt continued, 'I've been thinking, while you were out. Simon is a beautiful little boy, but he is holding you back. You are not yet nineteen, and should be out enjoying yourself, having a good time. You have taken on the responsibilities of a mother without having had a child.' She shook her head dolefully.

'What do you suggest I do with him?' Flora enquired coldly. She didn't remind her aunt that she'd been out enjoying herself that very night.

Her aunt didn't reply. She merely shrugged uncomfortably, and Flora went to bed.

Luke came next morning, out of breath from carrying the fire engine up the hill. So far, the toy hadn't spent a single night at Aunt Winifred's.

'It wouldn't be a bad idea to keep this at our house,' he gasped. He kissed Flora modestly on the cheek.

'Actually,' she said, 'it's a very good idea; I've no idea where it can be kept here.' They were standing in the hallway.

Simon appeared, grinning happily at the sight of his new toy, and all three of them went down the hill to the park. He didn't seem to mind that he and the fire engine slept under different roofs. Flora and Luke sat on a bench while the little boy pedalled his new toy up and down the path. They were being very stiff with each other, sitting a good foot or so apart, talking about last night's party, the weather and Luke's course at university. Flora had yet to understand what chemistry was all about.

Then Luke said, 'What our Millie said, about being a bridesmaid; let's not think about that sort of stuff yet, eh?'

'Absolutely not,' Flora said, relieved. 'Let's just carry on the way we are.'

They edged towards, each other, kissed sweetly and left it at that.

Later, Luke said, 'Do you know where the gangster lives? Mum told me he's come back to live at your end of the road.'

'The gangster?' Flora queried.

'Yes, horrible chap. During the war, he stole from houses that had been damaged during the air raids; took money and jewellery and other valuables. Sometimes the inhabitants were actually dead, having been killed in the raid. Fortunately the police caught him, and he was sent to prison. *Un*fortunately, he must have got out over Christmas, and he's back living in the same house. Mum said one of our neighbours had seen him.'

Flora's imagination was a mile wide. A horrible suspicion entered her mind. She thought about the phone call in the middle of the night and the man's voice in the kitchen which, in fact, thinking about it now, was much rougher than the one

on the wireless had been. 'What's the gangster's name?' she
asked Luke.

'I've no idea. I'll ask Mum, she'll know.' Suddenly, he put
his arm around her shoulders. 'Shall we go out to dinner
tonight and celebrate?'

'Celebrate what?'

'Oh, everything,' he said gaily. 'That we're still alive after a
horrible war, for instance, that we're young and have long
futures ahead of us, that we are both extraordinarily attractive
people, that we *know* each other . . . Oh, there's so many
things we can celebrate.' He laughed out loud. 'And I shall tell
our Millie that she definitely can't come.'

'All right,' Flora agreed, quite caught up in the moment.
'Where, and what time?'

'Have you ever had a Chinese meal?'

'No.' Chinese people ate loads of rice; that much she knew.

'Neither have I, so shall we go to that new place in Crescent
Road, The Blue Moon? I'll call for you at seven.'

'Make it half past. Aunt Winifred insists on Simon being
asleep before I go out.' She was already looking forward to it.

Flora had half expected Luke to discuss their relationship,
and was pleased when he did no such thing, just made fun of
politicians and told her about his experiences at university in
Manchester. He'd got into a few scrapes, had climbed things
he shouldn't have climbed, been discovered playing cards for
money in the middle of the night and done other things he
was too embarrassed to tell her about.

'Yes, but have you *learned* anything?' Flora wanted to know.
After finishing the meal, they were now having coffee.

'A bit,' he conceded. 'In fact, in between all those terrible
acts, I studied really hard.' She swore she believed him, and
he followed this by saying that he had learned something of
interest that very day, though it was nothing to do with
chemistry. 'That gangster I told you about, the criminal who's

come back to live in our road, Mum told me his name. It's John Lucas, more commonly known as Johnnie.'

Flora didn't speak for quite some time. Yesterday she had smelled tobacco in the living room. Then there'd been the man's cough she'd heard in the middle of the night that she assumed had come from the man next door, though she'd never known it to be so loud before. Aunt Winifred had been in a strange mood, very quiet, very thoughtful. Flora had spoken to her a few times and she'd claimed not to have heard.

If Johnnie Lucas was back living in Nelson Road, it could only be in her aunt's house. And he was there now, while Simon was lying asleep and helpless upstairs. And he had been there last night, too.

Flora told herself she was being silly. Her aunt would never allow Johnnie Lucas to touch Simon, or harm him in any way. But he was evil enough to have stolen from houses damaged by Hitler's bombs, and in some houses the people had been dead, or so Luke had said. She recalled how much she'd hated him, how frightened she had been, when she'd lived there as a child – the way he'd stared at her, the way he'd spoken in a deep, coarse growl. He was like a gypsy, with his black greasy hair and dark glittering eyes. In 1936 after Isobel, with her lovely clothes and delicious scents, had left – to return to Liverpool, Flora had since learned – Aunt Winifred had advertised for a new tenant in the window of the paper shop only a few doors away from the restaurant where Flora and Luke were sitting right now. Instead of turning away the unpleasant individual who had responded to her advert, her aunt had taken him in. Surprisingly, they had got on well together.

Flora also recalled the strange thing her aunt had said the night before, about Simon being a burden; that she'd be better off without him. Who had put that idea into her head? She jumped to her feet, pushing her chair away so hard that it made quite a clatter. She had a real and horrible feeling that something was very wrong. It was imperative that she go home immediately.

'What's the matter?' Luke looked up at her in surprise.

'I have to go.'

He still looked surprised. 'Let me pay the bill first.'

But Flora wasn't willing to wait. She grabbed her coat and was out of the restaurant before Luke had had a chance to call the waiter. Once outside, she made a beeline for Nelson Road. By the time she reached her aunt's house at the top, her breath was hoarse and rusty in her chest. She had to cling to the gate for quite a few minutes until she could breathe easily again. Then she took the key out of her bag, unlocked the door and went inside.

Her intention had been to race upstairs and make sure Simon was fast asleep, undisturbed and perfectly all right as he had been last night, except the first thing she heard when she entered the hall was a man roaring with laughter in the living room, and the answering chuckle of a child.

Simon! Simon had been brought downstairs, and he and Johnnie Lucas were laughing together. Flora felt tears come to her eyes. She was full of a mixture of rage and fear. She changed direction and made for the living room. Pushing open the door, she saw her aunt sitting smiling in the armchair on one side of the fire, and Johnnie Lucas in the other, holding Simon, in his striped pyjamas, on his knee.

Fiona had no idea what to say. She stood there staring at the child she loved more than anything else in the world, and the man she hated. Simon chuckled again, and waved when he saw her.

Aunt Winifred said, 'He woke up, Flora, and Johnnie brought him down. I was going to make him some milk in a minute. Would you like a drink, dear?' Flora ignored her.

Johnnie Lucas jiggled Simon up and down on his knee. The little boy shrieked with glee. 'He's a bonny little chap,'

44

Johnnie said. For the first time, Flora realised he had a Scots accent. 'Win told me how you came by him, Flora. You know, he'll have folks somewhere, relatives; grandads, aunts and uncles, rich ones, possibly, with his mother speaking English, like, and seeing as how he's probably a little Jew boy, very refined for a little 'un. I reckon you could get a big reward if you advertised in the papers, the American and British ones, at least three figures, even four. After all, you know his name, and you can describe his ma.'

Flora sprang forward and snatched Simon off Johnnie Lucas's knee. Simon, frightened, began to cry. She rushed upstairs, slamming the bedroom door behind her, wishing it had a lock or a bolt or something, half falling on to the bed and pressing Simon so, tightly against her that he began to cry even more.

'I'm sorry, darling,' she wept. She stroked his cheek and kissed away the tears until his sobs subsided. 'Oh, Simon,' she whispered, 'what are we going to do now?' She had laid him in bed and was tucking in the bed clothes when there was a light knock at the door.

'What is it?' she hissed.

'I truly wasn't expecting Johnnie back, dear.' Aunt Winifred turned the handle but didn't open the door; she must have had second thoughts. 'I didn't think I would ever see him again, but he came the other day asking for his old room back, I thought to myself, well, the money's a big help, and it's always useful to have a man about the house.'

Flora didn't say anything, and minutes later her aunt went away.

She couldn't sleep. She couldn't imagine ever sleeping again, at least not in this house. She just had to get away. But where?

At one point – she had no idea what time it was – she heard a noise downstairs, a whispering, a door opening and closing. After a while, Flora got up and went out on to the landing. On the floor below, from her aunt's room, there came a curious panting noise, heavy breathing, loud grunts and soft sighs.

'Oh, God, oh God, *oh God!*' Aunt Winifred cried.

Flora remembered hearing the same sounds years ago when she'd lived there as a child. Back then, she hadn't realised what they meant. But at the school in Switzerland, Else had told her how babies were conceived, what a man and woman did together and that for most of them it was an overwhelmingly enjoyable experience.

Well, that was certainly true if the sounds coming from the bedroom downstairs were anything to go by, at least as far as Aunt Winifred was concerned.

When she woke next morning, Flora felt as if she had hardly slept at all. She sat up and pulled the bedclothes around her shoulders. It was icily cold in the bedroom. Simon was still dead to the world in the bed across the room. He looked so at peace with the world, unaware of the danger from which he had once escaped and the danger that he was in now.

But was it danger? Would it be such a bad thing if he was reunited with his real family, his grandparents, aunts and uncles, possibly older brothers and sisters, even a father? Flora wriggled uneasily in the bed. Did these people exist? And if they did, did they have more of a right to him than she had? Certainly, well almost certainly; yet no one could possibly care for him as much as she did. She was the only person who could replace his mother in spirit and in love. In fact, she already had.

She imagined Johnnie Lucas putting an advertisement in the newspaper – in several newspapers, including some in English-speaking countries like America and Canada – and hundreds of letters pouring through the letter box, or queues of people forming outside the house wanting to claim Simon as their own. Men and women, families who had lost a child during the war, would want him, would be prepared to lie to get him, even if he wasn't the little boy they had lost. One of these people would give Johnnie Lucas hundreds of pounds, or even thousands, and Simon might be taken away from the woman, from Flora, who he thought was his mother. Another woman, whom he might or might not remember, had already vanished out of his short life.

I shall never let him go, Flora swore; *never!*

An hour later, everything she and Simon owned was packed into the stout leather suitcase that Else and Andrew had given her when she left St Thérèse's. She dressed Simon in his warmest clothes: thick coat and leggings, little boots, woollen hat covering his ears, a scarf around his neck, mittens on his hands. He stood regarding her solemnly while she covered up every single bit of him apart from the little circle that was his face.

She kissed his nose. 'It's time we were off,' she told him.

'Off,' he echoed. 'Is it a long journey, Flo?'

'Not quite as long as the other journey we made, darling.'

'Where is Rufus?'

'Here he is, still fast asleep in bed.' She gave him the bear and he hugged it to his chest.

In the breakfast room, Aunt Winifred was setting the table. Flora noticed there were four places. It looked as if Johnnie Lucas would be joining them from now on, that he would become part of the family. Except half the family wouldn't be there.

Aunt Winifred regarded them with astonishment, Simon decked out as if he were about to visit the North Pole, Flora wearing her sealskin coat. 'Where on earth are you going, all dressed up like that?'

'To Casablanca, to live with Else and Andrew,' Flora said confidently. 'Else says it's lovely and warm there. Andrew is starting a school, and I can help him teach. I was quite a good teacher during the short time I did it.'

'Oh, but Flora, there is no need to leave so suddenly, without any warning at all.' Her aunt managed to look both flustered and annoyed, but not exactly upset.

She wants me to leave, Flora thought. *She's sorry in one way, but in another she's glad me and Simon will be out of the way and that she and Johnnie Lucas will have the house to themselves.*

'Johnnie didn't mean what he said last night, you know. He was just joking.'

In the kitchen, the kettle whistled and Aunt Winifred left to make the tea. Flora was reminded how much she longed for a cup. And Simon always enjoyed his first cup of tea of the day. But they would both have to wait until they reached the station. She remembered the ration books, and removed hers and Simon's from the little drawer in the sideboard.

Her aunt returned with the teapot covered with an intricately hand-knitted cosy. 'Will you at least stay for a drink, Flora?'

If she did, Johnnie Lucas might appear, and she would prefer to avoid coming face to face with him. 'No, thank you. We'll be off now. Come along, Simon.'

And so Flora and Simon left the house in Nelson Road. It would be very many years before one of them returned.

Chapter 5

Twenty five years before, Joshua Lewin, Martin's father, having made the decision to expand his small jewellery business, had engaged a young woman, Lenka Gorski, who lived in the same brownstone in Bleecker Street, to be his secretary. Lenka had been taking lessons in shorthand and typing and was pleased to get such an important job at such a young age. She was only sixteen.

She had served Joshua well over the ensuing years as he built up what was to become a million-dollar company, known simply as Lewin's, importing diamonds from South Africa and gold from India, the precious stones and metal that would be turned into jewellery exquisitely designed by Joshua himself. It was then made by hand by workmen mainly from Poland, from where Joshua's father, a watch- and clockmaker, had emigrated at the end of the previous century. At that time, the Lewins surname had been a virtually unpronounceable jumble of mismatched letters. It was Joshua who had changed it to the simpler version.

Throughout all those years, Lenka Gorski had been a faithful and loyal employee, the perfect secretary, until 1941 when America joined the war on the side of the British against Germany and Japan, and she had enlisted in the United States Army Air Force, immediately becoming a sergeant.

Perhaps it was the loss of Lenka that had prompted Joshua to retire. He was approaching eighty, was reasonably fit and decided that, in the future, he would devote himself to promoting various charities. The company, lock, stock and barrel, as it were, was handed over to Martin, his eldest child and only son, a remarkably handsome man, impressively tall, dark-eyed and dark-haired, with an unpleasantly fierce expression.

Now the son instead of the father sat behind the elegant rosewood desk, his feet on the carpet imported from Italy with the name *Lewin's* woven into the pattern. It was Martin who gazed at the glorious Impressionist paintings hanging on the walls, though he had never been able to understand what anyone saw in them.

In the late afternoon of New Year's Eve 1945, Martin leafed through the following year's desk diary. It was bound in black leather, gold-tooled, very thick – a page for each day – the most expensive diary on the market. His secretary, Harriet Vine, had filled in the appointments that had already been made, some extending as far ahead as next December: dinners, meetings, fundraising affairs, political functions. At the bottom of the pages were written reminders of personal events, such as his wedding anniversary, his wife Lilith's birthday, his father's eighty-second, his mother's seventy-fifth, his son, Josh Junior's, twenty-first, which would be a major occasion. And of course, his own, in July, when he would be fifty-three.

There were other birthdays. One was actually Lenka Gorski's own, adorned with half a dozen asterisks: ★★★*Lenka Gorski*★★★. The reason for the adornment was that this was how Lenka had always written it in the diary until she'd left. It had been a joke between her and Joshua; he would buy her a single red rose. Other secretaries had followed suit: Harriet Vine was Martin's sixth secretary in four years, and he was likely to get rid of her pretty soon. Not one secretary over the years had the forethought to check if the people whose birthdays they were copying from the year before were still alive.

Aunt Ruth, for instance, had died peacefully in her sleep three years before: Martin's nephew, Gerard, had been killed when his plane was shot down over Berlin at about the same time. Yet their birthdays were still there, in next year's diary. It was out-and-out incompetence.

'Stupid bitches,' Martin growled. He turned to 28 February, and there it was: *Grace's birthday*. Damn it! He closed the book and hit it with his fist.

She was dead. She was bound to be dead. After all the turmoil in Europe, the situation in France, where she had gone to live, the rounding-up of Jews, the concentration camps, the final solution, the unmitigated savagery of the whole damn thing: after all that, surely she would have written after the war was over to let him and her mother know if she were still alive.

He should have gone to look for her when the war was still only in Europe, before America had got involved. Or he could have at least engaged other people to do it on his behalf. The trouble was, he was too stubborn and so was she. Lilith, his wife, Grace's mother, was too hopelessly weak and lacking in initiative to do anything. The battle had been between him and her – Martin and Grace, father and daughter – enemies since she was a small child.

He hadn't wanted her to get married at eighteen. It wasn't because the guy was a gentile, but that he was a jerk, a no-hoper. Martin could see it in his eyes. A failed writer from Boston, he'd had short stories published in the odd magazine, but mainly supported himself by waiting on tables and doing other odd jobs. He'd written a couple of novels that he couldn't sell, and had been unappreciative when Martin had offered to let a publisher friend take a look at them. 'He might be able to suggest changes, make them fit for publication.'

'They don't need changing,' the guy had growled. 'They're already fit for publication.'

Martin frowned as he tried to remember the guy's name. Edmund something. Edmund MacLaine, that was it. His family were Irish Catholics. He'd tried to track him down a few times, in case he and Grace had split and he'd returned to the States on his own and could provide information as to her whereabouts, but without success.

It had been Grace's idea that they go to Paris. She was going through her Ernest Hemingway phase, reading everything he had written. She was young and in love, and life was fiction, nothing was real. There were no words Martin could use that would change her mind. Hemingway had lived in Paris, and other writers, artists too. The great Pablo Picasso had been one of them.

'But that was then and this is now,' he raged at her. 'It's 1938. All those people left a long time ago.' Germany was already gearing up for war in Europe; things didn't look good over there – not that America had intended taking part in those days.

But she wasn't interested in anything he said. Her mind was made up. He should have chained her up in the cellar, done something to keep her in this country, if not in New York.

He stood and went to look out of the window onto the busy Manhattan street. Below, the traffic was nose to tail, horns honking endlessly. He stuffed his hands in his pockets. Perhaps he should have been gentler with her. The more he insisted on something, the more she prevailed against it. Had he pretended not to mind what she was about to do, the whole thing with Edmund MacLaine might have blown over and she'd have married someone else and had a couple of kids by now. He recalled that Lilith had tried to argue along those lines.

Martin crossed the room and flung open the door to his secretary's office. 'Book me a seat on a plane to Paris the day after tomorrow,' he barked.

'Yes, sir.' Harriet Vine jumped. She was blond, beautiful and anxious to please, but it cut no ice with Martin. She scrabbled frantically for her notebook and wrote down his demand with a shaking hand.

Martin slammed the door shut. He never used her name, never said 'please'. He was aware of his shortcomings as an employer, but he didn't care.

Two days later, he arrived in Paris, a place he'd never been before. It showed little evidence of having been occupied for five years. London hadn't been occupied, but he understood it had been bombed like crazy by the Jerries. Downstairs, an extraordinarily rowdy party was going on that he got the impression was the continuance of one that had started on New Year's Eve.

Martin was aware of the beautiful buildings in the area of his hotel, Le Bristol on the Rue du Faubourg Saint-Honoré, off the Champs des-Élyées, but remained unmoved. The Eiffel Tower was visible from his sitting-room window; the Sacré Coeur from the bedroom. But he hadn't come to sightsee. He'd come to look for his daughter, Grace Lewin, or Grace MacLaine if she really had married that son of a bitch – or at least to discover what her fate might have been.

He'd already engaged a private eye for tomorrow – *un détective privé* – who would show him around the city. He had two addresses for his daughter; she'd written a few times to her mother but he'd flatly refused to read the letters. She'd moved to a different place after a couple of months, and he would call at both.

It was evening, just gone six. He sat by the window, a French cigar in his mouth. In a minute, he'd take a shower if there was one, a bath otherwise, have dinner and go to bed. He wouldn't be joining the party downstairs. There would undoubtedly be all sorts of exotic delights available in Paris, but he wasn't in the mood for any of them right now.

The private eye was called Félix Brun. He arrived at the hotel early the following morning, and they met in Reception. His face was long and thin and his moustache looked as if it had been drawn above his lip with a crayon. He wore a tight-fitting velvet jacket and a black beret. It was a strange costume, the sort a private eye might wear in a play or a movie. Even his English had a stagey quality about it, as if the guy was playing a part.

Martin mentally shrugged. What did it matter what he looked or sounded like? All he wanted was assistance in finding the whereabouts of his daughter, and to know if she were alive or dead.

They went outside. It was a lovely fresh morning in Paris, though the drains smelled pretty bad and it was achingly cold. Brun opened the passenger door of a shabby Citroën and indicated for Martin to get inside. The guy hadn't bothered to clean it and it was full of old newspapers, books and a few toys. He had to fold his long body into an uncomfortable, cramped position to fit on the front seat. From the floor, a ragged teddy bear glared at him and Martin glared back. He cursed his daughter, as he had done so many times in the past, and wished he'd thought to demand they travel by taxi.

The first address was in the Rue Pierre Fontaine, off the Boulevard de Clichy. It was on the seventh floor of a narrow building that didn't have a lift. Martin could hardly breathe by the time they'd reached the sixth floor where a door prevented them from going any further.

Félix rang the bell, and after a while an old woman answered. The pair jabbered away in French for quite a while.

'Merci, madame,' Félix said eventually. He lifted his beret half an inch. 'Merci,' he repeated and the door closed.

'There are eight rooms to let on the top two floors,' he explained as they returned downstairs. 'That woman has been the concierge here for more than thirty years. She actually remembers your daughter.' Martin's heart lifted, but quickly fell as Félix continued. 'She moved out after six or seven months, but the old woman has no idea where she went,

54

though it'll almost certainly be the other address you have in the Boulevard de Magenta.'

'Was there a man with her?' Martin asked.

'Yes, but she couldn't remember his name or what he looked like.' Martin had given him a description of the guy: long face, limp wrists, hunched shoulders, funny-coloured hair . . .

'Did she say if they were married?' he enquired.

'I asked, but she didn't know.'

The place in the Boulevard de Magenta was a big improvement on the first. It was actually a hotel, Le Continental, small and narrow; nevertheless, just inside there was a guy behind a desk and there were two stars on the door. There were pictures on the walls, a decent carpet on the floor, brasses gleamed. Martin wondered how his daughter and the idiot could have afforded the increase in rent. At first, Lilith had sent money, but had stopped after hostilities had begun on the assumption that the postal service had ceased.

Félix launched into a conversation with the desk clerk, but turned to Martin almost straight away. 'Monsieur Tillier speaks reasonably good English,' he said. 'You can ask the questions yourself.'

Monsieur Tillier appeared anxious to help. A small plump-faced man with untidy grey whiskers and rheumy eyes behind a pair of wire-rimmed spectacles, he insisted they sit in the tiny reception area that conveniently held just three armchairs. He shouted something down a dark stairway. They had been seated only a few minutes when a smiling woman appeared with a tray holding a coffee pot and three doll-sized cups.

'I remember your daughter well, Mr Lewin,' he said when all three had been provided with coffee. 'She stayed with us for almost three years.'

'With a man?' Martin asked gruffly. He reminded himself that Monsieur Tillier was not an employee or an enemy, and was not to be interrogated. He was being helpful, and must be treated with respect and gratitude. 'With a man?' he repeated in a softer tone.

The man looked at him in surprise. 'Yes, with her husband, Monsieur MacLaine.'

'So they were married?' Martin felt slightly sick.

'They called themselves Monsieur et Madame MacLaine. She wore a ring, but I did not ask to see a certificate. It was none of my business.'

'Did Mr MacLaine have a job?'

'*Oui*, yes. Yes, he did. He was a waiter in La Bohème restaurant across the road. Six days a week. He worked the evening shift from six until midnight, later if the weather was warm. During the day he would write. He had brought a typewriter with him, and after Madame MacLaine had gone to work, you could hear him typing away, hardly stopping until his wife came home and it was almost time for him to go to work himself.' He nodded approvingly. 'Monsieur MacLaine was a very hard-working gentleman. They both were.'

Félix Brun must have felt it was time he took part in the discussion. 'Where did Madame MacLaine work?'

'In Lucille's, *une modiste*.' The other man looked lost for a moment while he tried to think of the word in English.

'Milliner,' Félix Brun supplied. 'She made hats.'

'Hats!' Monsieur Tillier slapped his knee triumphantly. 'That is it. Lucille made the hats, and Madame MacLaine, she sold them.'

Martin's mouth felt unnaturally dry. What he fancied was an ice-cold beer, but he couldn't have walked away from this conversation. He pointed to the coffee pot and asked for more. The older man responded, refilling the cups, along with an apology for not having offered before. The tiny cups only held a mouthful, and Martin's mouth felt scarcely less dry after he'd swallowed the drink.

There was silence while the other two men sipped theirs.

Martin wondered what to ask next. Where had Grace and the idiot gone after finally leaving the hotel? Had the Germans rounded them up, put them on a train and sent them to a concentration camp? The idiot for being an American, and Grace for being an American as well as a Jew? He was wondering how to phrase the question when Monsieur Tillier spoke.

'For your information, Monsieur Lewin, your daughter led a very happy life,' he said kindly. 'On Sundays, the only day they had all to themselves, she and Monsieur MacLaine would leave the hotel early and walk in all directions around Paris. In summer, they would eat in the parks, have . . .'

He gabbled something at Félix Brun.

'Picnics,' Félix supplied. 'In summer, they would picnic in one of the parks.'

The other man nodded. 'Then, after lunch, they would go to a concert, a recital, a performance of some sort. At around five or six they would return, change their clothes and have dinner with their friends, Monsieur and Madame Maillol. On Saturday nights, without fail, her friend, Mademoiselle Berry would call for your daughter – her husband would be hard at work across the road at La Bohème – and they would visit the opera or the cinema. Mademoiselle Berry was a delightful young woman.' His rheumy eyes shone. 'It would be early when she called and she, your daughter, and I would sit in these very seats and discuss politics and the state of the world – and the miserable state of Paris, for by then the hated Boche had invaded and we were a cruelly oppressed city. It was me,' he added proudly, 'who arranged for your daughter and Monsieur MacLaine to obtain false passports.'

'In what names?' Félix Brun enquired.

'Edmond – spelled the French way – and Marie Laurent,' the man replied.

Martin was aware that he was in a chair in which his daughter might once have sat. A strange feeling possessed him. He wanted to cry. He really, genuinely, truly wanted to cry for

Grace, for the daughter he had loved more than any other human being. He could actually feel the moisture collect in his eyes. He was vaguely aware that Félix Brun was questioning the other man about Mademoiselle Berry. Did she still live in Paris? Was she French? Berry was an unusual name.

Oh, Berry wasn't her real name, Monsieur Tillier was saying. She too was Jewish like Madame MacLaine. Her name was long and complicated, and she just liked being called Berry. 'Katriona Berry and Grace MacLaine, two such pretty names.' The Frenchman sniffed nostalgically.

'What happened to her, Mademoiselle Berry?' the detective asked. 'To them both? And Monsieur MacLaine, too?'

The other man uttered a long, tragic sigh. 'The Boche took Mademoiselle Berry. One Saturday, it was late summer in 1943, she just didn't turn up, Madame MacLaine went to look for her and came back to say the neighbours reported that she had disappeared, been taken away by the Boche in a truck, along with her family. A week later, Mr Lewin, your daughter and her husband had gone too.'

'In a truck?' Martin's voice was hoarse, and it hurt to speak.

'No, Monsieur. To Italy.'

Martin had to ask to visit the john. The bathroom was clean, but the john was a hole in the ground and there was nowhere to wash his hands. He almost wished he hadn't come to Paris, hadn't heard all this stuff. And while it was good to know Grace had been so damned happy, it hurt, too, that she could manage so well without him. She'd made a proper life for herself in a foreign country thousands of miles away from the one in which she'd been born.

He returned to Reception, pleased to find that more coffee had arrived, as well as a carafe of water and some tumblers. 'Why Italy?' he asked as he sat down. He poured a tumbler of water.

'Because Mussolini, monster though he was, refused to send Italian Jews to Germany and their death.' The older man's voice was almost a croak. He was tired now. He leaned back in the chair, breathing hard. Martin leaned across and squeezed his arm. For him, it was an uncommonly friendly and generous gesture, but he was feeling highly emotional. The door of the hotel opened and a bell rang. An elderly couple had arrived carrying a suitcase each. A woman came to the desk to deal with the newcomers.

'And don't forget,' Félix Brun put in, addressing Martin, 'in September, Allied troops had invaded Italy, landing in Sicily. Perhaps, Mr Lewin, your daughter and her husband hoped to meet up with them. I'll do my best to follow their trail for you, Mr Lewin, and will get back to you in New York as soon as I have anything.'

Martin spent another lonely evening in the hotel; not that he would have wanted to spend it any other way. He was flying home the next day, there seeming to be no point in staying any longer, though he wouldn't have minded returning to Le Continental to have a further conversation with Monsieur Tillier. He wanted to know more about what had been said between him, his daughter and Mademoiselle Berry. Just mundane stuff, idle chatter; what movies and shows did they see, what sort of clothes did they wear, how did they do their hair? Grace's was halfway down her back when she'd left New York; she'd been threatening to have it cut for ages. Of course, her father had been against that, too.

He lay on the bed and stared at the ceiling. He'd ordered a bottle of Jack Daniel's to be sent to his room and it was already a quarter gone. He had a feeling that if he went to see old man Tillier, he would cry his eyes out, make an utter fool of himself. And it wasn't fair on the poor guy, who'd been upset enough that afternoon. Martin was glad he and Grace had known each other in Paris. And it looked as if the idiot hadn't turned out too bad either, though his writing career had shown no signs of taking off.

If he drank any more Jack Daniel's he'd be sick. He'd never had a very good relationship with liquor. It had been of benefit at college, when he hadn't spent half his time as drunk as a skunk like his pals. It left him with a clear head at lectures.

Martin swung his feet off the bed. He'd go for a walk. It was dark outside and even he, without an artistic or appreciative bone in his body, couldn't deny that brilliantly lit Paris was a truly magnificent sight.

And if he walked far enough for long enough, he might just accidentally come across Le Continental, and he and Monsieur Tillier could have that talk, though it was most unlikely.

Chapter 6

Flora had lost track of everything. She had forgotten it was New Year's Eve when she and Simon left the house in Nelson Road that morning. It had been a lie, telling Aunt Winifred she was going to Morocco to live with Andrew and Else. Instead, she caught the bus to Euston station and boarded the train to Liverpool. She didn't trust Johnnie Lucas not to track her and Simon down if they were merely at the other end of the country. They would be safe if he thought they were miles and miles away on another continent.

She had no idea what sort of welcome she would get from Isobel Devlin. She'd been invited to visit, but people often said things like that without really meaning them. Isobel could well faint from shock when Flora turned up on her doorstep accompanied by Simon, who she knew nothing about. And Flora didn't want to stay just for a day or two, but until she could sort herself out and find somewhere of her own to live.

Perhaps Morocco would be the best idea – Andrew and Else would welcome them with open arms – but that would have to wait for the future; she didn't have nearly enough money for the fare.

It wasn't until they were on the Liverpool train, where an atmosphere of gaiety reigned, that she realised it was New Year's Eve. The Carrs were having a party that night that she'd been looking forward to. Oh, and she hadn't said goodbye to

Luke, or to Millie. Flora was beginning to feel frightened at the enormity of what she'd done, but what choice did she have? Simon wasn't safe living under the same roof as Johnnie Lucas. She could never have brought herself to leave the house again, not even for five minutes, without taking the little boy with her. And even if he never left her side, Simon still wasn't safe from whatever plans Johnnie might have to make money out of him.

She noticed Simon was sucking noisily on a lollipop that had been given him while she'd been lost in her worrying thoughts. The compartment was crowded, and a man with a giant red face on the seat opposite was smiling at him broadly.

'What's your name, kiddo?' he asked.

'Simon.' He managed to speak around the lollipop.

'He's a fine little chap,' the man said to Flora, She nodded.

'I think it's bloody flippin' marvellous that this is the first New Year's Eve for seven years when there ain't been a war on,' a woman commented. The cigarette in her mouth emitted smoke at a furious rate.

There were murmurs of agreement. 'I remember one year when an incendiary bomb came down the chimney just as we were toasting in the New Year,' a man reminisced. 'All of us were out the house like a shot, except for our old gran who's eighty if a day, and always had a bucket of water ready for emergencies. She emptied it on the fireplace and the flames went out. Should've got a medal, our old gran,' he finished fondly.

'Where do you come from?' Flora was asked. 'You haven't got a Liverpool accent.'

She wasn't absolutely sure. Her mother had been Scottish, her father came from London and she wasn't exactly sure where she'd been born. Almost half her life had been spent in Switzerland.

'London,' she replied. It was the simplest answer.

Simon finished the lollipop and was given a stick of

liquorice. Flora wanted to protest, but he was obviously enjoying himself. The red-faced man took a bottle of what looked like whiskey out of his pocket and drank a mouthful. His face got even redder as the journey progressed. The people in the next compartment started to sing, and Flora's compartment joined in. Pretty soon the entire carriage was singing Christmas carols and songs that she'd never heard before about the war, something about hanging out the washing on the Siegfried Line, and rolling out a barrel. A ticket inspector turned up completely the worse for drink and stood on everyone's feet.

Outside, the sky was dull and full of sludgy grey clouds. By the time the train drew into Lime Street station, it was almost dark. As they got off, everyone in the compartment wished each other a Happy New Year. Cheeks were kissed, hands shaken, backs slapped. During their four hours together, they'd become best friends in the whole world.

'Feel thick, Flo,' Simon claimed tearfully when she lifted him into his pushchair. He often lisped when he was overtired or not feeling well.

'I'm not surprised, darling,' she said, patting his head worriedly. He'd been eating sweets of one sort or another all the way from London. She picked up the suitcase. She'd already been advised how to get to Bootle. She had to walk to Exchange station and catch an electric train to a place called Marsh Lane. First of all, though, she felt it necessary to visit the Ladies, and Simon announced he needed a wee-wee too.

It was only then, after getting off at Marsh Lane, that Flora felt she could very easily panic as she stood in the dark under a bridge outside the station without any idea which way to go. She rarely cried, considering it a weakness, but now she could quite easily have bawled her head off. Simon was fast asleep in the pushchair. Although he was warmly dressed, she should have brought a blanket to tuck around him. At that very moment, he opened his eyes, glanced around and began to cry, scared at the blackness that surrounded them, and possibly cold.

'Don't like this journey, Flo,' he sobbed. He hid his face behind his mittened hands.

'Neither do I, darling.'

What was she doing to him, this helpless little boy? Why was she in this strange place, where the only person she knew was a woman she'd last seen when she was nine years old? She might not recognise Isobel if she saw her now, and Isobel would certainly not recognise her.

And, perhaps because her mind had sunk to a place where it had never been before, she began to think of her life, and the way it had gone over the last two years, in a completely different way; coldly, logically. Simon, she realised, would be much better off with a family who had plenty of money and a nice house for him to live in. That was a fact, and it couldn't be argued with. With Flora, he had nothing; no home, no money and no family apart from her. He had her love, as pure as gold, as clear as diamonds. But you couldn't buy food or clothes or pay the rent with love, no matter how pure and clear it was.

It wasn't Fate that had brought them together, but chance, a different thing altogether. The woman on the train would have handed him to anyone, young or old, male or female; anything to save her little boy from the gas chamber. By keeping him, Flora was being undeniably, unbelievably selfish, putting her own wishes and desires before those of a helpless child.

A man riding a bike appeared out of the shadows to interrupt this despondent chain of thought. He stopped and got off. Flora wasn't sure what he was doing, but next minute, the area where she and Simon were standing was illuminated by a flickering orange glow. He was a lamplighter. She remembered reading about people like him in a book.

'Are you all right, luv?' he asked. Flora became aware that she was cowering against the wall, wondering where to go next.

'Could you please tell me the whereabouts of Pearl Street?' she asked.

The man grinned. 'The whereabouts? That's a posh way of putting it. It's just along that way, love.' He pointed. 'Third on the left. Hurry up now, and get the little lad indoors. There's a fog rolling in.' As if in confirmation, a ship on the nearby river hooted mournfully. Liverpool was on the Mersey, Flora remembered.

She thanked the man. Her head cleared just a little and she felt almost human again as she pushed Simon in the direction the man had indicated.

Pearl Street proved to be long and narrow and packed with small terraced houses, the front doors opening directly on to the pavement. Flora was looking for number sixty-three, and the further she walked, the more alarmed she became. These mean little houses were nothing like she'd imagined Pearl Street would be, or where someone like Isobel Devlin would live. The street lamps cast a ghostly glow on the cobbled surface. The fog was getting thicker, and she had to peer at the numbers as she passed.

Number sixty-three turned out to be in the worst possible place, at the very end of the street next to a huge wall. She could hear trains running on the other side.

Heart sinking, Flora knocked at the door. 'Coming,' a woman shouted.

The door opened. 'Hello, luv. Come in, whoever you are. It's dead miserable out there, and that little boy of yours looks as if he's freezing.' The woman bent down and plucked Simon out of his pushchair. Flora was left with no alternative but to fold the pushchair and follow the woman into a narrow hallway.

65

'Are you Isobel?' she asked, slightly dazed by the warm welcome given to a complete stranger. The woman was pretty enough, and was wearing a smart blue dress.

'No, I'm June. Our Issy's in the kitchen. I'd take you out there, but there's five of us already, not including Nana, and it's dead noisy. I'll fetch her, shall I? Who shall I say it is?'

'Flora – and Simon.'

'Won't be a mo, luv. Take a seat in the parlour. I'll put the light on.' June pushed open a door, switched on the light, then disappeared with Simon in her arms. He seemed perfectly happy with the situation. He waved to Flora over the woman's shoulder as they left. Shrieks of female laughter were coming from elsewhere in the house.

Flora sat down. The contrast between the dark little street outside and the inside of the house couldn't have been greater, at least in this room. Paper with a pattern of huge pink cabbage roses covered the walls. The armchair in which she was sitting was beige velvet, luxuriously soft. There was another chair and a settee to match scattered with little embroidered cushions, a glass-fronted cabinet full of ornaments and a highly polished table folded against the wall with dining chairs to match tucked underneath. Rose-pink satin curtains hung at the window, a subtly patterned carpet covered the floor and a fire burned in the grate with a fancy wooden surround. It was like a miniature palace.

There were more gales of laughter outside. She jumped to her feet when another woman entered. Isobel! As lovely as ever in purple satin, just about two stone heavier and almost a decade older.

'Flora, luv, I could hardly believe me ears. It's really lovely to see you.' Flora was almost smothered in a pair of plump arms and pressed against a frilly breast. Isobel smelled of musky flowers and face powder. She pushed Flora away and held her by the shoulders, studying her face. 'Lord, girl, you've grown up to be a real bobby-dazzler. But saying that, you look dead

66

haggard, and you're much too thin. Hasn't that auntie of yours been feeding you proper? She always was stingy with the grub. Sit down, luv, before you fall over, and tell me why you're here.'

Flora was steered back towards her armchair and Isobel sat on the other, staring at her intensely. Flora felt too full up to speak. 'It would take so long,' she whispered, 'and it's so complicated. Can I tell you another time?'

'Of course, luv. Does your auntie know you're here?' Isobel asked gently.

Flora tiredly shook her head. 'If she contacts you, please don't tell her. She thinks I've gone abroad.'

'Me lips are sealed, Flora.'

'Is it all right for me to stay a few days?'

'You can stay as long as you like, luv. Look, come into the other room and have a cuppa. You look as if you need one, and it's warmer out there. Me sisters are here, and we're getting ready for a party tonight, it being New Year's Eve, like. We're mostly doing sarnies, jelly and custard and fairy cakes. You can sit and watch.'

'Where is Simon?'

'Nana's got him. Everyone's madly in love with him already. Is he yours, luv?' She looked at Flora keenly.

'Only in a way.' It was no good saying he was her cousin, not to Isobel, who knew her family history.

'Come on.' Isobel led her into the other room. It wasn't as posh as the parlour, but was still cheerful and nicely furnished, with yellow flowered wallpaper and lots of pictures on the walls. A table covered with a beautifully embroidered cloth was laid with several plates of food, the food itself invisible beneath napkins embroidered to match the cloth. An even bigger fire burned in the grate.

She looked for Simon, and saw that he was sitting on the knee of a much older woman with pure white hair. He was trying to remove her wedding ring, without success.

Isobel was introducing her to her four sisters: June, whom she had already met; Noreen, Lillian and Beattie. All were tall like Isobel, and could have been models too, with their beautiful brown hair, blue eyes and smooth, satiny skin. Like Isobel, they were dressed for a party. She couldn't tell if they were younger or older than Isobel, who, it turned out, fell in the middle. Noreen and Lillian were older, and June and Beattie younger. They'd each been born a year after the other. Noreen had turned forty last September, and already had two grandchildren.

Finally, 'This is Nana,' Isobel said. 'She's our grandma; her real name is Mary O'Shea. You know I left London to look after me mam? Well, sad to say, she died in 1942, by which time Nana had had a stroke, so I stayed to look after her.' She raised her voice. 'She can hear you if you talk loud, but she can't speak. Nana's nearly ninety, aren't you, darlin'?'

Nana nodded, smiling broadly and revealing a set of very white, very shiny false teeth. Flora half smiled back. She felt tense and nervous; if she smiled too much, her face would crack in two.

Isobel returned to the kitchen after telling Flora to sit on a little narrow settee. One of the sisters – it might have been Noreen – brought her tea and a sardine sandwich. Simon was seriously examining one by one the fingers on Nana's old, wrinkled hand, while the women continued to work in the kitchen, bringing in more and more food to put on the table. After Flora had drunk the tea and eaten the sandwich, she began to doze off, coming to from time to time, though nothing seemed real and she was convinced she was in the middle of a very strange dream.

It was next morning, and the house was eerily quiet, so quiet that Flora could almost feel, even hear, the seconds and the minutes ticking away on an invisible clock. She opened her eyes; more flowered wallpaper, this time little blue flowers on a white background, pale blue curtains at the windows. It was still dark outside.

Simon was asleep beside her in a double bed; someone had brought him upstairs and laid him down. She had vague memories of Isobel leading her upstairs not long after the party had started, helping her to undress, saying something about bringing Simon up later. Apparently he was enjoying being made a big fuss of.

She stretched her arms and the springs on the bed creaked. It was the most comfortable bed she'd ever slept in, soft and yielding like a jelly. After a while, she began to hear noises outside; trains passed, there was the *clip clop* of a horse's hooves, the rattle of bottles – the milkman was early. Downstairs, she heard water running and the sound of a match being struck, a stove being turned on.

Minutes later, the door opened and Isobel peeped in. 'Morning, luv. I had a feeling you'd be awake. I've brought you a cuppa.'

'Thanks,' Flora said gratefully. She pushed herself to a sitting position. 'You're being really kind.'

Isobel came into the room and sat on the bed. Without make-up, her face looked pale and there were metal curlers in her hair. Despite this, she still maintained an air of glamour. It was something to do with the way she carried herself, as if she were parading along a catwalk.

'Did the party keep you awake?' she asked. 'The last person went home – that was Uncle Hughie – at about five o'clock this morning.'

'I kept waking up, but I soon fell asleep again. I was so tired, you see.' Flora was gratefully sipping the tea. The sound of music and laughter had been more comforting than disturbing. 'The night before in London I hardly slept.' She'd been packing clothes and thinking about Johnnie Lucas and what he'd said about Simon, too scared to close her eyes.

She knew Isobel was entitled to an explanation as to why

she was there. She took a deep breath and told her about the morning in Switzerland when she'd accompanied Mrs Charlesworth to the station so she could catch the train to Zurich, and the other train that had come snaking through, silently so she thought, until she'd heard the sounds of the people on board, and the way some of them had broken the wooden laths to make space for the woman to give her baby to Flora.

As she spoke, Flora could see tears in Isobel's beautiful blue eyes. 'Oh, Flora, girl,' she gasped. 'You must have felt very blessed.'

Flora had never thought of it in quite that way before. 'Oh, I did, I did,' she confirmed. 'But yesterday, for the first time, I realised how selfish I was being by keeping him.'

But apparently Isobel didn't think so. 'All babies need is lots of love, Flora. Simon is a happy little soul, that's obvious.' She looked fondly at the little boy who, as if he was aware of being watched, opened his big green eyes and stared at them blearily before closing them again. 'Anyroad, luv,' the older woman continued, 'what brought you this way? I must admit, your Auntie Winifred is a bit odd, but I can't imagine why she'd object to having a delightful little chap like Simon on the premises. Personally, I'd've thought she'd appreciate your company, an' all.'

'Oh, she did at first,' Flora said emphatically, 'but then over Christmas Johnnie Lucas came to live there and started talking about advertising Simon in the newspapers and possibly getting a big reward.'

'Jaysus!' Isobel gasped. 'Has that bastard come back?'

'You've met him?' Flora was surprised.

'I went back to London once for a friend's wedding,' Isobel explained, 'and stayed with Winifred over the weekend. I didn't like him when she introduced us, and you could've knocked me down with a feather when I realised he was actually *living* there. I got the impression he had some sort of hold over her. Anyroad,' her voice rose in anger, 'I thought he'd been sent to prison for robbing corpses during the air raids, or something equally disgusting. It was in one of the newspapers, and I recognised his name. I considered writing to Winifred about it, but decided it was best not to, more tactful, like. I sent a Christmas card later in the year, but didn't mention Johnnie.'

'He was released just before this Christmas,' Flora explained.

'And went straight back to Nelson Road and Winifred, it would seem.'

Flora nodded. 'I had to leave. I was worried about what might happen to Simon.'

It was Isobel's turn to nod. 'You did the right thing, luv.'

'This is the only place I could think of coming to,' Flora added. 'It's a beautiful house, Isobel. I didn't realise *how* beautiful until I was inside.'

'You won't find another one like this in Pearl Street,' Isobel said modestly. 'Years ago, when I came back from London, I had more money than Mam had seen in her life before. I bought the furniture and had the place done up especially for her so she could die in luxury. But some folk in the street are dead poor. Me conscience was pricked, spending so much on furniture, like, but I put our mam first.'

Someone had started to play a tune with the knocker on the front door, and Isobel went downstairs to answer it.

It was the first of many knocks that New Year's Day. Visitors arrived by the front door, family came in the back. Noreen, Beattie, June and Lillian popped in at one time or another; June came three times and Lillian twice. They all lived nearby, Flora was given to understand, in the neighbouring streets.

The visitors came bearing gifts – bottles of wine or spirits, chocolates and cakes, little knitted garments for Nana: hats, scarves and gloves, though Isobel had said earlier that, with one exception, she only went outdoors in the summer. 'There's a wheelchair in the wash-house in the back yard.' The exception was going to Mass every Sunday. It was then that Flora remembered Isobel was a Catholic.

One aspect of the house she didn't like was the lavatory in the back yard. She shuddered whenever she thought about it. At Aunt Winifred's there'd been a lavatory upstairs and one downstairs, off the kitchen.

It had been a really horrible experience last night when she'd been about to go to bed and had asked the whereabouts of the lavatory, and was told its situation. The yard itself had been doused in a freezing fog. Simon had enjoyed standing on the wooden seat and aiming at the hole from which a cold draught blew.

'I've put a po under your bed,' one of the sisters had said. Flora couldn't remember which, only that it wasn't Isobel. She had no idea what a 'po' was.

That morning, she had peeped under the bed and discovered that a po was a chamber pot; quite a pretty one with rosebuds around the rim. She had never used one before, but it was a distinct improvement on the lavatory, particularly if you were obliged to use it in the middle of the night.

It was a strange day altogether. Flora tried to help in the kitchen, but the sisters arrived with food already made and she realised she was in the way. All the visitors wanted to know who she was and where she had come from. Some looked at her doubtfully, even disapprovingly, when she explained that Simon was her cousin. She was obliged to describe the accident in which his parents had been killed over and over again.

'And it happened in Switzerland, you say?' some people queried.

'What sort of car were they driving?' someone asked.

'A Mercedes-Benz.' She was conscious of telling numerous

lies, sometimes making things up as she went along. Her voice grew hoarse.

Early in the afternoon, she wrapped Simon up warmly, put him in his pushchair and went for a walk. They ended up by the river where a wind blew, so icy that it completely took her breath away and she dearly wished her mother's sealskin coat was considerably longer. Simon pulled the blanket she had borrowed over his face.

'Me cold!' he spluttered.

Worried that she was about to lose her breath altogether, Flora hurried back to the Devlins' house to face more questions from more people.

As one of the cousins, Tommy O'Shea, explained that afternoon, Isobel was the only Devlin left. Tommy, a handsome chap in his forties, was smoking a cigar and the smell felt familiar to Flora; she had vague memories of her father having smoked cigars when she was small.

'Nana's my gran too,' he told her. 'She married Bernie O'Shea in 1876, that's seventy years ago by my reckoning. The same year, they left Ireland for Liverpool. She bore eight live children, two girls and six lads.

'One of the girls,' Tommy continued, 'me Auntie Mary, married Peter Devlin, who was killed in the war – not the one just over, but the one before. By then, he and Mary had had five daughters. As they grew up, the Devlin girls became famous throughout Bootle. Five more beautiful lasses would have been hard to find in any part of the country, let alone one small town.' He blew a perfect smoke ring and stopped talking while he and Flora watched it float up to the ceiling, where it fell apart and the bits floated away in different directions. 'In fact,' he said thoughtfully, 'when I was a lad and we were growing up together, I planned on marrying one of the Devlin girls, I didn't care which one, except it turned out I couldn't because we were related. Anyroad, when I was eighteen I met

Pauline O'Reilly and married her instead. We've had eight kids all told, and the eldest, our Katie, is getting wed in the not-too-distant future. You'll find an awful lot of Nana's descendants still living in Bootle, girl. There was around a hundred at the last count. By now, it'll be even more.'

At about five o'clock, Isobel appeared, beautifully dressed in a black costume with a white lace blouse underneath. Her face was perfectly made up and her hair shone. She carried a fur coat over one arm and a black lizard-skin handbag on the other. She looked just like the model she used to be except a bit heavier.

'I'm going to work,' she explained to Flora. 'I'm manager-ess of the New Look, a cocktail bar in Bold Street. We open at six o'clock. I work there every night apart from Sundays. They let me have last night off knowing that the customers would get so drunk no one would notice I wasn't there.'

She managed a cocktail bar! It seemed such a comedown after being a model in London. Perhaps Isobel could see something in her expression because she took Flora's arm and squeezed it. 'It's just the way things go, luvvie,' she said in a low voice. 'Our mam fell ill, then Nana. I was the only one of me sisters not married, so who else was there to look after them? Look at you and Simon. What would you give up for him?'

'Everything,' Flora whispered. 'Absolutely everything.'

Chapter 7

Flora had lived with the Devlins for a month, and she didn't like it all that much. She felt she was the most ungrateful person in the world because everyone was being so kind; too kind, and far too nice. If people had been less nice, she wouldn't have felt so much of a burden. She quickly came to realise that the sisters had a pattern to their lives in which there was no place for her.

Isobel often didn't finish work until as late as two in the morning. She would return home in a taxi, exhausted, having been on her feet for hours, and go straight to bed, getting up at about eleven. While she was asleep, Noreen came at around seven to rouse Nana, who slept in her chair in the living room at night – it was a special chair that, with a bit of manipulation, could be turned into a bed – washed and dressed her, made her breakfast and helped her down the yard to the lavatory. The dishes would be washed, the fire lit and Flora's offer of assistance would be turned down flat.

'It's all right, luv. I've got me own way of doing it,' she was told again and again.

At one o'clock, by which time Isobel was up, Lillian would arrive with dinner, including Flora and Simon's. June, who did the weekly shopping, had already taken their ration books.

Dinner over, the other sisters would arrive for a 'jangle' and a cup of tea, taking turns to bring the tea with them. They would sit around the table and discuss their children, their husbands, their neighbours, what was happening in Bootle and the rest of the world. All Flora could do was sit, not contributing a word. This was a tribe that she didn't belong to.

One sister would start the jangle. 'I see Josie Reilly has had her baby at last,' she would say, or something similar. It would seem there were babies being born in the area almost every day.

'Crikey! It seems like she's been up the duff for almost a year. Did she have a boy or a girl?'

'No one knows yet.'

'I might go and see her in hospital. Her mam was our mam's friend when they were young.'

The conversation would change. 'Does anyone know what my birthstone is?'

'Diamonds. April is diamonds.'

'Oh, well, so there's no chance of getting a diamond necklace for a prezzie this year.'

'How about diamante? We'll get you one between us.'

'No, ta, I fancy real diamonds.'

'Well, you'll go on fancying for ever, girl.'

'Maybe our Peter'll get promoted at the Co-op and he'll buy us one.'

'Eh, does anyone know anyone who's seen that picture, *Double Indemnity*, with Fred MacMurray?'

'No, is it good?'

'It's supposed to be. If it comes on around here, will someone come and see it with me? Our Ernie can't stand the flicks. As for me, I'd have it off with Fred MacMurray like a shot. He could have me any way he wanted and as often as he liked.'

'Really! Personally, I think he's an ugly bugger. I'd prefer Gene Kelly any day.'

'He's much too young for you, sis.'

And so it went on. Every now and then Nana would snigger and Simon would echo it. Throughout, he would be sitting on Nana's knee, which appeared to be his favourite place in the world nowadays. The minute he would enter the room, Nana would open her fat arms and Simon would run into them. He would be scooped up and pressed against her enormous breast. Flora was worried he would suffocate.

Oh, it was horrible, really and truly horrible, but she couldn't stand Nana, yet all the woman ever did was smile at her, smile at everyone, in fact. She must be the happiest invalid in the world. Flora couldn't even think of a reason for her dislike, other than blaming herself for being a truly horrid person.

The jangle over, the sisters would go home and Isobel would start preparing a light tea which was eaten early, so she would have time to get ready for work at the cocktail bar. Getting ready took ages, and she came downstairs looking as beautiful as a film star, her make-up and clothes perfect, her hair beautifully styled, expensive perfume filling the room.

'Do I look all right?' she would ask in a loud voice for Nana's benefit.

Nana would nod her head furiously and Flora would say in an awed voice, 'You look gorgeous.'

From then on, a couple of the sisters might return for half an hour or so, as would other women, the wives of Nana's sons and grandsons; neighbours would call, old friends. Children would drop in on the way home from school, some bringing pictures they had drawn or things they had made like pincushions and plasticine figures. Even if Flora hadn't been there, there wasn't a minute when Nana would have been left alone.

It was a wonderful, friendly atmosphere, yet sometimes Flora wanted to stand in the middle of the room and scream. She felt trapped. The house was small, always full of people and claustrophobic. She wasn't used to crowds and noise and never having a minute to herself. She couldn't breathe after spending so many years surrounded by bracing fresh air and miles of emptiness. Sometimes she took Simon for walks, but it was much too cold to be out without a purpose, such as shopping. She would have liked to catch the train or a tram into town and look around the big shops, but very soon every penny of the small amount of money she'd brought with her would be gone. And what would she do then? So far, she hadn't paid anything towards her and Simon's keep.

It had always been her intention to look for a job when Simon started school, by which time she would have learned to type and do shorthand – there'd been a little commercial college over a shop in Crouch End. Nothing she had been taught at Andrew's school in Switzerland had prepared her for a life of work. Younger pupils were taught how to read and write and do simple sums. Classes, if you attended them, consisted of arguments, discussions on a bewildering array of topics, lots of games for those who felt like them, climbing trees for the most adventurous, drawing more or less anything you pleased, thinking – they were encouraged to think a lot – and having snowball fights in the winter. Andrew was intent on making sick people well. He concentrated on their bodies, while their brains were allowed to flower in a most unscholarly way.

So what was she supposed to do now, Flora wondered desperately? She had heard that people could obtain loans from banks, but they required something to set the loan against, like a house, for instance . . .

It was such a hopeless chain of thought that she didn't bother following it any more. But perhaps there was another way of acquiring a loan.

Later that day, she wrote to Luke Carr at Manchester University and suggested they meet on Saturday morning in the waiting room on Central station, from where the trains ran to and from Manchester. Why hadn't she thought of that before!

★

It was February, and still very cold. Today, the sun shone and the air glittered as if tiny icicles were floating in it. She took Simon with her in his pushchair. She wore her black sealskin jacket over a thick pink woollen frock given her by Isobel – these days it was too small for her. The dress had a cloche hat to match. It was rather old-fashioned, but Isobel said Flora was young and pretty enough to carry it off. 'People will think that style has come back in fashion,' Isobel had said. After paying for the return train ticket, Flora was left with tuppence in her purse.

A small fire giving off hardly any heat burned in the station waiting room. Luke had already arrived. He wasn't wearing nearly enough clothes for such a cold day, merely a tweed sports jacket, flannels and a black beret that covered only one of his ears, yet he looked extraordinarily healthy with rosy cheeks and bright eyes. His only concession to the weather was a long knitted scarf of many colours that wound twice around his neck. Other occupants of the waiting room were eyeing his outlandish outfit with amusement. He jumped to his feet and hugged her fiercely. When he broke away, she could see tears in his eyes.

'Flora! What happened to make you disappear like that?' He pulled her back against him. 'I was desperately worried. We all were. I went to the house next day and your aunt said you'd gone to Morocco.'

Simon was agitatedly kicking his pushchair with both heels in an effort to be noticed. Luke released Flora and lifted him out of the pushchair and held him up in the air. The little boy wriggled joyfully.

Flora felt awful, really awful, and terribly guilty at the same time. She'd felt much the same since leaving Crouch End because all she'd done was sponge off people, taking advantage of their goodwill and generosity. She'd scarcely thought about Luke since coming to live in Bootle, yet he'd been entitled to an explanation for the way she'd vanished so suddenly, dashing out of the restaurant, if she remembered rightly, not even waiting for him to pay the bill. And it was only because she wanted something from him that they were meeting now.

The reason for the meeting – that she needed to borrow money – was negated when Luke next spoke. Fishing in his pocket, he brought out a small box of Terry's All Gold chocolates, Flora's favourite.

'Bought you these,' he said with a grin. 'Would have got a bigger box, but I'm afraid I'm nearly skint, Flora. I tried to borrow a few bob this morning, but most of the chaps are in the same boat. But I can just about afford to buy us a coffee in the station restaurant right now, and a meal later, though not somewhere posh. Do you fancy a drink?'

Flora nodded. 'Yes, please.'

They went across to the restaurant, a high-ceilinged, rather depressing room where they were the only customers. Here, a slightly larger fire had been lit, and Flora sat as close to it as she could. Luke bought two coffees and a glass of milk and brought them to the table.

'I remembered Simon always had milk rather than a fizzy drink when we were out,' he said.

'I like dandelion and . . .' Simon looked to Flora for assistance. 'What do I like, Flo?'

'Dandelion and burdock, darling,' Flora told him. It was Nana's favourite drink. 'Years ago,' she said to Luke, 'it was made out of real dandelions, but I don't know if it is now.'

'It sounds extremely interesting.' Luke ruffled the little boy's hair. 'I'm sorry I didn't get you some. Can you manage to drink that milk?'

'I'll do me best,' Simon said gravely. He had very nearly acquired a Liverpool accent.

'You've grown, Si,' Luke told him. 'You've grown enormously since I last saw you. Soon you'll be as big as me.'

Simon puffed himself up importantly and looked pleased. He and Luke had always got on well together.

'How will you live for the rest of the term without money?' Flora asked Luke now.

'Oh, Dad sends a five-bob postal order every Monday that just about sees me through the week. Tomorrow, Sunday, somebody somewhere will feed us. I'm not the only one short of funds. Some kind soul will make a monster stew, and we can help ourselves. I've been on the lookout for a part-time job,' he went on, 'but there's not much work about and what jobs there are, full or part-time, should really be left for the servicemen being demobbed.'

'I know you worked down the mines, Luke, but you are in effect an ex-serviceman who's not long been demobbed.'

'I know, but I've got folks with enough money to help me through my three years at university. These other blokes might have wives and kids to support. They need the money more than I do. I could easily keep myself on Dad's five bob if I didn't spend so much on beer.'

He grinned again, and Flora felt her heart lurch just a little. Looking back, the time she'd spent in Crouch End with Luke and his family had been light-hearted and enjoyable, with little to worry about. She had fallen, just a tiny bit, in love with Luke. But it could only have been a very tiny bit, otherwise she would have contacted him long before now – and for a more flattering reason than wanting to borrow from him.

A woman came into the restaurant with two young boys, both a little older than Simon, who regarded them with considerable interest.

'What happened, Flora?' Luke asked in a low voice. 'Why did you run away?'

'I can't tell you,' she whispered.

'It could only have been because of that chap, Johnnie Lucas.' He took hold of her hand. 'We discovered later that he was staying at your aunt's house. Everyone was astounded that she let him come back.'

Flora licked her lips. She didn't know what to say. Luke

had never known the truth about Simon. Aunt Winifred and Isobel apart, and of course Johnnie Lucas, everyone else she knew had been told they were cousins.

'I just didn't like us living in the same house,' she told Luke now.

He squeezed her hand. 'I can understand that, but it doesn't account for you disappearing the way you did so suddenly, without saying goodbye. After all,' he said with a tremor in his voice, 'we did mean rather a lot to each other. At least, you did to me. Perhaps I didn't to you, I was broken-hearted, Flora. I nearly didn't go back to university.'

She didn't speak, and after a while Luke squeezed her hand again. 'Flora?'

'He made a pass at me,' she mumbled. 'That night, the night we went out to dinner, when I got home he made a pass at me. I hardly slept all night – there was no lock on the bedroom door, you see. I just knew I had to get away, so I left with Simon first thing next morning.'

Luke scowled. 'Next time I go home, I shall give the bloke a good thumping,' he said angrily.

'No, no. Please don't do that. My aunt has – well, she has a sort of relationship with him. Yes, I know, it's terribly sad,' she added in response to the look of shock on Luke's face. 'It's just that she's lonely.'

'OK.' He sighed. 'But that bastard making a pass doesn't account for the way you went rushing out of the Chinese restaurant, Flora.'

Across the restaurant they were in now, one of the boys was playing rather clumsily with a yo-yo. Simon was watching, starry-eyed. He looked at Flora, and she nodded slightly. If they could be bought for tuppence, he would have one that afternoon. She turned her attention back to Luke. 'What would you have done if you were me?' she asked. 'By then, I knew there was a man staying in the house. Then you said it was this terrible criminal living somewhere in the road who had just been let out of jail. My first thought was for Simon, that the man might cause him harm.'

'And had he?'

'No, but he'd been taken out of bed. He was on the man's knee.'

Luke contemplated this, frowning. 'Why did your aunt say you'd gone to Morocco?'

'Because it's what I told her. It's where Andrew and Else from the school in Switzerland have gone. They'd wanted us to live with them. Please don't tell anyone where we are.'

'Of course not.' He sighed. 'I knew you couldn't have gone somewhere like Morocco at such short notice. At first, I was worried you and Simon had been murdered, but Mum said not to be silly.' He put both his arms on the table and looked at her – it was almost a glare. 'So, what are you doing in Liverpool?'

She was beginning to resent the endless questioning. He didn't own her. She wasn't beholden to him in any way. When she answered, her voice was cold but polite. 'When I first went to live with my aunt, I was six, and there was a lady from Liverpool there. I really missed her when she went back. I wrote to her a few months ago, and she invited me to come and stay. It seemed the obvious – the *only* – place for me and Simon to go when I had to leave my aunt's.'

Luke contemplated this for a few seconds before shrugging and saying, 'I suppose you're right.'

I *am* right, she wanted to snap, but managed not to. He just didn't understand how desperate she had felt that day, how imperative it was that she and Simon get away. And he wasn't likely ever to understand when he didn't know the truth about her relationship with the little boy.

They finished their drinks. Luke suggested they walk down to the Pier Head. Flora agreed, but halfway she announced she could go no further and would rather go back to the city centre, where they would be protected from the Arctic wind

83

that was howling up from the river penetrating her clothes, even the sealskin coat. She knew that Simon was unhappy in this wretched weather.

'I can't understand why it's so cold in Liverpool, when the temperature was lower in Switzerland,' she complained.

'The air here is damp and penetrating, that's why,' Luke explained. 'In Switzerland, it's dry. It's fine for people with chest complaints, whereas damp air does them harm. However, the moisture in the Lancashire air was really good for the cotton trade when it existed. That's why there were so many cotton mills in the North-West.'

Flora was impressed. 'You learn something new every day.' It was a mundane comment, and it seemed to her that the conversation became duller and duller as they walked back in the direction they'd come from. She realised that this was the end of her relationship with Luke. Today would be their final day together.

Luke must have sensed it too. He had become very quiet. Central station wasn't very far away when he said quietly, 'Would you prefer it if I went back to Manchester, Flora – straight away, that is? We won't bother with a meal. It wouldn't be up to much, anyway.'

'Oh, Luke. I don't know,' She didn't like the thought of him spending the last of his money on a meal and having to wait until Monday for more. 'Would it be all right if we just had another coffee?' If only she had enough to buy the coffee herself!

'This was a silly idea, wasn't it? Us meeting.'

'It was *my* idea,' she pointed out. It was her fault he looked so unhappy. 'I wanted to see you again, but life has changed so drastically and it seems I don't feel the same as I did before.' He must never know the real reason why she'd written to him. He was such a nice young man who didn't deserve to be hurt. 'Life seemed very different in Crouch End. Perhaps if we met again in another few months it might feel like that again.'

'Perhaps,' he said sadly. They both knew it would never happen.

They had one last coffee together, and he concentrated his attention more on Simon than on Flora, telling the boy that he would grow up to be very clever. 'I can tell, Si. You've got a first-class brain inside that handsome little head of yours.'

When it was time for him to go, he shook hands with Flora and kissed her lightly on the cheek, then hugged Simon very hard. He didn't speak, didn't ask for her address in Liverpool, just nodded briefly and hurried through the ticket barrier without a backward glance.

On the way back to Bootle, Flora could well have cried the entire way had she been that sort of person. Instead, she stared at Simon, on the seat opposite, thinking what a difference he had made to her life. Without him, she might have been engaged to Luke by now, making plans for the wedding when he achieved his degree, or having an exciting time in Morocco with Andrew and Else.

Instead, a miracle had happened, and she was tied for ever to this beautiful little boy. She wouldn't have wanted it any other way, though a means had to be found of earning money – and found quickly.

Chapter 8

Saturday afternoons, and the house in Pearl Street was always full of women, the men having gone to a football match either in Liverpool itself, or on the train or in a charabanc if their team, Everton, supported by Catholics, was playing in another part of the country. When Flora and Simon arrived home after meeting Luke, he made straight for Nana's lap. The old woman had been asleep. She blearily opened her eyes and hauled Simon onto her knee, falling asleep again straight away. She had also celebrated a birthday recently, her ninetieth, and had been off colour ever since. It was as if her body had decided it had lived long enough.

A wedding was on the horizon. It would take place the following Saturday when Tommy O'Shea's daughter, Katie, married Jimmy Watson, a lad from an area of Liverpool called the Dingle. Jimmy's brother was a priest and would conduct the ceremony in St James's church on Marsh Lane. The women had been talking about it for days. Flora and Simon had been invited as a matter of course.

'That's a good job Katie's got – a barmaid in the Crown on Stanley Road,' Lillian observed. 'It's not just a pub but a hotel too, and dead respectable, not like some places I could mention. I mean, it hasn't got sawdust on the floor. A good number of the customers are guests at the hotel – travelling salesmen, businessmen and the like. It's a pity Katie has to give it up. The tips she gets are ever so generous.'

June turned and spoke to Flora, who was perched on the arm of the settee. 'Katie and Jimmy are moving to the Dingle to live with Jimmy's dad,' she said, 'so it'll be too far for her to come. Me, I'd do the afternoon shift like a shot. It means I can earn a few bob and be at home for when the kids get back from school. Though I couldn't manage the evening shift an' all.'

'I'm sure the manager wouldn't mind having someone different of a night,' Lillian put in. 'Splitting the job in two, as it were. A woman with a little kiddy, for instance, whose husband could look after it.'

'Or a relative.'

'Or a friend.'

There was a pause. This particular subject, taking over Katie's barmaid job, had been discussed before. There was a long silence, which was rather odd, as normally when the women were together, silences were rare and never lasted more than a few seconds.

The conversation had turned to something else – Katie's dress, which was being made by a dressmaker but which she wasn't too pleased with, before the penny dropped and Flora realised that the silence was for her benefit. She was supposed to have grasped that the job of evening barmaid would suit her perfectly. While one or other of the sisters sat with Nana, they could listen out for Simon, who'd be asleep upstairs and rarely woke during the night, and Flora would be working behind a bar in a respectable hotel on Stanley Road, which was only a short walk away from Pearl Street.

Oh, lord, she would loathe it, hate every minute, but she would share the job with June, who would do the afternoons. After all, it wouldn't exactly kill her, and she would have money of her own for a change.

'I'll do it,' she gulped. 'I'll do the evening shift. When would I have to start?'

★

87

The interior of the Crown was painted a miserable green that looked almost khaki, as if the paint had initially been meant for a military facility. It had nine bedrooms, decorated with a total lack of imagination. The reception area wasn't particularly inviting, but apparently the hotel was reputed to be a comfortable place to stay, the staff were friendly and the food – it offered breakfast and an evening meal – was excellent. The bar, a large square room with the inevitable green walls, was furnished with low tables and plenty of easy chairs and a sickly oatmeal-coloured carpet. The bar section was plain and functional – no polished brasses, shining mirrors or coloured lights. Nor was there a piano, as there was in most public houses, and the piped music was subdued, coming mainly from 1930s shows written by people like Cole Porter, Jerome Kern and Irving Berlin, creating a rather romantic atmosphere, particularly if you narrowed your eyes and saw only smudges of colour and people.

The clientele, mainly male, were either staying at the hotel or locals who preferred conversation to a rowdy sing-song. As for the job, it wasn't too bad at all. Flora discovered she wasn't averse to numerous men telling her in various ways that she was beautiful – a cracker, a bobby-dazzler, a nice piece of stuff, a sight for sore eyes – she remembered once Else had used that same phrase.

She was cold with any man who made remarks about her figure, and downright rude to those who told her what they would like to do to her in bed. During her first week, she refused to serve a man who asked how much she charged.

'What for?' she had innocently asked.

'A good long screw. A blow job would do, if you're busy.'

Flora had no idea what a screw or blow job was, but didn't like the sound of it, nor the way the man had licked his lips. She told him to go away and buy his drink elsewhere. As he didn't argue, she reckoned she had done the right thing.

The manager of the Crown, Lloyd Francis, had advised her

not to put up with any nonsense. 'You tell 'em, girl. You're here to serve them drinks, that's all. They have no right to be offensive.' He grinned. 'Mind you, it was the reason I took you on, despite your having no experience, like, because you look as pretty as a picture behind that bar.'

Isobel had loaned her a couple of blouses. 'I bought them in Harrod's, and they cost the earth, even with my model's discount. I'd give them to you, luv, except one of these days I hope to lose all this extra weight and wear them again.' She patted her generous hips hopefully.

By the time it was Easter, Flora was paying for her keep, had returned the blouses to Isobel and bought half a dozen of her own from a shop whose prices were a mere fraction of Harrod's. As only her top half was visible behind the bar, she mostly wore a plain black skirt and a pretty top. She had bought a pale pink lipstick, and Isobel had advised her to rub Vaseline on her lashes to make them look longer.

'Me, I use mascara, but you don't need it, luv. Nor do you need powder on that lovely clear skin of yours.'

They were in Isobel's bedroom, that had white lace curtains at the window and a dressing table adorned with a frilly flowered skirt. The older woman showed Flora how to put up her silvery-blond hair using combs and a couple of hairpins. 'Looking at you,' she sighed, 'I don't half wish I were young again. I had the time of me life in London.'

'Maybe you'll go back there one day,' Flora said encouragingly.

'No one wants a model this old and this size.'

Flora had no idea what to say to that. As far as she was concerned, Isobel was as beautiful now as she had ever been.

On the first of February, Flora had turned nineteen. She hadn't told anyone it was her birthday, but thought it was time she wrote to Andrew and Else in Morocco to inform them where she and Simon were living. They would recognise the date, realise it was her birthday and wonder – and worry – where she and Simon where. They were probably already worried. She really should have written to them before.

She didn't tell them exactly what had happened in Crouch End, or mention Johnnie Lucas's name, just that life there had become impossible and that she'd moved to a place called Bootle in Liverpool.

Remember I told you about Isobel, the model who used to live in my aunt's basement flat? she wrote. *Well, it's her we're living with now. We are very happy here. It's like belonging to a big, noisy family.* She also asked that they not let Aunt Winifred have her present address under any circumstances. Finally, she added that she hoped in the not too distant future to come and visit them in Morocco, bringing Simon with her.

It wasn't long after Easter that she met Kieran O'Shea. 'Everyone calls me Kerry,' he told her. A glorious smile sort of danced across his boyishly handsome face and his brown eyes twinkled. He had black curly hair, was slim of build and very tall.

'Are you Tommy O'Shea's son?' Flora asked. She found him exceptionally attractive.

'No, Billy's.'

'Why haven't I seen you before, at some event or other?' She would have noticed him had he been there. She recalled meeting Billy a couple of times.

'I've been in a seminary in Ireland,' he explained. He played a tune on the bar with his long, thin fingers. She got the impression he was the sort of person who couldn't sit still. 'I've been there since just after Chrimbo.'

'What's Chrimbo?'

'Liverpudlian for Christmas.'

'Are you training to be a priest?' What a terrible waste! Catholic priests weren't allowed to marry. While she wasn't planning to marry Kerry O'Shea after knowing him for only a matter of minutes, it still seemed a waste.

'Good Lord, no. I'd make a hopeless priest. I've been recuperating. I used to be in the Merchant Navy, and I had a sort of accident.' He beat his chest with his fist, making a hollow sound. 'I'm better now. I start a new job on Monday.'

'I didn't come to Liverpool until New Year's Eve. You would have left by then.'

'I know.' He beamed at her. 'I know all about you; me dad told me. Your arrival caused quite a stir. This is my first day back home, and I came especially to have a look at you. "She's working at the Crown on Stanley Road," me da said. And now I'm looking at you, and I really like what I see.'

For the first time in her life, Flora felt herself blush. 'What would you like to drink?' she enquired.

He rolled his eyes. 'Sorry, am I being a pain? I'll have half a pint of Guinness, please. I hate the stuff, but apparently it'll turn me into Mr Universe. "Guinness is good for you". Isn't that how the advert goes?'

'I think so.' He was perhaps a bit too slim; thin would be a better word, and rather pale. She poured the drink. He paid and turned to look for a seat. It was early on a Tuesday night and not particularly crowded.

'You're not being a pain,' she said hurriedly, not wanting to lose him. 'Why don't you sit on a bar stool and talk to me?' My, she was being forward tonight.

He looked delighted at the suggestion. 'Don't you mind?'

'I wouldn't ask if I did.' There were times when she did find it a pain if someone, often a commercial traveller, sat on a bar stool and monopolised her every free moment telling her about his racing pigeons back home, the fact that doorstep selling was on the way out, or that his wife didn't understand him – the most popular subject of all. But she welcomed being monopolised by Kerry O'Shea for as long as he was willing to do so.

He was still there when Lloyd Francis rang the bell and called time. 'Can I take you home?' he asked. 'It's a pity we can't dance the last waltz. Do you go dancing?'

'I've never learned.' They'd sort of danced at the school in Switzerland. Andrew had advised them to hop, skip and jump around the room while he played rousing marching music on the wind-up gramophone.

'I'm a tip-top dancer.' Kerry leaped off the stool and did a little whirl. 'Fred Astaire has nothing on me. Would you like me to teach you?'

She quite fancied it! 'When? I work five nights a week.'

'What nights d'you have off?' he enquired eagerly.

'Sundays and Mondays.'

'We'll go next Monday to the Locarno. But I can't possibly wait until then until I see you again. How about I take you to the pictures somewhere in town tomorrow afternoon?'

She quite fancied that idea too. The sisters would be there to look after Simon.

Leaving him sitting by the bar, she went to collect the dirty glasses, conscious of his dark eyes following her around the room. It would be nice to have a boyfriend again, but this time she would endeavour not to let it get as serious as it had become with Luke Carr.

She walked back to the bar with the tray of glasses. As she neared, he shouted, 'Will you marry me, Flora?'

Flora laughed. 'I'll think about it,' she shouted back. There was little likelihood of that. All she wanted was a boyfriend, not a husband.

When she arrived home, she found Lillian sitting with Nana. The older woman was fast asleep in her chair, breathing heavily. She had gone off her food and lost a lot of weight. Any mention of going into hospital caused her enormous distress, and she would cry for ages. The sisters had resolved to care for her for as long as it took.

'I don't like that sort of rattle in her throat,' Lillian said worriedly. 'What does it mean, I wonder?' Flora said she thought it sounded more like a snort than a rattle, and Lillian sighed. 'I'm dead ignorant about medical things. Perhaps I should stay with Nana until our Isobel comes home.'

'I'll stay up and wait for Isobel if you like,' Flora offered.

'Oh, would you, Flo? Ta very much. I'm dead tired, if the truth be known. And I've got to be up early tomorrow to take our Theresa to the dental hospital in town.' Theresa, Lillian's youngest daughter, had fallen over and broken two of her front teeth on the kerb.

Nana appeared to stop breathing for the space of seconds and the two women regarded her anxiously, then relaxed when the breathing began again in a rush.

Lillian went to fetch her coat from the hall. 'Well, I'll be off. Thanks again, Flo. Tara. I'll see you tomorrer.'

'Goodnight, Lillian.' Flora couldn't quite bring herself to say 'tara' back. Possibly one day she would do it naturally, without thinking.

Flora had got undressed and was in her dressing gown ready for bed. She was reading *Woman's Weekly* when she heard Isobel's key in the front door. It was almost half past two. Upstairs in the box room where Simon now slept alone, she heard him utter a little cry, followed by the creak of the bed as he turned over.

Isobel looked tired as she came through the door. Flora knew she always made herself a cup of tea when she came home and took it with her to bed.

'Go upstairs,' she whispered. 'I'll make the tea.'

Isobel removed the pin out of her white felt hat. 'How's Nana?'

'A bit restless, that's all.'

Flora crept past into the kitchen, where she put the kettle on. Minutes later, she carried two cups of tea upstairs. Isobel had already changed into a glamorous nightdress drenched with lace, and was hanging the costume she'd worn that night in the wardrobe.

'When I'm ready, I'll go down and sit with Nana for the rest of the night,' she said. 'You never know, I might fall asleep in the chair.' She sat on the padded stool in front of her dressing-table mirror and began to remove her make-up, first layering on soft cream, then removing it with a lump of cotton wool. 'How did you get on tonight?' she asked.

'I met an O'Shea I'd never seen before.' Flora found herself smiling at the memory of the delightful young man. 'His name's Kerry.'

'Billy's lad? Oh, he's a real charmer. If I were twenty years younger and we weren't related, I'd go out with him like a shot.' She paused in front of the mirror. 'Did he ask you out? Lucky girl!' she said in response to Flora's nod.

The cream had softened her mascara and it was smeared like tragic shadows beneath her eyes. For a moment, before wiping the shadows away, she looked briefly grotesque. 'It's a wonderful feeling, isn't it, luv? Meeting a new chap.'

'I've only been out with one chap before.'

Isobel twisted round on the stool until she and Flora were facing. 'Have a nice time with Kerry, Flora, but don't let it get serious.'

Flora had already made up her mind about that, but was interested to know why Isobel should offer such advice. 'Why ever not?'

Isobel turned back and began to rub, a different cream on to her face, 'Kerry O'Shea joined the merchant navy as an ordinary seaman in 1936 when he was just fourteen,' she said. 'While the war was on, he sailed in some very dangerous waters, accompanying Royal Navy convoys across the Atlantic numerous times. He must have sailed across every ocean and big sea during his young life, always returning home safely to Coral Street and his mam and dad when he had a bit of leave.' She picked up a metal curler and wound a length of hair around it, then reached for another. 'About eighteen months ago,' she continued, 'with the war almost over, Kerry's ship had picked up cargo in the Russian port of Archangel and was sailing home when it hit a floating mine. It exploded and sank. Most of the crew drowned, but Kerry and two other men managed to haul themselves into a lifeboat. The temperature of the water was below freezing, and they were soaked. By the time they were picked up, the only man left alive was Kerry O'Shea, and then it was a close call.' She paused, hands in mid-air, about to use another curler. 'His health is shot. He has a weak chest, and his immune system doesn't work any more. I don't understand these things, but one day he might catch a cold and it could kill him.'

'But he might not catch a cold, and live until he's ninety like Nana.'

Isobel nodded. 'I suppose that could happen. Only Himself up there knows the answer.' She rolled her eyes heavenwards as she tied an ugly thick pink net over the curlers.

Flora said, 'He looked perfectly healthy to me.' He was undoubtedly too thin and pale, but that was hardly a death sentence. He had claimed to have been a bit run-down, but plenty of sunshine and some decent food, and he'd improve no end. She stood, went over to the window and moved the curtain to look out. As expected, the street was deserted, the railway line silent. The yellow lamplight picked out the cobbled surface, making it look more bumpy and uneven than it actually was. No one was about, and the trains weren't running at this time of night. For some reason she found the view infinitely depressing.

She sighed, let the curtain go and returned to sit on the bed. Isobel was watching her carefully in the mirror. 'What are you thinking about?'

Flora just shrugged. 'Nothing, really.' She was about to tell Isobel that Kerry had proposed, but decided not to. Anyway, it had only been a joke.

Isobel picked up her tea. It must have been stone cold by now. 'I'll just drink this, then go down to Nana.'

Chapter 9

As promised, Kerry called for Flora the following afternoon, but by then it was obvious that a visit to the cinema wasn't on.

Early that morning, Nana had been taken unconscious to Bootle hospital, and by midday the entire O'Shea clan had been alerted. Isobel had woken Flora just after six to say she'd made Nana tea but, although she was still breathing, had found it impossible to wake her. Would Flora please run as far as Marsh Lane where there was a telephone box, and ring for an ambulance?

From that moment on, as if a bush telegraph was in operation, the house had been deluged with relatives, most of them in tears. Because she wasn't one of Nana's numerous descendants and Nana was ninety, Flora didn't feel too upset that she was nearing her end. She'd had a long life, and had been greatly loved.

As the hospital only allowed two visitors at a time, the bulk of the family remained in the house in Pearl Street. Flora and Simon apart, every single person was related by blood or marriage to Nana. Flora was making tea. There weren't nearly enough provisions to cater for them all, the weekly ration having long been used up, so people were bringing their own tea, sugar and milk. It would get even more crowded when the children came home from school and the men returned from work.

Kerry was with Flora in the kitchen. As Nana was his great-grandmother, he was as distressed as anyone that she was gravely ill and unlikely to recover. He was leaning against the back door, arms folded, watching Flora at work and taking the tea to whoever was next on her mental list.

'This is for Betty O'Shea,' she said. 'I don't think I've met her before. Someone asked for it.'

'She's me mam,' Kerry said. 'And you must've met her, 'cos she's met you.'

'Then I'm bound to recognise her when I see her.'

He took the tea just as Simon wandered in, a brightly coloured sponge ball under one arm and his teddy bear under the other, looking desolate. He was getting too much attention from people who didn't matter, and none from the two who did; Nana and Flora. He took hold of Flora's leg and laid his head on her hip.

'Me fed up, Flo,' he sniffed.

She dropped to her knees and took him in her arms. 'I don't blame you, darling,' she whispered. 'We'll go for a walk along the Docky later, shall we?' With the arrival of spring, the weather had improved enormously, and she and Simon had discovered they really loved the Dock Road where great ships arrived from all over the world. The different noises, the exotic smells, the colourfully dressed foreigners speaking strange languages fascinated them both.

He laid his head on her shoulder. 'Yes, please, Flo. But not in my pushchair.'

'Not if you don't want to.'

'I'm too old for a pushchair, and too big.'

'I know you are, darling, we'll leave it at home.'

'Flo, when will Nana come back?'

She hugged him closer. 'Oh, Simon, love, I really don't know.'

He sighed. 'Has she gone on a journey?'

She grasped at that. 'Yes, darling, a long, long journey.'

'Is she there yet?'

'Not yet, but she will be soon.' She stood and patted his head. 'Why don't you play in the yard with your ball for a little while? It won't be long before we can go for our walk.' She opened the back door and he went outside, only slightly cheered.

'Can I come on the walk too?' Kerry O'Shea had returned, and Flora's heart leaped with pleasure.

'Of course. The very minute someone comes and takes over in the kitchen, we shall go.'

Half an hour later, they were walking along the Dock Road, or the Docky as it was mostly called. Kerry's mother, Betty O'Shea, had taken over in the kitchen – Flora suspected that Kerry had asked her to. She hadn't introduced herself, just said grimly, 'I'll do a turn now,' and jerked her head at Flora to go. A tall woman, she was good-looking in a stern, patrician way – handsome would be an appropriate word to describe her. Flora remembered meeting her a couple of times, and had got the impression that the woman didn't like her, an impression confirmed by their encounter that morning. She would rather Kerry's mother had turned out to be one of the nicer O'Sheas.

Simon was still unhappy. Flora knew it was because he'd thought they would be going for a walk together, just the two of them, but this strange young man had tagged along and in his opinion, was taking up too much of her attention. She was holding Simon's hand and Kerry was walking along on her other side, not touching.

'Where's Luke?' Simon had asked loudly when they first set off along the busy, bustling road that was full of people and traffic.

'In Manchester,' Flora answered.

He was about to say something else, but was distracted by the sight of two French sailors coming towards them in their round hats, tight jerseys and flared trousers. 'Funny,' he giggled after the men had passed.

'Dead funny,' Flora affirmed, nodding solemnly.

Simon's attention transferred to a grey dappled horse that ambled slowly past, pulling a cart piled high with old furniture. 'Horsey,' he announced. 'Nice horsey.'

'Who's Luke?' Kerry enquired from her other side.

'He lived in the same road as we did in London, before moving to Manchester.'

'I see.' He stuffed his hands in his pockets and sort of skipped along beside her, kicking at stones on the way. It was hard to believe there was anything wrong with him. Flora felt differently about him today. Perhaps it was because the house was so crowded and there was no romantic music in the background that it had been quite flat when they'd met again. Or because she'd expected they'd be at the pictures by now, the only people they had to concentrate on being each other. And he didn't seem to be showing much interest in Simon. What had his mother told him about the little boy? Perhaps he suspected Simon wasn't her cousin. Quite a few people did. No one had ever said anything, but she could tell by the look on their faces that they believed he was her illegitimate son.

'*Bambi*'s on at the Trocadero in Lime Street,' he said suddenly.

'*Bambi*!' She knew what it was about, but surely he wasn't suggesting they go to the pictures to see a full-length cartoon about a baby deer? In London, when she'd gone with Millie Carr, they'd only watched heavy dramas with stars like Bette Davis and Joan Crawford, or the occasional thriller with Humphrey Bogart. Cartoons, they considered, were for children.

'I thought if we managed to get there over the next few days we could take Simon with us.'

What a wonderful idea! Why had she never thought of

taking Simon to the pictures herself? 'I'd like that,' she said. 'We'd both like it, wouldn't we, Simon?'

'Like what?' Simon asked crossly, having no idea what she was talking about. He was watching two Chinese men ride past sharing a bicycle while arguing furiously.

'Going to the pictures.'

'Nana used to show me pictures in books.' He looked unexpectedly tearful. 'Want to go home to Nana.'

'She won't be there, darling.'

He looked up at Flora pleadingly. 'Won't she be back yet from her journey?'

'No, Simon.' She made a helpless face at Kerry, as if to say *I've no idea what to tell him.*

'Are you hungry, Simon?' Kerry asked.

'I don't know,' Simon replied, a touch despairingly.

'We're just coming up to a chippy, and I think a few pennyworth of chips each would go down well, don't you, kiddo?'

Simon looked at him cautiously. 'P'raps.'

The chip shop came into view. The dinner hour over, the place was almost empty. Kerry went inside and reappeared with three parcels of chips wrapped in newspaper. He handed one to Simon.

'Here you are, kiddo.'

'Do I have to eat the paper?'

'No, just the chips.' He grinned and looked at Flora. 'I asked for salt and vinegar; hope that's all right.'

'That's fine.' She'd never eaten chips out of newspaper before. The O'Shea sisters were above that sort of thing. She ate her chips, feeling much happier.

There weren't any conventional shops in the road, only those connected with industry, like chandlers and shipping. Kerry became Simon's friend for life when he bought him a tape measure from a tool shop. The tape pulled out an entire six feet from its case, rewinding rapidly when a button was pressed. The little boy had never been so delighted with a gift before. From that day on, the tape measure went with him everywhere, and Rufus spent most of the remainder of his life sitting on the dressing table in his bedroom.

They returned home. On the way, they decided to take Simon to see *Bambi* as soon as possible. Kerry reminded Flora that he was starting a new job on Monday. 'So we can only go to the pictures on Saturday or Sunday afternoons.

'It's in Critchley's, the job, a men's outfitters in Strand Road,' he said ruefully when she enquired about the job. 'I've got to wear a *suit*! It's a bit different from the merchant navy.'

'Well at least it's on dry land,' Flora said. 'The job, that is.' He was giving Simon a piggy back, and both seemed to be enjoying it, which was a relief.

In the short time they'd been away, the house in Pearl Street had turned into a house of tears with the news that, virtually on the stroke of three, Nana had passed away peacefully in her sleep.

She returned the following morning, this time in a coffin that went into the parlour. Hardly a minute of the day would pass without a number of people there saying prayers, usually with rosary beads threaded through their fingers. A priest, Father Doyle, came twice a day, early in the morning and late at night, to say more prayers, joined by any members of the family who happened to be present, often quite a crowd. Quivery voices sang hymns, sometimes in Latin. Candles burned, and the room and then the house smelled strongly of sultry flowers and melting wax. There couldn't have been more fuss if a member of royalty had died, Flora thought.

People called with more flowers, messages of sympathy and Mass cards. Old friends of Nana, ladies eighty and ninety years old came to talk about old times with anyone who would listen. Nana's obituary went into the *Liverpool Echo* and the *Bootle Times*, which alerted even more people to come and pay their respects. Simon managed to get into the parlour, though Flora had done her best to prevent him. Some tactless soul lifted him up so that he could view Nana in her coffin, clothed in white and surrounded by lilies, hands crossed on her chest. He was strangely undisturbed.

'Nana's gone on a long, long journey,' he remarked, and the person was so impressed with this childish wisdom that the words were passed on and on, so that Father Doyle used them in his prayers that night.

Flora wasn't sure if she was glad she wasn't a Catholic or wished she were. It was like belonging to a secret society, with special benefits for members when they went to heaven, the only possible destination for a Catholic who had obeyed all the rules. She had no idea what the disadvantages were for non-Catholics; were they allowed into heaven, or not?

She astonished herself when, early on Monday, the day of the funeral, there being fewer people about than usual, she went into the parlour to say goodbye to Nana and found herself in floods of tears at the sight of her suddenly frail figure in the coffin. The lines on her face seemed to have melted like the wax, and she looked very young. It was so terribly *sad*. She would never see Nana again because Nana was dead, and it was impossible to imagine the house in Pearl Street without her.

It was Isobel who rescued her. She was already wearing black. Upstairs, there was a hat with a black veil to cover her face. All the sisters had them. 'Don't cry, luv,' Isobel stroked her hair. 'Are you sure you won't come to the funeral?'

'I'd sooner not, if you don't mind,' Flora sobbed. 'There's Simon to look after, and I promised to have Evelyn's twins.' Evelyn was Noreen's daughter, and the twin boys, Tony and Terry, who were three, were Nana's great-great-grandsons.

She was grateful to have an excuse, glad to be left behind when the carriage pulled by four black horses with black feathers in their manes arrived to collect Nana and take her on her very last journey on this earth. It was a grey, dreary day, and mountains of black clouds were massed in the sky. Rain hung in the air; it was like being wrapped in a wet mist.

The curtains at the windows of every single house in the street had been drawn when the carriage left for the church, which was only a few minutes' walk away. It was followed by at least a hundred people on foot, dressed from head to toe in black.

Flora closed the door, glad to shut out the sound of the carriage wheels on the cobbles and the clatter of so many feet; glad that it was almost over and that soon everything would return to normal. The children were arguing over something in the kitchen. Despite their presence, the house felt uncannily empty, and their voices unnaturally shrill. Unable to help herself, Flora paused in the hallway to have another heartfelt cry, then threw back her shoulders and went to join the children. She was going to read to them from *Rupert Bear*, Simon's favourite book.

It wasn't until late afternoon that Evelyn came to collect her boys. She was only two years older than Flora, and the pair of them had become friends of a sort – there never seemed to be much opportunity to see each other privately and have a proper chat without family present.

'Oh, lord it was miserable,' Evelyn complained. 'Not so much the Requiem Mass, I quite enjoyed that, what with all the hymns and the lovely atmosphere, but it was cold and windy in the cemetery and really horrible. All those dead people! I mean, I know for certain that one of these days I'll end up there meself, and so will me two little lads.' Tony and Terry were perched one on each of their mother's knees, glad to have her back. 'Are you going to the wake?' she asked Flora.

'I don't think so, no.' Flora didn't want to go anywhere that she didn't *have* to. A wake sounded awful.

'I would if I were you. It's in St James's church hall, and there's some smashing food there – I dropped in for a couple of minutes for a sausage roll and a glass of wine. I'll look after Simon until someone else turns up. Why not go and let your hair down? It's Monday. You don't have to work tonight.'

'Let my hair down, at a wake!'

Evelyn winked. 'There's wakes and wakes, Flo. I'd go and see what Nana's is like, if I were you.'

The first thing Flora noticed when she entered the church hall was the barrel of beer on a table just inside the door. People were sitting quietly on seats that lined two sides of the room. The beer apart, she couldn't see any other signs of jollity. Someone was playing a sad Irish song on a piano, and a few people were singing along in a desultory fashion. There weren't enough seats, so Flora joined the crowd in front of the stage where Isobel stood. Someone gave her a glass of wine and a ham sandwich. After five days of tears, or being on the verge of tears, it was a relief to see Isobel and her sisters acting quite normally and talking about quite ordinary things.

Flora actually witnessed the event that was about to turn the wake into something approaching a riot.

Two elderly women, sitting facing each other across the room, slowly and deliberately got to their feet. Lifting their skirts slightly with both hands, they began to approach each other, shuffling two steps one way and two steps the other, each one's eyes fixed on the woman opposite. Noting this, the pianist began to play a series of chords in time to the shuffling, and some people started to clap. The women reached each other, though remained about a foot apart. From somewhere there came a deathly scream, and the women's hands moved to their hips and they began to jump from side to side, faster and faster, then, linking arms, they began to whizz each other around, very energetically for two such elderly ladies.

The room exploded into movement and sound. There were

more screams, the piano player was going berserk on the keys and everyone in the room apart from an astonished Flora was dancing what she now realised was an Irish jig. Nana's life couldn't have been celebrated in a happier and more jubilant way.

She would have liked to have stayed longer, danced more jigs – she soon learned how – sung more songs, listened to the jokes and joined in the laughter, but it was nearing Simon's bedtime and she wanted to be there when her little boy went to bed. She hurried through the streets, wondering when she would see Kerry again; there'd been no sign of him in the church hall.

She found him in the house in Pearl Street, helping Simon measure the furniture with his new tape measure. Both were kneeling on the floor, and Kerry was writing the numbers down in a little notebook.

' 'Lo Flo,' Simon murmured absently when she went in. 'Kerry's teaching me to count up to ten.'

'That's kind of you.'

Kerry grinned. 'Well, I've not long learned how to do it meself.'

He got to his feet and they gazed at each other, he and Flora, soon to be alone at last. She wasn't normally shy, but she felt shy now. Words were locked in her throat, refusing to be said.

'Time for bed, Simon,' she managed to say.

Simon pressed the button on the tape measure to close it. 'Can Kerry come up and say goodnight?'

'Of course,' she assured him.

'And can I look at the figures in bed?'

Flora was nonplussed for a while, until she realised he meant the figures that Kerry had been writing in the notebook. 'Of course,' she said again.

'I'll bring them up with me,' Kerry promised.

The little boy obediently went upstairs. He chatted about his day while he undressed – by himself, with Flora only giving him an occasional hand. He had enjoyed playing with Tony and Terry, and wanted to know why he wasn't a twin.

'Because babies normally only arrive in ones,' Flora explained. 'Twins like Tony and Terry don't happen very often.' He was astonished to learn that, although it was even more unusual, babies could arrive in threes and fours. 'And about eight years ago, in Canada,' she told him, 'a woman had five little girls all at the same time. They're called quintuplets.'

'Don't want to be a quintuplet, Flo,' Simon said with a shudder.

'Well, I'm glad you're not. Let me button your pyjamas and you can get into bed.'

He turned away. 'Want to button them myself,' he said mutinously.

Kerry came in. 'Is it time to say goodnight yet?'

'In a minute.' Painstakingly, because his fingers were only small, Simon fastened the buttons on his pyjama jacket, slid under the clothes and eyed them mischievously. ' 'Night, Flo,' he said. ' 'Night, Kerry.'

Kerry laughed. 'Goodnight, little man.'

Flora kissed Simon's nose and said nothing.

Downstairs, it just seemed natural that he would take her in his arms. They didn't kiss, just stood in the middle of the room fitting together so perfectly it was as if they'd been born for it. Flora felt as if she could stay there for ever and never move again, even if it wasn't exactly practical.

'Well,' Kerry said after a happy sigh, 'I suppose this is it.' He stood back and held her face in his hands, staring deep into her eyes, before pressing his lips against hers. He would kiss her many times again, more passionately and for longer, but the first kiss was always the sweetest and would never be forgotten.

'When shall we get married?' he whispered after a while. 'Tomorrow? Next week?'

She needed more time than that to make up her mind. Although she hadn't planned on it becoming a serious relationship, it seemed she had no choice. She was pretty sure she loved him, but not *entirely* sure. It was only seven days since they'd met, and it frightened her to make such a big decision after such a short space of time. She remembered how differently she'd felt about Luke after not seeing him for a mere few weeks. 'It doesn't have to be in such a rush,' she said. 'I think we ought to get to know each other better.'

He looked disappointed, but she didn't care. She'd made the wrong decision by going to live in London with Aunt Winifred, when she and Simon would have been much better off in Morocco with Andrew and Else, and she didn't want to make another wrong decision now.

Chapter 10

Isobel arrived back from the wake just after ten, very slightly tipsy, at which point Kerry went home. 'I'll see you tomorrow,' he whispered at the door.

'Don't forget I'll be working at the Crown,' she reminded him.

'I'll be standing outside the bar waiting for it to open,' he assured her. He blew her a kiss and walked quickly down the street, turning to wave until he reached the corner and disappeared.

Flora closed the door and went inside to find Isobel in the living room, having poured two glasses of sherry. Another time and Flora might have found this rather odd, but today, like so many days recently, wasn't a normal day. She picked up her own glass and took a sip. She still felt slightly drunk, though she had only had a single glass of wine at the wake. She'd had little experience of alcohol.

'Let's drink to us both,' Isobel said. She raised her glass. 'May both our futures be happy ones.'

'I'll second that.' Flora took another sip of sherry. 'Does that mean you're planning on changing your own future?' Isobel had made it obvious she didn't like working at the club.

'I am indeed.' The other woman's cheeks were pink and her blue eyes twinkled. She looked extraordinarily happy, considering there'd recently been a death in the family, as well as more beautiful than ever in her tasteful black costume. 'Today is the first day of the rest of me life,' she cried.

Flora smiled. 'You could say that about everybody.'

'Maybe, but with me it's different.' She finished off the sherry and poured another. 'Pretty soon, I shall leave Liverpool and go back to London. I intend to lose weight and take up modelling again. Mam's gone and so has Nana, so there's no reason for me to stay in Bootle a minute longer.'

'But what about your job?'

Isobel snorted. 'Sod me job. Anyroad, I gave me notice the minute Nana died. Last night was me last time there. From now on, I'm as free as a bird.' She flapped her arms as if about to fly away.

Flora's eyes unexpectedly filled up with tears. It had been happening a lot lately. 'But I'll miss you.'

'No, you won't, luv. You'll have Kerry – not forgetting our little Simon. And if you're worried about where you'll live when I go, you can have this place.' She wagged her finger. 'But you'll have to get married first. The landlord will only pass it on to a relative. Once you're Mrs O'Shea, it's all yours. If Kerry hasn't proposed yet, then he will do soon. He's obviously mad about you.'

'But it's not long since you warned me not to feel seriously about him,' Flora reminded her. 'According to you, he hasn't long to live.'

'And according to you, he could live until he's ninety.'

'I can't marry someone just to get a house!'

Isobel grinned. 'I've known women marry a chap for far less than that.'

'But it doesn't seem proper,' Flora argued. Nothing about it seemed proper. 'Anyway, one of your sisters has more right to the house than me. One of them should have it. They'll think it most unfair if you give it to someone else.' The sisters had houses of their own, but none was as pretty as this one.

'But this is *my* house,' Isobel insisted. 'I'm the one who says who should have it. I'm the one who gave up me career to look after Mam and Nana, but they didn't give up a thing. Furthermore, it was me who had the place decorated and bought the posh furniture, and Mam had the landlord turn the rent book over to me.' She paused for breath. 'And which sister, pray, should I give it to? It'd cause bad feeling if I picked one over the others. Our Noreen, being the eldest, might expect to get it, and June'd think it should be her for being the youngest, like. Lillian's husband's out of work, so she might think *she* has the right. Yet if I was going to give it to a sister, it'd be our Beattie, 'cos she's me favourite. Whoever I choose, it'd cause never-ending griping. They'll resent you getting it, Flora, but it won't last for long, and it's better than them resenting each other. Anyroad, you'll be an O'Shea, one of the family, when you and Kerry are married.'

'I haven't said I'll marry him yet.'

'Has he proposed? I wouldn't be surprised if he had. Kerry's not the sort to hang about if he wants something – in this case, you.'

'He's asked me to marry him twice, actually,' admitted Flora.

'Well, you'd better make your mind up soon.' She picked up the sherry, drained the glass and poured one more. 'Of course, with you not being a Catholic, it'll be a mixed marriage and cause all sorts of ructions.'

'Oh, dear,' Flora said sarcastically.

'Kerry's mam, Betty, is a fanatical Catholic, in and out of church by the minute, attends Mass every single day, does the altar flowers of a Sunday. She'll do her nut when she finds out you and her favourite son are about to get hitched.'

'Her favourite son!'

'Well, he's the youngest and he's got this – what would you call it? – this medical problem I told you about. Favourite son or not, she'd kill him before letting him get married in a registry office. And there's Simon. I bet she's one of the ones who thinks you're his mother. She's got that sort of disbelieving nature. Oh, and she won't approve of you being a barmaid.'

Flora finished her sherry and put the glass on the table with a bang. The objections Isobel listed against her marrying Kerry had only served to help her make a decision. She *would* marry him. In her heart, she was convinced he would make a good husband and a perfect father for Simon – and it was Simon who she was most concerned about. Alone, she would have managed by herself with nothing to prevent her from doing whatever she wanted. And, she reminded herself, feeling rather uncomfortable about it, she would be getting a husband *and* a house. Not that she was influenced by the house. At least, she hoped not.

'Oh, all right,' she said loudly to Isobel. 'When Kerry comes round tomorrow I'll agree to marry him.'

'I just knew, when I first saw you in The Crown – gosh, was it really only last week? – that we'd get married eventually,' Kerry said jubilantly next day when Flora rather gravely accepted his proposal. 'I think I'm in what's called seventh heaven.'

Flora had the distinct impression that she might be in seventh heaven too, though she had never felt so confused.

Three days later, Kerry's mother, Betty, called. 'To talk about the wedding,' she said to Isobel, who opened the door.

Isobel insisted Betty and Flora use the parlour to talk in. 'You need your privacy,' she said. Her sisters were present, and Flora and Kerry's wedding was none of their business. 'They'll only stick their oars in.'

Betty refused to take off her coat, and also turned down the offer of a cup of tea. She sat on the edge of the settee and stared at the younger woman in a way that Flora could only describe as baleful. She was shabbily dressed in a too-short maroon coat with frayed buttonholes and wore a woollen headscarf over her rather nice brown hair. An imitation-leather handbag was clutched tightly on her knee.

'I would have expected you and Kerry to come together and tell us you were getting married,' she said gruffly. 'Not for him to tell us by himself.'

'I was coming on Sunday for that very purpose,' Flora assured her. She was seated in an armchair opposite, feeling nervous. 'Kerry said he would ask you to invite me – and Simon – to tea, and we would tell you then.'

Betty acknowledged this with a jerk of her head. 'Our Kerry could never keep a secret,' she conceded. 'Anyroad, consider yourself invited, and the boy.'

'Thank you.' Flora had expected objections, and was pleased to receive an invitation instead.

'There's lots of things I want to say,' Betty continued. 'You not being a Catholic is a really big problem. You can take instruction, become a Catholic, but it can take years. Kerry said you'd like to get married soon.' Her eyes narrowed. 'Is there any particular reason for that?'

'No reason at all.' Does she think I might be pregnant, Flora wondered? And it's Kerry who's keen to get married soon, not me. Though there was the house. It was important to become an O'Shea soon, so Isobel could bequeath it to her.

Betty continued to eye her suspiciously until something, perhaps Flora's look of indignation, convinced her she was wrong. 'There are priests around who are willing to officiate over mixed marriages,' she said, 'but they're few and far between. Billy, me husband, knows of a little church, St Kentigern's, in Waddicar Lane near Melling, on the very edge of Liverpool where the parish priest will do it. You wouldn't be able to have a Nuptial Mass, just an ordinary service. But at least it means you'll be married in the eyes of God, not like getting wed in one of them heathen registry-office places.'

She *wants* me to marry Kerry, Flora realised with a slight

113

shock. She wants him to be happy, and she thinks he'll be happy with me and Simon. Impulsively, she leaned forward and clasped the woman's cold hands in her own warm ones. 'I love Kerry,' she assured her. She genuinely did. She loved him very much, though she wasn't *in* love with him.

'Do you?' The woman's eyes were watery when they met Flora's. 'Do you, really?'

'Really.' Flora squeezed her hands again.

'What about this Simon?' Her voice had become hard. 'How did you come by him?'

Flora removed her hands. She'd thought they'd been getting on well. 'Simon is my cousin. His parents, my aunt and uncle, died in a car accident in Zurich just before the end of the war. As his only living relative, it seemed natural that I should bring him up.'

There was a long silence. Flora leaned back in the chair, waiting for Kerry's mother's reaction.

'I don't believe you,' Betty said bluntly after a while. 'Every word of that's a bloody lie. He's yours, I can tell he's yours. Our Kerry believes you, but he'll soon know the truth once you're married and he finds you're not a virgin. But by then it'll be too late, and you'll have copped him.'

Flora felt her stomach curl as she listened to the hate-filled words. She wanted to run from the room, but found herself glued to the chair, unable to move. How could someone as joyous as Kerry have such a dreadful person for a mother?

'I tried to talk me son out of marrying you,' Betty went on. 'We stayed up till after midnight arguing, but he wouldn't listen. You've really got your claws into him, haven't you, miss? So,' she got to her feet, 'me and Billy will do all we can to help with the wedding – our Kerry's happiness is our only concern. But you're not the sort of girl I wanted him to marry, not the sort of girl at all.'

Without saying another word, she left the room and let

herself out of the house, closing the front door quietly behind her.

Isobel came in. 'Has she gone without saying tara? She's dead peculiar, that Betty O'Shea.'

Flora assumed her face must have been as white as a sheet because Isobel glanced at her and gasped, 'Jaysus, Flora! You look as if you've seen a ghost. What did she say to you?'

'Horrible things; really horrible things.' Flora couldn't bring herself to list them. She wasn't sure if she wanted to marry Kerry and have Betty for a mother-in-law. 'At first, I thought she actually wanted me to marry him, but afterwards I realised she hates me.'

The sisters must have been listening. They piled into the parlour, and all four squeezed together on the settee. She was assured that while all mothers-in-law weren't nearly as bad as Betty, quite a few were, and some were even worse. They actually knew a woman from Chaucer Street who'd tried to poison her son's wife.

'I think it was arsenic – whatever it is you kill rats with,' June said ghoulishly.

'And Cissie Adams attacked her ma-in-law with a brick for being such a bitch,' Lillian recalled. 'I used to sit behind Cissie at school, and she was the sort of person who wouldn't have hurt a fly.'

So many examples of awful mothers-in-law were quoted that Flora accepted she could have had far worse than Betty O'Shea, and that the best thing to do was take no notice of her, or at least try not to. 'It's Kerry you're marrying, not her,' she was assured over and over. 'If it comes to it, just refuse to let her in the house.'

These assurances, along with the warmth of the sisters, knowing that all five were on her side, made her feel better. Life would never be perfect. Johnnie Lucas had driven her away from London, and she wasn't prepared to leave Bootle on account of Betty O'Shea. Oh, and there was no way she would go to tea on Sunday, either.

That night, she told Kerry about the morning in Zurich, just over two years ago, when a cattle train had glided into the station, the wooden laths had been torn from one of the carriages and a baby handed to her through the space that had been made.

'"His name is Simon," his mother said – I assumed she was his mother.' Flora's voice faltered as she recalled the way the sun had shone on that glorious spring day, and the dread she had felt as the train slipped slowly by. 'I just knew I had to look after him. He'd been entrusted to me personally – he was *mine*.'

'And he'll soon be mine too,' Kerry said softly. 'I promise I'll be a really good dad.'

They were strolling home from the Crown and Flora laid her head on his shoulder. 'I know you will,' she said. 'Please don't tell anyone about Simon, will you? Isobel is the only person in Liverpool who knows the truth. I don't want Simon knowing until he's much older.'

Kerry promised not to tell another soul. 'I'm sorry about me mam. Dad told me she'd been to see you this avvy.' She was physically conscious of his deep sigh. 'She's not a happy woman. Me dad's been a lousy husband – not that you could blame him.' He sighed again. 'They've just got this dead awful marriage, and I'm not sure who's most to blame.'

The landlord of the house in Pearl Street was consulted, and agreed to change the name on the rent book to Mr Kieran O'Shea as soon as Isobel left for London.

A date was fixed for the wedding; the last Saturday in May, which was convenient for the church in Melling. Flora and Kerry went to see it and discovered it was nestled within a little forest of trees that were covered with tiny new leaves as they prepared for summer.

During the day, the building was used as a school. At weekends, the folding doors in front of the altar were opened and it became a church. They spoke to the jovial, red-faced priest in the sacristy who said he trusted Flora to give serious consideration to becoming a Catholic one day, and insisted that any children they had be raised in their father's faith.

As Flora could see no objection to this, she promised on both counts.

Since Nana had died, the most senior O'Shea in Bootle was her eldest son – Uncle Hughie, who was seventy-one and lived only a few doors away in Pearl Street. Hughie was a bachelor who'd gained a reputation as a womanizer, in the course of a life in which he claimed never to have had a boring minute. He'd been a boxer in his youth, and later a croupier in a casino in Monte Carlo. He'd fought in two wars, and had been an air-raid warden in the war that had only recently ended. The glamorous woman in her fifties, Ada, who lived with him – a bottle blonde, according to Isobel – was introduced to people as his 'housekeeper', though hardly a soul believed it.

Now that Flora was about to become a genuine O'Shea, Uncle Hughie saw it as his job to welcome her into the family. He visited at least twice a day, usually wearing either a yellow or a poppy-red V-necked pullover that Ada had knitted for him. He was still an attractive man with a healthy pink face and a head of pure silver hair. His ties falsely indicated that he'd led an even more interesting life, such as attending Oxford, belonging to an exclusive London club or a top regiment. He taught Simon how to play snap and held Flora's hand for far longer than necessary when they chatted. As she had no male relatives, he had offered to give her away at the wedding.

'I see it as me duty, luv,' he said solemnly.

Flora graciously accepted, feeling she had no choice, particularly as Uncle Hughie offered to provide a car to take them to the church on the day. It wasn't that she had any objection to the man, just that it would have been nice to have been given away by a male member of her own family, had there been one. Andrew had been like a father to her, but although she'd written to tell him and Else that she was getting married, she didn't expect them to come all the way from Morocco for the wedding.

Uncle Hughie wasn't the only one to come round and make her acquaintance. Aunts, uncles, cousins, people who, until now, Flora had only been briefly introduced to since coming to live in Pearl Street also came, as well as some she'd never met at all. Everyone took it for granted that they would be invited to the wedding, arriving with the intent of their getting to know each other better and having a good look at Simon. He was apparently regarded as a somewhat mysterious child, whose relationship to Flora wasn't accepted by all, yet she didn't look like the sort of girl to have had him on the wrong side of the blanket. Unlike Kerry's mother, no one was even vaguely offensive, despite what they might have thought in private.

Auntie Hilda came, a sweet little lady, Hughie's younger sister, who offered Flora a pretty cameo brooch to wear at the wedding. 'Have you heard the saying that a bride should wear "something old, something new, something borrowed, something blue", when she gets married?' she asked. Flora confessed that she never had. 'In that case,' Hilda went on, 'you can wear the brooch for something old, but not borrowed, because I'd like you to keep it. You must make sure you get the other things. Albert, my husband, bought me that brooch as a wedding present. He got it second-hand from a pawnshop. I'm afraid it only has silver trimming, not gold.'

'I prefer silver.' Flora fingered the brooch. It felt very

precious, despite only being silver and not gold. She was beginning to feel precious herself as she was drawn into this very special family. Very soon she too would be an O'Shea.

Isobel's present was a white evening dress that was being turned into a wedding dress by a local dressmaker. It was satin with a sequined, strapless bodice. The dressmaker was making little puffed sleeves out of the cape that went with it.

'I wore that dress to all sorts of grand events,' Isobel said, 'I never imagined that one day someone would get married in it.'

Isobel was on a diet and doing exercises every day. Flora felt, dizzily, that she was about to take her place in her family, live in her house, almost become one of her famous sisters.

Chapter 11

The day dawned at last, a lovely May morning with the sun rising brilliantly in a perfect blue sky. Isobel brought Flora a cup of tea in bed, though she had been awake for hours wondering if this was a dream, a very pleasant dream, but one that was about to end soon.

But no: she sat up, drank the tea and the dream continued, and she realised she was already awake and that this was real; that in five hours' time, promptly at midday, she would become the wife of Kerry O'Shea. As if to confirm this was about to happen, a telegraph boy arrived with a telegram from Mrs Charlesworth in New York, wishing her and Kerry good luck on their wedding day.

Then, one by one, the sisters arrived to help her get ready. June did her hair, Isobel applied just a tiny bit of make-up, Lillian helped arrange her dress and Noreen the veil that she had worn at her own wedding more than twenty years before. Beattie gave Simon a hand to put on the pageboy outfit that another small boy had worn at another wedding, a wartime one. The outfit consisted of long black velvet trousers and a white shirt with a floppy velvet bow instead of a tie. Simon really fancied himself in it.

There would be bridesmaids; Flora wasn't sure how many. So many girls and young women had asked to be a bridesmaid, or their mothers had, that she had invited anyone who had the appropriate dress to follow her down the aisle when the day came. The dresses wouldn't match, but what did it matter? They had to supply their own flowers. All the bridesmaids were travelling to the church in a Bootle Corporation van driven by Bernie O'Shea, who worked as a supervisor of something or other.

The sisters left to get ready themselves – they had to catch a bus to the church in Melling. Bernie O'Shea called for Simon, who was going with the bridesmaids. Only Isobel remained, and she went upstairs to get ready. She had hired a taxi to take her to the church, along with Auntie Hilda and two other elderly aunts.

Flora sat in the maroon moquette easy chair that had replaced Nana's special chair clutching her tiny bouquet of white roses. She stared out of the window at the bare brick walls that surrounded the little yard at the back of the house in Pearl Street. Quite out of the blue, she was possessed with a feeling of terror at what she was about to do. She was about to marry a man she hardly knew, about to promise to spend the rest of her life with him, a man with a truly awful mother. She would have liked a much longer engagement, but they had to marry quickly in order to get the house.

Was this the future she genuinely wanted? Was it too late to back out now? And what would happen if she did? Where would she and Simon go? No – she had to marry Kerry, who was actually a very nice person she thought she might possibly love very much, if not now, then at some time in the future. She would do it for Simon's sake. And anyway, she'd had no particular future in mind for herself.

'I'm off now.' Isobel appeared in the doorway, looking lovely in a powder-blue linen costume. The fitted jacket had an embroidered collar and cuffs. She had lost so much weight that she was able to squeeze into some of the clothes she had once worn as a model. 'Are you all right, luv? You look as if you've lost a pound and found a sixpence. Shall I wait with you until Uncle Hughie comes?'

'I'm fine,' Flora assured her through dry-as-a-bone lips.

Outside, a car horn beeped. 'That's the taxi. I'll see you at the church, Flora. Are you sure you're all right, girl? Hughie should be here any minute. I'll leave the door open for him.'

'I'm fine, honestly. Bye, Isobel.'

The door closed. At that moment, as far as she knew, she and Uncle Hughie were the only ones expected at the wedding who weren't already on their way. Flora's mood changed and she suppressed a chuckle. Say if the old man had forgotten all about it, hadn't ordered a car and she ended up not being present at her own wedding!

But there were footsteps in the hall. 'I've come for the bride,' Uncle Hughie shouted. 'Are you ready, luv?' He came into the room looking magnificent in a morning suit and a shiny top hat.

Flora swallowed hard. 'I'm ready.' She was ready to face anything.

Outside, she gasped, for quite a crowd stood waiting for her appearance. There was a long *Aaaahhhh!* of appreciation when they saw her, and some people clapped. There were cries of 'Doesn't she look lovely', 'What a beautiful bride', and 'Best of luck, luv.'

She waved and climbed into the back of a large black car that looked as if it might have been one of the first ever made. Hughie got in the other side. It didn't come as all that much of a surprise to find that Ada, wearing a massive straw cartwheel hat, was the driver.

'Morning, luv,' she sang.

'She drove an ambulance in the first big war,' Hughie said, as if this explained everything.

And now here she was, walking slowly down the aisle of the crowded church, her arm linked through Uncle Hughie's. She hadn't realised that there would be an organist playing 'Here Comes the Bride', or that the tiny church would be quite so packed. Kerry was grinning madly as he waited for her in front of the altar. She'd seen little of her future husband, of late. He'd thought it important to spend the nights she was working in the Crown at Pearl Street, putting Simon to bed, reading him stories so that the little boy wouldn't mind him becoming part of his life.

The bridesmaids followed Flora down the aisle. There were six altogether, ranging in age from five to twenty-one. They looked like flowers in their pretty pink, blue, yellow and green dresses. Simon was supposed to be holding a corner of the bride's veil, but had dropped it.

Flora managed to smile as she walked towards the man who looked a total stranger, yet whose wife she would shortly become.

It was over, and she could hardly remember a thing about it, but she must have said all the right things because here she was outside the church having her photo taken – with the guests, without them, and in all sorts of combinations, including with Kerry's mother and father. Betty murmured, 'Congratulations,' through frozen lips and Flora nodded and wished the woman wasn't there.

People wandered among the trees of the tiny forest, the leaves greener now and larger than they'd been when she and Kerry had come to see the priest the month before. The sun shone through the branches, making dappled patterns on the grass, and girls picked buttercups and made chains with the little moon-faced daisies. The boys played tick and tried to climb the trees in their best clothes, receiving a slap on the legs from their irritated parents for their daring.

Flora was vaguely aware of a car – it turned out to be a taxi – stopping in the road outside the churchyard, and a couple getting out. As they walked down the path, she uttered a little cry. It was Andrew and Else, so sunburned that they were hardly recognisable.

She ran towards them. It was lovely having friends there, *her* friends, people who proved she had a past and had lived another life before she'd come to Pearl Street.

Else's face, when she kissed it, felt warm, as if she had rays of the sun stored inside it. 'Our boat docked half a day late,' she explained. 'We had intended coming to Liverpool yesterday afternoon, but couldn't get here until this morning.'

'Oh, but you're *here!*' Flora gasped. She turned to Andrew, who lifted her up and twirled her round and round until she felt giddy.

'Oh, it's lovely to see you,' they all said together.

'You look like a Greek god,' Flora said to Andrew. He had grown a little white beard and his blue eyes appeared much bluer than she remembered.

Kerry was standing nearby, looking mystified. She linked his arm, pulled him to her and introduced her new husband to her old friends. Then Isabel came, and her sisters, and Hughie and Ada. Everyone came to be introduced to the charismatic strangers. Flora had never been so happy; it was like being queen for a single, magical day.

There was a yell. It was Simon, stuck up a tree, having seen Andrew and Else and wanting to be rescued. Andrew lifted him down and hugged the little boy as if he were his own lost son whom he hadn't seen for a long while – perhaps that was how he genuinely felt.

'He recognises us,' Else said emotionally. 'I thought he might have forgotten who we were.'

The sun went behind a cloud, only for a minute, but it seemed to remind everyone that it was time to return to Bootle for the reception, which was being held in the Co-op hall just around the corner from Pearl Street.

The day continued to be magic. The food was delicious, or so Flora was told – she couldn't possibly have eaten a thing – and she lost count of the number of times she was kissed and hugged. When the speeches ended, telegrams were read aloud that had come from O'Sheas she'd never met who lived in faraway places in the British Isles, as well as from at least half a dozen in Ireland.

At six o'clock, she went home to Pearl Street to change into her going-away outfit – a neat lilac linen costume and a white halo hat, both from C & A Modes in Lord Street. She and Kerry were spending their honeymoon just a few miles away in Southport; three days in a posh hotel overlooking the Irish Sea. Lifts had been offered, but Flora had insisted they go on the train. She loved the modern electric trains with their sliding doors and complete absence of smoke.

Isobel had intended to look after Simon, but now Andrew and Else had accepted the offer to stay and sleep in Flora's bed, and all three would look after him together.

Flora felt quite breathless at how rapidly things were happening and life was changing. She might have been jealous seeing the way Simon clung to Else when she and Kerry left for Southport, but she was pleased that the presence of Else would prevent her little boy missing her so much while she was away.

They sat opposite each other on the train, Flora and Kerry, just married, just staring, Flora at least wondering if it were really true. This man, this handsome, funny, charming man, was her husband. He was also, possibly, a very delicate man in poor health. *He's not long for this world*, Isobel had said – or something like that. *He could die any minute.*

But he could live until he's ninety, Flora had argued. She hoped that would be the case.

Kerry moved forward, capturing her legs within his own. He squeezed them and she giggled. A woman on a nearby seat frowned disapprovingly, so Flora arranged her hands so that her wedding ring was visible, but the woman continued to frown.

They registered at the hotel. 'Mr and Mrs O'Shea,' Kerry said to the smartly dressed man in Reception. 'We have booked a double room.'

'Yes, sir,' the man said, exquisitely courteous, 'would you please sign the register?'

Kerry looked sideways at Flora and hid a grin as he carefully signed the book with a pearl-handled pen.

Their bedroom overlooked a vast expanse of silvery water. It had just gone eight o'clock and the sun was setting, a huge flaming orange ball as it sank out of sight. Yet it could be seen somewhere else, in the other half of the world, waking up on that side as this side prepared to sleep.

But Flora wasn't ready for sleep. It wasn't that she was worried about going to bed with Kerry, but she preferred to put it off until it was properly dark. Also she was hungry, having hardly eaten a thing all day.

'I really fancy eating fish and chips out of newspaper,' she announced after they had unpacked the few things they had brought with them; so that was what they did, eating the food in what was left of the sun on a bench on the fragrantly smelling promenade planted with what looked like millions of flowers. People were walking on the wet sands, dogs ran in and out of the water, two young men were kicking a football to each other and a handful of children were building sand-castles.

'What exactly did your mum and dad do?' Kerry asked. His food had been eaten, but Flora's was only half gone. He didn't know all that much about her, whereas she'd been told dozens of stories about him from people who'd known him all his life, had gone to school with him or had lived in the same street, even sailed with him on the same ships.

'They were actors; I thought I'd told you that,' Flora said. 'My father used to direct plays and act in them as well.' She threw a chip to a pigeon that had landed at her feet. 'They died when their car crashed.'

'But what sort of actors?' he persisted. 'Were they in plays in the West End of London, for instance, or in Liverpool theatres?'

'I don't think so; I doubt it.' She knew very little about her parents' acting careers, whether they'd gone to acting school, for instance. Aunt Winifred was the only person she could talk to, and she was always very unforthcoming. 'I think my father was a more experienced actor than my mother. She was from Scotland, he came from London and they met in a repertory theatre in Edinburgh. Their names were Frederick and Rose and they fell in love, married and started their own touring company.' The pigeon had been joined by a friend, and she threw more chips.

Kerry put his arm around her and she laid her head on his shoulder. 'And you were in the car when it crashed?' It was a question, not a statement.

'Yes. They often travelled to wherever they were performing next after that night's play was over, and there were no lights in the little country lanes.' Flora closed her eyes, remembering. 'There was a mattress and an eiderdown kept for me on the back seat of the car where I slept. I've no idea what happened the night of the accident as I didn't wake up until it was over. Either the brakes failed or my father fell asleep, and we just raced down a hill and crashed into the wall of a big house at the bottom – no one ever told me that. I had to work it out for myself a long time later. I woke up to a lot of noise and a man lifting me out of the back and carrying me into a house.'

The birds had become a flock. Flora emptied the rest of the food on to the path, then rolled the newspaper into a ball and placed it on the seat beside her to put in a rubbish bin later. 'I enjoyed those,' she said. She got to her feet, wanting to escape the birds. 'Shall we go back now? Will the hotel serve tea and coffee in the bar?'

'I expect so.' He paused to kiss her, and they linked arms as they began to stroll along the promenade to the hotel.

Flora assumed she had finished talking about her parents until, inexplicably, she began to cry. 'No one told me they were dead,' she wept. 'I knew there'd been an accident, but I thought they were in hospital. I was only six, and I kept waiting for them to come back.' All she could remember was a feeling of total loss, of emptiness and childish despair. 'After a while, I realised people were trying to find relatives. But my mother's parents and an older sister had died in the flu epidemic after the war, and mum had been brought up in an orphanage. Eventually they tracked down my father's sister, Aunt Winifred, who lived in London, and I was sent to live with her.'

'And that's where you met Isobel?' He was holding her tight, stroking her hair.

'Yes.' She had stopped crying and let out a long, tremulous breath. 'By then, I knew I would never see my mother and father again. Isobel helped me get used to the idea. My aunt was hopeless.' Aunt Winifred had been incapable of warmth and understanding. Then Isobel went away, and Johnnie Lucas had come along. Two years later, Flora had been sent to the school in Zurich; she assumed she'd been in the way.

Tea was served in a pretty china pot with matching cup and saucer on a silver tray with a lace cloth. Flora sipped the drink, feeling better, yet still a bit peculiar as she was deluged with memories of long ago. Why? Why had they all come to the surface now? Perhaps it was because it had been a highly emotional day, stirring up memories of other days, just as emotional but not nearly as pleasant as her wedding day. She could see the faces of her parents more clearly than she'd ever done before and was surprised at how young they were.

Looking back, she recalled that they had still been in their twenties when they'd died.

Poor Kerry felt responsible for his new wife's tears. 'I shouldn't have asked about your mam and dad,' he said, full of remorse. 'It was dead tactless.'

'Don't be silly,' Flora said bluntly. 'It's only natural that you should want to know everything about me.'

It was midnight by the time they lay in bed together. The room was in darkness, with just the moonlight visible through the closed curtains. Traffic could still be heard on the road outside, and music came from downstairs in the hotel where a dinner dance was being held.

'I love you,' Kerry whispered.

'And I love you,' Flora whispered back. She felt embarrassed. She had been warned by quite a few of the women that the first night could well turn out to be a disappointment. 'Sex isn't all it's cracked up to be,' someone had said. 'It takes a bit of getting used to,' said someone else. But then Kerry started to touch her in places where no one had ever touched her before, and Flora's embarrassment fled and she rose up to him, gasping with delight, crying out with pleasure because the feelings, the sensations she was having were beyond description. Her body was on fire, and she never wanted the fire to go out.

Chapter 12

At first, married life was like a game; an exciting, entertaining, very enjoyable game. They had only been back in Bootle a few days when Isobel left to live in London, Andrew and Else returned to Morocco and Flora and Kerry slept in the bedroom with lace curtains at the window and carpet on the floor. Flora had given up her job in the Crown, otherwise she and Kerry would hardly have seen each other, she having to leave the house straight after tea, not returning until close on eleven o'clock.

Flora hadn't imagined she would find looking after a house so agreeable. She actually got pleasure from doing the washing and hanging it on the line in the little back yard, or on the rack in the kitchen if it happened to be raining. When she took Simon shopping, they sometimes walked as far as North Park, where he played on the swings, or they went on the see-saw together. Food was still rationed, and it could occasionally be a nuisance having to stand in queues when a rumour flashed around that tomatoes were available in the greengrocer's or the butcher had in some very nice pork chops.

Cooking turned out to be an unexpected talent. She found herself able to turn out sponge puddings that melted in the mouth, grill meat to the precise degree of tenderness required and make perfect shortcrust pastry.

Housework she found a chore, but she dusted and polished everywhere regularly and the place always looked spick and span. She had visions of Isobel turning up out of the blue one day and finding her house no longer up to the standard that she herself had kept it in.

Every Friday – payday – Kerry would bring flowers, so the place always smelled of the countryside, despite being only a few feet away from a busy railway line and there not being a tree in sight.

It was a lovely game, this perfect version of married life, and it lasted for just over a month until Flora discovered she had spent all the money she had saved from her work as a barmaid along with what was left of the bounty Kerry had received when he left the merchant navy.

It came as a shock to realise that his wages were barely sufficient to pay the rent – the landlord had put it up by half a crown when Isobel's name on the rent book had been changed to his – and to buy food, fuel and all the other odds and ends required for day-to-day living such as sanitary towels for Flora, clothes for Simon, who was growing rapidly, and Kerry's occasional visits to the pub for a pint or two of Guinness. From now on, they would no longer be able to afford the pictures, and gave up on the idea of going to the Locarno so that Kerry could teach her to dance. Flora felt obliged to forgo the coffee for herself and lemonade for Simon when she did the main shopping on Fridays. Kerry, though, continued to bring flowers on Fridays, and she didn't like to insist he stop because it was such a lovely gesture, though much too extravagant.

Life was going to be very different. 'We're just going to have to tighten our belts,' said Flora. 'But it doesn't mean we can't be happy, darling.'

'I know,' he sang, not seeming the least put out. He wasn't much good at belt-tightening.

They would always be happy, even if they had to live under straitened circumstances until they were very old. She discovered mincemeat; fried it, boiled it and used it in casseroles.

She made scouse with it – with brown sauce on top, it was delicious. Flora still sang as she did the housework, and occasionally even did a little dance.

It would be Simon's third birthday on the first of August, the date she had made up for him. Of late, he'd begun to demand he play in the street with the other children, and she'd felt obliged to let him. It was cruel to keep him indoors. The back yard was too small for him to play in, and the only real fresh air he got was when she took him shopping or to the park.

It worried her, letting him out. Some of the children were really rough, poorly dressed and – quite frankly, there was no denying it – incredibly dirty. Would Simon, cossetted and cared for, healthy and well dressed, be able to hold his own with these street children?

Kerry only laughed when she discussed it with him. 'I grew up in the streets,' he told her. 'Most kids round here do. Simon's not a rare flower; he's a normal little boy, though he probably needs to be a bit tougher. You're a snob, Flo. You think you and Simon are better than other people.'

She flatly denied she was a snob who considered herself better than anyone else, but agreed she considered Simon to be far superior to other little boys.

On the first day Simon played outside, not long after they'd had dinner and Kerry had returned to the shop, she hid behind the curtains in the parlour watching as Simon ventured into the street on his own. By now, June was nearing its end and the days were sunny and hot. Only small children, the under-fives, were playing outside, the older ones being at school.

Simon, wearing his oldest clothes, stood shyly on the pavement watching five boys about his age play football with an ancient leather ball that had no air left in it. A goal had been chalked on the railway wall. The point of the game appeared to be that everyone prevented everyone else from scoring.

The deflated ball suddenly landed at Simon's feet, and he

kicked it towards the goal and scored. At this, a boy wearing only a vest, swimming trunks and wellington boots launched himself at Simon, knocked him to the ground, kneeled on top of him and proceeded to punch him in the face. Flora screamed and made for the front door. But by the time she'd opened it, the positions had been reversed and it was Simon who was sitting on the other boy and holding him firmly on the cobbles by his shoulders, though thankfully not hitting him. Flora resisted the urge to leave them like that and hauled Simon to his feet.

A woman appeared out of a house across the street – most of the front doors were left open in the summer. She was a small woman, young and scrawny, wearing a filthy cotton frock that was much too big. Her hair looked as if it hadn't been combed in weeks. Flora swallowed, assuming this was the other child's mother, who was gearing up to have a fight. The boy who had attacked Simon was now standing, and the woman slapped him across his face so hard Flora could've sworn his neck creaked.

'I saw you, Liam Brannigan,' she shrieked. 'You hit this little lad without any reason.'

She was about to hit the child, Liam, on his other cheek, when Flora seized her hand and said impulsively, 'Please don't, I'm sure he didn't mean it. Maybe Simon shouldn't have interfered in the game.'

The woman's hand fell to her side. She turned to Flora, who could have sworn the woman almost bobbed a curtsey. 'I'm sorry, missus, but he's a bad lad altogether, our Liam.'

'I'm sure he isn't,' Flora said warmly, though she had no reason for doing so. From what she had so far gathered, Liam was a horrible, unfriendly child who had attacked Simon un-provoked – a fact confirmed by his mother – though behind the dirt she was aware that he had the face of an angel, with enormous blue eyes and dirty blond hair.

'He kicked our ball without asking.' The angel glared at Simon.

'Well, he'll ask next time, won't you, Simon?'

Simon shrugged. 'Yeh!'

Yeh! Not 'yes' or 'all right', but 'yeh'! Flora would take that up with him later, but it was important now that his first time on the street got off to a better start. 'I tell you what,' she said, impulsive again, 'let's go inside and have a cup of tea. Would you like one?' She smiled at the woman, who appeared flustered.

'Alice, me name's Alice Brannigan.' She yanked nervously at her long stringy hair. 'Yes please, I'd love a cuppa, ta.'

'I'm Flora O'Shea.'

'I'll be back in a mo, Flora. I just need to collect the baby and wipe me face over with a flannel, like.'

'While you're doing that, I'll put the kettle on.'

Flora hummed 'There'll Always be an England' as she threw a small lace cloth over the table and set it with milk and sugar, two pretty cups and saucers and a plate of the broken biscuits she'd recently taken to buying — they were considerably cheaper than the unbroken sort. The kettle boiled and she made tea. Simon and Liam, should the boy choose to appear, could have a glass of Tizer. Simon was presently lying on the floor in front of the empty fireplace, filling in his magic painting book. So far, his experience of playing outside had lasted only a few minutes.

It was a good quarter of an hour before Alice Brannigan appeared. During that time, she had combed her hair and tied it back with a ribbon, washed her face and changed into a frock that was clean but hadn't been ironed. Liam had also had a wash and was wearing a shirt and shorts that were much too small — Flora took from this that she hadn't the money to buy her son clothes to fit. The baby was a pretty little girl of about six months, whose name was Meriel.

'It's an Irish name,' Alice explained. 'Liam is, too. Me

husband, Gerard, is from Ireland. Me, I was born in Bootle, in the very next street.'

'It's a lovely name, Meriel,' Flora said. The baby clapped her tiny hands in agreement.

Alice smiled. 'Flora's lovely, too.'

'It's a Scottish name. My mother came from Scotland.' Flora gestured towards a chair. 'Sit down and I'll pour the tea.'

Alice's eyes were as round as pennies as she surveyed the room with its pretty wallpaper and curtains. 'I'd been told about this house, that it's dead posh, but I never dreamed it was as posh as this. It's like a little palace.'

'That's what I thought when I first came. It was my friend Isobel who had it done up.' Flora didn't want the woman thinking she could have afforded to have the house decorated and furnished the way it was. She wasn't in any way superior to Alice, just luckier.

She gave the boys their drinks. Liam was lying next to Simon on the floor, having a go with the magic painting book. He picked it up and showed it to his mother.

'Look, Mam. You just paint water on it and it turns into colours. It really is magic.'

'I'll get you a book like that one of these days,' his mother promised.

'Actually, Simon has quite a few. Liam can take one when he goes home. Can't he, Simon?'

'Yeh,' said Simon.

Despite the 'yeh', Flora felt pleased. It looked as if Simon had already made a friend.

There was a noise outside, a man was shouting and across the table Alice flinched. The shouting came nearer, into the house, in fact, as a man tore down the hall and into the room where they were sitting. He was young, unshaven and wore a flannel shirt without a collar. Frayed braces held up a pair of old corduroy trousers. He smelled strongly of alcohol.

'There you are, you damned bitch!' he yelled.

Flora jumped to her feet. 'Just who do you think you are?' she demanded in her sternest voice.

But she may as well not have spoken; the intruder didn't even glance in her direction. Instead, he lifted up a cowering Alice by her hair and dragged her from the room. Meriel banged her head on the door frame and began to scream, Alice was crying loudly and the man still shouted.

'I've told you before, bitch, that I expect youse in the house when I get home, with me dinner on the table, not out bloody gallivantin'.'

In the street, Flora was running after the man, trying to catch him so she could rescue Alice, who was being dragged along on her heels, or at least to save the baby from another bang on the head.

'It's no use,' a voice said quietly from behind. 'The only way to stop him from beating Alice is to kill him.'

By now, it was too late to do anything; the man, Alice and the baby had disappeared into the house. The door slammed.

Flora turned in the direction of the voice. It was Sheila Reilly, a friendly, nice-looking woman of about thirty who had loads of children and who Flora already knew a little. Her husband, Calum, was in the merchant navy, and had once sailed on the same ship as Kerry. Weeks ago, when Calum had been home, he and Kerry had gone out a few times together for a drink.

'But how can it be allowed?' Flora could hardly believe what she'd just seen. 'Isn't it a crime? Shouldn't someone go and tell the police about it? I'll go right now, in fact.'

'There's no use, luv.' Sheila shook her head. 'The bobbies aren't interested. As far as they're concerned, Alice and her kids are Gerard's property. He can do whatever he likes with them.'

'But that's terrible. There should be a law against it.'

Sheila smiled ruefully. 'There should be a law against an awful lot of things, luv, but I'm afraid there isn't one that stops a husband from hitting his wife. Look, I can see you're upset, why not come in and have a cuppa with me? It's nice and quiet in there, but very soon the kids'll be home from school. Bring your little boy with you.'

Simon, Flora saw, was in the doorway of her own house. He too looked upset. 'I'd just made tea for Alice. Why don't you have a cup with me?' she suggested.

'I'd like that, ta.'

They went into the house and found Liam Brannigan lying on the floor, absorbed in the magic painting book. He must be so used to his father's violence that the recent contretemps hadn't disturbed him in the least.

That night, Kerry was horrified when she told him what had happened. She waited until after Simon had gone to bed before she told him. 'You mean he came in here, right into the room?'

'He came roaring in like an animal and yanked poor Alice out by her hair. The baby – oh, she was such a sweet little baby, Kerry – banged her head on the door.' She shivered at the memory that kept playing over and over in her mind. 'I shall never forget it.'

'Did he touch you?'

'He completely ignored me, even though I chased after him,' Flora said indignantly. 'I didn't manage to catch him, though.'

Kerry looked at her, astounded. 'You chased after him? And what did you intend to do if you caught him?'

'Hit him, of course, try and make him let go of Alice and the baby.'

He snorted derisively, 'Apart from what he might have done to you, do you think that would stop him from attacking Alice again? If so, you've got another think coming. It'd only make him worse. Anyroad, what made him look for her in our house?'

'Someone must have told him Alice had come in here. Oh, and Kerry, Sheila said that the only way of stopping Gerard Brannigan would be to kill him.'

For some reason, this amused Kerry and he grinned. 'Well, if someone ever gets round to killing the bloke, I'll point the bobbies in your direction.'

At that point, Flora lost her temper. 'It's not a laughing matter. It's serious – *dead* serious, as Liverpool people would say. Gerard Brannigan has no right to beat up his family like that.'

Kerry merely shrugged. 'He's not the first bloke to hit his wife and kids.'

Flora turned angrily on her husband, aware that they were on the point of having their first real row. 'How can you take it so lightly?' she demanded.

'Because I've come across it before, loads of times.' Kerry was beginning to get annoyed. 'Me dad wasn't slow at giving me mam a crack when us kids were little.'

'And you just let him?'

'I said, when we were little. He didn't try it once we were grown up.'

'He must be a coward then.' Until now, she'd really liked Kerry's cheerful, good-natured father, Billy – and his behaviour might be the reason why Kerry's mother was such a sourpuss.

'It could be that me dad learned sense. Look, luv,' he said, trying to be reasonable. 'It's the sort of thing that goes on all the time. You've got to learn that life isn't easy for some people.'

'But I don't have to accept it. And it doesn't mean I shouldn't try and do something to stop it.' She began to pick up the tea things and take them into the kitchen, making more noise than was necessary. 'I wish I'd never come to Liverpool,' she snapped, regretting it immediately. Kerry understandably took offence.

'Oh, so you'd sooner we weren't married? Well, that's nice to know, Flora.' He stood, and she guessed he was about to collect his coat from the hall and go for a drink, something that nowadays he only did at weekends. 'Didn't you leave London on account of some bloke who lived with your auntie? Liverpool isn't the only place in the country where men are violent.'

He was in the act of putting his coat on when she ran into the hall and flung her arms around his neck. 'I'm so sorry, I'm being horrible. It's just that this afternoon really upset me. As far as I know, Johnnie Lucas was never violent, I just didn't know men like Gerard Brannigan existed.'

'I'll have a word with him tomorrow.' He picked her up and carried her into the parlour, where they lay together on the velvet settee. After a while, he whispered, 'Don't ever leave me.' She could feel his lips against her ear.

She was shocked to have hurt him quite so much. 'As if I would!' She turned her head and kissed him.

'You don't need me as much as I need you, Flo. I never realised till now how tough you were. You were all prepared to take on that animal across the road. You'd manage much better on your own than I would.'

'I couldn't live without you, darling,' she assured him, meaning it with all her heart.

Chapter 13

Simon had a party on August the first, his third birthday. Evelyn brought the twins, Tony and Terry, and Sheila Reilly, who had six children altogether, brought her two youngest, Mary, six and Ryan, seven.

Alice Brannigan and her children were there, and her husband made no objection to them coming. After Kerry had spoken to him and warned him on no account to enter his house again, Alice had reported that Gerard was deeply sorry for his recent bad behaviour, but only on account of the fact that, in his drunken rage, he hadn't realised whose house it was he'd invaded.

It appeared that not only were the O'Sheas a popular family in the area, but Kerry's experience as the lone survivor when his ship sank in a foreign sea no one had heard of had been reported in the press – the *Liverpool Echo* and the *Bootle Times* – where it had been on the front page, along with a photograph of Kerry when he joined the merchant navy at fourteen.

'Gerard's only sorry for selfish reasons,' Flora said cynically when she told this to Kerry. 'He doesn't want to get on the wrong side of the local hero.'

'It's too late; he's already on it,' Kerry said, just as cynically.

The table looked most attractive when the children sat down to eat. Flora had reckoned it would be silly to bring out the beautiful blue-and-white damask cloth that Isobel had left behind, and had used the pink-and-cream-checked second-best one instead. Sheila had contributed a dozen small jellies sprinkled with hundreds and thousands, and Evelyn had brought an entire loaf of meat-paste sandwiches. Alice apologised for not bringing anything. 'The larder's a bit bare at the moment,' she said, but Flora had assured her it didn't matter. 'We have plenty of food,' she told the woman. For herself, she had made fairy cakes and an eggless sponge filled with lemon curd.

The children behaved themselves perfectly, though Simon was just a bit too loud and showed off rather a lot, but this was put down to the fact that it was his birthday and only to be expected.

Liam Brannigan was a model guest, as if his mother had impressed on him to be a good boy, but Flora couldn't help noticing the eagerness with which he helped himself to the food, no doubt a feast compared with what he was used to.

'How do they live, people like the Brannigans?' she had asked Kerry.

'On handouts,' he told her. 'There's charities around that'll give them a few bob a week, but asking can be really degrading. Gerard does odd jobs when he's sober – if a slate falls off the roof, he'll borrow a ladder and put a new one back, or unblock a drain, that sort of thing.'

After the children had eaten and gone out into the street to play, the women sat down to demolish the rest of the food. Meriel, the baby, who was in fact an undersized nine months old, not six months as Flora had thought, ate jelly for the first time in her young life and gave the impression of enjoying it immensely. Flora cut herself a big slice of lemon-curd sponge but, to her annoyance, had to rush out to the lavatory in the yard to be sick.

'It keeps happening a lot lately,' she complained when she came back. 'I must have a badly upset stomach.'

The other three women looked at her with amusement. Flora felt annoyed, having expected sympathy. Sheila even laughed. 'Your stomach isn't upset,' she cried. 'You're almost certainly pregnant.'

Flora looked at her stupidly. She'd heard of the word, naturally, but why was it being applied to her? 'What?'

'Pregnant, girl.' Sheila laughed again. 'Pregnant, preggers, up the stick, in the club, got a bun in the oven. You're having a baby, Flo. Congratulations.'

'A baby!' Flora whispered.

'It often happens when a woman gets married.' Sheila was having enormous fun with Flora's confusion.

'I didn't think it would happen so soon. I didn't think it would happen to *me*!' She hadn't had a period for quite a few weeks, and had merely thought she was late, as sometimes happened. How on earth could she have been so silly?

'I don't know why, but I thought it would take much longer to get pregnant,' she said to Kerry that night. 'Andrew and Else wanted a baby, and they'd been married for years and years but never managed it. Anyway, the thing is, are you pleased?'

'Me? I'm over the flippin' moon,' he assured her. 'How about you?'

'I'm over the moon too.' And still in a bit of a daze.

'When's it due, our baby?'

'Sheila thinks I must have "copped it", as she put it, just after we got married, so he or she should arrive sometime in February. She said I must go to the clinic to see a nurse or a doctor who'll book me a place in Bootle Maternity Hospital.' Flora rubbed her hands together excitedly. 'Just think, a little boy or girl has actually started to grow inside me. It's like a miracle.'

It seemed a bit less like a miracle as the days and weeks passed and she continued to be sick; in the morning, during the day and before she went to bed at night. It wasn't until halfway through September that the sickness disappeared and she began to feel extraordinarily well. Her cheeks, normally pale, turned a beautiful rosy pink; her grey eyes sparkled and her silvery-blonde hair shone. She was in love with life, with Kerry and Simon and the baby that was slowly growing in her stomach.

At quiet times, she would sit and think what a strange journey had led her to end up in this particular spot. Most of the people she knew in Bootle had been born within walking distance of where they lived now. Whereas she, according to her birth certificate, had been born in a nursing home in a place called Inverness in the north of Scotland, she had been raised in London and then Zurich after her mother and father had died, had eventually returned to London and from there had arrived here, a little town on the fringes of a great city called Liverpool which she never wanted to leave. Though sometimes she would stand in the little back yard with its smoke-stained walls and long to be on a mountain in Switzerland able to see, from whichever way she turned, for miles and miles and miles, to smell grass and to hear birds sing. But the feeling never lasted for long.

With winter, there came serious worries. It snowed. The people of Bootle and the entire British Isles had never seen such snow before. It arrived, with its eerie silence, usually in the middle of the night, so that people would wake to find it halfway up their walls and windows. They would open the doors and the snow would either fall inside or, having frozen, would present an apparently solid white wall and they would have to dig their way out.

The snow itself didn't bother Flora. She had spent seven years living up a mountain in Switzerland. Had she owned a pair of ice skates and not been pregnant, she would have skated around Bootle. What concerned her about the weather

143

were the freezing temperatures, and the fact that Kerry appeared to catch cold so easily yet insisted on going to work.

Before he left for Critchley's shop, she would wind a heavy woollen scarf around his neck, pull his woolly hat over his ears and insist he wear gloves and thick socks. She would have bought him long johns, had he been willing to wear them, but he laughingly refused.

Flora wanted to cry with frustration, as he wouldn't even consider taking the day off when one of his frequent colds was at its worst. 'I'll lose me job, Flo. You know I'm dead lucky to have one.'

He was right. The war had seen many thousands of women take over men's jobs; in the factories, as drivers, tram and bus conductors and delivering letters. They were reluctant to give up the jobs when the men returned home, particularly if they were now the only breadwinner. And what Kerry really wanted was to return to the merchant navy. He wasn't cut out for shop work and badly missed life at sea, but he knew he would never be taken back due to his weak chest. Even if they had taken him, he wouldn't have wanted to live without Flora and Simon, who he thought of as his son, for months on end – and now there was the baby to think of.

Whenever he had a cold, in the middle of the night Flora would lie beside him listening to his hoarse breathing, praying he would get better soon and that the awful winter would soon be over.

Rose O'Shea, named after Flora's mother, arrived effortlessly and painlessly at the end of February 1947 in the middle of a snowstorm. She weighed seven pounds, three ounces and, after being washed, it was revealed she had a full head of golden curls. She was the most beautiful baby ever to have been born at Bootle Maternity Hospital, at least so Flora and Kerry thought, and also the best behaved.

Simon was fascinated with her, which was a relief, as Flora

had worried he would regard a baby as an intrusion into their lives. When eventually the snow melted and the earth returned to being its normal self, he insisted on helping to push the pram when they went for walks in the park where snowdrops were thrusting their heads through the freshly enriched soil.

'She's me sister, like Meriel is Liam's sister,' he told people. He now possessed a distinct Liverpool accent.

Flora didn't contradict him. One of these days Simon would have to be told the truth about his birth – or the truth as far as she knew it. It was something she was dreading. There were times when she felt enormous guilt for having kept him when, somewhere in the world, grandparents or other relatives of the young woman on the train might be searching for him. This would be followed by an argument she had with herself. The young woman had put the baby into her arms, and at the time Flora had felt that she was being entrusted with his destiny. It was pure Fate that had brought her, the woman and Simon together, and they would remain linked until the day Fate might force them apart, something else that she was dreading.

After the dreadful winter, spring was particularly lovely that year. Kerry's health improved and life returned to normal. Rose proved to be a model baby, sleeping throughout the night from the start.

'You're dead lucky,' Sheila Reilly told Flora. She had called one morning while Flora was breastfeeding Rose. 'With a couple of mine, I didn't get a decent night's sleep for months on end. Mind you, I was on me own; Calum was at sea. After I'd had Mary, we decided not to have any more kids while the war was on.'

'How did you do that?' It was something Flora was extremely anxious to know.

'Do what, luv?'

'Decide not to have any more children? I mean, how do

you *not* have children, if you're married?' She had conceived Rose directly after marrying Kerry. If the pattern continued, by the time she was forty she could well have twenty or more children. She explained this to Sheila, who burst out laughing.

'Oh, Flora, you are incredibly naive. Didn't this Else woman you lived with not tell you the facts of life? Good lord, girl, you must have got a surprise on your wedding night.'

'Oh, I knew what would happen, of course I did.' Else had told her that making love with the right person would be absolutely wonderful, and it had turned out to be true. 'It's not that I don't want any more children, but I'd like a bit of a gap between them – a couple of years, say.'

'There's ways and means,' Sheila said. 'One way is not to do it at certain times of the month when you're at your most fertile, which happens in between your periods, I think. Ask at the clinic, they'll know. It also helps to have your husband away at sea for about ten months of the year, like Cal was.' Sheila pulled a mournful face. 'The Germans took him prisoner once; I'll tell you all about it one day.' She folded her arms and looked thoughtful. 'The man can use a French letter, though they don't enjoy it as much with it on, or the woman can put a sponge soaked in vinegar inside her, which personally I think is disgusting and I'm sure must smart. There's some things the man can do, but quite frankly, luv, I'd find them too embarrassing to describe. Anyroad, whatever method you use to stop having babies, the Pope will disapprove.'

Flora transferred Rose to her other breast. The baby gave a tiny sigh before settling down to a noisy sucking. 'What's the Pope got to do with it?'

The other woman's eyes narrowed. 'You know, Flo, watching you and Rose is making me feel dead envious. I'll have a talk with Cal next time he's home. It's about time we had another kid.'

Flora reminded her friend that she'd asked about the Pope.

'Well,' Sheila said, grinning, 'as you will have gathered, the Pope's a Catholic, and he wants as many Catholics to be born as humanly possible, so he strongly disapproves of women who do anything to prevent it. Mind you, the good Father doesn't have to feed and clothe the babies once they come, or worry about having his sleep disturbed or where the next meal's coming from.' She nodded towards Flora. 'Anyroad, what you're doing right now is one of the best ways of avoiding getting pregnant, and the Pope's not likely to complain about that.'

'You mean breastfeeding?'

'It's the best contraceptive there is.'

Flora reminded Sheila of her words on Boxing Day when, after a tortuous labour, she gave birth to Andrew O'Shea, a long, thin baby with an angry red face and lovely blond hair who'd arrived two weeks early. Within a minute of his birth, he took over where his exhausted mother had left off and proceeded to scream the place down.

Flora had given birth to two babies in the same year, an achievement she might well be proud of one day, but not just yet.

What made matters worse was that by the time she'd left hospital, Andrew had been converted to Andy not only by Kerry, but by every other visitor. It was something she had specifically not wanted to happen.

She was *so* tired! Rose had been such a good baby that it came as a bit of a surprise to Flora, despite what Sheila had told her, that there were some, and Andy was one, who never slept for more than a few hours a day and would wake up with a howl of rage then cry non-stop, no matter how much he was kissed and cuddled and told what a beautiful boy he was – which he undoubtedly was. The nurses at the clinic were loud in their admiration of his length, his strong limbs and thick blond curls.

'He'll turn into a handsome young fella and break dozens of young girls' hearts when he's older,' one of the nurses predicted.

All Flora wanted was for her son to stop crying, to let her have more than a few hours' sleep. Simon was already cross with him for waking everyone up, including himself and Rose. Flora borrowed a cot from Evelyn – Rose still needed hers – and put it in the middle room, where some nights she slept in her old bed, closing the door to lessen the sound in the rest of the house. After all, Kerry had to go to work and was unable to catnap at odd minutes of the day like she was. Anyway sleeping in a separate bed meant they could avoid making love, which she was dreading.

She'd got a leaflet from the clinic, but it seemed that because her periods had never been regular it was hard to work out precisely when she was at her most fertile – or least fertile, which was more important. As far as she could tell, the only safe time to have sex was for a few days after her period ended. She discussed the matter with Kerry and he told her not to worry; from now on he would use French letters.

'But the Pope won't approve,' she warned him, remembering Sheila's words.

'What His Holiness doesn't know, he won't grieve over,' her husband said enigmatically.

The day came when Andy stopped screaming and turned into a normal, four-month-old baby boy. His hair was just like his mother's and his eyes were a lovely dark brown, like his dad's. The energy he had put into screaming was instead put into attempts to sit, stand, then walk months before babies were expected to do so. He didn't demand attention, but was constantly in receipt of it either from his family or from strangers on the street who were impressed by his ability to put both his feet in his mouth at the same time, or his efforts to climb out of his pram despite being firmly strapped in. Flora would emerge from a shop with Simon leading Rose by her reins, to find that Andy had managed to discover a hole in his knitted leggings and was undoing the wool with enormous skill.

Simon still didn't like him. He had stopped requesting that Andy be taken back to wherever he'd come from. Now he wanted to know how long would they have to keep him.

A letter came from Else and Andrew. At forty-one, Else was pregnant, and they were returning to England. 'Somewhere warm like Brighton or the Isle of Wight,' Andrew wrote. 'It won't be as hot as Morocco, but it's a healthier place to bring up a child.'

In London, Isobel hadn't quite reached the heights she'd scaled before, but was making a comfortable living modelling for catalogues and knitting patterns. She returned to Bootle from time to time to see Flora and her sisters. She was still beautiful. 'But older,' she sighed. 'Too old for the catwalk and to be photographed wearing the latest creations from Chanel or Balenciaga. Still, I can live the sort of life in London that I never could in Bootle.' She winked when she said this, and Flora could only guess at what she meant.

Things weren't quite the same as they'd been before. It was as if there was a blot on one of the pages in the story of Flora and Kerry's life. It was to do with sex and French letters, and the lack of spontaneity when they wanted to make love. Kerry could no longer just turn over and take his wife in his arms when they were almost asleep. Flora had to think before touching him in the morning when they first woke up, realising he would have to reach for a contraceptive and put it on, and it was all a bit of a palaver as well as being rather clinical.

They didn't love each other any less, but some of the excitement had gone out of their marriage.

Flora discussed it with Sheila, who said it was inevitable.

In the summer of 1948, down in Brighton, Else gave birth to a little girl, Georgina, who was undersized and underweight, 'but very strong', Andrew wrote hopefully to Flora. 'Please pray for her, my dear girl. No one will listen to the prayers of an old atheist sinner like myself, who has denied the existence of God virtually all his life.'

So Flora prayed, aware that she was getting nowhere with her promise to become a Catholic. Dutifully, she went to Mass on Sundays with Kerry and the children. Rose and Andy had been christened in a Catholic church, but she had done nothing apart from read a few books that she didn't understand. She conducted another of her tortured conversations with herself, and decided it didn't really matter. Not becoming a Catholic seemed more honest and acceptable than becoming a reluctant Catholic, at least in her own eyes.

Anyway, her prayers apparently worked because a few weeks later Else wrote to say that Georgina had begun to thrive and was drinking milk by the gallon. 'I had no milk of my own, I'm afraid. Oh, but Flora, isn't being a mother wonderful?'

'Absolutely wonderful,' Flora wrote back.

Suddenly it was 1950, by which time Simon had started school, Rose was almost three and Andy would reach the same age before the year ended. Flora had worried that Simon would be bullied, but he was taller than the other boys and they seemed more to want his approval than to hit him. The teachers were impressed with the fact that he could already read a little and knew the alphabet as far as the letter M. At home, he was teaching Rose.

On Easter Saturday that year, Flora and Kerry went to a party – it was Lillian's daughter Annie's twenty-first. Both drank just a little too much, returned home, thanked Sheila Reilly for watching over their children and went to bed, where they lazily made love.

'It's all right,' Flora giggled. 'I'm at my most infertile.'

Constance O'Shea, known for the rest of her life as Connie, was born the following January. Flora and Kerry were delighted. There'd been a long enough gap since Andy was born for Flora to get her breath back. But she resolved that Connie would be her final child. She was directed to a clinic next to Liverpool University where women were fitted with rubber caps to insert in the womb, making pregnancy near impossible. From now on, she would have control over her own body.

Two years later, the manager of Critchley's men's outfitters retired and Kerry was promoted to manager in his place. His wages were increased, and for a while he and Flora considered buying a car, but decided against it.

'I'd sooner the money was spent on food and clothes and toys for the children,' Flora said, unsure whether she was being reckless or sensible. 'After all, love, you can walk to work, I can walk as far as the shops and we can always get the train or the tram into town. What money's over we can put aside for a rainy day. In fact, I'll start an account with the post office tomorrow.'

Life wasn't perfect. Flora knew that Kerry would have preferred a more exciting job, and she had an undeclared longing for some sort of nameless adventure that she knew would never happen. But they were happy. They loved each other, loved their children and their children loved them back.

But Flora knew that one day things would change, for better or for worse. It was inevitable. After all, nothing lasted for ever.

Chapter 14

Unlike women, the vast majority of men weren't interested in owning more than one really good suit. Why bother? Most couldn't care less being seen in the same suit, no matter how many times in no matter how many years. They didn't mind having a suit for second best, if they could afford it, in which to go shopping with their wives or to the pictures or other trivial outings. But the best suit was for weddings, funerals, christenings, Mass on Sundays and other really important events – the theatre ranked higher than the cinema – until the seat of the pants became shiny, the buttonholes frayed and the jacket just seemed to lose its shape, all things that seemed to happen overnight, and the suit would be demoted to second best. Then the wife or mother or girlfriend had to begin the enormously difficult task of talking her husband, son or boyfriend into buying a new one.

Kerry O'Shea, now manager of a rather boring men's outfitters who received commission on his sales, knew it was no use trying to persuade men to set foot inside his shop to buy a suit unless they genuinely wanted one.

How could he increase his customer base, as he called it after reading a book called *How to Run a Small Retail Business*. ('Written by an expert', it said underneath.) He decided to offer different sorts of suits to different sorts of customers.

Down in London, Teddy boys were making themselves known. Kerry read about them frequently in the *Daily Mirror*, and viewed them in colour in the *Picture Post*. They were in some way connected to this great American music, rock 'n' roll, that he considered the gear when played by Bill Haley and His Comets, who he was occasionally lucky enough to catch on the wireless. Teddy boys wore a style of suit never seen before, with large draped jackets, tight trousers, and chunky shoes with thick crêpe soles known as brothel creepers. The jackets had velvet collars, often black, in contrast to the colour of the suit, that could be any colour on earth. No longer were men forced to dress in dark, sober colours; if they wanted they could wear vivid purple, lime green or eye-wincing red.

Kerry obtained such a suit from a supplier in London. It was royal blue, not as outrageously bright as some. A shop dummy was selected to wear this super-modern outfit along with a pair of black suede shoes. Flora did something with brilliantine to a wig so that it resembled a duck's arse, the amusingly named style the Teddy boys were all wearing.

Critchley's shop was lucky enough to have two front windows, usually occupied by a couple of dummies wearing formal suits, insipid shirts and ties and shoes and socks that didn't exhibit a single shred of imagination.

The Teddy-boy dummy caused quite a stir in Bootle. There were times when a crowd, admittedly only a small one, gathered outside to admire, sneer or wonder what the world was coming to when men were willing to stroll the streets dressed like a prat.

There was even a photograph of Critchley's window in the *Bootle Times*. The following week, in the letters to the editor, someone asked if this was what the recent war had been fought for. When a reporter asked the same question of the manager of the shop selling the offending suit, Kieran replied, 'It's exactly what it was fought for, so that people could dress as they please, not be told what or what not to wear by some fascist-type government.'

As Kieran O'Shea was considered something of a war hero in Bootle, no one dared argue with this point of view.

Despite the fuss, or more likely because of it, Teddy-boy suits were being bought from Critchley's at the rate of at least one a day, and occasionally two. The shop had never done such good business before. The increase in commission was enough for Kerry to put down a deposit on a Dansette radiogram that cost thirty-one pounds, ten shillings and sixpence. The first record Kerry bought was Bill Haley's 'Rock Around the Clock', which he played non-stop every night for a week until Flora swore she would leave, taking the children with her, if he didn't give it a rest.

'After we've paid for the radiogram, shall we buy a television?' she suggested. 'It's like having your very own cinema in the house.' Sheila Reilly had one, and Connie went over the road every day to watch *Muffin the Mule* and other children's programmes.

The following week, a van stopped outside the house and a Murphy television was delivered and placed in the parlour next to the radiogram.

Flora put on her coat and unfolded Connie's pushchair. 'We're going to see your dad,' she announced. By now Connie, three, was the only child not at school. Andy had gone at four and a half, bored out of his mind at home and anxious to be with his sister, Rose, whose attention he and Simon vied for.

It was afternoon. Nowadays, Kerry no longer came home for his dinner, after deciding to keep the shop open all day – other shops still remained closed between one and two. He hadn't told her to expect a television. Flora would have thought it a mistake, had his name not been on the delivery note.

This week's Teddy boy wore an acid-yellow suit with a chocolate-brown velvet collar and brown brothel creepers. Kerry had managed to bend one of the dummy's knees so that it looked as if it was doing a crazy sort of dance.

He grinned when she went into the shop. 'The telly's come, I can tell from your face. I bet you're dead pleased.'

'Well, you're wrong,' Flora said crossly. 'I'm dead cross. We've hardly payed anything off the radiogram.'

A young lad worked there as his assistant, a somewhat distant cousin but an O'Shea all the same. 'Go for a walk along the Docky or somewhere, Eric,' Kerry told him affably. 'Me and the missus won't be long.'

'You mean,' Flora said after Eric had gone, 'you genuinely ordered the television, it hasn't come by mistake?'

'Well, it hardly seemed fair me getting a radiogram, like, and you and the kids getting nothing.' He spread his hands, palms upwards, as if this indicated the unfairness of the situation. 'I knew how much you wanted a telly, so I thought, why not? After all, we only live once.'

'Are we buying it on hire purchase, like the radiogram?'

He picked up Connie, sat her on the counter and began to tickle her ears. 'Well, of course, luv. I didn't exactly have seventy-two pounds, eleven and a tanner to spare, did I? We can easily pay back the instalments. Can't we, Connie?'

'Yes, Dad,' Connie confirmed.

'*That* much!' Flora was aware of her blood turning to ice. 'But Kerry, that means we owe more than a hundred pounds! Can we send it back? Oh, please, darling, send it back.'

'We don't owe anything like a hundred, Flo.' It was the voice of reason. 'More like ninety, after the deposits have been taken into account. And haven't you got a bit saved in the post office?'

'That was for Christmas presents.'

'Well, we won't have prezzies this Christmas; we'll just sit and watch telly instead. Won't we, Connie?'

Connie giggled. 'Yes, Dad.'

In the days ahead, Flora continued to argue that they couldn't afford the payments, but Kerry merely produced columns of figures to prove that they could. His wages were this much, and his commission was that much, and increasing weekly. They were definitely in the black, he insisted.

'But other shops will soon start selling those horrible new suits,' Flora raged. She had no idea what 'in the black' meant, but was determined to find out. 'You won't be the only stockist in Liverpool for much longer. Your sales will inevitably go down.'

'I know that,' he said calmly – he was never anything but calm. 'In fact, they've already got them in T. J. Hughes and Lewis's, but I was the first and I've already got a loyal customer base.'

'A *what*?'

'A loyal customer base – you must read that book, Flo, it'll help you to understand what I'm about.'

'I know what you're about, Kerry O'Shea, you're about getting your family mired in debt. You'll end up in a debtor's prison, mark my words.' She burst out laughing when he made a face and began to whimper at her fearfully.

He was incorrigible and she couldn't possibly have loved him more.

Christmas approached. It was only the second ration-free Christmas since the war had begun in 1939. At last, most types of food were available to buy and the shops were stocked with plenty of clothes and children's toys. As she had anticipated more money being available this year, Flora had been looking forward to being extravagant, not just with food but with presents too. But the hire-purchase payments for the television – the ones for the radiogram she could cope with – felt like a heavy chain around her neck and she was determined to pay off both as soon as possible. Instead of being extravagant, now she was determined that this Christmas she would spend as little money as possible, and just hoped the family wouldn't notice.

She baked things she had never baked before, such as a Christmas cake and two puddings, and even made something that bore a slight resemblance to a Yule log. She began to call in at second-hand shops looking for clockwork toys and books. It was suggested to the children that they make the decorations. Flora made it sound as if it was a big treat.

It was such a lovely sight, all four of them sitting around the table cutting streamers out of crêpe paper, making cardboard stars and bobbles out of milk-bottle tops and odds and ends of wool to hang on the tree; Simon was so serious, Andy frowned angrily though in fact he was merely concentrating hard, and Rose and Connie looked as if the whole thing was a marvellous joke. It was one of the memories that Flora would treasure until her dying day. She only wished she'd had a camera to record it.

In the lead-up to Christmas, Kerry embarked on a bid to make Critchley's men's outfitters stand out from the neighbouring shops in Strand Road. The current Teddy-boy dummy was appropriately dressed in scarlet. Spotlights were directed on it from front and back, and the wall behind was covered with silver paper. Tiny lights snaked haphazardly across the floor. The window dazzled like a grotto.

'It looks spectacular,' Flora enthused when she went round to have a look. Connie clapped in appreciation.

'I'd like to put more lights outside.' Kerry rubbed his hands together excitedly. 'I bought a set of special outdoor ones from Woolies this morning.'

'Did you, now!' Flora said, a touch sarcastically. He bought all the extras to promote the shop out of his own money, when it was the owners who should have paid. The owners were a somewhat mysterious family who lived over the water in Greasby, and only communicated by letter.

'In fact, Flo, I'll put them up now while you're here to hold the ladder.'

'Have you bought a ladder too? And why not send Eric up it? He's supposed to be your assistant.'

'Don't be daft, Flo. He's only little, and it'd be irresponsible.' He disappeared out of the back of the shop and returned carrying a wooden ladder that looked far too old and dangerous to contemplate using.

Flora was so angry she stamped her foot. 'Take that back immediately. Tomorrow, you can bring the stepladder from home and use that to put your damn lights up. And when you do, *put your coat on*. It's freezing out here.' Strand Road led straight to the river, and an icy wind blew.

'But the stepladder isn't tall enough, Flo,' he protested. 'I wanted to string the lights over the shop's name.'

'Well, you'll just have to string them underneath the name instead.'

Honestly, you'd think I'd married a child, she said to herself several times on the way back to Pearl Street with Connie in the pushchair. *Simon's got more sense than he has, and so has Andy and he's barely five.*

At home, she glared at the bowl of fruit on the table. It was wonderful having such an assortment of fruit available, but the trouble was the children ate it, the contents usually disappearing within a day. She would have to start only having fruit at weekends.

'Damn you, Kerry,' she whispered. She felt like going into the parlour and breaking 'Rock Around the Clock', his only record, into bits, but the children were there watching television and would be upset. Well, more than upset. She visualised their reaction if she snapped the record in two in front of their eyes, and wasn't sure whether to laugh or cry.

She made tea and drank it alone in the living room, glowering at the chrysanthemums that Kerry had bought the Friday before; six huge russet and gold blooms that must have cost the earth. Exactly how much money had Kerry wasted on flowers over the years? They still appeared, every payday without fail, even though she had tried to persuade him that once a fortnight was enough. In fact, there was a vase of lovely red Christmas roses from the week before last in the parlour right now. She could probably have bought a couple of Christmas presents for the children for the cost of the stupid flowers.

Andy appeared. 'Will tea be ready soon, Ma?'

'It'll be ready when you are,' she snapped. There was a cottage pie in the oven. 'And stop calling me "Ma".'

'OK, Ma.' He winked at her cheekily and returned to the parlour.

The parlour door closed and for a few moments, Flora couldn't comprehend what she was doing in this strange house, in this strange town, with a husband and three children. Simon, she understood. He'd become part of her, but these other people were strangers. The room felt strange too; flickering, as if it were on fire, and she could have sworn that the chair she was sitting in was moving and about to collapse. She was finding it hard to breathe.

There was a knock at the front door and a creeping awareness spread through her, making her tingle from head to toe. She knew that the hand on the knocker belonged to someone who had brought devastating news. Her shoulders sagged because her head was too heavy to support. One of the children must have opened the door, and she imagined the bad news entering the house, walking down the hall, a big black monster without a face, on its way to tell her that something terrible had happened.

Eric O'Shea, Kerry's assistant, entered, sobbing his heart out, followed by all four of the children, who were exceptionally pale, as if they too were aware that Eric brought a message no one wanted to hear.

It appeared that Eric was crying because Kerry had asked him to hold the ladder while he put the lights up outside the shop. But the ladder had broken in two when he was halfway up, and he'd fallen right through the window.

'Where is he now?' Flora whispered.

'Bootle hospital,' the boy said wretchedly.

'I'll go and see him straight away.' Her voice sounded quite sane and sensible, as if the words had come from someone else.

'But he's . . .' Eric paused. He looked down at the faces of the children surrounding him. Although no more than fourteen himself, he was conscious of the fact that these children were considerably younger and should be treated with caution. He leaned over and murmured in Flora's ear, 'But he's already dead, missus.'

Chapter 15

The smoke signals or the jungle telegraph, whatever it was that helped spread information like wildfire through the O'Shea family in Bootle, worked at their swiftest that day.

Flora had barely digested the news that her husband was dead before June and Noreen were in the kitchen making tea for the visitors who had already begun to arrive, and Lillian had taken the children back to her own house for their tea. Beattie was trying to locate Betty O'Shea, Kerry's mother, who it was thought was out shopping somewhere, possibly Waterloo. His father, Billy, was on his way home from the factory where he worked. Other relatives had been alerted. From all over Bootle, people with serious faces were making their way towards Pearl Street. Uncle Hughie had brought a bottle of whiskey acquired for Christmas, but available now for those that needed a nip.

Flora refused. Her preference would have been to hit Uncle Hughie with his whiskey. She was furious, really furious, with everybody, apart from her children, and furious most of all with Kerry O'Shea. Left to herself, she would have wrecked the house, thrown the dishes against the walls and the ornaments in the bin. Had she been able to drag the furniture into the street, she would have started a bonfire and destroyed everything the way Kerry had destroyed himself. How could he have been so careless? He probably considered himself invincible, the only man left alive when his ship had sunk.

Or perhaps he had been tempting fate, daring God to let him die if he did something stupidly dangerous like climbing a rotten ladder, or went out without a hat and scarf when it was freezing cold.

Idiot! Idiot! Idiot! she cursed silently. 'I hate you, Kieran O'Shea,' she breathed.

But of course, she didn't. She had loved him as much as it was possible for a woman to love a man, and she knew for certain she would never get over losing him. Now he was gone, and once again she would have to manage on her own. The only difference was that this time, she didn't have just one child, she had four.

Betty O'Shea, Kerry's mother, arrived deeply distressed. She and Flora had met many times over the years, but the two women had never got on. Flora was quite prepared to be nice to her mother-in-law, but not if she continued to be horrible to her. Now, she managed to stay civil while arguing that it was a bad idea to have her son's body laid out in the parlour.

'It would confuse the children as well as upset them terribly,' she said patiently. Fortunately, Betty seemed able to acknowledge that this was likely, and went on to say that she had an insurance policy for her son that would pay for his funeral. Flora thanked her and hoped she would remember to thank the woman again, more graciously, in a few days' time when she had got over her all-consuming rage and felt calmer.

It was a gloomy, grey day when her darling Kerry was buried beneath six feet of earth in Ford Cemetery; Nana's grave was only a short walk away, as were those of many other O'Sheas. Afterwards, Flora only returned to the church hall for a sandwich and a cup of tea. She didn't know if perhaps all funerals turned into wakes like Nana's, that eventually people would stop feeling sad and start singing and dancing Irish jigs. Would jokes be told? Would people *laugh*? Her rage had gone and been replaced with a feeling of overwhelming sadness, as well as, sometimes, an inability to believe that her husband was genuinely dead, that it wasn't all a dream, followed by cold horror when she realised that it was real. She would never see Kerry again.

Sheila Reilly had been looking after the children while the funeral took place. School had broken up, and they were on holiday for the next two weeks.

'Hello, luv.' Sheila greeted Flora with a hug and a kiss. 'I hope you don't mind, but we've put the Christmas tree up. It looks the gear, doesn't it, kids?'

They trooped into the parlour to look at the tree that Flora had bought the day before Kerry's death. It stood in the corner, festooned with the decorations they had made.

'It's beautiful,' Flora said, her eyes brimming with tears.

The children must have taken this as a cue to shed their own tears, and all five of them threw themselves on the settee. Flora found herself covered with children, all talking and crying together, telling her how much they had loved their dad, including Simon who hadn't got a dad, but had found a perfect substitute in Kerry O'Shea.

The dreadful Christmas over, Flora knew they couldn't mourn for ever. There were practical issues to deal with, and it was time she sorted out their future. Her first decision was to get rid of the television and the radiogram. But although only a fraction of the cost of each had so far been paid back – interest had taken up almost half of the payments – she was reluctant to sacrifice the money. And the children loved the telly. And how could she possibly get rid of the radiogram Kerry had been so fond of? What's more, they would no longer be able to play 'Rock Around the Clock' half a dozen times a day, as they did now. No: by hook or by crook, she would continue paying for both the damn things.

After working out the finances, it came as a comfort to realize that they weren't about to starve. She was already in receipt of Family Allowance at eight shillings a week for each of the three youngest children, and was due a widow's pension. It wouldn't be enough to live on, but if she worked for a few hours a day she would be able to feed and clothe the children and keep them warm, as well as make the payments on the television and radiogram.

She was lucky compared with most people in the street, though this wasn't how she had imagined life would go. But beggars can't be choosers, as the saying went.

She returned to work weekdays behind the bar at The Crown from midday until three o'clock. The hotel was shabbier than it used to be when she'd worked there the first time, and not quite so busy. It was rumoured that Lloyd Francis, the manager, was seriously thinking of selling up, and Flora indulged herself by imagining the colours she would paint the walls and what sort of curtains and carpets she would buy if, by some miracle, Lloyd put her in charge of a complete makeover, with money no object.

That aside, the hours were perfect and would be even better once Connie started school. Connie was an amenable, uncomplaining little girl, and was happy to spend her afternoons in the office of the hotel drawing pictures of angels.

As the Crown was where she had met Kerry, Flora felt as if she had completed a full circle in her life and was now commencing on another. She knew in her heart that something would happen that would change the course of things yet again; whether for good or bad, she had no idea.

It was 1955, three years since Kerry's death, when the letter came from Andrew. It had been sent to Morocco, he informed her, and the person who had taken over their apartment had redirected it to him in Brighton. *Luckily, I left them my address in case something like this might happen,* he wrote. *It's for you and it's from a solicitors' in London – their details are on the back of the envelope.* He reckoned it was something to do with Aunt Winifred, and his Moroccan address was the only one to be found in the house by which Flora could be contacted. *They refer to you as 'Miss Flora Knox', so clearly don't know you are married.*

Flora opened the envelope with a mixture of interest and dread – somehow a letter such as this could only contain bad news.

She sighed as she read it. The news *was* bad, but not terribly upsetting. Messrs Rush, White & Dangerfield, whose office was in Crouch End, were requesting that she contact them immediately regarding the estate of the late Mrs Winifred Harriet Lucas. It had been written six weeks before, in March.

So, Aunt Winifred had married Johnnie Lucas! Now she was dead, and her funeral would be well over. Flora wished she could feel sorrier, but was unable to raise a single tear. She couldn't imagine why the solicitor wanted to speak to her, unless it was merely to inform her that her aunt was dead. If there was a will, Flora was unlikely to have been left anything – not that she wanted a single item from that miserable house. As for the house itself, she had no idea whether Aunt Winifred had owned or rented it. Whatever the case, it was nothing to do with her now.

She would telephone the solicitor later from the Crown. Lloyd wouldn't mind, as long as she paid for the call, and it would be easier than using a phone box.

'Ah, so *there* you are!' said the woman who answered when Flora dialled Rush, White & Dangerfield's number that afternoon and announced who she was. 'I'll put you through to Mr Dangerfield.'

'Miss Knox, at last!' Mr Dangerfield had a warm, plummy voice. She visualised a small, plump gentleman with rosy cheeks. 'We were about to hire a private detective to find you.'

She explained about Andrew and Else and their move to Brighton, and the fact that she had never been anywhere near Morocco. 'What did my aunt die of?' she then enquired.

'Heart trouble, my dear. Apparently, it had always been weak. It just gave up one night when she was asleep.'

Flora hadn't known that her aunt's heart hadn't been all it should be. 'I'm terribly sorry,' she commented, which she was, in a sort of way.

Mr Dangerfield must have taken that for granted. He went on to suggest that she come to London at the earliest possible opportunity. 'This afternoon, Miss Knox, if you can make it. If not, then first thing tomorrow. Out of interest, where are you speaking from?'

Flora hastened to explain that she was no longer Miss Knox, but a married woman with four children who lived in Bootle, near Liverpool. 'My name is O'Shea, Mrs O'Shea. And why do I need to come to London?'

'It's in connection with the property in Nelson Road,' the solicitor replied.

'But surely my aunt left it to Mr Lucas?'

'She did indeed. Mr Lucas produced the will, properly drawn up by a firm in the next road to us, leaving the property and all its contents to her husband,'

Flora was puzzled. 'Then why do you want to see me?'

'Because the property wasn't your aunt's to leave, my dear. It belonged to your father, and as his only living heir it has belonged to you ever since the day he died.'

'I must say,' James Dangerfield remarked two days later after Flora had managed to arrange for the children to be looked after so that she could spend the day in London, 'you don't look at all like the mother of four children. Had I not known better, I would have thought you were still in your teens.'

His eyes shone with admiration. She had told him she was a widow, so wasn't offended by the open regard.

He didn't look at all like Flora had imagined, either, being tall and slim with an interesting pallor and considerably younger than *she* had expected. She had spent so many years being a mother and, latterly, a widow, that she had forgotten she had once been considered beautiful. She responded to his compliment with an embarrassed smile.

'I'm afraid it smells rather musty in here,' he remarked as they entered Aunt Winifred's house in Crouch End, which it turned out had been hers, Flora's, house all along.

'When I returned from Switzerland, she gave me twenty-five shillings a week to live on and I felt enormously grateful,' she said when they were inside, the door closed. The hall seemed very dark, the only light available seeping faintly through the stained-glass window in the front door.

'How old were you when your parents died?' he enquired.

'Six. They died together in a car accident. As far as I know, Aunt Winifred was my only relative.'

'Then she would have been entrusted to deal with the estate. He left money too, your father. Did you know that? Though I'm afraid it's mostly all gone,' he added hastily. 'Just a few hundred pounds left. We tracked down his will.'

Flora went into the living room that led on to the garden, now very overgrown and looking rather like a jungle. The lovely spring sunshine was struggling to get through. 'I didn't know about anything,' she said. She stared at the sideboard, somehow reluctant to open the drawers because it felt like spying.

'If Mr Lucas hadn't tried to sell the property the minute your aunt passed away, no one would have known it wasn't his. He could have lived here, undisturbed, for years until he decided to sell. But the solicitor he approached quickly discovered the deeds weren't in your aunt's name.'

'Where is Mr Lucas?' Flora asked.

'Gone!' The solicitor shrugged. 'Just disappeared. Very disappointed, I should imagine. Tail between his legs, I reckon, though it was hardly his fault the house didn't belong to his wife. Did you ever meet him?'

'Yes,' Flora said shortly. She wasn't about to describe her brief experience with Johnnie Lucas. It wouldn't surprise her if he'd only married her aunt to get his hands on the house; that she hadn't wanted, or had even been too scared to tell him she didn't own it. It would have been easy for Flora to let her imagination run wild and wonder if Aunt Winifred had really had a heart problem and her death was as natural as it appeared. She dismissed the thought as soon as it came, resolving never to go near the place again.

James Dangerfield took her back to his office to discuss what was to happen next. 'Do you want to keep the house?' he asked when they were seated and had been provided with coffee and cheese sandwiches – Flora had turned down the offer of a proper lunch, as she didn't have the time. 'It would accommodate four children nicely. Or you could let it out at a good rent.'

'I'd prefer to sell it,' Flora said. 'I was never happy there.' That day, she had found it dark and full of bad memories. 'Anyway, my life is in Liverpool now.' She could have sworn he looked disappointed.

'Would you like Rush, White & Dangerfield to deal with the sale? It would be arranged through an estate agent, of course.'

'Yes, please.'

'And what about the house contents?'

Flora vigorously shook her head. 'I don't want them. I'd like everything sold.'

He frowned. 'What about letters, photographs, personal items like that?'

'Oh, yes.' There might be papers concerning her parents. 'Would it be too much trouble for them to be sent to me?'

'No trouble at all,' he said heartily. 'I'll send you particulars of the house as soon as the estate agent has them prepared. I should imagine the asking price will be in the region of four and a half thousand pounds.'

That much! Flora swallowed. Oh, if only Kerry were still alive! He could have bought all the rock 'n' roll records in the world, gone to America to hear Bill Haley and His Comets in person, even started his own band . . .

But the solicitor interrupted these lovely thoughts. 'What do you think you will do with the money, Mrs O'Shea?'

'I think,' Flora said slowly, 'I'm not quite sure, but I think I might well buy a hotel.'

Part 2

Chapter 16

Martin Lewin glimpsed the face across the palatial dining room of the Plaza Hotel. It was a man's face, and it was someone he knew from way back, but he couldn't think who it belonged to for the moment. Someone spoke to him and he answered, then looked for the face again, but it had disappeared.

He sat, bored out of his mind because the event he was at was so tedious, and he'd only come to please his wife, Lilith. It was a dinner being held to raise money to build libraries and provide books for disadvantaged children in cities and towns throughout the country – a worthy mission, but boring nevertheless. The charity had been established by his father, but Joshua had died two years ago and Lilith had taken over the fundraising side. It was an admirable and impressive post for someone of her retiring disposition, but Martin found it hard to muster much sympathy for his wife – for anyone, in fact.

They were seated at the top table, which he particularly hated. It meant he would be eating in full view of an audience. He drummed his fingers impatiently on the white tablecloth. Most of the thirty or forty circular tables were full, but a few people were still standing around talking.

Edmund MacLaine!

The face had belonged to Edmund MacLaine, the idiot his daughter had become involved with, who'd carted her off to Paris from where she'd travelled to Italy and then disappeared. The realisation caused his heart to pump inside his body at a dangerously fast rate. Recently, his doctor had advised him it was time he started to take things easy.

'You're in your sixties,' he'd been reminded, as if he didn't already know.

He'd been keeping an eye on the book charts for years to see if Edmund MacLaine had made it as a writer, but there'd been no mention of him.

'Are you all right, darling?' Lilith enquired, noticing his racing fingers.

'Fine,' he snapped. She looked at him reproachfully, but he didn't care. If he hadn't been sitting at this table, he'd have gone in search of the chap, but didn't want to be stranded on the other side of the room when the dinner started and then have to make his way, very noticeably, back to the top table.

A gong sounded, the people standing rushed to their seats and scores of white-clad waiters emerged from the kitchen, trays aloft. Martin felt almost ashamed of his sudden feeling of triumph. That's what MacLaine was doing here; he was a waiter! *Still* a waiter! His ambition to become a writer had failed miserably.

A bowl of soup was placed in front of him. It was the thin sort, which he hated. It tasted like dishwater. Or how he imagined dishwater would taste. Lilith, who knew how much he disliked it, looked at him nervously.

Martin ignored the look and the soup. He was only interested in locating MacLaine the waiter, but there were too many faces to examine next time they emerged en masse from the kitchen to collect the soup bowls, and later when they brought the main course; beef something-or-other – he couldn't recall the fancy name.

After his visit to Paris ten years before, he'd stayed in touch with Félix Brun, the private detective, for quite a while. The chap had gone regularly to Le Continental hotel to see M. Tillier.

'He likes to talk,' he had written to Martin. 'I go in case one of these days he comes up with something new. Also, I rather like this old-fashioned gentleman.'

Nothing new had turned up. Martin had suggested he go to Italy to see if he could find any trace of Edmond and Marie Laurent, the couple, using their new names. Brun had gone, but it had been a wasted journey. Two years ago, not long after Joshua had died, Brun had written again to say that M. Tillier had also passed away. It was strange, but Martin had felt almost as upset at his death as he had been over his own father's. He too had rather liked the old-fashioned gentleman, and had been grateful knowing that his daughter had lived in the guy's hotel; that he'd been there to keep an eye on her, that he was happy that she was happy.

The meat was tough; he found it hard to chew, though no one else seemed to be having trouble. It was just him, unable to digest the food properly, his mouth too stiff. Once swallowed, he could feel it lying heavily in his stomach in hard, gristly balls. He took a mouthful of wine and it tasted like vinegar. He swore under his breath. Lilith heard, and sighed. How long would this disgusting meal last? There was dessert to come, coffee to drink, speeches to be made.

The waiters came pouring in again to collect the plates, but every face looked the same.

It was another hour and a half before the meal and the speeches were over. Only a handful of people stood to leave, the rest remaining at the tables to gossip and order drinks from the bar from the circling waiters.

Martin, his nerves almost on fire, hurried into the kitchen where pandemonium reigned and there was enough steam for a Turkish bath. He stood inside the door, in everybody's way, scanning faces.

'Can I help you, sir?' The chap wore tails and was probably the head waiter or maître d' or something.

'Edmund MacLaine, I need to speak to him,' Martin said brusquely. 'Where is he?'

The man was exquisitely polite, 'I'm sorry, sir, but there is no one of that name here.'

'How the hell do you know? Hardly any of these guys work here all the time. You must have got them from an agency.' He couldn't possibly know all their names.

'You are right, sir, but it is an agency that employs only Mexicans. I doubt if there are any Mexicans with an Irish, or is it a Scottish, name?'

It was Irish, but Martin couldn't be bothered telling him. He turned on his heel and went back to the dining room, where he stopped at the first table he came to and surveyed the room. He was one hundred per cent positive he had seen Edmund MacLaine earlier.

He became aware that from the other side of the table a man was regarding him solemnly. He looked to be in his late thirties, and had a decent head of reddish-brown wavy hair, green eyes and what Martin had always considered an offensively humorous mouth that even now was curved in a smile.

'MacLaine!' The name emerged like an oath. He strode around the table, but before he could reach the guy, another man rose from his seat, blocking his way.

'Nice to meet you, old chap.' A Southern accent; lazy, elongated vowels, fruity voice, the product of an almost certainly slave-owning family in the previous century. The speaker had a veritable haystack of pure silver hair, icy blue eyes and thin lips. Martin hated him on sight; the looks and the voice, not to mention the hair. 'Just wondering what act of violence you had in mind for our bestselling writer. I can see the threat in your eyes, and thought I'd better stop you before you got within striking distance.'

'It's all right, Hugo.' Even after all these years, Martin actually recognised MacLaine's Boston twang. 'I don't think he means any harm.' He got lazily to his feet. 'Shall we chat in the bar?' He nodded to Martin to follow him into the adjoining room, where at least half the tables were empty. He chose a small, corner table, sat down and signalled for a waiter. 'White wine, please,' he said when the man came. 'And for you, Martin?'

White wine was a woman's drink, Martin thought contemptuously. And there'd been a time when he was 'Mr Lewin' to his daughter's boyfriend. 'Scotch,' he snarled. 'Neat.'

'What's with the "bestselling writer"?' he demanded after the waiter had gone. 'I've never heard of you.'

'Shortened my name; reduced the Edmund to "Ed" and the surname to "Laine". I'm Ed Laine now, author of a dozen thrillers that have each sold in their hundreds of thousands, yet to reach millions. Two have been turned into movies, and I've just sold the rights to a third.' He shrugged casually. 'It's not the sort of literature I wanted to write, but I make rather more than waiting on tables.'

Martin scowled as he contemplated this news. He didn't know what to think. He knew he was being unreasonable to resent this loser's turning out to be a winner. He decided not to comment. After all, his only interest was to find out about Grace. He blurted out the question starkly. 'Where's my daughter, MacLaine? What happened to her?'

'I'm sorry, Martin, but she's dead. The Nazis came when we were in Italy and took her to Auschwitz.' The tone was gentle, not wanting to hurt. 'Surely you must have realised that a long time ago?'

Martin stared at his shoes. 'I suppose I did.' He raised his eyes and looked accusingly at the man. 'You could have told me. As soon as you were back in this country, you could have come and told me.'

'To be punched in the nose? Roughed up in some other way? Verbally maligned?' He shook his head. 'No, thanks. I took it for granted that you would have guessed Grace's fate when she didn't come back once the war was over – or tried to find out for yourself.'

'I went to Paris after the war for that very reason.' Un-expectedly, anger curled like black smoke in his chest, choking him. 'I'd like to kill you, MacLaine,' he spat. 'Fuck Hugo. If I had a gun, I'd shoot you right through your thick, stupid head.'

Edmund MacLaine leaned forward and said in his quiet, pleasant voice, 'Not half as much as I'd like to kill you, you bastard. You are responsible for Grace's death. If you'd had a brain in your own stupid head, you would have understood that every word you said to her when she and I first met made her even more determined to stay with me and leave this country. It was through your pig-headed stubbornness, your crass idiocy, your perverted need to be in control of every single person around you that *drove* your daughter away. If you hadn't objected so violently and unreasonably, then she wouldn't have wanted to leave this country. We would have got married and remained in the States. I hate you with all my heart and soul. All due to you, I lost my wife and son.'

Martin was halfway out of the chair before the final words had sunk in. He sat down again with such force that he could have sworn his bones crunched. 'Son? Grace had a son?'

'Yes.'

The two men sat in silence. Their drinks arrived, but neither acknowledged the waiter. Martin downed his Scotch in a single gulp. He had never been spoken to so offensively before and had been about to leave and never to see this man again, but now he wanted to know more. If he sat there long enough, Edmund MacLaine would tell him.

'We called him Simon,' the man said after two or three minutes had passed in complete silence. 'He was born in September 1943. We were living about ten miles outside Rome in a big house that had belonged to some minor member of the Italian royal family; we called it *Il Palazzetto*. We'd left Paris because Grace became frightened when the Nazis picked up her best friend, who was Jewish, and she was sent to a con-centration camp.' He paused to pick up his wine and take a few sips, but from the cloudiness in his eyes and the expression on his face, it was obvious he was miles away, years back in war-torn Europe with Martin's only daughter.

'Apparently,' he went on, 'Mussolini had nothing against Jews, so we thought we would be safe in Italy. Trouble was, we hadn't been there long when the Allies invaded, Italy surrendered and Mussolini left, leaving the Germans in control of most of the country. Now *they* could get rid of the Jews. But even so, Grace felt secure in that house. Not a single German ever came near. About twenty of us lived there; old and young, communists, socialists, misfits. Two of the others were Jewish, a lawyer and an artist – a sculptor, in fact. The women looked after Grace when she got ill late in the pregnancy, and afterwards when Simon was born.'

There was another pause and Martin said gruffly, 'What did you live on? Where did the cash come from?'

'Well, we didn't need all that much. We grew our own vegetables, had our own hens, a couple of goats, but some things had to be bought, so three of the men worked, including me. Inevitably, I went back to waiting, but Christ,' he almost chuckled, 'it was very different from Paris, where we used the best china and the guests ate by candlelight. In Rome, I only worked lunchtimes and it was scrubbed tables, the cheapest wine, plates heaped with spaghetti. I've never been able to eat pasta since. Anyway,' he sighed, 'everything seemed to be going about as smoothly as it possibly could while living in a country under enemy occupation. The Allies were having a hard job making progress, but we knew they would reach Rome one of those days. So we felt safe . . .' He paused again. 'But it turned out to be a damn foolish thing to do. I arrived home one afternoon, it was just before Easter forty-four, and the place had been ransacked. Three of the old people had been shot, just left lying there, on the floor and in the garden. The rest, including Grace, had been taken away. I searched the house, looked in cupboards, everywhere. I thought there was a chance Grace might have hidden Simon, knowing that I would search for him.

'But he wasn't there?'

Edmund MacLaine shook his head hopelessly. 'He wasn't there. After a while, the other two men who worked came home. Their women had been taken too.' Now his eyes fluttered with panic as he relived that desperate day. 'We stole a car, drove into Rome and found Gestapo headquarters, but weren't allowed in, which wasn't surprising. So we went back to the house and found this kid had come back, Alfonso. We'd forgotten about him; he was twelve and had been at school, and now he found his parents had been taken away. Next day, his mother returned, but his dad had been sent to a work camp in Germany, as had one of the other men who'd been in the house that day. Then another woman came back. That's all there was left; two women, a kid and the three men who'd been at work – one was my friend, Vittorio Papallo, a hard-line communist whose girlfriend, Assunta, had been taken – she was a Catholic. The Nazi's position on Catholics wasn't exactly friendly.' He shook his head as if it was all beyond him.

'We buried the old folk and went out every day for a week trying to find what had happened to Assunta and Grace and, of course, Simon. No, that's not true.' He slapped his knee. 'We were trying to find out what *hadn't* happened to them. Does that make sense?' He glanced at Martin as if waiting for an answer before continuing. 'We'd suspected on that first day that they'd been sent by train to a concentration camp in Poland along with the two Jewish guys who'd lived there. We were hoping to find out that it *wasn't* true, that perhaps they were in prison somewhere in Rome, but the time came when we had to give up. It was confirmed that a train full of Jews and misfits had left Rome two days after the raid on the house. We were left with no reason other than to believe that Assunta, Grace and Simon had been on it.'

There was another long silence. Martin hadn't noticed how

crowded and noisy the bar had become. A young girl approached MacLaine and asked for his autograph. He signed the paper napkin without speaking. Graham, the Lewins' chauffeur, whispered to Martin that Mrs Lewin was about to leave.

'Let her,' Martin said cuttingly. 'I'll make my own way home.'

'Yes, sir.' The man glided away.

'What did you do next?' he asked MacLaine.

The man blinked and seemed surprised when he became aware again of his surroundings. 'I made my way down through Italy,' he said in a voice that was hardly more than a whisper, 'and caught up with Allied troops around the Anzio bridgehead. I tried to join up, but they said it wasn't on; I'd have to return to the States and enrol there, which I wasn't prepared to do. It would have been too safe back home, and I'd have had too much time to think about my wife and son. I rather hoped that if I hung around some German bastard would kill me, though it was obvious the battle in Italy was nearing its end. I tagged along with the advancing troops and sent reports of the fighting to a little local paper in Boston where my pop knew the editor. After a while, my articles were taken up by the nationals. That's why I found it so easy to get published when the war was over; I'd already gained a reputation as a writer.'

He drained his glass and got to his feet. 'I've talked enough for tonight, Lewin. I'm going home.'

'When will I see you again?' He wanted to talk some more about Grace, but the man was already lost in the throng and Martin found he was talking to himself.

When Martin entered his house on 98th Street on the edge of Central Park, the only illumination came from the lamp on the ornamental table in the grey marble hall. The place was silent; his wife and the servants had gone to bed. His son, Josh,

181

no longer lived at home. Martin had virtually disowned him on account of the drug-filled, disgusting life he was leading. Last he'd heard, Josh was living in LA with some porno actress. He'd return home one day, be forgiven and the pantomime would start all over again.

As he climbed the stairs, he noticed a light showing beneath the door of Lilith's bedroom; she was watching television without the sound. She often had the set on all night. It helped her sleep, she claimed.

Martin opened the door and went in. He didn't knock. He had never understood why he should be expected to knock on a door in his own house. Lilith was sitting up in bed, a book on her knee. She was still beautiful in her early sixties, though painfully thin. She looked at him questioningly with her huge brown eyes.

'Are you all right?'

'Why shouldn't I be?' he growled.

'It's just that Graham said you were talking to Ed Laine, and I wondered what it was about.' She removed her glasses, slipped a marker in the book and closed it.

Martin found himself totally confused. How come Graham, the chauffeur, knew Edmund MacLaine? And why did he and Lilith refer to him as 'Ed'? He stammered something, but afterwards couldn't remember what it was.

Whatever it was, apparently Lilith understood. 'He came to see me, Ed did,' she explained slowly, as if to a child, 'almost exactly ten years ago, right after the war in Europe was over. He came here because he wanted to tell me about Grace and Simon, making sure first that you weren't present, naturally.'

'You've known about Simon all this time?' Martin stuttered. 'Tonight, MacLaine didn't mention he'd told you.' He'd actually been *here,* set foot in his house.

'I expect he was worried you'd get angry with me for not telling you – he knew I hadn't spoken to you about it, that I'd kept it to myself.' His complete bewilderment must have shown on his face. She said kindly, 'We meet for coffee every few months, Ed and I. After all, I am his mother-in-law. And Graham always takes me to his signings – book signings, that is,' she added. 'In fact, Graham has read all his books. He's a real fan – as am I.' She nodded towards a small bookcase in the corner of the room. 'His books are over there, all twelve of them.'

Martin wasn't sure if he wanted to burst into tears or throw the books, every damn one of them, out of the window. 'Why didn't you tell me?' he asked in a choked voice.

Her face melted and she became her soft, gentle self. She leaned towards him. 'Oh, darling, because I wanted to think about Grace and our grandson without you spoiling it by ranting and raving, swearing and calling Ed names he really doesn't deserve. He's a lovely man, who did his best by our daughter. I wanted to savour the thought of the little boy I would never know, never touch, without your interference. I wanted it to remain pure and simple, unsullied by your black looks and insults.' She held out her arms towards him, something she hadn't done for more years than he could remember.

Martin couldn't help it. He fell into her arms and burst into tears.

Chapter 17

He would go to Italy!

The decision wasn't exactly surprising, Ed Laine thought as he unlocked the door of his apartment, in view of the long conversation he'd just had with Martin Lewin, during which he'd actually felt as if he were *there*, in Italy, reliving the panic and the heartbreak of that hellish time. The war over, he'd felt guilty about letting his good friend Vittorio down, just disappearing out of his life without a word. There was no way Vittorio could have got in touch since, as he'd known Ed as Edmond Laurent, of whom no record existed anywhere apart from on a false passport long ago destroyed.

He went into the kitchen and made coffee. He had never been much of a drinker – of alcohol, that is. He had been aware of the look of scorn in Lewin's eyes earlier when he'd ordered wine rather than 'a drop of the hard stuff', as his pop used to call it. There'd been a time when the look would have bothered him, but success had brought a measure of confidence that he'd never had before. He no longer felt inferior or a bit of a dolt in front of anyone, Martin Lewin included.

Ed sighed. He would always miss his mom and pop who'd both died in the years since the war had ended. Fortunately he'd remained close to his sister, Laura. In fact, Laura had come to New York from Boston to help him choose furniture for this place – an apartment consisting of the second and third floors of an old brownstone with vast windows at the front.

It overlooked Washington Square in Greenwich Village, where a street market was held on Sundays. The furniture was ordinary, comfortable stuff. There was no stainless steel or black plastic like in Hugo's, his publisher's house, or expensive antiques, as in the Lewins'.

He took the coffee into the room where he did just about everything except sleep – ate, read, listened to the radio, watched television and, most importantly, created his books. His desk was extra long, one section where he wrote by hand, jotting down ideas, making notes, and another section where he typed. There was a telephone and filing cabinet in between, and bookcases at each end. He sat on one of the office chairs and twirled it around; this was his most favourite place in the world. The chair had wheels, and could take him to any part of the room. There were times when he used it as a toy.

Photographs of his family were scattered around; his mom and pop, Laura and her husband, Pete and their two kids in various poses. But none of Grace and their son. They'd collected a few during the years in Paris and Rome, but Ed hadn't thought to remove anything from *Il Palazzetto* after Grace and their baby had been taken. Lilith had given him a photo of a young Grace, but it was too painful to look at, and he kept it in a drawer.

He sat still in the chair to contemplate the here and now. It would be a while before he could leave for Italy. He had a book to finish, and another about to be published that he would spend a few weeks promoting around the country. After that, he would be off to California – Hollywood, to be precise – where he would be working with a couple of writers on the script for the movie of one of his books. He looked at the calendar; it was February, and now likely to be July or August before he could get away. The height of summer wasn't a good time to visit Italy, but nor was it the best time to be in New York – or California, come to that.

★

He flew to Italy on the first of September. His publisher's secretary had booked the flight and arranged for the five-star hotel in Rome where he would stay. They had a representative there, Arthur Benton, an American, who would meet him off the plane and be of assistance while he was there. They had even discovered Vittorio Papallo's address and occupation – he was a Communist party official employed at the Rome headquarters. Ed found it extraordinary that in Europe someone could quite openly be a communist, when in his own country hysterical anti-communist feeling had reached ridiculous and terrifying proportions.

Arthur Benton turned out to be a small, tubby individual who'd married a girl he'd met in Italy while in the army during the war. They took a taxi to the hotel, where Ed changed his shirt, ordered a pot of coffee from room service, had a chat with Arthur about their war experiences and then shook the man's hand, thanked him and promised to get in touch should he need assistance during his visit. Looking disappointed, Arthur made his departure. He'd clearly been looking forward to the company of a fellow American for more than the couple of hours they'd just spent together.

Ed studied the map of Rome. It was just gone three o'clock in the afternoon. Italians worked strange hours, he remembered. They had an extra-long period for lunch, calling it a siesta. The office where Vittorio worked was on the outskirts of the city, and the hotel where Ed was staying was at the top of the Spanish Steps, in the centre. He decided it would be a good idea to telephone to make sure his old friend was available rather than risk a wasted journey.

As he'd learned a good bit of Italian during his time in the country, he had little difficulty getting through to the office and asking to speak to Vittorio Papallo.

Seconds later, there was a stunned silence after he was put

through and had announced who he was, followed by a shout of joy.

'Edmond Laurent!' Vittorio bellowed. 'I swear I have thought of you every single day since 1944, or was it forty-five when we last met?'

'Forty-four,' Ed said awkwardly. They'd gone through so much together; he should have got in touch before. 'I've been busy,' he said lamely. It was a hopeless excuse. 'Can we meet soon?'

'How about today? Are you staying in Rome?'

'I'm at the Hotel Hassler,' Ed told him.

Vittorio whistled. 'The Hassler, eh? You have done well, my friend, during the intervening years. Can we meet there? I've always wanted to see inside, but was only prepared to do so as a guest, not a gawper, to see how the other half lived.' He'd been a language student when they'd first met and his English was excellent, as was his French and German.

'Sure thing. When?'

'Now – as long as it takes me to get there.'

'Aren't you supposed to be at work?'

'I am at work, but I am also my own boss. See you soon, friend – in the bar.'

Vittorio had always been a slight, wiry individual, with barely an ounce of spare flesh on his tall, lanky body. Ed hadn't given much thought to how he might look now, but if he had, would have expected him to have put on a bit of weight since; instead, the man actually managed to look even thinner. Like a walking skeleton, though with a huge grin and a loud laugh, nothing like the picture painted in the States of grim-faced, ultra-left-wing men and women intent on turning the entire world into a colony of Russia.

'Don't you eat?' he enquired when they shook hands half an hour later in the bar of the Hassler with its gold mirrors, rich red carpet and brocade chairs, Vittorio, not satisfied with a handshake, hugged Ed ferociously in his wiry arms.

'I am one lucky individual,' he boasted. 'I eat like an elephant, but it never shows.'

'Like a horse,' Ed corrected. 'You eat like a horse.'

'No, no, Edmond. I eat like an elephant, I can assure you.'

After a few minutes of backslapping and congratulating each other for having survived the war all in one piece, it was time to get serious. Ed had ordered a bottle of red wine, which stood on a silver tray on the black lacquered table; it was a good wine and a good year, Vittorio said knowledgeably as the waiter filled their glasses.

'I tried to get in touch,' his friend assured him, 'but couldn't trace an Edmond Laurent in America fitting your description. In my position, I have all sorts of means at my disposal for checking such things.'

'It's MacLaine; my name is Edmund MacLaine. There seemed no need to tell you that at the time.' Ed shrugged. 'Afterwards, I didn't want to be reminded. I never planned on visiting Italy again. Too much bad stuff happened here.' Both men were silent, lost in their own thoughts. 'What happened to Assunta?' Ed asked after a while. 'Did you ever hear from her again?' He took it for granted the answer would be 'no', so was surprised when Vittorio nodded vigorously.

'Yes, I did. She returned after the war was over, looking not much different than when she went. She'd spent the year in a work camp.'

'Did you two get married?' He'd noticed Vittorio was wearing a wedding ring.

'No.' The man shook his head as vigorously as he'd nodded 'My wife is Anna. We have three children, two boys and a girl. No; somehow, with the war over, Assunta and I no longer hit it off – I think that's how you say it in English. After just a few weeks together, we went our separate ways. She married a lawyer and still lives in Rome, though she hasn't had kids.' He paused. 'I don't suppose you heard anything of Grace?'

'No.' Ed stared at his shoes. 'I never really expected to, though I tried to find out through the Red Cross. There was no record of a woman with a baby arriving at any camp around the date she and Simon disappeared.' He refilled both their glasses. Unusually, he felt like getting extremely sozzled tonight.

'I doubt if their records are complete,' Vittorio said.

'It doesn't matter whether they are or not.' Ed shrugged. 'She's dead, and so is Simon. I can't understand how knowing the grisly details would help.'

'You're right. Mind you, it might be worth your while talking to Assunta. When she came back, she was upset that you couldn't be traced. She said she had something to tell you – something she wasn't prepared to tell me.'

Ed wasn't sure if he wanted to hear it. Grace and Assunta had left Rome together, presumably on the same train. What news could Assunta possibly have that stood the remotest chance of being good?

'I think you should visit her, for old times' sake.' His friend's voice was slurred. Was this the first or second bottle of wine they'd had? He had a feeling he might have ordered a third. 'We come across each other occasionally. She would be upset if she discovered you'd been in Rome and hadn't been to see her. I have her address and telephone number,' he added encouragingly.

Ed left it to Vittorio to arrange the meeting with Assunta. His friend called the following morning and announced in a hurt voice that she would be happy to meet Edmond, but not himself. 'She wants to speak to you alone. She works for the United Nations in the Viale delle Termi di Caracalla, and has invited you to a private lunch at her office. Oh, and she married an Englishman, a lawyer, so her English is perfect.

189

Remember how poor it used to be? Her name's Thompson now; Signora Assunta Thompson.'

'What time do I have to be there?' Ed wasn't looking forward to it.

'One o'clock.' Vittorio sniffed. 'I shall take you in my car, and wait for you in a very nice restaurant where I will eat like an elephant.'

'Thanks, Vittorio. See you later.' If Assunta offered wine, he would refuse. His head was bursting after last night.

A uniformed guide took him to Signora Thompson's office on the second floor of the hugely impressive United Nations building — Mussolini had built it as a palace for himself, according to Vittorio. Ed couldn't remember seeing it in his only other visit to the city — there was nothing so far that he recognised from that time. It was like coming to a place he'd never been before.

The guide knocked and opened the door. The woman inside was already standing, smiling at him from behind a desk. 'Edmond!' she said huskily, before stumbling across the room and embracing him. 'Oh, Edmond.'

She buried her head in his shoulder. She was even more beautiful than he remembered, but so different now in her smart black suit and sleek hair. Her scent, her black, flashing eyes, took him back almost physically to a previous time when her hair was loose, her legs were bare and she wore cotton skirts and not a trace of make-up. He recalled the smell of the blossom on the trees and the feel of the hard soil beneath his bare feet, the sun beating down on him in a way it never seemed to have done since. He could almost sense the feeling of danger, of knowing the enemy was outside the gates of their little paradise, their *palazzetto*. Yet they just knew that they were quite safe there, that guardian angels were looking after them, that they would never be touched. 'We are blessed,' Grace used to say, though it had turned out not to be true.

And then, clearer than he had ever done before, as clear as it had been in real life, he saw his son, Simon, lying in his cot in the garden, a sheet spread over it to provide shade, laughing and cooing and he, Edmund, removing the sheet and picking him up, his hands almost meeting around the small, plump body . . .

'Edmond,' Assunta whispered, breaking into this vision of sheer happiness, 'Did you hear from the girl? There wasn't time to get her name. Did she manage to find you?'

He had no idea what she was talking about. He didn't know why, but he felt irritated. 'What girl?' he asked, rather pettishly he thought afterwards.

He was aware of Assunta's soft body stiffening against him. 'The girl who took Simon,' she hissed. 'The train had slowed down. We were at a station and there was a girl on the platform. We managed to break the wood, and Grace handed him through. She spoke in English. She shouted, "I've got him," as the train left. I remember she was pretty with lovely blonde hair, almost silver.' Assunta pushed him away, but left her hands on his shoulders. She shook him roughly. 'Simon is still alive, Edmond. Somewhere or other in this world you have a son who will be about fourteen by now.'

There was a tray of food on Assunta's desk, but neither could eat a thing. They emptied the coffee pot and she ordered more. Ed asked why she hadn't told Vittorio about Simon, and she replied that she couldn't bring herself to talk to him about anything that had happened during the time she was away.

'I didn't go into a work camp,' she told Ed, her voice bitter. 'I was put into a brothel used by German officers. I had two abortions while I was there. It's why I haven't had children – I am physically unable to conceive. If I'd told Vittorio, he would have insisted on our getting married as planned, out of sympathy or a sense of duty; one or the other. But I didn't think that was fair. I told him I didn't love him anymore.'

'Was that true?'

She smiled slightly. 'No, but it is now.'

'Does your husband know?'

'Yes, but I told him on our first date, giving him plenty of time to change his mind about seeing me again.'

'But he didn't.' Ed was glad.

She shook her head and poured more coffee for them both. 'What are you going to do now, Edmond?'

'First, I shall go to that station you mentioned and ask if anyone remembers what happened.' She had described the whole episode again, the second time in more detail. She had been astonished, she said, as had all the people on the train when, instead of crossing the border into Germany, it had passed through Switzerland. 'I learned later that this was unusual, but that it did happen occasionally.' At one station it hadn't stopped, merely slowed down until it was hardly moving. The station was small and didn't look important. It seemed only minutes later that it had thundered through Zurich, and about fifty miles later they'd entered Germany. They had travelled on and on, for days and days, or so it seemed, without food, without water, not knowing where they were or where they were going. At one point they had stopped and been transferred into trucks. She and Grace had managed to stay together until they'd arrived at Auschwitz, where they were separated, Grace going into the camp, Assunta to the place that served as a brothel.

'It was loathsome there, but better than death.' She began to weep. 'I never saw Grace again.'

Assunta gave Ed permission to discuss Simon's possible whereabouts with Vittorio – 'But not the other thing,' she said. Ed promised never to breathe a word.

She refused to go down to the restaurant to meet her old

lover. 'It would be too moving, much too sad, the three of us together after all this time, but without Grace. I would only cry even more.'

'I think I might cry too,' Ed admitted.

They said goodbye and promised faithfully they would meet again one day. 'Promise to let me know if – when – you find Simon,' she pleaded.

Ed promised, but found it hard to believe that he would ever find his son.

'I'll come to Zurich with you,' Vittorio announced when Ed had told him what had happened to Simon. 'In fact, I'll drive you there.'

'There's no need. Assunta telephoned the airport, and I am booked on a plane to Zurich leaving at midday tomorrow.'

'I will still come with you – can you afford another ticket?'

'You've got a cheek,' Ed said amiably. He could easily afford for both of them to go, and welcomed the idea of having Vittorio's company – and he could act as interpreter. He was pretty sure they spoke German in Zurich. 'I'll book another ticket.'

'Thank you, Edmond.' Vittorio made a face. 'I think I'd better spend tonight at home with Anna and the children. Would you like to come with me?'

'Another time.' He would quite like to take a look at the Vatican. He didn't visit church much, but was still a Catholic and might even go into St Peter's and say a few prayers, even light a candle.

The following day, all they saw of Zurich was what they glimpsed through the window of the taxi that took them from the airport to the main station, where Vittorio found out about the station that Assunta had described.

'It's what I think you might describe as a "stop" in your country, rather than a proper station. It's used mainly for guests at a hotel there, the St Aloysius. Shall I buy two tickets, or shall we hire another taxi?'

'Let's go by train. I would like to ask if anyone on the station remembers the train passing through and a baby being handed out.' It seemed most unlikely after fourteen years, but it had to be done. He was approaching the search for his son much too negatively. Perhaps it was because to find him would be a miracle and, despite being a Catholic, Ed had never believed in miracles.

The uniformed young man on the tiny station had only worked there for two years, and had no idea who'd done the job before. Vittorio, who was translating, said, 'But he knows that whoever had his job before has joined the army, so is not easy to contact. Shall we ask at the Hotel St Aloysius? Apparently there is a bus waiting outside. It only runs when a train arrives, and is due to leave right now.' He beat his chest and attempted to yodel when they left the station and went outside. 'The air here is very bracing. I feel at least ten years younger,' he remarked before they got on the bus.

The hotel resembled a massive log cabin and was pleasantly cool inside. The middle-aged receptionist was exceptionally helpful. Not only had she worked there since before the war, she was able to unearth the hotel records for April 1944, but couldn't find any guests who'd stayed there with a baby.

Oh, well, that's it, Ed thought. He almost felt relieved that the short search for Simon was already over, unsure if he was actually strong enough for the emotional journey as well as experiencing the discovery of his long-lost son.

The receptionist spoke helpfully in French once she realised Ed could understand the language. 'I remember there was a baby at the school,' she remarked, 'a boy. We used to see a lot of the pupils, and the couple who ran it were often in and out of Zurich and would sometimes catch the bus from here. I remember we had a party when the war ended, and all the children came. The baby was no longer a baby, but about eighteen months old by then. His mother – if she was his mother – was a really lovely young woman with beautiful blond hair. I'm afraid I can't remember her name, or the child's.'

Ed felt as if his heart had turned a somersault. 'Where is the school?' he asked.

'Further up the mountain, though nowadays it's run by two French sisters, the Clemences, and it's a different sort of school. The other couple left years ago.'

'How much further up?' Vittorio enquired.

'A few hundred metres. Our driver will take you there without charge, though he would appreciate a generous tip. Seeing as it's summer and there is no snow, you will have no problem walking down again this far. The bus leaves for the station on the hour.'

Ed, used to built-up, noisy, crowded cities, found it hard to imagine living in such an isolated spot. The dazzlingly clear air was not sufficient compensation for the loneliness and deafening silence of this part of the world. He would prefer to live with a choking fog to this, and be surrounded by buildings and unending, honking traffic.

The hotel limousine drew up in front of a cold stone building nestled within a circle of exceptionally tall trees. He felt as if they were committing a crime when Vittorio pulled on a rope outside the front door and a bell rang inside.

Almost immediately, the door was opened by a sweet-faced woman with short-cropped hair. 'Hello,' she said, holding the door open to allow them in. In French, she added, 'Madame Hubert from the hotel has already telephoned and told me about the information you require.' She showed them into a low-ceilinged room with large windows, through which nothing could be seen except trees and endless grassy hills. Ed hid a shudder.

The woman introduced herself as Juliette Clemence. 'We aren't used to being quite so peaceful, but the girls are having their afternoon nap. Any minute now they will wake up.' Even as she spoke, voices and subdued laughter could be heard elsewhere in the building. She showed Ed a card on which was printed a name, *Andrew Gaunt*, followed by an address in Brighton, England. Next to it, an address in Morocco had been crossed out.

'I'd like to keep this, so have copied the new address for you.' She handed him a piece of paper with *École Clemence* printed in heavy type at the top. 'We took over this building in 1945, not long after the war was over. Then, it was an entirely different sort of school, and Mr Gaunt was the principal. We have remained in touch ever since, usually sending cards at Christmas telling each other how we are getting on. There were hardly any pupils left at the school when my sister and I first saw it. I remember the girl with the baby was called Flora, though he was no longer a baby when we met, but a child aged about two. His name was Simon, and he was remarkably intelligent. I wasn't sure of Flora's position, whether she was a pupil or a teacher. Andrew mentions her and Simon from time to time in his letters, but I'm afraid I have no idea where they live.'

It was night, quite late and very dark, by the time Ed arrived back at the Hassler. He lay on the bed fully dressed, trying to adjust to the consequences of the day.

He was a father; he had a son who he thought had died fourteen years ago. Tomorrow he would fly to London, take the train to Brighton and possibly meet this son, or at least be told where he lived.

And what would happen then?

He fell asleep while mentally in the throes of turning

the spare bedroom in his apartment into a room suitable for a teenage boy. There would be posters of sporting heroes on the wall, and a baseball glove hanging behind the door. Saturday mornings they would play catch in the nearest park, and they would see movies together. Oh, and he would definitely encourage his son to enjoy modern jazz and vote for the Democratic party.

His heart raced as he thought about it, but when he thought about Simon's mother he wanted to cry.

Chapter 18

Vittorio drove him to the airport the following morning. He claimed to be distraught that Ed was leaving so soon. 'We have had hardly any time to talk, Edmond,' he complained. 'You must come back again – promise to come again, and we can talk more. Or you might find me on your doorstep in New York one of these fine days.'

Ed doubted it. America was doing its best to rid itself of communists, not allow them in. He had, however, enjoyed being with Vittorio, and vowed he would return to Rome. He had been there twice now, and still hadn't seen the place properly.

He wondered if London would turn out to be the same; that he would see very little of it, as the subway train forged its way beneath the bowels of the earth towards Victoria station, where he got off and caught another train to Brighton. He hoped Andrew Gaunt would be at home. He should really have contacted him before presenting himself at the man's house, but there was just a chance that, if he'd been approached first, he might have found a reason to refuse to see him.

A taxi took him to Gaunt's address, a small house overlooking the English Channel where the air was fresh and cool. A petite blond woman in her forties answered the door, and invited him into a room where the white walls were lined with books and paintings while she went to get her husband.

'He's in his studio and won't be a moment.' She had a slight accent, and he thought she might be Swedish or some other Nordic nationality.

Gaunt appeared, wiping his hands on a rag that smelled of turpentine. He had a smear of yellow paint on his bushy white beard, and his hair was longer than his wife's. She had followed him into the room.

'You're an artist,' Ed remarked to Gaunt.

'No, I'm a painter. I find "artist" rather a pretentious word, too easily used to describe people, not necessarily talented, who follow quite ordinary pursuits.' The man's broad smile was enough to smooth the edge off this rather cynical remark. He had a deep, musical voice and a strong accent that Ed was unable to identify. Despite the white hair, his face was youthful and unlined. 'Anyway, how can I help you, Mr Laine? I won't shake hands – you'll understand why. And my wife is called Else, and I am Andrew, by the way.'

'I'm Ed.' He swallowed, wishing he'd rehearsed how to explain why he was there. 'I understand you spent some time in Zurich during the war.'

'My wife and I ran a school there, yes.'

'And one of your pupils was a young woman called Flora, who had a son called Simon?'

There followed what could only be described as a stunned silence. Andrew Gaunt and his wife stared at each other. She opened her mouth to speak, but he beat her to it.

'You're a relative of Simon's, aren't you? Perhaps his father.' He collapsed in a chair. 'We've always had a feeling that something like this would happen one day.'

Else laid her hand on his shoulder and squeezed it. 'And it seems we were right.' She turned to Ed. 'How on earth did you find out about Simon?'

He explained about meeting Assunta a few days before, who'd been on the train with his wife and son. 'We hadn't met since the war was over, and she had no way of tracing me. I used a different name when we lived in Italy. I had assumed Grace and Simon had died in one of the camps.' He smiled awkwardly. 'So yes, I am Simon's father.'

'Grace – is that Simon's mother?' When Ed nodded, Else went on, 'Knowing her name makes her feel very real. Flora only got a glimpse of her, and described her as a "shadowy figure".'

Andrew unexpectedly buried his face in his big hands. 'What are we going to do now?' he said wretchedly.

Again, Else squeezed his shoulder. 'We are going to tell Ed where Flora and Simon live, darling, and he will go and see them. That's what you want to do, isn't it, Ed?'

'Well, yes.' What he would say when he came face to face with this Flora, he had no idea.

Else stood and announced she was going to make tea or coffee, whatever they preferred, then collect their little girl from school. 'Her name's Georgina, and she's nine. Perhaps, Andrew, while I'm away, you can tell Ed everything there is to know about Flora and Simon.'

After Else had gone, Ed sipped his coffee and told Andrew he'd sooner not know anything about Flora or Simon. 'Absolutely nothing; I'd rather find out for myself,' he said. 'Their address is all I need.' He didn't want his head filled with pre-conceptions.

At this, Andrew looked impressed. 'What a wise chap you are! But I insist on telling you this much; Flora was orphaned at six, and handed over to an aunt who didn't want her. She lived with us in Zurich from the age of eleven, and was seventeen when your wife put Simon into her arms and she regarded this as a miracle, something ordained by Fate, if that makes sense. At last she had someone of her own, a real relative. She and Simon belonged to each other, and I can promise you that he couldn't possibly have been more loved.'

'I see.' Ed wanted to argue with this, but declined to do so. 'All I need is their address,' he emphasised.

When Else arrived back home with Georgina, a delicate but intense and lively little girl, Ed was in the studio admiring her husband's paintings. They were mainly of weather conditions – tropical storms, snow scenes, mountain floods, trees bending in a gale as well as numerous sunrises and sunsets. They were rough, vibrant works that appealed to Ed greatly.

'Do you sell many?' he enquired.

'Just a few. I guess about one a month on average.' He made a face. 'We just about scrape by, and wouldn't manage at all if Else didn't work part-time as a nurse at the local hospital.'

'How much do they cost?'

'I usually charge about fifty pounds each.'

'I wouldn't mind a couple for my apartment in New York. My sister helped furnish it, and she bought mainly Impressionist prints which are good, but hardly exciting.' He stared at the walls. 'These are so . . . *alive*! And I'm sure my publisher would like one. He has all sorts of wealthy people in his office, and it would be a good advertisement for your work.'

'Publisher!' Gaunt looked at him in surprise. 'You're a writer.'

'Yes – sorry, I didn't mean to show off.'

'My dear chap, if you're a writer, you're a writer,' Gaunt said in his blunt way. 'Admitting it isn't exactly showing off.'

Else, who had been in the kitchen, came into the studio. 'Would you like to stay to dinner, Mr Laine? It's nothing elegant, just a stew followed by apple and custard.'

'I'd like that, thank you.' He had definitely warmed to the family. 'Oh, and please, do call me Ed.'

★

He didn't just stay for dinner, but overnight too, the invitation extended when the Gaunts realised he hadn't booked into a hotel and the small bag he was carrying contained everything he had brought with him.

He got up very early the following morning with the feeling he had made lifelong friends. He had bought three paintings, that Andrew would arrange to despatch to New York. Else drove him to the station, and he promised to let them know what happened in Bootle, Liverpool where apparently his son lived in a hotel called Haley's.

'Flora's bound to get in touch with us once she knows who you are,' Else told him. 'We're the nearest thing to a mother and father she's had since her real parents died. She'll be devastated,' she added, half to herself.

'Do you intend telling her I'm on my way?' Ed enquired. Perhaps *warning* would have been a better word.

Else frowned. 'Of course not. We won't mention your name to Flora until she lets us know that you have been. This is something that has to be dealt with between you and her. And Simon,' she added after a pause.

Liverpool bore a close resemblance to the dock area of New York, where he'd once lived. Gulls squawked angrily, swooping down like avenging angels in search of food. He was appalled at the wreckage left by the German bombardment of the city, still apparent so long after the war had ended.

He was dropped off outside Haley's hotel in Bootle, glad to escape the garrulous taxi driver, who had given him an account of the history of Liverpool from the day the first brick was laid until now.

The hotel was a largely unattractive, two-storey building with identical cream curtains at every window, the frames freshly painted white. He stepped inside onto a highly patterned carpet. Facing him was the receptionist's desk, presently unoccupied.

He stopped, taken aback at the sight of the painting on the wall behind the desk – a larger than life-sized figure of Bill Haley, the singer, wielding a guitar. So that's where the place had got its name from. Ed loved music, every sort of music: classical, New Orleans jazz, modern jazz, the new rock 'n' roll; but if there was one person in the trade he couldn't abide, it was Bill Haley, with the silly little kiss curl on his forehead. A massive cat was sitting on the desk, and began to purr when he tickled it beneath its fluffy chin.

'He's called Tabby.' A young woman had appeared from somewhere at the back, another startling figure with a white face, jet-black hair and eyes made up so heavily they looked like cockroaches. She was dressed from head to toe in black.

'Oh, hello, are you the Yankee Doodle Dandy?' she asked.

'Well, yes, I suppose I must be,' Ed stammered.

'We were all wondering what you would look like – me auntie June took your booking on the phone – and whether you'd be young or old, like.'

'And what am I?'

She smiled roguishly. 'Somewhere in between, I reckon.'

'Thank you.' At least she didn't think him old.

'Is that all you've brought with you, all the way from America?' She nodded at the travelling bag.

'That's all,' he agreed. 'What is Bill Haley doing on the wall behind you?'

'Oh, me cousin Kerry was mad about him.' She put her elbows on the desk and regarded Ed coyly. 'Y'know that record, "Rock Around the Clock"? He played it all the time. In fact, it was the only one he had by the time he died. Now Flora has every single rock 'n' roll record there is. They're played in the bar every Sat'day night. Will you be here Sat'day?'

Ed hoped not. 'I'm not sure of my plans,' he explained. He wasn't even sure what day today was. What relationship had the deceased Kerry had to Flora?

'Anyroad, if you'd like to sign the book – sir – I'll show you to your room.' The 'sir' had been added as an afterthought, as if she'd been instructed to address the guests as sir or madam, but wasn't something she would have done normally.

Ed duly signed the leather-bound book and followed the girl upstairs, Tabby padding softly behind. The walls were painted in an assortment of loud colours, following some sort of pattern, reminding him of a half-finished jigsaw.

His room was lime green, with a rose-pink door and a slightly paler pink ceiling. The curtains may have looked cream from outside, but inside they were wildly spotted. The room reminded Ed of a building in a fun fair, and he couldn't help but smile at the craziness of the colour scheme. Had it been painted like this in an attempt to cheer the guests up? If so, the attempt had succeeded. The cat had entered the room with him and leaped on to the bed. It began to purr again.

He opened a door expecting to find a john, but it turned out to be a wardrobe. The bathroom must be elsewhere. He found it along the corridor, returned to his own room, unpacked a few things and decided to go for a walk.

After depositing his key with the girl on the desk who was striving to be a beatnik – dinner would be at six, she told him – he left the hotel. There was a park on the other side of the road that the vivid sun had turned almost blindingly green.

Ed crossed the road and wandered through it. Despite the sun, it was cooler in Liverpool than it had been anywhere since leaving New York. His grandparents, married but hardly out of their teens, had sailed from Ireland to the United States via Liverpool, a journey the old couple had been fond of describing to their young grandson, so Ed had a yearning to see the River Mersey and pay his respects.

He left the park and walked under an old railway bridge that, although he didn't know it, was the same one under which Flora had sheltered with Simon on their arrival in Bootle twelve years earlier.

It was as if he was being drawn towards the river by its smell and the feathery touch of a soft salty wind, so was pleased eventually to turn a corner and find himself on a road lined on the far side with the high walls and tall gates of a series of docks. Behind them rose the funnels of ships, and the shouts of the dockers could be heard as they loaded or unloaded their cargoes.

Ed felt as if he had been transported back three dozen years or more to a time when he'd walked along a similar road in Boston, with his own father. He wandered along the busy pavements, hands in pockets, enjoying the familiar aromas and sights of his childhood. He had almost forgotten such places existed since leaving for Paris with Grace. He had lost contact with his roots.

He had also lost contact with the present, he realised when he glanced at his watch and remembered dinner would be served at six o'clock. If he didn't hurry back, he would be late. The walk and the fresh air had given him an appetite.

In the dining room, the same mad artist had been let loose with a paintbrush – or perhaps there was a whole team of them. It was like eating in a jungle, as the walls were decorated with leaves of various sizes and in several different shades of green, joined together with gold branches on which perched the odd exotic bird. There were only five other guests there – an elderly couple and three men who appeared to be commercial travellers. The young beatnik acted as waitress. Her name, he discovered, was Shirley.

He wondered when he would come across Flora and Simon, and whether Flora owned the hotel or merely managed it, and how on earth the place could make money with so few guests.

He discovered how when he emerged from the dining room stuffed to the gills with shepherd's pie – or so it said on the menu – and sherry trifle, and found that the lounge, which he hadn't noticed before, was slowly filling with customers. He went inside and discovered that it was in fact a bar, and that the barmaid was a spectacularly beautiful woman with silver-blonde hair.

Flora! For a moment, Ed could have sworn his heart stopped beating. This woman had stolen his son, and in reality he should hate her, but he had no idea how he felt.

It was then that he noticed three boys playing snooker on a table in the corner. Once again, his heart missed a beat, did something possibly dangerous. He edged closer and watched. The game wasn't exactly snooker, but something they must have made up for themselves so that all three could play. One, clearly the youngest, had hair the same colour as the stunning barmaid. Was she married – the barmaid, that is? Married to the late Kerry, perhaps, the Bill Haley fan? If that had been the case, then she was now a widow. He was sorry he hadn't let Andrew and Else fill him in a little on her history.

There was an altercation at the table; the blond boy had thrown down his cue, crying angrily, 'You cheated, Simon. You always bloody cheat.' His cheeks were pink with anger.

'You can't cheat at snooker, Andy. You always say that when you lose.' The speaker was a thin boy who looked decidedly undernourished.

The third boy, Simon, looked up and met Ed's eyes. He was the tallest of the three. His son, Simon, had been born in September and would be fourteen this month. This boy's name was Simon, and seemed about fourteen. Ed felt strongly as if he was looking at his own face when he was the same age. They had the same reddish-brown hair and green eyes. The boy smiled at Ed, a smile that he could only have inherited from Grace, and said, 'He only says that when he loses.'

Ed stepped forward. His feet were unsteady and his throat felt tight; this could only be his son he was addressing. 'It is possible to cheat,' he mumbled. 'I've heard of magnets being used, both in the ball and by the pockets. But I doubt if there are any magnets here.' It was only a cheap table, and it was also a stupid thing to have said.

'Are you the American Mam was expecting?' It was Andy who had asked the question. He seemed to have recovered his good humour.

'Yes, I'm Ed Laine. I was born in Boston, but have lived most of my life in New York.'

'New York!' All three spoke together in awed voices with strong Liverpudlian accents. They gathered around him, Simon the only one to reach higher than his shoulder. 'Is it the same as it's shown in the pictures?' the thin one enquired.

'Depends on the picture – we call them movies over there. There's one called *Blackboard Jungle*, you must try and see it sometime, it shows how tough it is in some schools in New York.' He remembered something. 'Oh, and it features "Rock Around the Clock" with Bill Haley.'

Andy literally jumped with excitement. 'Hey, that was our dad's favourite record. We sang it at his funeral; the priest nearly did his nut.'

Ed felt a soft hand on his arm. It was the barmaid. 'Leave Mr Laine alone, boys. You're probably making him feel embarrassed.' She led him towards the bar, and the boys groaned at having lost him. 'Everyone's so thrilled to have an American guest that you must feel like a film star. My name's Flora O'Shea, and I own this hotel. Can I offer you a drink, on the house?'

'That'd be nice, thank you.' Ed was feeling odder and odder; there were too many confused emotions to identify, and he didn't know which was uppermost.

She indicated for him to sit on a high stool, and made her way behind the bar. 'What would you like?'

'White wine, please.'

When she put the glass in front of him, it was full to the brim. 'That is the best we have,' she said. 'Welcome to Bootle, Mr Laine.'

'Thank you. You have three fine sons there, Mrs O'Shea.' He thought this a rather clever remark. It would oblige her to explain her relationship to Simon. Would she claim him as her son?

'Oh, only one is my son – Andy. He's really big for his age, and will be ten in November. Liam is the son of a friend; we used to be neighbours.' She folded her arms and leaned on the bar; he could smell her flowery perfume and admire her eyes, that were grey with shreds of silver and gold. 'Simon, the tallest, is in fact my cousin. His parents died in a car crash in Zurich, where we were living at the time. He was only eight months old, and as his only living relative the obvious thing to do was raise him as if he were my own. I was seventeen, old enough to be his mother.' She spoke quickly, as if it was an explanation she had given many times over the years, and had got it off pat.

'We also have two daughters,' she went on. 'Rose and Connie. They're upstairs, doing their homework. The boys have homework too, but have to be nagged to do it.' Her lips twisted. 'I said "we" – sometimes I forget I am a widow. My husband, Kerry, died five years ago.'

'I'm sorry.' He didn't say he was a widower, deciding to leave it for another time – if there was one. 'So you have three children, a cousin and a hotel to manage on your own!' He was genuinely impressed.

'Yes, but Kerry's family is very supportive. Virtually every employee is an O'Shea. Shirley, his niece, who's currently working temporarily as our receptionist and waitress, will be returning to art college next week. It was the students who painted the interior of the hotel. Don't you think it's beautiful?' She laughed. 'You don't have to answer that. Some people think it's awful. But at least it's cheery.'

'Very much so,' he stammered. 'But I admire it, too.'

'Excuse me.' She turned away to serve a customer. The room was becoming more and more crowded. It was hot, and the air was thick with smoke. To Ed's horror, his head fell forward and he realised he had briefly fallen asleep. Not surprising, when you thought about it; he had visited three European countries in a matter of days, travelling by plane. He was probably thoroughly exhausted. No wonder his emotions were in such turmoil; his life had been turned completely upside down, and he would have had even more difficulty coming to terms with it had he been fully alert.

When Flora turned back to speak to him, he claimed he had work to do in his room, and wished her goodnight.

Chapter 19

Next morning, he woke up to the sound of shrieking gulls and heavy traffic, if not exactly refreshed, at least more in control of himself, better able to think clearly about the situation. A bright sun glimmered around the edges of the curtains.

After a breakfast of eggs, toast and an entire pot of coffee to himself, he left the hotel and made his way to the docks. There'd been no sign of Flora or Simon. He tried not to think about them as he strolled along the crowded pavements in the dazzling sunshine – he seemed to be the only person who wasn't in a hurry, and he didn't care that people were dodging and dancing along behind him, trying to pass.

He came to a café, where he bought a cup of tea that tasted like tar. For some reason, although it was horrible and things were pretty weird at the moment, it made him feel extraordinarily pleased with life. For rather too many years, things had been too comfortable. He'd never been cold, never hungry, his clothes had been washed and pressed and he'd gone everywhere by taxi, where before he'd used a bus or the subway. The tea had reminded him of his early days in New York when he couldn't even sell a short story, let alone a novel. It made him realise just how far he had come.

Eventually he came to the point where the docks ended. He veered to the left and walked until he arrived at the business district of Liverpool, and from there to the city centre and the big stores. He noticed a movie house showing a double bill:

Bride of the Gorilla and *Francis Goes to the Races*. Back home, he only saw movies that the critics had given favourable reviews to, something he doubted either of these films had received – Francis was a talking mule! He bought a ticket and sat through both movies, emerging three hours later into the dazzling sunshine feeling more like a basic human being and less like a cosseted, overpaid writer.

He recalled that tram cars rattled past Haley's Hotel in their dozens, tracked down the one for Bootle so that there was no need for a taxi, and returned to the hotel.

It had been a weird and wonderful day, but not exactly what he had come to Liverpool for.

Simon was in the lounge playing snooker, the only person there. He looked up when Ed went in. 'Hello.'

'Hi there. Where are the other boys?' Ed enquired.

'Andy and Liam? They're in the Scouts; me, I'm not interested.' *I am above such boyish interests*, he seemed to be saying.

'Do you three boys go to the same school?'

'No, Liam's at the local secondary modern.' He aimed the white ball at the red, but missed. He muttered something underneath his breath that Ed couldn't quite catch. If it was a curse, he hoped it was a mild one. 'Me, I passed the eleven-plus and go to St Anthony's grammar school in Waterloo. Next year, Andy will sit the eleven-plus. Right now, he's at junior school.' He stopped playing, saying thoughtfully, 'I'd sooner go to a secondary modern, though Flo wouldn't stand for it. At St Anthony's we're taught Latin – I mean, who needs Latin in this day and age?' He twisted his mouth in disgust. 'Only doctors, and I certainly don't want to be a doctor. Liam's taught far more useful stuff.'

Ed idly picked up a cue. 'What would you like to do when you're older?'

Still thoughtful, Simon rubbed chalk on the end of his cue

and blew off the surplus. 'I don't really know. Sometimes, I want to join a group like Bill Haley's.'

'Good luck!' Despite not being a fan of Bill Haley, Ed approved. He removed his jacket and nodded at the table. 'Would you like a game?'

Simon's green eyes brightened – Ed's eyes, not Grace's. 'Gosh! Yes, please. Do you play much?'

'Years ago, I worked as a waiter and there was often a table in the place.' These were the cheaper, rowdier establishments. 'I played something called pool, not too different from snooker, but the table's smaller. Sometimes I'd stay long after the place had closed.' In winter, it was preferable to being in his cold-water flat. 'I'm very much out of practice. You go first.'

Ed quickly regained the hang of things, and he beat Simon hands down. He had no intention of going easy on him, of allowing him to win. If he revealed his identity, he didn't want the boy thinking his pop was a loser.

If?

Simon was anxious to play another game. He made the break, and Ed was conscious of Flora having entered the room. She didn't speak, and he affected not to notice she was there. Out of the corner of his eye, he could see that she was dressed all in white and wore her hair in a ponytail. A strange atmosphere developed, and he wondered if she and Simon were aware of it, as if they were joined together as a family; mother, father and child, and there was no need for words.

It wasn't until the game was over that anyone spoke. It was Simon, who had lost again, though Ed had deliberately missed a few easy balls so it wasn't such a sound thrashing as before.

'I'm not as good as I thought I was,' Simon said dejectedly.

'You could do with some coaching,' Ed said encouragingly. 'You've definitely got a flair. Another thing – these cues are too heavy.' He threw his a few inches in the air and caught it.

'You need lighter ones, and the table needs to be re-covered. It's a bit lumpy here and there.'

'How much is all that going to cost?' Flora asked.

'I'll find out.' He wished he hadn't said anything now; he was merely adding to her burdens.

She sighed. 'Thank you.' She seemed to pull herself together. 'Would you like a drink, Mr Laine? I haven't stayed in many hotels in my life, but what I disliked was being unable to have a drink whenever I felt like it – I mean, tea or coffee. Though I'll get you a real drink, if you want,' she added hastily.

'Coffee would be great, thank you.'

'I'll go and make it. Would you like something, Simon?'

'No, ta, Flo.' The boy was at the table again.

They were easy with each other. You could tell they'd been together for many years.

After the coffee, Ed lay in the tub for half an hour. Twice, someone knocked on the door. He shouted 'taken', the first time, and 'still taken' the second, in case it was the same person.

Getting dressed, he thought he'd have to buy himself a few new outfits if he stayed much longer – or ask the hotel, in other words, Flora, to launder his soiled clothes. It wasn't the sort of situation he'd ever faced before.

That afternoon he'd bought a book, Evan Hunter's *Blackboard Jungle*, which he would leave behind for the boys. He didn't fancy spending the evening reading in his room, so instead sat in a corner of the bar with Tabby curled up on his knee. The other customers respected his privacy and left him to read undisturbed. Every now and then, he would find himself peering over the book and watching Flora behind the bar. She fascinated him.

★

She was in the extremely noisy foyer the next morning dressed in white again, along with Simon and Andy and two extremely attractive young girls wearing pretty dresses, and Shirley, with her ghostly make-up and black clothes, Ed hadn't realised it was Saturday. There was a basket on the floor containing buckets and spades and a cricket bat, and another with soft drinks and packets of what were obviously sandwiches. The children looked excited, including Simon, who was holding a large, brightly coloured ball.

'We're going to Southport for the day,' Shirley announced. 'Why don't you come with us, Mr Laine?'

'Shirley!' Flora said with an embarrassed shudder. 'He's a guest, not a member of the family.'

Shirley grinned. 'I dunno why, but he feels like an O'Shea.'

'My grandparents were called MacLaine,' Ed informed her. 'They hailed from Ireland.'

'Did they really?' Flora looked interested. 'Oh, look. Rose is longing to talk to you. She's ten, and wants to tell everyone at school she's met an American.'

'Hi there, Rose.' Ed shook hands with the dark-haired girl. 'It's nice to meet you.'

Rose actually curtsied, and Simon groaned; it was his turn to be embarrassed. 'It's nice to meet you too,' the girl said politely.

Flora looked a trifle harassed. 'I'm sorry, but will you please shake hands with Connie too, or she'll feel ignored.'

As if to contradict this statement soundly, Connie hid behind her mother until Simon scooped her up in his arms and carried her across to Ed. 'She's shy,' he said, 'but you still want to meet the nice man, don't you, Con?'

The little girl nodded. 'Hello,' she said timidly, reluctantly holding out her small hand for Ed to shake. Afterwards, she buried her head in Simon's shoulder and Ed felt a jolt of hot anger. *The nice man!* He felt riled at the closeness of the family that included his son, yet he, the son's father, was totally excluded.

'How are you getting to Southport?' he enquired.

Shirley answered. 'On a charabanc; it'll be here any minute.'

What the hell was a charabanc? It turned, out to be a deluxe bus that drew up outside the hotel as they were speaking. The family piled on, and the deathly silence that followed almost made it feel as if the world had ended.

Ed thought he was alone until a voice behind him said, 'Can I help you, luv?'

He turned to find that a woman he'd never seen before was now the receptionist. He didn't doubt she was an O'Shea. 'I'm all right, thank you. I'm about to go out myself.' He waved. 'So long.'

'Tara, luv. Have a nice time.'

He left the hotel, crossed the park and passed under the railway bridge before coming to the docks, that were as crowded as ever, despite it being a Saturday. He joined the pedestrians jamming the pavements and began to walk.

How would all this end?

There was no need to ask himself that question; he already knew. Tomorrow, the day after, or one day very soon, he would return to New York, not having told a soul apart from Andrew and Else in Brighton that he was Simon's father. It would be too cruel. His son had become an O'Shea. It made no sense to remove him – *try* to remove him; he might not want to leave – from the only family, the only people, he had ever known. The chances were he wouldn't want to live in another country with a stranger, albeit that the stranger was his father. The best thing for Ed was to return in another few years, three, say, and reveal the truth then, when Simon was eighteen – a man. He debated with himself whether to tell him at all, but the boy had the right to know the true facts of his birth at some time. And the ghost of Grace had to be acknowledged as the mother of a fine son. Simon was living proof that Grace herself had actually lived.

He was too lost in thought to hear the bicycle bell, or the voice at his rear yelling, 'Get out o' the bleedin' way!' Afterwards, all he could remember was being hit from behind and thrown into the road, but not the lorry that mowed him down.

He woke up from time to time; he had no idea for how long, whether it was minutes or hours. He became aware that he was in hospital, and that the other patients, or at least some, were very noisy. They sang loudly, complained bitterly and swore eloquently, sometimes using words and expressions he'd never heard before. The man in the next bed, for instance, told anyone who went near to go and 'piss up your kilt, mate'. Ed planned to use it in a novel one day. He wasn't in pain, and felt agreeably light-headed and extremely happy just lying there, able to sleep whenever he felt like it.

A doctor, who only looked about eighteen but must surely have been older, appeared at his bedside – Ed didn't know whether it was morning, afternoon or evening. 'Ah, you're awake,' the doctor said in a pleased tone. 'Do you think you'll manage to stay awake until I've finished explaining what's wrong with you? I did try before.'

'Try me now,' Ed said.

'It would appear that two days ago you were walking along Regent Road in Bootle, more commonly known as the Docky – and where this hospital is situated, as it so happens – when a bicycle knocked you into the road, whereupon you were nearly run down by a lorry.' He looked at his notes. 'You have a broken leg, which has been set in plaster, two broken ribs and your back is badly bruised. You are heavily sedated, which is why are sleeping so much. We should be able to let you out in another seven to ten days. Do you understand all that? I can see you're still with us.'

'I understand; thanks.' Ed snorted. 'I bet all this is going to set me back a tidy sum.' He was pretty sure his health insurance didn't cover injuries acquired abroad.

'My dear sir,' the young man stated with a mixture of gravity and pride, 'you are now in the land of free medicine, available to every citizen from the cradle to the grave. You will not be charged a penny, though I understand that if the same thing were to happen to me in your country, without proof of a healthy bank balance I would go untreated and end up on the streets.' He sounded a bit like Winston Churchill.

'How did you know I was from America?'

'Several people from your hotel have been in to enquire about your condition; they were informed after we found the address in your pocket.'

At about that time, Ed floated back to sleep. When he woke up, there were visitors by all the beds, and Flora was sitting in a chair beside his. She looked worried.

'How do you feel?' she enquired.

'Marvellous.'

She looked even more worried. 'Are you being sarcastic, Mr Laine?'

'No, I really do feel good. I'm enjoying not doing anything. No phone calls or mail to deal with. I don't have to go anywhere.' He remembered his leg was broken. 'I *can't* go anywhere.' He sighed blissfully.

'I feel guilty,' she confessed. 'I feel as if we should have looked after you better than we did.'

'I have been old enough to look after myself for a long time,' Ed said mildly.

'Yes, but you're a stranger in a strange land. As a guest in my hotel, I feel responsible for your welfare.'

Ed laughed, and was surprised when his face hurt. 'I think you should look for a different business, Mrs O'Shea, or you will find yourself committed to a life of non-stop anxiety.'

She changed the subject. 'Do you have a wife, Mr Mac-Laine?'

'I did once, but she's dead.'

'I'm so sorry. What was her name?'

'Grace.'

'That's a pretty name.'

'So was she.'

She looked down at her flowered skirt and began to make tiny pleats in the material with her fingers. She was trying to think of something else to say, and Ed didn't have the energy to think of anything himself. The situation was saved by the arrival of Shirley, who blew him a kiss and said, 'See, if you'd come with us to Southport, you wouldn't have had an accident and you wouldn't be in here!'

'I'll always regret it,' Ed said, grinning. That hurt too.

Next time he opened his eyes, both women had gone.

There were fourteen beds in the ward. A few were occupied by ancient gentlemen who looked as if they were barely alive; the rest by men whose ages ranged from the very young to the not quite so old.

After the visitors had gone, a nurse appeared with a tea trolley and sandwiches. This was supper. The same nurse came back about ten minutes later to collect the plates and empty cups, shortly followed by a bad-tempered sister and a harassed junior nurse who tucked the patients in. The curtains were drawn and everyone was curtly ordered by the sister to go to sleep immediately.

The curtains were thin and it was still light outside, so it was possible to see perfectly. The man in the bed opposite Ed sat up and began to read the paper. Three others gathered around the bed of his neighbour to play poker.

'Fancy a hand, wack?' one enquired of him.

'Too tired, I couldn't concentrate,' Ed replied. 'But thanks for asking.'

There was laughter from the far end of the ward, where alcohol was being passed around. An earnest young man sat on Ed's bed and began to complain about the United States government.

'After the war was over, they wouldn't grant us a loan because we had a democratically elected socialist government in this country,' he said angrily. 'Yet we'd won the war together.'

Ed expressed his sympathy. 'I know; I'm sorry. It was very bad of us.'

'Now we've got the Conservatives in, and it's all the fault of the USA,' he claimed.

Ed faintly remembered apologising a second time. When next he opened his eyes, the ward was in darkness apart from a single red bulb burning over the door to the exit. Snores, coughs and groans were coming from all directions. He urgently needed to visit the bathroom. He started to get out of bed, and discovered that he couldn't. With a sigh, he pressed the buzzer over the bed and waited for the nurse to come.

As the days passed, he felt less tired and more awake. His injuries began to hurt as his medication was gradually withdrawn. Now he was finding it difficult to sleep, and in the darkness of the night he thought a lot about Grace and how they'd met in New York, at a party over a music store in Bleecker Street. He recalled the first time he'd been introduced to her odious father. Martin Lewin had made no secret of his dislike for the waiter with ambitions to be a published writer. His only daughter had picked a loser, as well as a Catholic, for a husband.

Flora came to see him every day, as did other O'Sheas, some he'd met before and some he hadn't. They brought him fruit and flowers. Simon, Liam and Andy came twice. They talked about snooker and American gangster movies.

He was allowed out of bed to practise walking with crutches, and discovered it was a talent he'd never known he had. The plaster would come off in another six or seven weeks, he was told, and he wondered if he would be able to negotiate his third- and fourth-floor apartment in Washington Square until that time.

By now he was longing to be home, with his life returned to normal. Two men had died in the ward since his arrival, and others came and went; he was becoming one of the long-stay patients. He had listened to numerous life stories, and had made up a simple, manufactured version of his own to tell in return.

At night, left to his own thoughts, he returned to his life with Grace and became more and more angry with Flora. Something he had been greatly looking forward to since meeting Assunta, and discovering that Simon was still alive, was telling Lilith that she had a grandchild. He was extremely fond of Lilith. Married to that tyrant Lewin, she hadn't had much of a life. She would be delighted to know about Simon, but it would be as cruel for Lilith to know she had a grandchild in another country that she wouldn't be able to see for another few years as it would for Simon to find out that he wasn't a Knox or an O'Shea, but half a MacLaine and half a Lewin.

It was almost time for him to leave, but he felt helpless. Without a telephone, how could he arrange his flight home? He had a few things to collect from Haley's, but had no intention of going back. In desperation, Ed wrote out a telegram to send to Hugo Kingsbury, his publisher. It said, *Am stranded with broken leg in Bootle hospital. Please arrange flight back to New York.*

He asked a nurse to send it for him. She read it and said, 'Don't you want to tell him where Bootle is?'

'No. He'll find out easily enough.' He had utter faith in the indomitable Hugo to do absolutely anything.

Two days later, Hugo marched into the ward wearing a pale grey silk suit, silver hair gleaming, looking as if he owned the place. He was carrying a bag containing clothes from Ed's New York apartment. With the help of a nurse, Ed was quickly dressed and put into the taxi waiting outside.

'I've booked a suite at the Adelphi Hotel not far from here,' Hugo said. 'Once we're there, we'll sort you out.'

'I'm supposed to be signed out by a doctor,' Ed protested. 'I wasn't expecting you to come in person, just book me a flight home.'

'We can get the doctor to come to the hotel and sign you out tomorrow.'

Ed smiled, but didn't comment on Hugo's automatic assumption that there was nothing on earth that couldn't be acquired with money. He would arrange things more tactfully himself, and have his stuff collected from Haley's and transferred to this Adelphi place along with the bill for their services, which he would pay by cheque. He also wanted a letter delivered to Mrs Flora O'Shea, which he would compose tonight.

Hugo helped him sit on the elegant brocade-covered sofa in their suite at the Adelphi, and Ed landed with a sigh. This was luxury with a vengeance; flocked wallpaper, satin curtains, carpets as thick as a carefully tended lawn.

'What the hell are you doing here, Ed?' Hugo asked irritably. He was arranging a stool for Ed's leg. 'I thought you were going to Rome, not Liverpool.'

'I've been to Rome. I've also been to Zurich, and now I'm here.' He forgot to mention he'd also been to Brighton.

'Why?

'Order me some coffee and I'll tell you.'

★

Over Ed's coffee and Hugo's large Scotch, Ed told him the story of his life from the day he'd met Grace until now. He had known bits before, that Ed was a widower, for instance, but not the raw details.

'Phew!' Hugo gasped when Ed had finished. There was a long silence. His publisher had never been known to be stuck for words before. 'What are you going to do about it, pal?'

'For now, I shall return home and try to forget about it for a few years, but I'll tell Flora I'll be coming back one day.' He couldn't possibly forget about it. Perhaps 'ignore' was a better word.

'What's she like, Flora?'

Ed closed his eyes and visualised Flora behind the bar at Haley's and sitting by his bed in the hospital. 'Charming,' he said. He looked helplessly at his friend. 'Utterly captivating. And yet I can never forgive her for what she did. At least, I don't think so.'

'Really!' Hugo crossed his legs in his uniquely elegant way. 'It's a pity *you* didn't bother searching for Simon the minute the war was over. If you've found him now, and so easily too, then you would have found him then. Flora would have had him for a year or less. It's hardly fair to blame her for keeping him all this time, when you made no effort to find him yourself.'

Ed was outraged. 'But I searched everywhere at the time. After the war, I made enquiries of several different agencies and there was no record of an American woman entering Auschwitz, or any other of those despicable places, with a baby around that particular time. What else could I do?'

'What you did last week, pal,' Hugo said coolly. 'Gone to Italy; asked the same questions. It's what *I* would have done.' He shrugged laconically. 'Still, you've found him, and landed yourself in a sea of troubles, as Shakespeare said. In fact, I think it was *Hamlet*.'

Perhaps it was appropriate as Ed felt as if he were drowning.

Next morning, Hugo arranged to pay the night porter, Derek, a ludicrous sum of money to hire a taxi to take himself to and from Haley's Hotel in Bootle, collect Ed's stuff and deliver two letters, one addressed to Flora, the other to Simon, Liam and Alex containing ten pounds to buy billiard cues and have the table in the bar re-covered. Ed wasn't sure if ten pounds was too much or too little, and had to hope it was just enough.

Flora returned to the hotel from taking Connie to school, and was told about Derek's visit by Alice Brannigan, who was in charge of breakfasts and had swiftly packed Ed's bag. 'I've put the letters in the office,' she said. 'Our Liam's name's on one, along with the other lads, but I suppose we should leave them to open it together, though I'm dying to know what's inside. Would you like a cup of tea, luv?'

'No thank you, Alice.' Flora couldn't wait to read her own letter.

She went into the office and picked up the envelope with shaking hands. Her mind, her entire body had been in turmoil since Ed Laine had been knocked down on the Docky and taken to hospital. She had looked through the possessions in his room in case there was evidence of a relative or friend in America to notify that he'd been hurt.

In the pocket under the lid of his suitcase, she'd found his passport and the piece of paper that had nearly caused her heart to fail. It was a letterhead from the École Clemence in Zurich, on which had been written Andrew and Else's Brighton address. On the other side, in Andrew's barely legible scribble, was Haley's address in Bootle.

Was Ed Laine a relative of Simon? His uncle, perhaps? His *father*? Or was he just someone who'd been sent to track him down? She had liked him, really liked him. *Really!* He was the first man she'd felt attracted to since Kerry had died. She recalled the day she'd gone into the bar where he'd been playing snooker with Simon. The three of them had been the only people there, and she'd had the really strange feeling that they were connected to each other in a strange way, like a family.

Why hadn't Andrew or Else been in touch, she wondered, to warn her that this man was on his way? She recalled, all those years ago, that both had thought it wrong that she keep her little boy, that she should try to find out if he had relatives, get in touch with the Red Cross, for instance. After Ed's visit, they must have decided not to contact her, and were probably wondering what was going on. Well, she didn't feel inclined to tell them right now. They could just wait for an explanation.

'But he was mine,' she whispered now. The dark-haired woman had put her baby into Flora's arms – in other words, Ed's wife, Grace.

That's a pretty name, she'd said in the hospital.

So was she, he'd replied.

She opened the letter. It had been printed with a black pen, the letters large and angry, on paper from the *Adelphi* Hotel. So that was where he was staying! He hadn't put *Dear Flora*, but had just plunged in. She imagined him full of rage.

DO YOU KNOW WHAT A CONCENTRATION CAMP IS? DO YOU KNOW WHAT GOES ON THERE? WHAT DO YOU THINK HAPPENED TO GRACE, MY WIFE AND SIMON'S MOTHER, WHO SPOKE TO YOU FROM THE TRAIN THAT DAY IN ZURICH?

FOR MORE THAN FOURTEEN YEARS UNTIL A FEW DAYS AGO, I HAD THOUGHT MY LITTLE BOY WAS DEAD, THAT HE HAD DIED A TERRIBLE DEATH IN A GAS CHAMBER, HIS BODY THROWN INTO AN OVEN ALONG WITH MY BEAUTIFUL WIFE. I

HAVE VISUALISED THEIR DEATHS MANY THOUSANDS OF TIMES.

YOU HAVE KEPT MY CHILD FROM ME ALL THESE YEARS. I FIND IT HARD TO BELIEVE ANYONE COULD BE SO SELFISH. YOU HAVE ALSO KEPT HIM FROM HIS GRANDFATHER, ONE OF THE RICHEST MEN IN AMERICA AND HIS GRANDMOTHER. LILITH IS A DEAR, LOVELY WOMAN WHO WOULD BE DE-LIGHTED BEYOND BELIEF TO KNOW THAT SHE HAS A GRANDSON.

I AM RETURNING TO NEW YORK IN A FEW DAYS, BUT WILL COME BACK ONE DAY WHEN SIMON IS OLDER AND MORE CAPABLE OF DEALING WITH THE TRUTH ABOUT HIS BIRTH – THAT HE HAS A FAMILY OF HIS OWN AND THAT YOU ARE NOTHING TO DO WITH HIM.

I KNOW THIS SOUNDS OVEREMOTIONAL, BUT THAT IS HOW I FEEL. I SHALL NEVER FORGIVE YOU, FLORA.

ED LAINE

Chapter 20

Two years before Ed Laine had come to stay at the hotel, Flora had returned from London where she had discovered she would shortly be worth about five thousand pounds, from the sale of her father's house and the money in the bank, but had delayed telling anyone about the windfall until two months had passed, the house had been sold and the money was in her new bank account.

Although five thousand pounds sounded like a small fortune, she was well aware of how quickly money could lose its value — inflation, it was called. After all, the children were growing older and cost more to feed and clothe.

If she just left it in the bank to live on, a time would come when it would all be gone, the children would be even older and once again she would be looking for a job. What she needed was to make the money work for her — not buy shares or invest in schemes which she knew nothing about, but acquire a business and work for herself. And what better business to take on than the Crown, that Lloyd Francis was about to put on the market? Some years before, his only brother had emigrated to Australia with his large family and was building a successful life there. Lloyd's application to join him with his own family was currently being processed, and he was likely to leave quite soon.

Flora contemplated writing to Andrew and Else, or to Isobel, to ask their advice, but in the end she made the decision on her own. She was worried all three would talk her out of buying the hotel, when in her heart she knew she wanted to go ahead.

The place had been badly in need of renovation when she'd first worked there and met Kerry, and had become even shabbier since. On the day she signed the final contract and let everybody know, a small crowd of O'Sheas turned up to have a look round and remark on the courage, or sheer stupidity, of what this unusual young woman was up to.

'Our Kerry wouldn't have approved,' his mother remarked sourly.

'Our Kerry would have thought it a grand idea,' his father commented. 'Fancy having a hotel in the family! I think it's bloody marvellous.'

The younger children were out of their heads with excitement on their first visit, running from room to room, bagsying the ones they wanted. Flora had to remind them that the family quarters were downstairs, and that they couldn't just sleep wherever they wished. Nor would they be allowed the use of all three bathrooms; two were for the guests. Simon stayed aloof. He had discovered a snooker table in the bar, managed to track down the cues and balls and was quietly teaching himself to play.

Flora had acquired the hotel fully furnished and equipped. Lloyd had bought it with a win on the football pools and a large loan from the bank. He was willing to sell it for two thousand pounds cash, leaving her with plenty over to have the place decorated throughout and new furniture bought where it was required. Some pieces she would get rid of; other items only needed a good polish or a coat of paint. There was an airing cupboard full of reasonably adequate bedding and a kitchen full of dishes, including pots and pans and cutlery. The sisters were out there now, making tea.

There was also a magnificent cat. With a woeful lack of imagination, for obvious reasons it had been christened Tabby, and he was taking his time getting to know people. It could be because he badly missed his previous owners that he was still so distant. After all, as Rose had reasoned, cats had feelings like everyone else. The children adored him.

Flora rubbed her hands together, as excited as the children. She couldn't wait for everything to be done so that she could start running her own fully functioning hotel!

One of the first things she did was change the hotel's name. From now on, it would be called Haley's. The children thought it an excellent idea for it to be named after their dad's favourite person. 'Much better than the Crown,' said Andy. 'We could put up posters of Bill Haley and His Comets in the entrance.'

'It's called Reception,' Rose told him, sticking out her tongue.

'Where would we get the posters from?' Simon wanted to know, practical as always.

No one had any idea until one of Isobel's sisters, Beattie, suggested they ask her daughter, Shirley, who was at the art college. Shirley managed to come up with an even better idea.

'We could paint a picture of Bill Haley on the wall behind the reception desk, so people will see him as soon as they walk in.' Shirley's seventeen-year-old face shone with enthusiasm.

'Who's "we"?' Flora asked cautiously.

'Me and the students I'm at college with. Shall I bring some of them along at the weekend?'

They arrived on Saturday morning, three boys and three girls, including Shirley, bringing photos of Bill Haley in various poses for Flora to choose from. They regarded their task with a gravity befitting Michelangelo when he was commissioned by Pope Julius II to paint the ceiling of the Sistine Chapel.

When it was finished, it was odd, but the face looked more like Kerry's than it did Bill Haley's, though the kiss curl and the guitar left no room for doubt about who it was meant to be.

By then, the students were stripping wallpaper off the would-be guests' bedrooms, anxious to paint more walls. To be paid to display their talent so early on in their careers was like a dream come true.

O'Shea's young, old and in-between, as well as friends, were appointed to various positions in the business. Alice Brannigan was put in charge of breakfasts; her daughter Meriel, who went to school with Rose and Alex, helped at weekends. Calum Reilly, Sheila's husband, who'd recently retired from the merchant navy, was made manager of the bar and went on a management training course run by the brewery who would supply the hotel. Flora thought wistfully that it was a job Kerry would have taken to with enormous enthusiasm. The sisters took turns being laundry maids and chambermaids and managed to run everything smoothly.

The transfer of the liquor licence from Lloyd Francis to Flora O'Shea had already been applied for. Flora wanted the bar closed for the shortest possible time, otherwise she might lose long-standing customers. For the time being, she made do with the horrible oatmeal carpet, arranged to have the easy chairs re-covered ten at a time with hard-wearing tan velour, which toned in perfectly with the walls, now no longer a miserable green but daffodil yellow. The bar itself was framed with coloured lights.

Flora had taken advice offered by Andrew, and had made her employees part-owners of the business. 'If they are entitled to a share of the profits, they will be conscious that they are working for themselves, not just for you. This is a truly socialist idea, Flora, and I'm sure Kerry would have approved.'

Haley's bar was full to capacity the night it reopened, and an article appeared in the next day's *Liverpool Echo*. It included a photograph of the Bill Haley painting in reception, as well as some flattering remarks about the landlady, Flora O'Shea, and her get-up-and-go attitude. It was a venture *bound to succeed* according to the final comment.

Oh, but it was such a shame, thought Flora, having to give up the house in Pearl Street where she had lived with Kerry, and where their children had been born, and that held so many lovely memories. She had already discovered that it was possible to be happy again, but never as much as with her dear, darling husband.

Little in the house had changed over the years, apart from the colours on everything gradually fading so that it was now a lighter, paler, rather worn version of the one she had moved into all those years ago. She left behind the expensive furniture and pretty curtains that Isobel had bought for Nana. The sisters could sort things out for themselves.

When he was eleven, Simon had sat the eleven-plus, and a letter eventually arrived to say that he had passed and would attend St Anthony's grammar school in Waterloo. Although Flora was full of pride over Simon's achievement, she largely kept the news to herself, not wanting to make a fuss.

Long ago, Flora had realised that Andy was deeply resentful of Simon. As time passed, it became obvious that the resentment was turning to dislike. For a reason Flora was unable to understand or explain, unlike Rose and Connie Andy was unable to accept Simon as a brother, but saw him rather as someone who didn't really belong in the house and wasn't a real member of the O'Shea family. This was true, of course, but not another person in the entire O'Shea clan appeared to think twice about it – or if they did, they didn't care. Yet Andy would complain bitterly, actually make an unpleasant scene, if Simon had one more guest at his birthday party than he'd had himself, or been given a present more obviously expensive than his own, in particular from his mother. He was a big boy, the tallest in his class, as if he were feverishly urging himself to grow taller and taller until he caught up with his older rival. All in all, Simon and his friend Liam were more like brothers than Simon and Andy.

It was the one single factor in their lives that Flora found most difficult to deal with, having to weigh things out constantly to make sure Andy wasn't being given less favourable treatment than Simon. Occasionally she might remonstrate mildly with her son, realising that if she made a big issue of it, it would only make things worse and Andy would resent Simon even more. Yet of all the family it was Simon, young though he was, who never once referred to what was happening, who had helped her get over the death of Kerry, seeming to have an almost adult understanding of how she felt. Secretly, she deplored her real son's behaviour. It worried her sometimes that, if he were some other woman's son, she might not like him all that much.

When Andy learned that Simon had passed the eleven-plus and would attend St Anthony's grammar school, he behaved more or less as Flora had expected, stamping out of the room, swearing that he would do the same thing himself when the time came.

The first guests at the hotel were the familiar ones of old, the travelling salesmen who had used Haley's as their headquarters when it used to be the Crown. Flora was pleased to have them back, though they were fewer than they'd once been.

Selling from door to door – brushes, encyclopedias, medical supplies – was fast going out of fashion. Nowadays, people preferred to buy over the counter, where they had greater choice. As for cough medicines, iron tonics and the like that had once been so popular, they could be prescribed free by a genuine doctor through the National Health Service formed after the war.

Lots of things were changing. Across the country, a more liberal attitude prevailed. The Prime Minister, Winston Churchill, had resigned and been replaced by Anthony Eden, reputed to be very much a ladies' man who had actually been divorced, though Princess Margaret, the Queen's younger sister, had not been allowed to marry the man she loved because he was a divorcee. Most people, particularly women, thought that grossly unfair.

Only basic, healthy meals for the guests were so far served in the restaurant; stews of one sort or another, casseroles, chips or boiled potatoes with more or less anything, followed by apple and custard, bread-and-butter pudding or spotted dick. There was trifle for afters on Sundays. When Flora felt the time was right, she would employ a trained chef and promote the restaurant side of the hotel. She rubbed her hands together, overcome with excitement – it had become a habit. One of these days, she half expected there to be sparks.

They all became older, if not wiser, the children grew bigger and the hotel prospered. O'Sheas died and O'Sheas were born. They got married, made their First Holy Communion and were confirmed. They saw more of each other than they used to, as now there was an O'Shea with a hotel that had a bar, and what better place to hold a party, a wake or a wedding reception – or just go for a pint?

Flora felt indeed blessed for the day she'd met Kerry O'Shea in the same bar and had become a member of this noisy, boisterous family. Or perhaps it was Isobel she should thank, for being her friend all those years ago when she was still a child.

Simon was in his fourth year at St Anthony's, where he was doing well, but he didn't like the place. He didn't say anything, but she had a feeling he would have sooner gone to the local secondary modern with Liam.

They were just jogging along, contented with their lot, working towards a better future, when the American came to stay and everything changed. It really only changed for Flora, but she felt as if the entire world had shifted on its axis.

Now she was reading Ed Laine's letter, reading it again and again until she could have recited it off by heart. She turned the paper over. The words went away, yet she could still see them; when she closed her eyes and buried her face in her hands they were still there.

Of course she knew what a concentration camp was like. There'd been enough about them in the newspapers at the end of the war, and she'd seen them on the news at the pictures. They were unbelievably horrible places. She deliberately avoided thinking about what might – what would almost certainly – have happened to Simon if she hadn't been at the station in Zurich on that beautiful April morning.

What was she to do? What did Ed Laine intend to do? Return again in a number of years, if what he said in the letter was right, which she didn't believe. It was obvious he'd written it so consumed with rage that he probably couldn't remember what he'd said. His actions were unpredictable. Whilst he was still in the country there was a chance he could turn up at any moment. Or he might arrive when Simon came home from school. In a matter of hours, Simon's father could have taken his son away and she would never see him again.

She remembered the day Ed Laine had arrived – the Yankee Doodle Dandy, as Shirley had called him.

'He's here,' Shirley had hissed when Flora arrived home with a bag full of groceries. There'd been enormous interest when a man with an American accent had telephoned to book a room. 'He's very nice; dead handsome, in fact. A bit like Montgomery Clift; sort of quiet. I bet you anything he's dead clever.'

'Where is he?' Flora had asked.

'Gone for a walk.'

Flora had been too busy to seek him out until after dinner.

He was in the bar, talking to the lads. Shirley was right. He was good-looking, in a restrained sort of way, indeed more like Montgomery Clift than openly handsome types like Tyrone Power or Clark Gable, She took to him immediately, though not in the same way it had been with Kerry. Then, it had been a strong physical attraction. With Ed Laine, it was more a case of understanding, of just knowing they would get on well together. She could have sworn he felt the same. On the Saturday, when they were in Reception waiting for the charabanc to take them to Southport and Shirley had suggested he come with them, Flora had remonstrated with her but had secretly wished he would come – a ridiculous idea when the man was a guest.

And if he had come, then he wouldn't have broken his leg, she wouldn't have discovered the letterhead from the École Clemence in his room, and what would have happened then? She had no idea, and doubted if he did either.

Taking a deep breath, Flora got to her feet and went into the kitchen, where Alice was washing the dishes. 'Do you mind looking after things by yourself this morning?' she asked.

'Of course I don't, luv,' Alice said brightly. She was so grateful at having been given a job that Flora sometimes felt uncomfortably like Lady Bountiful.

'I need to go out for a while, but I shouldn't be long.'

'Take as long as you like, Flora. There's only four guests. And they've all had their brekkie. All I have to do is wash the dishes. After that I'll tidy meself up a bit and go on Reception.'

Flora blew her a kiss. 'Thank you. You're an angel, Alice Brannigan.'

Half an hour later, Flora left the hotel. She had pulled back her hair, securing it with a black and gold enamelled slide, powdered her face, painted her lips and lightly applied brown mascara to her long, pale lashes. The turquoise cotton dress she had changed into with its embroidered bodice was her favourite, flattering her slim figure with its stiff, white belt that she buckled as tightly as it would go. She put on a new pair of nylons and her white court shoes – the heels needed repairing, but Ed Laine was hardly likely to notice – if he was willing to talk to her, that is. No matter how smart she looked, there was a chance he wouldn't even allow her into his room at the Adelphi.

'We don't have a Mr Laine staying here,' the toffee-nosed male receptionist informed her when she presented herself at the hotel, so much superior to her own.

'But I had a letter from him this morning,' Flora told him in her poshest voice. She was secretly in awe at the grandeur of her surroundings: the beautiful tiled floor, the marble pillars, the massive staircase. 'He's American. He's waiting to see me,' she lied.

'Is he staying with Mr Kingsbury?' the man enquired, relaxing slightly. 'He's an American.'

Flora had no idea who Mr Kingsbury was. 'Yes,' she said.

'All right, then. Go on up. They're in Suite Four on the second floor. The lift's over there.' He nodded to somewhere behind her.

Minutes later, Flora was knocking on the door of Suite Four, hoping it was the right one. It was opened by a distinguished looking gentleman with silver hair, who regarded her coolly. 'Yes?'

'I'd like to see Ed Laine, please. Tell him it's Flora.'

'I'll ask him.' The door closed with a snap. It opened seconds later. 'He'll see you now. You're not to tire him.'

Flora entered the room where Ed Laine was seated on an elegant settee, his plastered leg resting on a stool. He wore striped pyjamas and a towelling dressing gown, and his hair was slightly ruffled. 'Hello,' she said nervously. 'How do you feel?'

'Lousy.' He nodded towards a small table covered with a

lace cloth on which stood a silver coffee pot, cups and saucers. 'Sit down, help yourself to a drink.'

Flora sat down, ignoring the coffee. The silver-haired man said, 'I'll be off now, Ed. I'd like to have a quick look around Liverpool while I'm here. The nurse should be along soon to help you wash and dress.' Flora was treated to another cool look. 'Goodbye,' he said, adding an unexpected smile.

'Goodbye,' she replied.

'So long, Hugo,' Ed Laine said. The door closed. 'Why are you here?' he asked Flora accusingly.

Flora wasn't sure. 'To say how sorry I am.' It was at least one of the reasons.

'You could be sorry for the rest of your life; it will never make up for what you did.'

Flora's mind went back to the day it had happened, as it had thousands of times before; the day Ed's wife had handed over her baby to a stranger. The memory was so real that she actually cradled her arms, looking down as if there were a baby lying there. She could almost feel his weight, smell his smell, sense how upset and uncomfortable he was.

'He felt like mine,' she said softly, 'as if she had genuinely given him to me; not just then, but for ever.' She looked at Ed. 'I don't suppose you believe that, but honestly and truthfully, I loved him straight away.'

Ed sighed. 'Have you never felt any guilt at all?'

'Oh, yes,' she cried. 'Often. But if I'd approached someone, the Red Cross, for instance, and told them about Simon, they could well have taken him away from me. He might have ended up in a home, his relatives never found. I couldn't risk that happening. I made a life for him. He's always been happy.'

'I think he would have been happier with me, his father.'

She looked at him challengingly. '*As* happy, possibly, but not happier.'

'How can you know that? You are unbearably arrogant.' His eyes narrowed. 'If I didn't have such difficulty getting around and my back didn't hurt quite so much, right now I feel so angry I could kill you.' He ran his fingers dejectedly through his hair. 'And just as easily love you.'

'I could very easily love you back,' Flora whispered. *Had she really said that?* Had he heard? And had he really meant what he'd said? She contemplated crossing the room to kiss him, but it was too soon. And anyway, she didn't have the nerve.

There was a long silence until he said, 'I'm sorry about the letter. I was just getting things off my chest. I'm as angry with myself as I am at you. It had never crossed my mind that Simon would still be alive.' There was another long silence, and again it was he who broke it. 'What are we going to do?' His tone had changed, become less emotional, more matter-of-fact.

It seemed he didn't intend taking Simon away, at least not immediately. She was about to mutter plaintively, 'I don't know', but decided she should match him and said firmly, 'See what happens next, I suppose.' Then she remembered something. 'Do you intend telling his grandparents that you've met Simon?' she asked.

He shook his head irritably. 'No, I can't think of any news that would make Lilith happier, but Martin, the grandfather, would be over here like a shot making one hell of a fuss. For Simon's sake, I wouldn't want that to happen.'

There was a knock at the door and Flora opened it. A woman in a nurse's uniform was standing outside. 'I'm here for Mr Laine.'

Flora let her in. She gave Simon's father a half-smile and left. It was a very sudden and not very satisfactory ending.

But *was* it an ending?

The first sign that it wasn't arrived that afternoon in the form of a bunch of perfect red roses sent from a florist's in the town centre. There wasn't a card or message of any sort. Flora had just arrived home after collecting Connie from school.

'You've got a secret admirer, Mum,' Rose remarked. She and Andy too had not long returned home. Connie was playing with the typewriter, with which she was fascinated.

'There's no card. They might not be for me,' There was little privacy in the hotel, particularly when the children were there.

'Can I have one to stick behind me ear?' Rose was an extremely pretty, extrovert child, full of confidence. She hadn't passed the eleven-plus and didn't care.

'If you like. Mind you don't prick your finger, or your ear, on a thorn.'

Andy appeared, looking bad-tempered as usual. 'Mam, when will Simon be here?' He was waving the envelope that had arrived that morning addressed to him, Simon and Liam.

'Same time as usual, love.' Simon didn't get home from Waterloo until at least half an hour after the others.

'Why can't me and Liam open this now?'

'Because it has Simon's name on it, as well as yours and Liam's. You'll just have to wait.'

He aimed a kick at the wall. 'That's not fair.'

'It seems entirely fair to me, Andy.'

'And me!' Rose made a face at her brother, and he scowled back.

Simon arrived about a quarter of an hour later, the envelope was opened and ten one-pound notes were discovered to be inside. There was a message on Adelphi notepaper to say that the money was for new cues and to have the snooker table recovered.

I hope there's enough, Ed had written at the bottom. He wished the three boys good luck.

'How much is that each?' Andy was counting the notes. Liam was eyeing them, dumbstruck, never having seen so much money before.

Flora took control of the situation. 'You can have a pound each to buy a cue,' she told them. 'I'll find out how much it will be to have the table re-covered, and you can share what's left over between you.'

'Ed must be out of hospital, and he's moved to the Adelphi. Why didn't he come back here, Flo?' Simon frowned. 'Does that mean we'll never see him again?'

'A friend has come over from America to help him get home with his broken leg,' Flora explained, assuming this to be the right explanation for Hugo Kingsbury's presence at the Adelphi. 'They're staying in a suite.'

'A suite!' Simon was impressed.

Flora couldn't wait for them all to disappear and for dinner to be over so that she could have the time to sit and wonder what the roses meant. And if they meant what she thought they did, what sort of return gesture should she make?

She would send Ed a photograph of Simon as a thank you for the roses. He'd had one taken last term, in which he looked thoughtful and serious; parents had been invited to buy copies. Flora had bought three; one for herself, one for Else and Andrew and one for Isobel. She hadn't yet sent Isobel her copy, and was reminded that it was quite a while since she'd had a letter from her.

'Will you write a little note to Ed,' she asked Simon, 'thanking him for the money?' She'd get the other two boys to write messages at the bottom. She thought about sending a photo of herself, but discarded the idea immediately. That would have been incredibly conceited of her.

'Mr Kingsbury and Mr Laine are leaving the day after to-morrow in the afternoon,' she was told when she telephoned the Adelphi.

'Thank you.' The day after tomorrow was Sunday, which meant the lads could go into town in the morning, Saturday, to buy the cues and deliver the letter and the photograph to the hotel. Simon was, of course, unaware that the tightly sealed envelope addressed to *Mr E. Laine, Suite 4* contained his school photograph. Flora knew that Liam Brannigan felt honour bound to buy a billiard cue, but was anxious to give his mother any money that might be left over. Gerard, his father, had moved out of the house in Pearl Street years before, leaving Alice to manage on her own, which she was managing to do successfully. Liam had grown up to be a lovely lad and a best friend to Simon, and Meriel was a sweet little girl.

They returned, Simon, Liam and Andy, in a boisterous mood, each carrying a billiard cue in a canvas case. It seemed that the doorman at the Adelphi had been disinclined to allow them in, even when shown the letter addressed to Mr Laine. He had insisted on taking it to the reception desk himself.

'But before he could take it, this silver-haired geezer butted in,' Liam explained to Flora, eyes bright and cheeks flushed with pleasure at the memory. 'He was just coming in and he told the doorman to let us in too, so we could hand the letter over ourselves.'

'Then,' Andy interrupted, eager to have his turn in the telling of the tale, 'after we'd delivered it, he said he was a friend of Mr Laine, and asked if we'd like afternoon tea.'

'But it was still morning,' Flora exclaimed. They'd left at about half past nine.

'I know, and that's what the hotel said, but *he* said, the silver-haired geezer, that it didn't matter that it was morning, we were to have afternoon tea. "And no stinting," he said to the waiter. What does "stinting" mean, Mam?'

'No holding back,' explained Flora. 'You were to have loads of everything. And did you, Simon?'

Simon rolled his eyes. 'We all felt stuffed by the time we'd finished. There were sarnies, about six different sorts, loads of dead gooey cakes, buttered scones and cream . . .'

'And strawberry jam,' Liam added.

'And as much tea as we wanted,' Andy finished with a satisfied sigh.

The silver-haired man was quite obviously Hugo Kingsbury, who had turned out to be much nicer to the lads than he'd been to her, though she recalled he'd given her a lovely smile before he'd left.

The snooker table was duly re-covered with smooth green felt. By word of mouth, the story of Ed Laine's generosity spread, including the provision of afternoon tea by his friend at the Adelphi hotel. His name became something of a legend at Haley's.

'Perhaps we should paint a picture of him on the wall as well,' suggested Shirley.

'I don't think so,' Flora said hastily. 'This hotel has hardly been open five minutes. Over the years, we might have guests who are much more interesting than Ed Laine.'

But hopefully not quite so troubling.

Chapter 21

In no time at all, it was December. The hotel was closed for Christmas Eve, Christmas Day and Boxing Day, though the bar remained open. Flora reckoned that on those three days, her children would require all her attention. Of course, during this time, various O'Sheas continued to drop in for a cup of tea or something stronger, often bringing presents. Every now and then, a new relative would appear that Flora had known nothing about: Auntie Mabel from the Old Roan, for instance. Mabel had never before appeared at a function due to the fact that her husband, Arthur, had cut himself off from the family because of a real or imagined slight many years before. But Arthur had recently died, and nowadays Mabel was able to go anywhere she pleased.

On Christmas Day, after dinner, Flora and her children listened to their entire collection of Bill Haley and His Comets records, singing along and jiving to songs like 'Shake, Rattle and Roll' and 'See You Later, Alligator' and wishing with all their heart that their dad could have been there to join in.

New Year's Eve, and Flora was busy from the minute she got out of bed until the time she got back into it at something like three o'clock the following morning, when the year had turned and become 1958. It had been an emotional day, with quite a few sad moments as well as many happy ones.

There'd been a name on the list of guests expected that day,

John Smith, and somehow she'd got it into her mind that it was a pseudonym for Ed Laine, though why he should do such a thing she had no idea. She'd been expecting to him to arrive all day, but when John Smith came after tea it turned out that he was there to see his elderly mother who lived nearby, and who already had a house full of relatives, so couldn't put him up. He looked nothing at all like the man she hoped he would be.

Then there'd been a Miss Devlin on the list, and it wasn't until quite late when the bar was packed and the clientele, who weren't normally given to singing, were belting out all the old war songs, it being New Year's Eve: 'We'll Meet Again', 'There's a Boy Coming Home on Leave', and 'Goodnight Sweetheart'. Some couples were dancing. Flora was finding the atmosphere quite heartbreaking when her name was called and there was Isobel, who she'd quite forgotten was also called Miss Devlin, pushing her way through the packed bar towards her.

From a distance, she looked more beautiful than Flora had ever known her, blue eyes shining and enormous, but as she got nearer it was obvious that Isobel's eyes looked so big because her face was considerably thinner – quite haggard, in fact, and close up it was plain to see that she was sick, very, very sick. She was also wearing far more make-up than usual, and it was possible to glimpse the wrinkles on her neck through the frill of her frothy lace blouse. Her cheeks were flushed – either that, or she'd gone mad with the rouge.

Flora came from behind the bar and threw her arms around her old friend. 'You look well, Isobel,' she lied. 'It's ages since we've seen you . . . or heard from you, either.'

'I've been busy; terribly busy.' She laughed. Even her voice had changed; it was deeper, huskier, rather breathless.

Flora led her out of the room and into the foyer, where it wasn't quite so noisy. Sheila Reilly witnessed this, and went to help Cal, her husband, who was in charge behind the bar.

'Your sisters will have a fit once they find you're staying here. Every single one of them would rather you stayed with them.'

'Which is why I'm staying here, Flora; then I won't hurt anyone's feelings. Or at least, it will hurt all their feelings equally.'

'Would you like to go to bed? You look dead tired.' Behind the glitter in her eyes, she looked exhausted.

'On a night like tonight? Not likely. I haven't gone to bed before midnight on New Year's Eve since I was about ten.' She laughed again. 'Anyroad, you just told me I looked well.'

'You do, you do, but you also look rather tired. Would you like something to eat then, or a cup of tea, maybe? Have you unpacked? Would you like me to help you?' Flora was at a loss to know what to do. This wasn't the Isobel she'd always known, that she was used to.

'No to everything,' she cried. 'What I'd like is a gin and It – and go easy on the It! Oh, and put it on my bill.' She giggled. 'Actually, I wouldn't mind a little sit-down before I go back into the bar, where I'll sing and dance and have the time of my life.'

'Go and sit in the office and I'll get you your drink.'

'Get one for yourself too, Flora,' Isobel shouted after her. 'I don't like drinking alone.'

Flora was back within minutes. Her own gin and It comprised nothing but water. Normally she only drank wine, and never touched a drop of anything while she was working. Isobel was sitting in the little easy chair where Flora sometimes sat to do the accounts and write letters.

'Who do you know in America?' Isobel asked. She was looking at the Christmas cards that had arrived from former guests at the hotel, and firms that Flora had dealt with – those from friends and family were in her private quarters.

'Mrs Charlesworth,' Flora said. 'I've told you about her before. She knew Simon and me in Zurich. Every year without fail I send her a photograph of him and she sends us a card.'

She also knew Ed Laine, but nothing had been heard from him since September, when he'd gone home. It could be years until he got in touch with her again – when Simon was older, as he'd said in his letter.

'I love her card; it's a photograph of Times Square in New York. Many years ago I actually spent New Year's Eve there. It was a riot.'

'Really?' Flora frowned. She recalled standing Mrs Charlesworth's card on the living-room mantelpiece. It had a teddy bear dressed like Father Christmas on the front. 'Which card are you talking about?' she asked Isobel.

'The one with the photo surrounded by holly.' Isobel reached for the card – it was clearly an effort – and opened it. 'It's from someone called Ed, and he wishes you, the kids and Shirley a very Merry Christmas and a Happy New Year. He ses he hopes the lads are managing to play better snooker with their new cues.' She paused for breath. 'Sounds like a guest who got to know everyone pretty well. Did you send him a card? He's written his address here.'

'Someone must have opened his and just put it there without mentioning it to me. It's been very hectic lately.' She was cross with whoever had done it. 'I'll tell you about Ed tomorrow, when it's quieter and we have more time.'

At midnight Connie was fast asleep but Simon, Rose and Andy were wide awake and had been watching television with Tabby, who was fascinated by the screen. If football was on, he would sit on top of the set and try to catch the ball with his paw.

She felt a sense of achievement after 'Auld Lang Syne' had been sung, everybody had more or less kissed everybody else, the evening had ended and most people had gone home, apart from a dozen or so O'Sheas who stayed behind for a little party of their own – Isobel included. The holiday period was nearly over. All in all, everything had gone extremely well.

Of those who had stayed were Beattie and June, and they regarded their sister worriedly. Over the last few hours, Isobel's eyes had become even brighter and her cheeks yet more flushed as she had joined in the singing and dancing with every bit of energy she possessed. She looked like a flower at the height of its beauty, on the day before it begins to wilt.

Until now, Simon hadn't realised she'd arrived. To Flora's surprise, he was clinging to her hand possessively, as if over all the years she'd been away he'd badly missed her. She recalled how much he'd loved Nana, and reminded herself in the morning to show him and Andy the card that had come from Ed Laine – and Liam, as soon as he arrived.

When Flora woke and looked at the clock – it was five past ten – she jumped out of bed with a yell, then fell back, overcome with dizziness. She had guests requiring breakfast, and when she'd left the bar in the early hours of the morning, it looked as if war had broken out in there. It urgently needed a good clean-up.

There was a knock at the door and Alice Brannigan came in. 'Are you all right?' she asked. 'I thought I heard a scream.'

Still dizzy, Flora looked at her through a cloud of stars. 'What's happening out there? I've slept in. Has everyone been fed?'

'Of course they have,' Alice said indignantly. 'I'm in charge of breakfasts, aren't I? Have you ever known me be late?'

'Oh, Alice, what would I do without you?' Her head was gradually becoming clearer, 'I'll get dressed straight away and start tidying up.'

'There's no need,' Alice said, blithely. 'The kids have already done it; your four and my two, I'm making them a nice big trifle as a treat. You stay there and I'll fetch you a cuppa.'

Simon brought the tea. He wore his oldest trousers and a brown hand-knitted jumper full of holes that was his favourite.

'I understand you've all been very busy,' Flora said. 'I'm really grateful, love.'

'It was fun. We had a game to see who could collect the most empty crisp packets.'

'Who won?'

'I made sure Connie did. She didn't realise it was fixed and is dead pleased with herself.' He was thoughtful beyond his years, as if he was only pretending to be a child of fourteen to please everybody and secretly he was twenty or even more.

'Are you happy, Simon?' she asked, and immediately wished she hadn't,

'Of course. What a funny thing to ask.'

'I sometimes wonder, that's all. I lost my mum and dad when I was six, much older than you were and have often wondered what it would be like to grow up with a mother and father, like most children. Do you ever wonder the same thing?' A few times over the years he'd asked about his parents. 'I hardly knew them,' she would tell him, hoping that would do. It seemed it had.

He sat at the foot of the bed, frowning as he contemplated his lot. 'I've had a family ever since I can remember, Flo; you and Kerry, Andy and my sisters – even Liam, in a way. I feel as if we all belong together, one big family. I mean, Kerry was like my real dad too.'

Flora squeezed his hand. 'That's good.' He sounded terribly old and wise. 'Oh lord!' She jerked forward, spilling the tea in the saucer. 'Isobel! I'd forgotten all about her. I wonder how she is this morning.'

'Alice knocked on her door, but she didn't answer. She thought it best to leave it till she wakes up of her own accord.' He looked at Flo curiously. 'She was acting dead weird last night.'

'I thought so too. I'll try and find out what's wrong later, when I can get her by herself.' Maybe a love affair had gone wrong. 'Oh, by the way, none of us realised, but a Christmas card came from Ed Laine. It's on the desk in the office. He's put his address on it. Perhaps you and the other lads would like to write back.'

His face lit up at the news. 'I'll go and find it.' He hurried out of the room. He'd really taken to Ed, which was as it should be since Ed was his father. Flora proceeded to torture herself; should Simon be told the truth now, or would it be better to wait until he was eighteen, an adult, and more able to accept the news, to react to it in a grown-up way? As usual, she had no idea what the right thing to do was. Things seemed to be going relatively smoothly; perhaps it was best to leave them that way.

For the first time ever, Flora lay listening to the sounds of her hotel being looked after by other people. A vacuum cleaner was being used upstairs, dishes were being washed in the kitchen, her daughters were chattering away some-where close and the boys were arguing; perhaps it was over Ed's card.

She got up at eleven, when she was told that Lillian and Noreen had arrived. They'd heard about Isobel from June and Beattie, and had come to see how their sister was this morning.

'Our June said she wasn't herself last night,' Lillian com-mented. 'Like she was at death's door, yet at the same time she was the life and soul of the party, and totally pie-eyed.'

Flora had no idea what pie-eyed meant – drunk out of her mind, the sisters explained. She agreed she would have described Isobel's behavior in exactly the same way. 'As far as we know, she's still asleep. We were wondering when we should bang on the door.'

Noreen offered to do it there and then. They went upstairs and she hammered on Isobel's door with her fist, as well as shouting her name with the strength of a fog horn. The girls came running to see what was happening; Connie was quite nervous.

'Coming,' called a calm voice, and the door was opened by Isobel wearing a royal-blue velvet dressing gown with slippers to match. A towel was folded over her arm and she carried a leather toilet bag. 'Good morning. I was just about to have a bath, if nobody minds.' She appeared to be perfectly well.

'Of course no one minds,' Flora stammered.

'Hello, Lil. Hello, Nor.' Isobel kissed her sisters affectionately.

'We were told there was something wrong with her,' Lillian said when the bathroom door closed, 'and it wasn't just the drink.'

'Well, there did appear to be something wrong,' Flora confirmed. 'But she seems all right this morning.'

Isobel's behaviour continued to be unpredictable over the days that followed. Sometimes, she would sleep for hours in the middle of the day, then Flora would hear her going back and forth between her room and the bathroom during the night. Her eyes either drooped with tiredness, or they grew huge and shone with a frenetic energy that had her going for walks for hours on end along the Docky wearing a beautiful sable coat. Simon would go with her.

'I've always loved the Docky,' she would say.

'Well, mind you don't get run over there,' Flora warned. 'That's what happened to our American guest; he had his leg broken.'

She had wanted to tell Isobel about Ed, about him being Simon's father and who had been living in Italy with Simon's mother, Grace, when the Germans came one day and took Simon and Grace away. In fact, ever since Isobel had appeared on New Year's Eve, she had been waiting for the right moment for them to have a talk. Andrew and Else aside, and now Ed, Isobel was the only other person who knew the truth. But there never seemed to be a right moment. Either Isobel would be asleep, or much too on edge and fizzing over with energy to listen, or she would be, quite frankly, pie-eyed after drinking half a dozen gin and Its. Anyway, she was nothing like the Isobel six-year-old Flora had met all those years ago in Aunt Winifred's house in London, or when she'd come to Liverpool, where Isobel had treated her with unreserved hospitality and kindness.

Flora hated to admit it, if only to herself, but she wished her old friend would go back to London. Yet Isobel swore to her sisters that there was nothing wrong, flatly refused to see a doctor, spent ages on the telephone in the office, insisting on privacy, so that no one else could use the room while she was there. Once, she sent Simon, who she seemed to talk to more than anyone, on a message.

'A message for what?' Flora demanded to know when he got back.

'Headache powder,' Simon replied. He held up a little white packet. 'I got it from a chemist on the Dock Road.'

'Powder!'

'She said it's like Beechams Powders.'

'We have tablets for headaches here.'

'Her headaches are very bad,' Simon said gravely. 'She explained it all to me. Tablets aren't strong enough, not like this powder.'

Why was she talking about headaches with a fourteen-year-old boy? And why hadn't she asked Flora or a grown-up to get the powders?

One afternoon, Isobel and Noreen, the eldest of the sisters, had a blazing row. It was the first time Flora had known the women have anything more than a mild argument.

There was snow on the ground, and the children were still on holiday from school. Connie was upset by the shouting. So was Simon, though he said nothing and went out alone, leaving Alex and Liam to play snooker by themselves, which was most unlike him.

'What was that all about?' Flora asked Noreen when she emerged from her sister's room.

'I'm sorry, Flora.' Noreen seemed embarrassed. 'It was about everything and nothing, I just asked what the hell was up with her, insisted she pull herself together, and she tried to pretend everything was perfectly fine. I mean, it's obvious something's wrong. Anyroad, she's just said she's going home.'

At that moment, Isobel poked her head out of her room. 'Flora, will you please phone for a taxi to take me to Lime Street station in about half an hour? Thanks, darling.' The door closed and Noreen burst into tears.

'Now what have I done? The others will kill me.'

Flora felt confused. She wanted Isobel to leave every bit as much as she wanted her to stay.

Isobel stayed in her room until the taxi arrived. She refused all requests to come out and talk. Flora hardly had time to say goodbye, just a quick peck on the cheek and a quick 'tara' as her friend rushed by, virtually falling into the taxi on top of her luggage. When Simon came home and found her gone, he was so upset that, for the first time in his life, he shut himself in his room and refused to come out.

The telephone rang about an hour later. Flora hoped it was Isobel calling from Lime Street station to say goodbye properly, or even apologise for her hasty departure. Instead, the caller was a man.

'Is that you, Flora?' Ed Laine enquired angrily.

'Yes,' Flora sat down with a thump.

'My mail has just arrived, and there's a letter from Simon. Are you aware you have a drug addict on the premises?'

'*What?*'

'A drug addict. Apparently, she's a lady who goes by the

name of Isobel. Simon seems to be quite attached to her. Do you know she sent him out for drugs? Cocaine, I should imagine.'

Flora had a strong urge to lose her temper and burst into tears at the same time, 'How on earth do you know Isobel is on drugs?' What was wrong with being on drugs, anyway? 'She's not been herself, that's for sure, but it's because she's ill, that's all. She takes powders for her headaches. Anyway, she's just gone back to London.'

'I'm glad about that, Flora, but she shows all the symptoms of being an addict. If she carries on doing it for long enough, it'll kill her.'

'I don't know what you're talking about,' she said pitifully. She'd never heard of cocaine before.

There was a pause, and when Ed Laine spoke again he was no longer angry. 'Of course you don't,' he said tiredly. 'I suppose I've lived in New York long enough to become familiar with all kinds of human weaknesses.' He paused for a moment and she heard him sigh. 'Taking drugs, and I don't mean headache powders or painkillers, but drugs that bend the mind, that induce feelings of amazing happiness followed by fits of hopeless depression, are quite common here. Eventually they can kill you. What does Isobel do for a living? Simon didn't say.'

'She's a model.'

'A model! Well, successful or not, she's part of a world, like show business, where drugs can become a big feature in some folks' lives. Another thing; not only is taking drugs against the law, but they cost the earth. I take it Isobel earns enough to fund her habit?'

'I would have thought so.' She couldn't be sure of that, having recalled Isobel saying she was now too old for the modelling jobs she used to get.

'How is Simon's snooker coming along?' Ed enquired,

thankfully changing the subject. 'I received his letter, obviously, and those from the other boys.'

'Well; very well, in fact.' She had no idea how Simon's snooker was coming along. 'I won't tell him that you called. I think that's best, don't you?' Simon was still shut in his room.

'Infinitely the best,' he said drily. 'We can't have his father upsetting the apple cart, can we?'

It had never crossed anyone's mind, not even her sisters, that Isobel was taking something harmful called cocaine. Though Flora couldn't help but wonder why Simon had mentioned Isobel in his letter to Ed. Was it because he could say things to him that he couldn't to Flora? Something about Isobel must have worried him.

It was still snowing when January neared its end. Connie had had a birthday, the children were back at school and everything had returned to normal, when one day Alice answered the telephone in the office and told Flora that a woman with a dead funny accent wanted to speak to her.

'I think she must be from London,' she said. 'She talks like Tommy Trinder.'

Flora picked up the phone and said, 'Hello.'

'Is that Flora O'Shea?'

'Speaking.' Alice was right; the woman had a Cockney accent.

'Hello, darlin',' she said. 'My name's Heather and I'm sorry to be ringing you out of the blue like this, but there's loads of addresses in Isobel's stuff, and yours is the only one we could find with a telephone number – apart from her agents and magazines, and the like.'

A warning bell began to ring in Flora's head. 'That's all right. Is something wrong?'

'More than wrong, darlin'. I'm afraid Isobel's dead. She died in her sleep last night.' The woman began to weep. 'It gave us a terrible shock.'

Flora tried to hold back her own tears. There'd be plenty of time to cry later. She went over and closed the office door. 'What did Isobel die of?' she enquired.

There was a pause, until the woman said tearfully, 'There has to be – what's it called – an autopsy, that's it.' She paused again. 'Me and the girls think it was a heart attack. Isobel complained she hadn't been feeling well lately, and she'd been to the doctor's with her heart.'

'I see.' Flora wanted to know if it was anything to do with the drug Isobel had been taking, the cocaine, but couldn't bring herself to ask. 'Thank you for calling,' she said politely, 'I'll let her sisters know.' She took Heather's telephone number, put down the receiver and burst into tears.

Isobel Devlin might not have had the O'Shea surname, but she was one of the most significant members of the family. Like Kerry, Flora's husband, Isobel's photo had been published, if not in the newspapers, then in numerous magazines. On several occasions, she had gone all the way to Paris and New York to show off the latest fashions to some of the richest women in the world. No one had suspected she'd had a problem with her heart.

Her distraught sisters composed a short history of Isobel's life and sent it to the *Liverpool Echo* and the *Bootle Times*, along with a photograph showing Isobel at her most beautiful; swathed in white lace with little diamonds in her ears.

And she was to be buried in Bootle; there would be no argument about it. It didn't matter how much it would cost to have her body brought from London to the place where she'd been born, and where she would be surrounded by people who had known and loved her.

The house in Pearl Street, the one at the bottom of the street next to the railway line, where Flora and Kerry had lived and where their children had been born, was now occupied by Evelyn and Gladys Moran, the spinster daughters of one of Nana's cousins. They were only too willing – honoured, in fact – to have Isobel's coffin placed in their parlour where people could come and pray.

Heather and four of her friends – Isobel's friends – insisted on coming to her funeral. As soon as she set eyes on them, Flora knew that these women weren't models – or at least, not the sort of models who appeared in classy magazines or trod the catwalk in major cities of the world. They had on too much make-up, and wore clothes that were cheap and gaudy without any sense of style. They were nice women with kind hearts, but not the sort who would be accepted into polite society. Had Isobel become one of these women too? Flora's heart bled for her old friend.

They had brought Isobel's valuables with them: her jewellery, a small amount of money, an unopened bottle of Guerlain's Shalimar scent and some clothes in a snakeskin suitcase with a handbag to match.

'We hope you don't mind if we don't stay for the wake,' Heather said after Isobel had been buried and the car had brought them back from Ford Cemetery to Haley's, where Alice had made mountains of sandwiches and numerous pots of tea. For the hundredth time Flora reminded herself that she must buy an urn for these sorts of occasions. 'It's important we get back to London tonight.'

'It was really good of you to come,' Lillian said emotionally. Isobel's friends, and her sisters, knew they were unlikely ever to meet again.

The friends departed for Lime Street station in a taxi. After they were gone, the sisters and Flora went into the office of the hotel.

'What's happened to everything?' Beattie wondered aloud as they stared at their sister's few possessions on the desk, including the sable coat. 'I mean, our Isobel had loads of dead expensive jewellery, real pearls, like, and some lovely rings with proper jewels. And she had three or four fur coats, not just one. Those women won't have taken them, surely?'

'They seemed awful nice,' June commented. 'I mean, if they've pinched her stuff, they wouldn't have come to the funeral, would they?'

'Let's face it, if them women are models, then I'm the Queen of England,' Noreen said sarcastically. 'I don't like to say it, but I reckon our Issy went right off the straight and narrow before she died. How long was it since we'd seen her before she turned up on New Year's Eve? It must have been at least a year.'

'And then she acted dead peculiar,' Lillian said.

Isobel must have sold her jewellery and her furs to buy cocaine, Flora concluded. Ed Laine had said it cost the earth. Flora felt convinced the heart attack that had killed her had been brought on by drugs. But she would never tell that to her sisters. And anyway, they were already suspicious.

'Don't cry, Flora, luv.' Lillian squeezed her arm. 'We're all upset, naturally, but our Issy had a good life.'

Flora wiped her eyes. She hadn't realised she'd been crying.

The wake wasn't raucous, not like Nana's. As with Kerry, this was a relatively young person who had died, a beautiful woman taken before her time, and it was not an occasion for Irish jigs or happy songs.

When everyone had gone, and Haley's had returned to being a hotel and the bar was full of guests and ordinary members of the public, Flora retreated to her office again, this time alone. There, she locked the door and telephoned Ed Laine. Rather oddly, he was the only person she wanted to talk to.

'What time is it there?' she enquired when he answered.

'Half three – in the afternoon,' he replied. 'Is that the reason you called, Mrs O'Shea, to ask the time?'

'Of course not,' she said tetchily. 'I was worried it might be the middle of the night.'

'New York is five hours behind Britain. We have several time zones in the States, and some cities are six or seven hours behind.'

'Why aren't you at work?'

'I *am* at work – I work at home.' He made an impatient sound, like a *huh*. He clearly found her irritating.

'I'm so sorry to have disturbed you, Mr Laine. I wanted to tell you something, but I'm obviously being a nuisance. Good—'

Before she could finish the word, he said hurriedly, 'You're not being a nuisance. Please tell me why you called.'

'Isobel's dead,' Flora blurted out. 'She died of a heart attack, and was buried today.' The autopsy had confirmed it.

There was a pause before he said gently, 'I'm sorry. How's Simon taking it? He seemed to be very fond of her.'

'He was. I was too. She was incredibly nice to us when we first came to Liverpool – we only came because of her in the first place.' A sob came to her throat, and she wondered what would have happened to her and Simon if it hadn't been for Isobel. 'She was the kindest person I've ever known.'

'I'm sorry,' he repeated. 'You must have had some adventures in your time, you and Simon.'

Flora nodded. 'We have indeed.'

'I met Andrew and Else,' he said. 'They are very fine people.'

She nodded again, then remembered her aunt and Johnnie Lucas. 'But there were a few who weren't so fine.'

At the other end of the line, far away in New York, she heard him sigh. 'When will we meet again, Flora?'

'Whenever you want,' she whispered. 'You're welcome to come any time.'

'Easter – shall I come then?' His voice was suddenly low and tender.

'Yes, Easter.' Easter would be perfect.

After the unexpected death of Isobel, and the ambiguities that remained over the precise reason for it, Flora could well have felt deeply depressed, particularly on those days when she imagined how unhappy her friend must have been not to be chosen any longer for the top modelling jobs. She had probably noticed every new wrinkle, perhaps the beginnings of a double chin, an increasing waistline. If only she had shared her feelings with her sisters, or with Flora, who would have told her that she would always be beautiful no matter how old she grew. Instead, she had resorted to cocaine to boost her failing confidence.

But Flora had far too much to do to let herself brood over things. At the end of February, the Lancashire branch of the Bill Haley fan club were coming to stay, all forty of them, for a long weekend. Initially she had turned them down. She only had ten bedrooms, and they weren't exactly large. 'I couldn't possibly take forty people,' she told the secretary on the phone.

But the secretary didn't care how few bedrooms she had. 'We've only just heard about your place,' he told her. 'There's nowhere else in the whole of England where we'd sooner stay. I mean, Haley's, a hotel dedicated to the King of Rock 'n' Roll! I understand you have a painting of him in Reception.'

'Well, that's true,' Flora conceded. 'But we still only have ten bedrooms, and the kitchen isn't big enough to fry forty sausages, let alone bacon and eggs as well.'

'We'll bring sleeping bags and sleep on the floor,' the man told her. 'Just give us cornflakes for breakfast and something simple for our tea – we'll pay the going rate. You won't be out of pocket.'

Knowing that Kerry, who'd been so mad about Bill Haley, would have welcomed all forty members with open arms, Flora knew she had no alternative but to take the booking.

She discussed the menu with Alice, and they decided on a

buffet breakfast; an assortment of cereals, gallons of milk, loads of toast and plenty of jam.

'As for their tea,' Alice said, 'we could give 'em mashed spuds and order steak and kidney pies from that fish and chip shop in Marsh Lane. I'd really enjoy making half a dozen trifles for afters.'

Flora gave her a warm hug. 'Oh, Alice, if I'm not careful the Adelphi will be poaching you to work for them.'

'Don't worry, Flo, I'll turn them down. I bet it's not half as much fun working there as it is here.'

A few days before the Bill Haley fan club were expected, Simon cornered her in the office, which had become the place where important things happened, critical decisions were made and vital matters discussed.

He threw himself into one of the chairs on the other side of the desk and informed her that he wanted to leave school. Flora moved to the other side herself and sat beside him. This was serious, and she didn't want a large piece of furniture stuck between them.

'But you're only fourteen,' she said. 'You can't officially leave school until you're fifteen, and at St Anthony's the leaving age is a year older.'

'I know, Flo,' he said a touch impatiently. 'I don't want to leave school altogether, just transfer to Liam's secondary modern where it's far more interesting and more *useful*,' he emphasised. 'I can't abide Latin.' He frequently complained about having to learn a dead language, which would be of no use to him until he was dead himself. He sighed, slouched into the chair and lapsed into a weary silence.

Flora regarded him, frowning. There were times when she wondered if he was getting too old for her – his voice was already starting to break. He needed someone much cleverer than she was to help with his homework, and to talk to about life and death and the world's great problems. He actually *looked* clever, *handsomely* clever, with green, curious eyes and a high forehead. He had a trusting, vivid face and people seemed to take to him immediately. With her encouragement, he'd never had a proper haircut, what was termed a 'short back and sides'. His dark red curls were allowed to flourish untamed and uncontrolled. She visualised the poet Byron looking much the same as a youth.

'You'd hardly be at Liam's school two terms when you'd be fifteen and have to leave,' she pointed out. 'What do you want to do when you grow up?' she went on when he didn't answer. This was something they really should have talked about before.

'I dunno,' he said with a shrug.

'You must have some idea. I mean, Rose wants to be a film star, and Andy a lumberjack.'

He managed a grin. 'What about Connie?'

'She wants to stay with me for the rest of her life, but I'm sure she'll change her mind when she gets older.'

Simon cocked his head to one side and thought. 'I know what I fancy,' he said after a while, 'but it might be a bit difficult to achieve.'

'What's that?' It couldn't be more difficult than becoming a film star or a lumberjack.

'Seriously, I'd like to have something to do with the law; criminal law. Become a solicitor or a lawyer or a barrister – I don't know the difference between the three.'

Neither did Flora, but there was one thing she did know. 'You'll need Latin to study law,' she advised him. 'In which case, you'd be mad to leave St Anthony's.' She was surprised he wasn't aware of that himself.

'I'm worried about Liam,' Simon said. 'He gets badly bullied at school. He's so small, smaller than most of the girls. Hardly a day goes by when he doesn't get a clout off some lousy bully. I thought if I went to his school, then I could protect him.'

So *that* was the reason he wanted to leave. Flora gasped. 'But that's awful! It's dead unfair. Does Alice know?'

Simon wrinkled his nose. 'He doesn't want her to because it'd upset her. If the bruise or the cut is visible, he tells her he fell over. Don't say anything to her, will you, Flo?' he said anxiously. 'There's nothing she can do about it.'

'She could complain to the school.' Flora wouldn't have minded complaining to the school herself on Liam's behalf. 'Anyway, Simon, it's very good of you to want to leave St Anthony's and help Liam, but it'd mean leaving at fifteen, which is the wrong thing to do if you want a career in the law.' She leaned across and patted his head. She felt proud of him; it was a noble thing he'd wanted to do for his friend.

'D'you mind if I write to Ed? He's a bit of an expert on the law. He has put a lot about it in his books.'

'You can write to Ed as often as you like.' She frowned. 'What books?'

'His crime novels. I've ordered two from Bootle library.' He left the room, and seconds later she heard him playing snooker in the bar with Andy and Liam. Ed Laine, a novelist! She'd thought he had something to do with newspapers.

On a Friday evening at the end of February, the Bill Haley fan club descended noisily on Haley's, and there was scarcely a quiet moment until they left at midday the following Monday.

There was huge excitement in Reception when they saw the painting of their hero on the wall. Quite a few genuflected, and others pretended to go into a trance. Some had brought guitars, and little concerts took place frequently in different parts of the hotel. Had Kerry had been there, Flora reflected, he would have been in his seventh heaven.

Things returned to normal on Tuesday after the fan club had departed. The hotel that had seemed much too noisy over the last few days was suddenly too quiet. However, the club had booked to come again in November.

Ed Laine would have been flattered to know how much the staff at Haley's were looking forward to his second visit to the hotel. The three boys were anxious for him to see just how much their snooker had improved with the help of their new cues and the re-covered table. Shirley, now working in an advertising agency in Bold Street, had announced she intended making a special visit to see the 'Yankee Doodle Dandy', as she referred to him. Rose had apparently acquired a bit of a crush on him. The other staff, who'd been sorry he'd had an accident and had left without saying goodbye on his first visit, were glad he was coming again.

As for Flora, she was unsure how she felt; in love with him one day, out of love the next. One of the problems was that she was still in love with Kerry, and it seemed like only yesterday that he'd died. She didn't think she could bring herself to let another man touch her. But did Ed Laine want to touch her in *that* way? And was it right to form a relationship with the man who was Simon's father?

If only Isobel were still alive! *She* would have known what to do.

He arrived at exactly the time he'd told her to expect him – mid-afternoon on the Thursday before Easter. The boys were wearing their best clothes in his honour; not that anyone had suggested it. They were in Reception, making a nuisance of themselves as they waited for his taxi.

'He's here!' It was Andy who first noticed the taxi, and they rushed outside to help with his luggage, though last time he'd only brought a small bag. This time the bag was slightly larger. His outfit, khaki trousers, check shirt and cream jacket, was much more informal than the average Englishman wore. His shoes were navy-blue cotton with cream laces. He looked casually handsome.

'Hi there.' He smiled at Flora over the boys' heads, though

Simon must have grown a little since September; the top of his head was level with Ed's ear.

'Hello.' She returned his smile calmly; at least she hoped she was calm. 'Would you like coffee?' She'd bought an expensive brand especially for him.

'Yes, please.'

'Boys,' she said sternly, 'will you please leave Mr Laine alone.' They were dancing around, all talking at the same time. 'He's had a long, tiring journey and would probably like a little rest before he watches you play snooker. Go into the dining room, Mr Laine, and I'll bring you your drink in there. Would you like a drink?' she asked the boys as they trailed after their hero. They all grunted something that she assumed was a form of 'Yes, please'.

'I'll get them.' Alice had been listening. 'You go and entertain our favourite guest. What those three lads need is a decent bloke in their lives,' she said as she was leaving. 'It's not much use having one who lives on the other side of the world.'

It was almost midnight. Only two couples remained in the bar. Apparently, they had met during the war, two boys and two girls, at a dance in Bootle town hall, had eventually married and as couples had moved to different parts of the country. Today was the fifteenth anniversary of the wonderful night they'd met – though Flora couldn't help but notice that one couple looked far less happy about it than the other.

She was in her office, tapping her fingers impatiently on the desk, not because she was anxious for the guests to go to bed so that she could go herself, but Ed Laine had gone out and she was waiting for him to come back. She hoped he hadn't been knocked down again or been attacked, his wallet stolen and was lying bleeding somewhere in a gutter. There were parts of Liverpool where it wasn't safe to be alone late at night.

The couples went to bed. She wondered if the pair who were unhappy wished they'd chosen a different partner.

Another half an hour had passed before the American came in. Without thought, she blurted out, 'I've been worried about you. I've been half expecting the police or a hospital to ring and say you'd been hurt.'

'I'm fine,' he sang. He looked extremely happy, and she wondered if he'd had a bit too much to drink. 'I went to a club called The Cavern and heard something called skiffle for the first time. Chap there by the name of Lonnie Donegan; "My old man's a dustman," he sang. I tell you, Bill Haley's got nothing on this guy. He's a genius. Fact, I was thinking of opening up a hotel along the road, calling it Donegan's and having a picture of Lonnie painted on the wall. Haley's will crack under the competition.'

She smiled. 'Do you think so?'

'No, not really.' He sat down. 'Is it all right if tomorrow I take the boys into town and buy them boxing gloves?'

'Boxing gloves!' Flora made a face. 'I think boxing is a brutal sport; men hitting each other mercilessly until one falls unconscious to the ground. Simon, for one, would hate it.'

'Simon approves,' he said surprisingly. 'I suggested it in my last letter. I don't know if you're aware that he worries about Liam. Apparently, the poor kid gets knocked about at school. But although he's small, Liam is wiry and quite strong. He might possibly make a decent boxer and be able to stand up for himself.'

'Simon mentioned he was having trouble.' She felt ashamed for having ignored the news about Liam, apart from the initial feeling of shock, when if it had been one of her own children, she would have gone to the school and raised hell. 'Are you a boxer yourself?' she asked.

He grinned and shuddered delicately. 'I'm a total coward. I'd be too scared to even wear the gloves, in case it gave some guy ideas. No, there's a gymnasium not far from here. The boys could go there as often as they want for as long as they want. I'll meet the bill.'

Flora felt obliged to agree that it was a good idea. 'But you won't be able to get the gloves tomorrow, it's Good Friday and all the shops will be closed. Make it Saturday instead.'

'OK, Saturday.' He reached across the desk with both hands and captured hers. 'Why don't you come with us?'

'I can't. I have a hotel to run.'

'Not for twenty-four hours a day, seven days a week, surely?'

'Something like that.' Her hands were tingling from his touch, her arms, all of her. She didn't know how to deal with this man.

Possibly he felt much the same, because he said, 'I don't know what to say to you.'

Flora thought of Kerry, and tears came to her eyes. As soon as he saw the tears, Ed released her hands. 'I'm sorry. Is it too soon?'

'It shouldn't be. It's years since Kerry died, but the thing is, I imagine him up in heaven keeping an eye on me.'

'Would he mind knowing you were with someone else?'

She shook her head. 'No, he'd be thrilled to bits, but it's me; I don't like the idea of him watching. Don't you feel the same about Grace?'

'Not after such a long time.' His expression sobered. 'Sometimes, the years with Grace seem no more than a dream. There was nothing normal about them. It was like being in a movie, playing a part.' He looked at her keenly, his eyes narrowing. 'But you do something to me, Flora, as the song goes.' He smiled, but it was a sad smile. 'Do you feel the same?'

'Yes,' Flora whispered. 'Yes, I do.'

'Let's wait, shall we?' He touched her cheek with his finger. 'Until the time comes, I shall think about you night and day, as another song goes.'

★

They made love a few days later.

It was Easter Monday. Flora had applied for an extended licence, and there was an unexpected event. Tommy O'Shea, Kerry's dad, had won £117 on the pools and had decided, only that morning, to throw a party. Since then, Flora and her staff had been busy getting things ready.

Ed Laine made the trifles, dozens and dozens of them in little round cardboard containers big enough for one person. He stood for ages in the kitchen – getting in everybody's way, though Flora didn't like to tell him – putting in a single slice of peach, a cube of pineapple, two grapes and a spoonful of chopped cherries in each carton and covering it with jelly. He used to do it for his mom, he explained, when he was a little boy and they were having a party.

It was such a nice gesture, and Flora liked the way he was mucking in, as if he were a member of the family, and also that, unlike many men, he didn't mind being seen in the kitchen surrounded by women.

She danced with him at the party. He *felt* like a member of the family, as if he was a close friend, even a boyfriend, and she'd known him for ages. The party over, it seemed quite natural to go back to his room, where they made love. Even that felt faintly familiar, as if they'd done it before. It wasn't earth-shattering or mind-blowing; more warm and hugely enjoyable, and there was something about it that made them laugh rather a lot.

He came to stay again within a few weeks, and they telephoned each other regularly. It wasn't exactly a courtship. They knew they would get married once Simon had been told the truth about his birth, and that Ed was his father.

Alice and Sheila soon became aware of their relationship. Flora tried not to make it too obvious, mainly because she preferred that the children didn't know, particularly Simon, and she didn't want it to become a talking point with the O'Sheas.

She frequently thought of how lucky she was; what a lovely life she was leading. It wasn't exactly perfect, but almost.

Flora also knew how foolish it was to think like this, for who knew what shocks and calamities lay waiting around the corner.

The next summer, everything fell apart.

Part 3

Chapter 22

New York,
June 1959

Mrs Rhona Charlesworth had always been glad that she'd moved from Zurich back to New York all those years ago. During her time away, she had forgotten what an *intimate* place the city of her birth was. How, even in quite expensive apartments such as her own in Gramercy Park, you could see right into your neighbours' windows and chat to them in the hall. And, in her opinion, it was such a classless city – she frequently held long conversations with shop girls and taxi drivers and waiters in restaurants. Everyone felt equal to everybody else.

Rhona's sisters and her brother had died over the years, leaving her on her own at the grand old age of seventy-five. Had she lived anywhere else, she might have felt lonely, but she had scores of friends and met with the closest on an almost daily basis.

Today, for instance, she was lunching with Kitty Oppenheimer, who she had known since childhood. Afterwards, they would go for a stroll in Central Park as long as the rain held off – it was early June, but they were experiencing a showery period. If it was wet, they would visit a museum or an art gallery.

It meant Rhona had the entire morning to prepare for her lunch appointment, leaving her with enough free time to watch one of her favourite programmes on television.

In Rhona's opinion, television was just about the best thing invented since the world began. A person would never be lonely if they had a TV set in the room. There was hardly a programme she didn't love to distraction: *The Jack Benny Show* and *The Andy Griffith Show*, for instance; *Perry Mason, Candid Camera*, *The Price is Right* – all were her favourites. When *I Love Lucy* ended, Rhona had joked she might well kill herself, she had loved it so much. But other shows had quickly taken *Lucy*'s place.

This morning, for instance, *Monica Martin Meets* . . . was on a local New York channel at half past ten. What made the programme interesting was that the person interviewed was always a woman who Monica would be very tough with near the end, asking revealing questions, sometimes even quite rude ones. The women who were in business or politics were capable of holding their own, and the film stars, actresses and writers were prepared for their interviewer's prying remarks and had their answers ready. Occasionally a woman was taken aback and became upset or justifiably angry – just after Christmas, millinery designer Talullah Pitts had thrown her glass of water in Monica Martin's face when it was hinted she was a lesbian. Rhona had cheered, and imagined all the other women in New York who were watching cheering along with her.

After showering, she wrapped herself in a towelling robe, made coffee and at twenty-five past ten, turned on the television and snuggled down on the couch to watch *Monica Martin Meets* . . .

The guest this week was Lilith Lewin, wife of Martin Lewin, owner of the jewellery company with shops all over the world. She looked in her sixties and Rhona had never seen her before, though Martin Lewin himself was a relatively famous personality, often appearing in programmes about the economy or politics.

From the bathroom window could be seen the narrow, square building on Seventh Avenue with more than eighty floors with the name LEWIN visible in coloured lights on all four sides. Rhona's wedding and engagement rings had been purchased five decades before in Lewin's jewellery store on Fifth Avenue. She held up her hand and looked at them, sparkling still, after spending all these years on a finger considerably more wrinkled now than when the rings had first been put there by the youthful, long-dead Ezra Charlesworth. It made her feel as if she had something in common with the beautiful, rather sad-faced woman on the small black-and-white screen.

Mrs Lewin was there to promote libraries. Libraries for poor children all over the country, libraries plentifully stocked with suitable books, libraries where children could sit and read and do their homework undisturbed and in perfect peace.

Rhona resolved to contribute towards this admirable objective later by writing a cheque and posting it that very day. She loved reading, had read daily to her daughter, Antonia, when she was alive and couldn't imagine life without books and the time to read them.

The interview was drawing to a close. Lilith Lewin was clearly a shy person, slightly withdrawn, but her eyes had shone with passion when she'd described her aim – to provide libraries full of books for needy children.

'Did you read to your own children, Lilith?' Monica asked when the interview was almost over.

'Oh, yes, indeed,' the woman replied in her soft voice. 'Josh, my son, got bored quickly, but my daughter Grace adored the books of Louisa May Alcott and Susan Coolidge. I read them to her over and over again until the time came when she could read them herself.'

The *Little Women* books and the *Katy* series! They had also been Antonia's favourite books. Monica Martin had asked a simple question, but Rhona hadn't liked the way it had been delivered, a way that suggested she was about to follow it with another more probing and unwelcome one.

'Your daughter and her baby son – your grandson – died in Auschwitz during the Second World War. Is that not the case, Mrs Lewin?'

To Rhona's horror, Mrs Lewin burst into tears. 'Yes, oh, yes,' she sobbed. 'We lost our darling Grace and her little boy, Simon. He was only six months old, and my husband and I had never so much as set eyes on him.'

Monica Martin had never looked so uncomfortable. She enjoyed shocking people, making *them* feel uncomfortable, but her interviewee's reaction indicated that this was a desperately vulnerable woman whom she had deeply hurt. 'I'm sorry,' she stammered. 'Would you like to tell us what happened?'

'Grace was living in Italy,' Mrs Lewin whispered, tears streaming down her face. 'It was 1944, and the Germans had overthrown Mussolini and were now in power. About Easter time, they came to the house where Grace lived with Simon and her husband, Edmund, as well as several other people and took them away. They were put on a train that it was assumed was going to Auschwitz. Edmund was out working. When he came home, everyone had gone.'

Rhona got up from the couch and switched the set off, unable to watch any more. She had understandably considered herself unfortunate enough to lose her own daughter at a young age, but at least she had been with Antonia throughout her illness, had held her hand as she drew her last breath, had been able to kiss her smooth white brow as she lay in her coffin and visit her grave by a little Swiss church. She suddenly felt the urge to visit the grave again, just once, before she died.

Poor Mrs Lewin. Such a nice, gentle woman. How terrible being left to imagine what her daughter and her little grandson's eventual fate had been, how greatly they would have suffered. Rhona wasn't sure if she could have borne it.

And what a coincidence, she thought later as she combed her hair in front of the dresser mirror, preparing to go out, remembering the school in Zurich with Andrew and Else, and young Flora who'd rescued baby Simon off a train on its way to Zurich. What a coincidence that Simon and Mrs Lewin's grandson should have the same name. And a further coincidence that it had happened at about the same time, Easter 1944.

Rhona laid down the comb and stared at herself in the mirror. Her face was a picture of shock and horror. She recalled that, at the time, Andrew had deduced the train had come from Italy and was likely to be on its way to Auschwitz. The family of *that* Simon had never been found after the war was over, for hadn't Flora sent her a photograph of him every Christmas since, including the last one, when he was fifteen?

She continued to stare at her stunned reflection in the mirror. Had Flora *tried* to find Simon's relatives? Rhona had always assumed that she had tried and failed. But what if she hadn't tried at all? She recalled how much the girl had loved the baby she had found – as much as any mother.

Could they . . . could they possibly be the same child?

Well, she certainly intended to find out. Rhona dressed quickly in her new dark green linen dress and white silk turban, changed her bag from the small crocodile-skin one to a capacious leather one, into which she put all the photographs and letters that had come from Flora over the years and been kept in a shoebox in her wardrobe. She telephoned Kitty and told her she would be late because something earth-shattering had come up and that she would tell her about it when they met, then set off, shaking badly, feeling quite wobbly, in fact.

She had no idea where Mrs Lilith Lewin lived, but she knew where her husband worked – in the building she must have noticed many thousands of times over the years from her bathroom window.

Lewin's didn't occupy the entire building, she was told by an amused doorman, but merely the forty-ninth and fiftieth floors. He held her arm and led her to an elevator that went to the appropriate floor. It took off at such speed that Rhona emerged in an even more wobbly state than she'd been in before.

A pair of large glass doors with LEWIN'S painted on them in gold were on her left, through which a young woman in black and white stripes was seated behind a vast wooden desk, typing. Rhona went through the doors, leaned on the desk and said shakily, 'I would like to speak with Mr Martin Lewin, please.'

The woman stopped typing and looked up. 'Do you have an appointment?' she enquired brusquely. She was black-haired, very young, with bright red matching lips and nails.

'Well, no, but it's extremely important.'

'You can't see Mr Lewin without an appointment.' She turned back to her typing, effectively dismissing the older woman.

Rhona wondered if she was expected to disappear into thin air. 'It's about Mrs Lewin's interview on television this morning,' she insisted. 'I have what might well be some quite vital information.'

'We have already had two calls this morning regarding that interview. Exactly how much are you asking for your *information*?' The last word came out like a sneer.

A woman, considerably older, was coming along a corridor towards the exit. She wore an outdoor coat and carried a bag over her shoulder.

'I wouldn't dream of asking for money,' Rhona gasped, by now breathless with indignation. 'How frightfully rude you are, Miss Whatever-your-name-is. Oh, dear!' She desperately needed to sit down before she fell down.

'It's all right, I've got you.' The older woman put a strong arm around Rhona's shoulders and led her into a waiting room with an assortment of easy chairs and small tables. 'Sit down Mrs . . . ?'

'Charlesworth, Rhona Charlesworth,' Rhona gasped. 'I do

apologise. I'm not normally so feeble. In fact, I'm very strong and healthy for my age. It's just that I've had an enormous shock this morning, and your elevator didn't help, nor did the young lady outside. She made me feel dreadfully flustered, on top of everything else.'

'I'm sorry about Miss Brandt. She's not been here long, and clearly needs a stern lecture on how to behave with visitors. Anyway, Mrs Charlesworth, my name is Lenka Gorski, I started work at Lewin's when I was sixteen, took time off to join the army, get married and have a baby, then returned, a widow, last year to become Mr Lewin's secretary again.' She pressed her hands against her heart. 'So I am quite trustworthy. In what way can we help you?'

Lenka Gorski had such a nice face and a kind voice that Rhona was starting to feel herself again. She told her about having watched Mrs Lewin on television that morning, then explained how she had known Flora in Switzerland during the war.

'Flora Knox, her name was. She was an orphan. Such a pretty girl. And it was around Easter, I remember that quite clearly. It happened – Flora rescuing baby Simon – after she had seen me off on the train back to Zurich.'

She told Lenka that she and Flora, who had lived in Liverpool for many years, had exchanged cards and messages every Christmas since, and that Flora had always included a recent photograph of Simon, starting from the age of two. 'I have them in my bag, every single one.' She patted her large leather handbag as if it provided proof that the photos were inside.

'May I see them?'

'Of course.'

One by one, Rhona laid the photos on a table, starting with Simon as an infant, up to the latest received only four months ago, now a handsome fifteen-year-old, nearly a man.

Lenka Gorski looked very serious as she nodded just once each time a photograph was laid down.

'I see,' she said when Rhona had finished. 'May I take these to show Mr Lewin?'

Rhona put her arms protectively on top of the photos. 'No,' she said firmly. 'These are very precious to me. Mr Lewin must come here to see them, or I will take them to him.'

'I understand, Mrs Charlesworth. I will fetch him immediately. While you're waiting, would you like tea or coffee?'

'I would love a coffee, thank you. With cream, if you don't mind.'

'I will ask Miss Brandt to bring you some.'

Miss Brandt entered minutes later with a tray bearing coffee, cream and sugar. 'Now you've got me into trouble,' she hissed.

'No, I haven't, young lady,' Rhona said pleasantly. 'You got yourself into trouble.'

Mr Lewin came in with a rush, as if he had been blown in by a strong breeze. He was terribly good-looking for an older man, Rhona thought. At least six feet tall, well built though not at all overweight, with a strong face and slightly thinning brown hair. She found herself standing up to shake hands when, at her age and of her gender, she should have remained seated.

'How kind of you to bring your photographs for me to see,' Mr Lewin boomed. There was something about his voice that made her suspect it wasn't always so full of bonhomie.

He sat down and moved the table with the photographs so that it was in front of him. After staring intently at them for a full, silent minute, he looked up at Lenka Gorski and said quietly and urgently, 'Get Lilith here.'

'Straight away.' The woman left the room.

When he had finished examining each photo closely, he raised his eyes and regarded Rhona with the same intensity. 'I know you have already told Lenka how you came by these, but now do you mind telling me? Please speak slowly, I am finding it hard to take this in.'

She realised then that he was overcome with excitement;

his dark eyes glittered, but he was trying to control the feeling. Had he been alone, she felt sure he would have thrown his arms about and run around the office shouting for joy. She knew then that *her* Simon was *his* Simon, that she had found his grandson for him, that for him and his wife, something unbelievable, unexpected and astonishing had happened. And to think it had happened because of her! Rhona felt quite dizzy with it all.

It was only then that she thought about Flora.

Flora had spent Sunday in the Floral Hall in Southport, where a day-long conference had been held with experts advising small businesses on their liabilities when it came to income-tax and employment law, and the benefits they were entitled to if they did things properly. Several short films had been shown, lunch had been provided and there'd been two breaks for refreshments. It was exactly five o'clock when proceedings came to a close. Alice Brannigan, who had become assistant manageress of Haley's two years before, had accompanied Flora to the conference.

On the way to the station to catch the train home, the women stopped for a pot of tea and a cream cake. 'I love me kids,' Alice commented, 'yet at the same time it's nice when they're not around, and I can hear meself think for a change. I've really enjoyed today.'

Back in Bootle, Sheila Reilly was looking after the younger children – at fifteen, Simon and Liam were old enough to take care of themselves. It wasn't a particularly busy weekend at the hotel.

Flora agreed. 'I like getting away from Haley's too, to think about something different. Did you notice the clothes in the shop windows in Bold Street? There were some gorgeous frocks there.'

'Well as far as I'm concerned, Flo, they can stay there. They were too posh for me by a mile. I reckon some probably cost a whole year's wages.'

Flora laughed. 'Oh, well, it's a good job the shops were closed, else I might've bought myself a couple!' She'd try to get into town one day soon and buy some summer frocks at normal prices. '*Idiot!*' she muttered.

'What did you say, love?' Alice asked.

'Nothing.' She'd forgotten for the moment that she was pregnant. Ed had come from New York in February for her birthday, bringing with him dozens of red roses, a bottle of the best champagne and a pair of gold hoop earrings that nowadays she wore all the time.

They'd made love quickly, passionately and unexpectedly after tea when everyone else was either washing up or watching television. Flora hadn't forgotten how easily she'd fallen pregnant in the past when she and Kerry hadn't taken precautions, but this time she hadn't minded. She was four and a half months gone, beginning to show and perfectly happy to be having another baby with Ed Laine at the age of thirty-three. As yet, no one knew, not even Ed himself, who she wanted to tell face to face, not in a letter or on the telephone. He was expected to arrive in Bootle any day now and she would tell him then. If they got an emergency wedding licence, they could be married before the week was out. Of course, there would be all sorts of whispers and dark looks from some of the O'Sheas when the baby arrived months too early, but she was fully prepared to brazen it out.

She and Alice got off the train at Marsh Lane station and walked to the hotel. Flora had barely set foot inside when Rose, Andy and Connie virtually threw themselves upon her, quite clearly distressed.

'Mam, a really horrible man came,' Rose wailed. 'He tried to steal Simon.'

Flora was thrown back against the wall by their combined weight. '*Steal* Simon?'

'Yes, honest, Ma.' Andy's face was red with anger. 'He spoke like Ed, but in a really loud voice. He said he was Simon's grandad.'

Flora was aware of the colour literally draining from her face. She began to shiver. 'Where is Simon?' she asked.

'He ran away, Mam, him and Liam ran away,' Rose cried.

'Where to?' Flora croaked.

'I don't know, Mam.'

Sheila Reilly appeared, her hand on her throat. 'I think they've gone to Alice's house,' she said. 'Oh, honestly, Flora, it's been a terrible afternoon. This chap, his name's Martin something and he's a Yank, like Ed. As Andy said, he claimed to be Simon's grandad. He was in a really vile temper. His wife tried to calm him down, like . . .'

'His *wife*!'

'Simon's grandma, I suppose,' Sheila shrugged questioningly. 'She was a lovely woman, Flo. I suppose she's what you'd call a gentlewoman. Anyroad, she said they'd come back later. I hope you don't mind, but I suggested they wait until tomorrow, give you time to get used to the situation and talk to Simon. He didn't half look sick, poor lad.' The look she gave Flora wasn't unfriendly, rather accusing, as if she thought it wrong that Simon should have been left to discover at the age of fifteen that he had American grandparents; that Flora should have prepared him for the discovery a long time ago.

Flora was in no doubt that she was right.

She turned on her heel and left the hotel, Alice running behind, assuming they were going to her house. Flora's children had started to follow, but she heard Sheila say, 'Stay with me, kids.'

She was seriously out of breath by the time she reached the Brannigans' in Pearl Street, where the front door was wide open. The baby she was carrying must be wondering what the hell was happening. Alice was lagging some distance behind.

'Simon,' Flora yelled as she rushed inside. Through the living-room window, she could see him and Liam playing darts in the back yard. She went outside, her hands pressed against the stitch in her side.

'Simon,' she said more quietly.

Soon he would be sixteen; he had shot up over the last year or so and was close to six feet. His voice had broken completely; there was a little growth of hair on his chin. The baby she had reached for on the little station just outside Zurich had become an extremely presentable young man. His long trousers were a fraction too short; she kept meaning to let them down.

'You should have told me.' He came into the kitchen, closing the door behind him; Liam stayed in the yard. Alice had reached the front door and was coughing and spluttering in the hall. 'You should have told me I had relatives. You had no right to keep me in the dark.' He spoke with a mixture of false patience and real anger, while remaining superficially calm. Unlike Flora, he'd had time to get over recent events, if not come to terms with them.

For the moment, Flora didn't speak. She only knew about the grandparents because Ed had told her – and Ed had only found out by accident that he had a son. Until he'd turned up, Flora had known nothing about Simon's background. 'I'm sorry,' she said eventually. 'I intended telling you everything I knew about you when you reached eighteen.'

'Didn't you think I had a right to know before?' he asked mildly.

'I didn't know you had grandparents until relatively recently, until Ed turned up and said he was your father. Before that, all I knew was that you were put into my arms in Switzerland just over fifteen years ago by a woman who I was led to believe was on her way to certain death. It could only have been your mother. I was only seventeen myself. If I'd told the authorities I had you, they might have taken you away, but I wanted you for myself. Your mother had given you to *me*! I felt that I was doing what she had wanted, and that she had wanted me to keep you for ever.' She would have loved to have sat down, but there wasn't a chair in the kitchen. Instead, she leaned against the sink for support, still struggling for breath. Simon was roaming edgily around the room. He turned on the tap and turned it off again. 'I know I've been dead selfish,' Flora finished.

'Not just selfish, but irresponsible too, according to my grandfather. He's really mad at you.' It seemed odd to hear him say *my grandfather*! Despite the critical words, he smiled at her. For the first time, he was speaking to her as if they were both adults. 'I haven't really believed for a long time that we were cousins,' he went on. 'I just let you think I did. It must make me a bit of a freak, not wanting to know such important stuff like who exactly I was, but you were all I cared about, Flo, all I needed. I was really happy with the way things were. And I knew you'd tell me the truth one day, but I didn't realise it would be so complicated.'

'Neither did I. I'm sorry it had to happen the way it did.'

He stuffed his hands in his pockets and stared out of the window, to where Liam was still playing darts. 'You know, they showed me photographs. There was one of my mother and father at a party – it was when they met, apparently. And there was Ed, who's been my dad all this time . . .'

Before she could say anything about Ed, Liam came in through the back door. He glanced at them both, and could tell he'd intruded on a private conversation. 'Is me mam around?' he asked.

'She's at the front,' Simon said.

Liam uttered a chirpy, 'Okey-dokey,' and left the room.

There was silence for a while, until Flora said, 'What do you want to do now?'

What she meant was, do you want to come back to the hotel for your tea, or would you prefer to stay and have it here, with Liam? She felt something very close to terror when Simon replied, 'If you don't mind, Flo, I think I'd quite like to stay in New York with my grandparents for a while.'

Of course she minded. She hated the idea with all her heart. The walk back from Pearl Street to Haley's on her own seemed to take ten times as long as it had to get there. At home, the children bombarded her with questions.

'Where's Simon?'

'Is he all right?'

'That horrible man isn't coming back, is he?'

'Simon's having tea with Liam,' she told them, though she wasn't sure if that was the truth. All she knew was that she'd left him behind and he hadn't followed her. 'He's quite all right.' More than all right, she thought, looking back; perfectly self-controlled and happy about things, it would seem, though clearly annoyed with her and Ed. As for the horrible man – Martin Lewin – Flora didn't care whether he came back or not.

Two days later, Ed Laine arrived. Flora had telephoned to put him in the picture. It was early afternoon and the children, apart from Simon who was in London with his grandparents, were at school. The Lewins, Flora explained, were at the American Embassy, to see about getting a passport for their grandson.

'They want him to become an American citizen.' She didn't know why she grinned, but she couldn't help it when she thought about Martin Lewin's shocked face when he learned that Simon's birth certificate and the passport that had got him to England after the war were forged. Andrew had arranged for them to be done.

It appeared Ed already knew where Simon was. Lilith had

contacted him. In fact, he had stayed overnight in London and met the Lewins at the embassy. 'I'm his dad,' he said to Flora when they were ensconced in her office. 'I'm the one who has the final say on passports, and that sort of thing. I told them that Simon's birth had never been registered. And that, in fact, he'd been born at the beginning of September, not in August as you had guessed.'

'And you don't mind him becoming an American citizen?' Flora asked.

'Yes, I do, actually. I want him to have dual nationality, British and American, and that's what I insisted should happen. Don't you approve?'

'Well, yes.' She sighed. 'How was he with you? Simon, I mean.'

'Fed up. He thinks I should have told him who I was as soon as I turned up two years ago.'

'And why didn't you?'

He looked at her in surprise. 'Because I gathered it wasn't what you wanted, that you wanted to tell him the truth when he was older.'

'Oh, yes.' It was as if her brain had been removed and given a good shake before being put back in again, slightly substandard. She was totally mixed up. A letter had arrived from Mrs Charlesworth in New York saying she had met the Lewins, *such charming people*, and to expect a visit from them soon. *They think Simon might be their grandson. Isn't that marvellous news?*

'Marvellous!' Flora had remarked sarcastically at the time. 'What do you think about Simon going to New York?' she asked Ed now. She tried not to sound as hurt as she felt.

'I think it's a good idea.' He smiled at her encouragingly, 'It'll only be for a couple of months. He's probably finding all this a really big adventure. I mean, not every young man's lucky enough to discover he has a millionaire grandfather he knew nothing about.'

Flora couldn't help it. She burst into tears. 'I can't *bear* him going,' she wept. 'I can't imagine life without Simon.' Right from the start, she'd felt as if they were meant to be together, that it had been ordained by God.

Ed was instantly on his feet. He knelt beside her chair and took her in his arms. 'If you love him, Flo, you should feel pleased he's got so many opportunities ahead of him. With the Lewins' money, he can do anything he wants.'

'But at school, he's just sat his O levels,' she cried. 'He took ten, and felt confident he'd passed them all. In another two years he'll take A levels, and at eighteen he'll go to university to study law. What does he need other people's money for?'

'He can still do those things, Flo,' Ed said patiently. 'The money will ensure he gets a place in one of the very best law firms.'

'You mean in New York?'

'Well, yes,' Ed conceded, 'in New York. You have three other children, Flo – lovely children. What would Kerry think if he knew you were fonder of Simon than the ones you had together?'

'Oh, I'm not, I'm not,' she assured him. 'Please don't think that.' She must never let anyone think that. 'I love my children with all my heart.' It was just that she'd felt she had a special link to Simon. So far, there hadn't been a right time to tell Ed she was expecting *his* baby, or to talk about them getting married. It just didn't seem all that important right now.

She met the Lewins several times. Martin Lewin was icily polite, and made her feel like a major criminal responsible for one of the worst crimes in the world. His wife, Lilith, was entirely different. Flora would have found it impossible to dislike her, had she wanted to. She thanked Flora for taking care of their grandson all this time. 'He's an adorable young man, Flora,' she said gratefully. There was something about the way she said it, no doubt unintentional, as if the time had now come for him to be transferred to his real family. Flora had done a good job, and her task was over.

But Simon was talking about the subjects he would take when he returned to St Anthony's for his final two years. Flora held on to that. As far as he was concerned, he was going to New York for a long holiday, not the rest of his life.

Simon's papers took over a fortnight to be organized. The Lewins stayed in London, close to the American Embassy, so as always to be available if there was a query. Simon went to London twice; first to have his photograph taken, then to prove his existence and answer questions asked him by an embassy official.

Ed was due to return to New York in another few days. He had a deadline to meet with the book he was writing, followed by a tour of the East Coast signing copies of the book he'd just had published. He was annoyed that the Lewins were taking over Simon's life.

'But it's only for the time being,' he impressed upon Flora – and himself. 'He'll be back home soon.' He laughed mournfully. 'He's definitely gone off me since he discovered I'm his dad.'

'No one could go off you for long,' Flora told him. 'You're too nice. And by the way, you'll soon be a father again quite soon. If we don't get married quickly, Ed, I'll become known as a scarlet woman, and some of the O'Sheas, the narrow-minded ones, will cast me into the outer darkness.'

Ed couldn't have looked more happy had he tried. 'We'll get married as quickly as we can.'

It was early July, and Simon was ready to leave for New York. Flora understood from her numerous in-laws that a party was expected.

'But he's not going for ever,' she argued. 'Two months, and he'll be back.'

'Yes, we know that, but what about you and Ed getting married on the sly? That's two good reasons for a party. And I reckon there'll be a third before the year's out.' Beattie winked as she nodded suggestively at Flora's swelling tummy.

Flora couldn't very well refuse. It turned out to be one of the occasions when not a single O'Shea happened to be away, or was ill or too old or too frail to attend. The weather was lovely, and everyone was in the mood. What's more, they all loved Simon, who wasn't an O'Shea but who had been taken into their generous, willing hearts. This was a lad who'd passed the eleven-plus and gone to a posh school, who wanted to be a lawyer when he grew up. They were proud of him, and not at all surprised that some dead rich New York toffs had turned out to be his grandparents.

The New York toffs attended the party, and Flora couldn't help but be proud that such a huge, noisy crowd had turned up. She could tell the Lewins were impressed that their grandson was loved by so many people, who tousled his hair, kissed him and stuffed ten- or twenty-shilling notes into his hand.

'That's to spend on your holiday, lad,' they said cheerily. Or, 'Don't do anything I wouldn't do.'

'Oh, and don't forget to change it into dollars,' someone added sensibly.

Simon and the Lewins left the following morning. They were travelling to Heathrow, an airport on the edge of London, in a chauffeur-driven limousine that seemed to float away from Haley's, the engine hardly making any sound at all, Simon waving madly from the back seat.

Flora, Rose, Andy and Connie waved madly back, until the big car merged with the traffic and was out of sight. The children went indoors, but Flora stayed, waving at nothing. 'Two months,' she whispered, 'he'll be back in two months.' After all, he'd promised. And Simon wasn't the sort of boy who would break a promise.

Chapter 23

So far, what Simon had enjoyed most about New York was getting to know his uncle Josh. He'd been told just to call him Josh — and his grandparents insisted on being Lilith and Martin. It must be the American way. Anyroad, Josh was thirty-five and wickedly handsome, with dubious morals. He took Simon regularly to the movies, always in the afternoon. *Movies!* It sounded so sophisticated, going to see a *movie!*

Simon wrote and told Liam about it — and about the house as big as Bootle town hall on 98th Street where he lived, about ice-cream parlours and diners and going by taxi all over the place. *Though over here they call them cabs.*

Josh showed him how to hail a cab. Just lean out a bit from the pavement and raise your hand. 'Yell "cab," if you think it helps.' Josh also showed him how to smoke little black Turkish cigarettes, how to drink whisky — *Scotch!* — in a single swallow. 'Just literally throw it down your throat, old chap,' And the way to judge how soon you could expect a woman to sleep with you.

'It depends on the colour and texture of her lipstick. The thicker and brighter it is, the sooner she'll let you into her panties.' He taught Simon how to play poker, and took him to places behind restaurants, or in cellars, where the game had to be played in secret because it was against the law. Simon would inevitably lose the ten dollars Josh had given him. Josh would inevitably lose too, and much more than ten dollars.

Simon didn't enjoy the black cigarettes, and would stub them out after a single puff. The one time he had swallowed the whiskey he had coughed and choked for about an hour and had refused the second time a drink was offered. As for women, he was a healthy, almost sixteen-year-old male and had frequent thoughts about them, but wasn't remotely attracted to the type Josh pointed out. In fact, he found them utterly terrifying.

An intelligent boy, he had realised from the start what Josh was up to. With the aim of upsetting Lilith and Martin, he was trying to turn Simon into a younger version of himself. From the odd things muttered by the servants, Josh had turned out to be a great disappointment to his parents who no doubt thought the arrival of a nephew in the form of Simon would inspire their son to turn over a new leaf.

Simon had no intention of being influenced by his repulsive uncle, but truth be told, he was finding the dark side of life very entertaining as well as interesting, though he wouldn't want to experience it for long.

'Just tell the old folk we've been to the park,' Josh advised, after they'd spent the entire afternoon gambling illegally in an old hut on the docks.

Simon did, not to oblige Josh but to protect his grand-parents, who he rather liked, in particular his grandmother. Lilith was gracious and kind and, he could tell, loved him with all her heart, despite only having known him for such a short time.

There were four servants altogether, all of them black: a housekeeper, Maria, who was married to Graham, the chauffeur-cum-odd-job man – they lived in an apartment over the garage; a part-time maid who lived out and a full-time cook who had a cosy apartment in the basement with her son, Lincoln. Lincoln was still at school, and was teaching Simon how to play basketball using the hoop attached to the back of the garage. Simon didn't like to tell him that it was called netball back in England, and was considered a girls' game.

Josh's plan to corrupt his nephew was discovered after he had taken Simon to see a porn movie in a shabby little cinema in an area called Soho, that was very bohemian with its interesting little shops and restaurants. Simon thought the movie uproariously funny. The actors were so excessively *serious*. Quite frankly, he wasn't terribly sure what they were doing. There was a lot of huffing and puffing going on in the entirely male audience. He was glad when the film – the *movie* – was over and they could go home.

That night, Josh threw the ticket stub from the porn movie in the waste bin in his bedroom and next morning, Maria found it and showed it to Lilith, who showed it to Simon over breakfast – Josh never rose before midday.

'Darling,' Lilith said in a shocked, shaky voice. 'Did Josh take you to see this movie?'

Simon grinned. 'Yes, it was dead funny. I could hardly stop laughing the whole way through.'

That was the day Josh disappeared out of Simon's life, though no doubt he would return again one day. 'He's gone to California,' Lincoln told him later, 'Hollywood.' The entire household knew what had happened. Martin had gone to work in a flaming temper, Lilith was still as white as a ghost. Josh had been banished, not for the first time, and wouldn't be missed. 'He always goes to Hollywood when he's banished,' Lincoln grumbled. 'Me, I get sent to bed with nothing to eat. Jeez! This world ain't half unfair, Simon.'

There'd been times in his life when Simon may well have considered the world a trifle unfair – when he'd been hungry but wasn't allowed a second helping of pudding, for example, though it was only because there hadn't been enough to go round. Or if he'd had to wear his shoes until the soles were so thin they began to hurt – Flo would be doing her best to get together the money for a new pair.

But nowadays he was living in the lap of luxury, and he couldn't identify a single thing about it that was unfair. He had enough to eat of more or less anything he wanted – steaks an inch thick, ice cream galore, varieties of fruit he'd never seen before. Lilith took him shopping, and money was no object. He owned more clothes than he'd ever had; he possessed a genuine silver wristwatch, a leather wallet with his name on and a guitar that he was learning to play. Should he casually drop a hint that he fancied a car, he felt sure one would appear the following day, not that he had any intention of doing so. In America, kids could drive at an incredibly young age, but the weight of traffic in New York was horrendous.

He knew that this exceptional life couldn't go on for ever. In September he would return to Haley's and begin his final two years at St Anthony's. He missed his brother and sisters, he missed Liverpool, but most of all he missed Flo. He wrote her short, stiff letters, not quite knowing what to say, not wanting her to know he was having the time of his life in New York. Anyway, he reasoned, *this* was his home now. This was where his real relatives lived; his grandparents, his uncle – and his numerous cousins. He couldn't help but be annoyed with Flo for keeping things back that he should have known.

Yet just imagine if she'd done what Martin, his grandfather, insisted would have been the right thing to do when he was a baby – handed him over to the Red Cross, or some other agency, after the war was over. Just imagine growing up without her, without living in Pearl Street or at Haley's, never having had Kerry for a dad or Andy, Rose and Connie as his brother and sisters, or knowing Liam, the best friend in the world. Was it possible he would have been happier living here with his grandparents, or with Ed in his apartment in Greenwich Village, than with Flo and all those other people? It was something Simon would never know.

Lilith's two sisters and three brothers were married with children, who by now were married with children themselves, which meant that twenty-five young people were now Simon's second cousins, ranging from small babies to a guy called Geoff, the eldest, who'd been first to reach twenty-one earlier in the year. Apparently there'd been a big party for him at the Waldorf Astoria Hotel.

The family had been in banking for more than a century – they actually *owned* their own bank! All of them lived in New York, as well as owning country properties in places like Nassau County on Long Island, or the Hamptons, further up the coast. As with the O'Sheas back in Bootle, there always seemed to be a reason for a party. Simon had already been to a christening and a wedding-anniversary party. He had picnicked on a beach in Martha's Vineyard, and paddled a canoe in the frothy waves of the Atlantic Ocean. There were times when life in Bootle no longer felt real.

On Sunday, Graham drove Lilith and Simon to Lilith's sister's house on Long Island. It was a searingly hot August day. Simon had brought his swimming trunks and couldn't wait to plunge into the water.

'What's the occasion?' he asked his grandmother on the way.

'It's a fundraising event for the election of the next president of the US of A,' Lilith said with a satisfied smile.

'You mean Senator Kennedy?' People talked about the Democratic senator from Massachusetts all the time. Simon had seen him on television on numerous occasions. His Republican opponent, Richard Nixon, didn't stand a chance. Kennedy was a charming and charismatic individual who promised a new frontier. Black people adored him for wanting equality of treatment for them in every aspect of their lives. He was bound to be elected. Had Simon had a vote, he would most certainly have cast it in favour of John F. Kennedy.

When they arrived at the large white clapboard house, stalls had been set up on the lawn and it was crowded. The Stars and Stripes hung limply from a flagpole – there wasn't so much as the trace of a breeze. There were burgers for sale, home-made cakes, sweets and lemonade, knitted things like tea cosies and Fair Isle mittens and photographs of the would-be president, as well as bric-a-brac – white-elephant stalls as they were called back home. It was like a dead posh jumble sale; Flo would have loved it.

Simon ignored all the hard work and effort that had gone into filling the stalls with goods to sell, and made his way round to the back of the house where acres of smooth silver sand stretched down to the flat, glistening ocean. People were already swimming in the water and throwing balls to each other on the beach. He found the changing room, put on his trunks, raced along the sand and flung himself into the water where, he thrashed about like a maniac until he was exhausted, then came staggering out and collapsed on to the sand. It felt hot and silky against his face.

'Phew!' he gasped. He couldn't recall ever having felt so happy, so *satisfied*. This was better than Bootle, any day.

'Phew yourself.' Nick Gallant lay down beside him. Nick was tall, painfully thin and a year older than Simon. Of all the cousins, Nick was his favourite. They had loads in common. 'Nice day,' he said contentedly.

'Great,' Simon murmured. In fact, it was perfect.

'We're dead lucky, you know, compared with the rest of society, not just in this country but in the whole wide world.' Nick intended going into politics after he'd been to university. Right now, he went to high school, the equivalent of second-ary modern and grammar schools in England.

'Don't I know it.'

After a while, with the sun feeling too hot on his back, Simon plunged into the water again. Nick did the same, and they sauntered back to the house, Nick muttering that he didn't want to get sunburned. 'I did once, and it was like torture and lasted for days.

'How long are you staying in New York?' he asked Simon when they were sitting on loungers on the veranda in the shade. A maid had gone to fetch them iced lemonade.

'Another four weeks,' Simon said, wishing he hadn't sighed quite so deeply. 'I've two more years to go before I take A levels and go to university.' He expected to receive his O-level results soon. Martin was trying to persuade him to attend university in the States. 'Harvard or Yale, young fella,' he said coaxingly. 'They're the equivalent of your Oxford and Cambridge.'

Simon had promised to think about it, and felt inclined to go along with his grandfather's wishes.

'Why don't you stay and graduate here?' Nick suggested. 'Come with me to Edinburgh Academy. It's a really great place.'

'Edinburgh?'

'It's where I go, and it's not in Scotland, idiot,' Nick snorted. 'It's only a few miles from here. We wear kilts and dance jigs on speech days and parent days, sing "Auld Lang Syne" at the end of term and worship Bonnie Prince Charlie.'

'*Worship* him?'

'I'm joking – only about Bonnie Prince Charlie.' He laughed, and Simon noticed that he had a very prominent Adam's apple. 'The head, Gideon Hart, is a real character. There's no religion, he doesn't believe in physical punishment, so no one is ever beaten. Though you can get expelled pretty damn quick for bullying or doing anything violent. You're taught mainly by discussion. It's a great place to be educated, Si.'

'I thought you'd've gone to a Jewish school.'

'I would, except I'm not Jewish. My Jewish grandpa married a Quaker and my ma married my pa, who's a Baptist, so there's hardly any Jewish blood left in me. Didn't your ma marry a Catholic? That makes you half a Jew. By the way, my ma knew yours back in the thirties. They went to matinees of all the Broadway shows together.'

The maid arrived with their drinks in frosted glasses with long striped straws. She was extremely pretty. Nick beamed at her. 'Thank you, Amy.'

Amy beamed back. 'Thank you – sir!' The 'sir' was accompanied by a wink.

'Did they really!' Simon's mother had married Ed Laine, known then as Edmund MacLaine, a Boston Irish Catholic. Martin, his grandfather, had explained the history of their relationship as far as he knew it; they'd married in Paris, and were separated by the Nazis in Italy . . .

Simon forgot about Nick. He got up and wandered into the house. He was looking for somewhere quiet where he could think. This was easily done back at his grandparents' place where, servants apart and with Josh in California, there were only three people present. But not here; there were loads of folks around.

He went into a ground-floor room that had two sewing machines on a long table heaped with lengths of brightly coloured material. There was a small flowered armchair in the corner, on which he sat. Had his mother perhaps once sat in the same chair? Whose house was this? Did it belong to Nick's parents? He couldn't remember.

Simon closed his eyes and thought about what Nick had just said. His mother and Simon's mother had been friends. They'd gone to the theatre together. Simon had already been to 42nd Street, home to a number of theatres. Not much more than twenty years ago his mother had done the same.

His *mother!*

Grace.

There were photographs of her all over the house on 98th Street; on tables, on shelves, on mantelpieces. She'd had long black hair and brown eyes. Martin was openly miffed that his grandson looked more like his father than his daughter, his beautiful Grace. It made Simon feel just a tiny bit uncomfortable.

Lilith and Martin rarely talked about Grace. Perhaps they were waiting for Simon to speak first, ask questions.

So far, Simon hadn't asked questions because she didn't feel real. In fact, it was hard to believe she had ever been part of his life.

But Grace had gone to 42nd Street with Nick's mother – Helena, her name was. Perhaps they'd strolled arm in arm, or held hands, shared chocolates together at the theatre. Perhaps she'd confided in Helena after meeting Edmund MacLaine for the first time, the man she would eventually marry.

Simon was clutching the arms of the chair, his body stiff, his eyes tightly closed, concentrating . . . concentrating . . .

Ah! There she was! His mother, girlish, not much older than he was now, walking along 42nd Street . . . heels tapping on the pavement, skirt swishing, talking very fast. *He could actually see his mother* . . .

He shouted something. It was just an anguished roar, and meant nothing.

Lilith came in. 'I've been looking for you everywhere, darling,' she said brightly. 'Someone said you'd come in here.' Her voice changed. 'Oh, Simon, dear, are you crying?'

She came and pressed his head against her breast, gently stroking his hair. 'There, there, darling.'

'I want my mother.' His tears were wretched, like those of a small child. He couldn't have felt more different than he had just a few minutes before, when he'd been on top of the world.

'And so do I, darling. So do I,' Lilith whispered. 'Your grandpa and I have missed her, our Grace, more than anything in the world. But having you here with us has made up a little for all those years of loss.'

He could understand that. He was his mother's flesh and blood, as she was theirs.

'Shall I ask Graham to take us home, dear?' Lilith suggested. 'You're obviously not very happy here. If you like, we could go see a movie and have supper afterwards.'

He would have liked to have gone back, but he knew how much she'd been looking forward to the day. She had been embroidering tray cloths to sell for weeks. 'No, thanks,' he said gruffly. 'I'll be all right. There's just one thing. Is it all right if I go to school here? High school, I think it's called.'

She sat on a wooden chair beside the table, her dark eyes a mixture of tears and joy. 'You mean, you want to stay with us, Simon, and not go back to Liverpool?'

'Yes, I would, if you don't mind. I'd like to go to Edinburgh Academy with Nick.'

Next day, Monday, he had lunch with his father for the first time since coming to New York, The strange feelings he'd had the day before had disappeared. He left early for lunch, strolling through Central Park, emerging on Seventh Avenue, from where he walked all the way down to Washington Square where Ed lived. On the corner of 42nd Street, he paused. The street looked tawdry in the brilliant sunshine, but at night when it was dark and the lights were on its character completely changed. On most nights in these theatres, magic was performed, haunting music was played, romantic songs were sung by performers whose only reason for living was to entertain people.

Simon closed his eyes and saw his mother coming towards him. He opened them quickly when he was nearly knocked off the pavement by a young man on skates.

He met his dad in a large restaurant a stone's throw from his apartment. He was already seated at a table on the pavement outside, and announced that he had just returned from Liverpool. He was back and forward like a yo-yo since he and Flo had married. Simon wondered if they would ever live together permanently in the same country.

'How is Flo?' Simon enquired. It was really weird, but Flo was expecting a baby, who would genuinely be his half-brother or -sister. What was even weirder was that Flo was now his stepmother.

A waiter came and they ordered; Simon a burger, Ed a medium-rare steak, both with chips and salad.

'I'm glad I found out who I was when I did,' Simon declared. 'Though I wish I'd known when I was younger.'

'Why's that?'

'Because I'm having a really great time, and I could have been having it for years and years.'

Ed was very slowly opening his napkin. He laid it carefully on his knee. 'That sounds,' he said cautiously, 'as if it's possible you're thinking of staying here.'

'I'm not just thinking about it, I've made up my mind. I *am* staying here. I'm going to go to Edinburgh Academy in September, with Nick Gallant. He's a cousin. And Martin's promised to get me into a good university.' He hadn't meant to sound quite so defiant.

'I know who Nick Gallant is.' Ed's face fell. 'Flo will be upset – that's putting it mildly.'

'I'm sorry, but my mind's made up.' Simon shrugged, though he didn't like the idea of upsetting Flo.

For the first time since they'd met two years ago, his father looked extremely cross. 'She knew you would leave one day, all children do, but she was expecting you back to take your A levels. Shirley's been in and decorated your room – it looks awful.' He glowered at his son. 'I hope it's your intention to go back to Bootle soon, to say goodbye. Lord almighty, son, Flo will be devastated if you don't,' he said thickly when Simon shook his head.

'I couldn't bear it,' Simon said frankly. 'I love them all too much. To say goodbye and realise it might be years before I saw them again would be truly horrible. I'd sooner take the coward's way out and not see them at all – it'll be better that way for Flo, Ed. You know it will.'

'I know no such thing,' Ed snapped. 'Tell you what, though, guess who's really upset you've gone – Andy! I always got the impression he resented the hell out of you. But he's still crying himself to sleep night after night because you're not there.'

'I'll write to him,' Simon promised. 'Send him a baseball glove, or something. How are the girls? How's Liam? I write to him often, but only get half a page back. Liam's no letter writer.'

'The girls are OK, but they miss you. I didn't see much of Liam. He still works out at that gym you used to go to. He's getting to be quite a decent boxer.'

'Good old Liam.' Simon sighed happily. 'Everything's worked out fine.'

'No, it hasn't, son,' Ed said soberly. 'Flo won't consider it fine. Nor do I. There's just one thing: you can come with your dad next time I do a book-signing tour. I shall enjoy showing off my son to my devoted followers. Do you fancy that? I might be going to Canada soon.'

Simon fancied it no end. With each day, life seemed to be getting better and better.

Chapter 24

Flora was sitting up in bed surrounded by cushions, three behind, one on each side and one beneath her knees. Her stomach was like a cushion, absolutely huge and very hard. She felt as if she had been blown up with a bicycle pump.

Her baby was due next month, and for most of the time nowadays she felt acutely tired. If she was on her feet too much, her ankles became swollen, Alice Brannigan had virtually taken over the running of the hotel. Ed was there a lot of the time, having bought a desk and a portable typewriter and put them in the smallest bedroom, which was now his study.

It was half past eight, dinner was long over and she could hear dishes being washed and the buzz of conversation in the bar. In the living room, Ed was watching television with Rose and Andy and Connie was fast asleep in bed.

Flora had the feeling of all being well with the world with her family around her, safe and sound, but right now there was one family member who wasn't present, and she had no idea when she would ever see him again. According to Ed, Simon had decided to stay in America. Any day now, he would start at a hugely expensive, terribly exclusive school in the state of New York, where he would be a boarder along with two of his new cousins. It sounded very different to St Anthony's, the school he'd been due to attend where the science laboratories were in a Nissen hut in the grounds.

She could hardly blame him for not coming home. He was having such a good time in his new home, which was like a small palace, or so he'd told Rose in one of his letters. He told the children far more than he did Flora in his polite little notes to her. In New York, there were so many exciting things to do and so many people to make a fuss of him, with Lilith and Martin at the top of the list. Ed had told her about the scores of aunts, uncles and cousins there were, forever socialising. 'Like the O'Sheas in a way.' But in a much grander way, Flora thought drily.

And then she realised that the more time that elapsed between them seeing each other, the more difficult it would become for them to meet. Already she would feel a little embarrassed if they came face to face, as well as rather annoyed. She imagined him having become very sophisticated, much cleverer, more sure of himself; a Simon she no longer recognised, no longer knew.

The baby gave her a vicious kick, bringing her back down to earth. After the pain had faded, she opened the book that had arrived that morning from Andrew; she'd been keeping it to read in bed.

I found this in a second-hand bookshop, Andrew had written. *Brighton is full of them. I don't know why, it's not the sort of book that interests me, but something prompted me to pick it up and look inside. And there, on the page I opened, were your parents' names, Frederick and Rose Knox and a photograph, if you please. I bought it straight away. It cost a whole sixpence!*

The book was leather-bound, dark green and bendy. It only had 153 pages. It was an autobiography of Charles Perrier, who had been a stalwart of the British theatre since before the end of the last century until the war, when the London theatre where he was performing had been bombed and the members of the cast on stage at the time had been killed, Charles Perrier among them.

Towards the end of the book, there was about half a page about her mother and father – Flora herself was actually mentioned, though she had no memory of the man. Charles Perrier had met the family in Edinburgh, where they were presenting a W. Somerset Maugham play, *The Letter*, in a small theatre on the edge of the city that normally housed the local Women's Institute.

They were an attractive couple with a small child in tow, the actor wrote, *whose love for and commitment to the theatre was much in evidence. I was told they toured Scotland and the North of England along with their little girl, mainly performing two-handers, only occasionally using an extra actor or two when required and very little scenery. I could easily have fallen in love with Rose, or with Frederick; it was hard to choose!*

I was upset when I learned a year or so later that they had been killed in a car accident. I have no idea what happened to the child.

'She's here,' Flora whispered. 'About to have her fourth baby.' Had Charles Perrier still been alive, she might have written and told him her life story, though he'd be close to a hundred by now.

The black-and-white photo showed a rather bare stage on which two people stood, one either side, a man and woman who looked nothing like the parents she only half remembered.

The door opened and Connie came in, rubbing her eyes. 'Can I get in with you, Mam?'

'Can't you sleep, love?' Flora threw back the bedclothes and her youngest daughter climbed in beside her.

'No. Why do I always have to go to bed first?'

'Because you fall asleep while you're reading your book, or watching television if you're not in bed by eight.'

'No, I don't,' Connie argued and immediately went to sleep, her head tucked underneath her mother's arm. When Ed came in, he'd carry her back to her own bed.

Flora began to doze herself, thinking what wonderful things children were. Whoever had invented them had done a good thing. She wished she had childish memories to look back on, but there were very few, none of them particularly pleasant. It wasn't until she'd met Isobel that she'd felt happy, then later Andrew and Else.

She half lay, half sat in the pillows, her arm resting on Connie's warm body, allowing dreamy thoughts to flit in and out of her head when, without warning, a ferocious pain ripped through her body and she screamed.

Connie woke up and began to cry. Flora pushed her out of bed. 'Fetch Ed, love,' she gasped. 'Tell him to come straight away.'

Her baby had decided to arrive early.

Two hours later and Flora groaned when yet another contraction, considerably longer and more painful than the one before, took possession of her body. She managed not to scream – after all, she was used to them by now – and contented herself with another powerful groan.

Ed was sitting beside her, in tears. 'I can't stand this, Flo,' he wept.

'You've already said that a million times.'

Sister Hilda entered the ward. She was in charge of things, and kept popping in and out to see how Flora was progressing. 'If you want to keep out of labour wards, Mrs O'Shea, you know what to do,' she'd said gruffly. 'Or what *not* to do.' She looked like a boxer, with her broken nose and the suggestion of a squint. 'I suggest you avoid copulating with a male of the species.' She threw a nasty glance at Ed.

'It's a bit late to tell me that now,' Flora said icily. She would have disliked the woman even if she hadn't been suffering the most painful delivery ever known. The woman totally lacked sympathy, and was devoid of understanding.

There was a terrific noise from outside, as if there was a fight going on. Once it had been known in the hotel that she was about to go to hospital because the baby had decided to come early, the customers in the bar who belonged to the O'Shea dynasty had taken to their cars, the buses and tramcars and had followed the ambulance to the hospital. A few had started to sing, 'There'll be bluebirds over, the white cliffs of Dover . . .' Sister Hilda sniffed disapprovingly, and Flora felt proud she belonged to such a loud and boisterous family.

There was a definite movement inside her body. 'I can feel the baby coming.' She desperately wanted to push.

The nurse pulled on a rubber glove and thrust her fingers inside her womb and announced there was still time to go. She removed the glove and appeared ready to go away again.

'But I *know* it's coming,' Flora said, panicking. She didn't fancy delivering the baby on her own.

'Jesus Christ!' Ed shouted.

The baby shot out of its mother and was caught just in time by the nurse, who picked the bloody little body up by its ankles and smacked its bottom. The baby yelled.

'It's a boy,' she announced laconically. 'What are you going to call him?'

'Freddie.' She looked tearfully at Ed. 'Do you mind? I only thought of it tonight when I read the book about my father.' They'd been stuck for a boy's name. A girl, and she would have been called Isobel.

'We've had a boy,' Ed repeated, and began once more to cry his eyes out. At that point, Sister Hilda ordered him outside.

About an hour later, Flora was sitting up in bed, Freddie cradled in her arms. Sister Hilda had gone and she was now being seen to by a young nurse called Sally.

'Eight pounds!' Sally said admiringly. 'Lord knows how big

306

he would have been if you'd gone full term. I hope you've got plenty of large baby clothes.'

'I've enough baby clothes of every conceivable size to last about three years,' Flora told her. Every single female O'Shea had knitted baby clothes, some actually big enough for a three-year-old. They were in several drawers at the hotel.

The nurse went away, and she was left alone in the delivery room. Other babies were being delivered elsewhere in the hospital. Soon she would be taken to a ward. Outside, the O'Sheas were still having a good time. Flora looked down at Freddie, who was clad entirely in white. She could have sworn she could feel his tiny heart beating against her breast. He had loads of untidy reddish-brown hair. Long dark lashes flickered on his cheeks and he was very pale. He looked very much like Simon when she'd first seen him, and like Ed too. Those blue eyes could well turn to green.

'You're going to play the piano really well,' she whispered, touching his white fingers; they were as thin as cake candles, but looked extremely long.

Flora shuddered and the baby stirred. She felt guilty for disturbing him, but oh, how careless it was to bring a helpless little human being into the world without planning it first, with scarcely a second thought! Now there was another life that would be her responsibility for the entirety of her days. Quite out of the blue, she thought about Grace giving up her baby to a complete stranger, and a feeling of depression, blacker than anything she had ever known before, crept over her and she had to make a physical effort to stop herself from shuddering again.

The door opened and Nurse Sally came in. She was young and rosy, nothing like the older nurse. 'Are you ready for your visitors?' she asked.

'Only the ones who aren't singing,' Flora said.

'I'll let your husband and children and your sisters in first.'

The door opened, and Ed came in with Rose, Andy and

Connie, followed by the Devlin sisters, Beattie, June, Lillian and Noreen.

'We claimed to be your sisters,' June said, 'I hope you don't mind.'

'Well, you're as good as,' Flora told them.

'Was I that ugly when I was born?' Rose asked.

'No, you were dead pretty. But you wouldn't want a pretty brother, would you?'

'No, Mam.'

'I think he's very handsome for a baby,' Andy remarked. 'It looks as if he's already got a moustache.' The baby really was sporting dark downy hairs on his upper lip.

'That will go away in time.' By now, Flora was feeling bone tired and longed to sleep.

Ed stroked her brow, kissed her softly and said he'd fetch the nurse to tuck her in and put Freddie in the nursery.

Flora looked at Connie who, so far, hadn't spoken. 'What do you think about your new brother, Con?'

'Me?' Connie's blue eyes shone with happiness. 'I think he's beautiful, Mam. Aren't we the luckiest family in the whole wide world?'

'Well, for some of the time,' Flora agreed.

The Lewins' drawing room was festooned with lengths of scarlet and green decorations and packed with young people, twenty-four to be exact, mostly male, all having a good time. The music was loud and came from Bill Haley and His Comets. They were Simon's records, and he'd bought them one day when he'd felt homesick, which seemed to be happening a lot lately.

Scarlet and green were the Edinburgh Academy colours, and looked rather gloomy on the walls, Simon thought, needing a dash of silver or gold. There really *was* a kilt of the same scarlet and green, hanging in his room ready to be packed in the morning before he left for the school. The kilt was making him have second thoughts, though it was a bit late in the day for doubts of any sort.

'We only wear them a couple of times a term,' Nick Gallant had assured him when Simon had first complained. 'I did tell you we wore kilts, didn't I?'

'Yes, but I thought you were joking,' Simon said through gritted teeth.

Nick laughed. 'I was only joking about worshipping Bonnie Prince Charlie. Anyway, you could have objected when we went to buy them.'

'It was too late then.' Lilith was over the moon that he was staying in New York, and he couldn't bring himself to disappoint her. Also, the kilt-wearing didn't seem so daft when it was six weeks off, but the reality of actually *wearing* a *kilt* felt dafter by the day as the date for starting the establishment neared. If his mates at St Anthony's ever found out, they'd kill themselves laughing.

And now the time to go was upon them, and this was his leaving party. Not just Nick, but a chap called Eric Sanderson, a grandson of one of Lilith's brothers, was also a pupil at the academy. Both boys had already been there a year. Simon knew he was lucky to be starting a new school with a couple of friends – relatives, in fact – already there.

Lilith had gone to bed and Martin to his club, leaving their guests to have fun on their own. Graham, the family chauffeur, had been left to make sure things didn't get out of hand; he was hovering in the hall, peering in at them from time to time.

Alcohol was limited, though inevitably some guests had brought their own, mainly Scotch, flat bottles tucked in their back pockets from which they swigged. Quite a few were pissed to the eyebrows, a phrase he'd never heard used in America.

Simon was being a real party-pooper, not having touched a drop of hard liquor. The last thing in the world he wanted was to turn up at Edinburgh Academy with a hangover. He had deliberately excluded himself from the atmosphere of jollity, only pretending to laugh when something funny happened.

He was relieved when Graham approached just after ten and laid his hand on his shoulder. 'There's a phone call for you in the library, Simon.' Simon had positively refused to be addressed as 'sir'.

'Thanks.'

'It's your father,' Graham added, as Simon followed him out of the room. 'He sounds highly delighted about something.'

That was a relief. It was about three o'clock in Liverpool, and he'd been concerned something awful had happened. Simon picked up the phone in the library which was full of books, not one of which he'd ever seen his grandfather read. 'Hi, Dad.'

'You'll never guess what's happened, son.' His dad loved calling him 'son'.

'Will I guess if I try?' he asked. 'I mean, have you won the Nobel Prize?'

Ed laughed, 'No such luck, I'm afraid.'

'You're writing the script for Rita Hayworth's next movie?' He'd professed to be madly in love with the beautiful red-haired actress, though that was before he'd met Flora.

'Wrong again. It's just that the entire family's just got back from the hospital, where we've been for hours; Flora had her baby early. It's a boy, I mean, *he's* a boy. We're calling him Freddie, after her father.'

'What's he like?'

'Like you, a bit − and like me too, same colour hair.' His dad's voice throbbed with excitement. 'His eyes are blue, but they might change to green.'

Simon moved around the desk and sat in Martin's chair. He felt unreasonably angry that he'd been left out of things. How dare Flo have a baby without him being there? His stomach did a somersault. He *had* to be there and join in the excitement.

'How do the others feel about it?' he asked. 'Rose and Andy and Connie?'

'Oh, they're overjoyed to have another brother — a half-brother, actually, but they already love him. Oh, and he's your half-brother too, son. You must come over and have a look at him one of these days.'

'Oh, I will, I will. Anyway, congratulations, Dad.'

'Bye, son.'

Very slowly, Simon replaced the receiver. He stayed in his grandfather's chair for a long time, thinking. At one point, Graham opened the door and asked, 'You OK, Simon?'

'I'm fine, ta.' He stood, left the library and went upstairs, where he knocked on Lilith's door. He could see the light was on and knew she read in bed until all hours.

She looked up, and he could see the hint of tears in her eyes. She'd guessed why he had come.

'I have to go home,' he said. 'I mean, I *want* to go home. I hope you don't mind. Ed rang — Flora's had her baby, a little boy called Freddie. I'll take my A levels at St Anthony's in Waterloo as planned.' The autumn term had started, but he felt sure they'd have him back. He sat on the edge of the bed and took Lilith's hand.

'You're right, darling,' she said emotionally. 'Of course I don't mind. I think Flo deserves to have you for another few years. Maybe Martin and I could come and see the new baby soon. After all, if he's your half-brother, then he's our half-grandson.'

'Flo would love that.' Simon nodded. 'Oh, and I haven't changed my mind because of the kilt, you know.'

'I know you haven't, Simon.'

'I'll be back in two years to take my law degree.'

He kissed Lilith goodnight and went downstairs. In the library, he looked through the telephone book and found the code for Liverpool in the United Kingdom. He dialled it, followed by the number of Haley's, which he could remember clearly.

He expected it to be Ed, but instead it was a girl who answered: 'Haley's Hotel.'

'Hello, Con. You're up early.'

'Oh, hello, Simon. I haven't gone to bed yet,' she said importantly. 'Alice is making us loads of toast. Would you like her to make you some?'

'Yes, please, but it'll be a while before I get there.'

It already felt as if he'd never been away.